W9-BTS-193

THE
Chaneysville Incident

BY THE SAME AUTHOR
South Street

THE
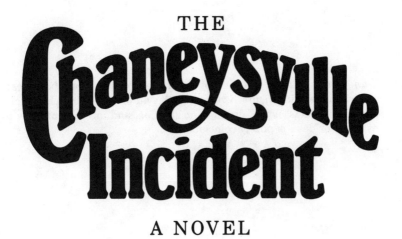

Chaneysville Incident

A NOVEL

DAVID BRADLEY

1817

HARPER & ROW, PUBLISHERS, New York

Cambridge, Hagerstown, Philadelphia, San Francisco,
London, Mexico City, São Paulo, Sydney

The Chaneysville Incident is a work of historical reconstruction; the appearance of certain historical figures is therefore inevitable. All other characters, however, are products of the author's imagination, and any resemblance to persons living or dead is purely coincidental.

THE CHANEYSVILLE INCIDENT. Copyright © 1981 by David H. Bradley, Jr. All rights reserved. Printed in the United States of America. No part of this book may be used or reproduced in any manner whatsoever without written permission except in the case of brief quotations embodied in critical articles and reviews. For information address Harper & Row, Publishers, Inc., 10 East 53rd Street, New York, N.Y. 10022. Published simultaneously in Canada by Fitzhenry & Whiteside Limited, Toronto.

Designed by Lydia Link

Library of Congress Cataloging in Publication Data

Bradley, David, 1950–
   The Chaneysville incident.

   1. Underground railroad—Fiction. I. Title.
PS3552.R226C5   1981   813'.54   80–8225
ISBN 0–06–010491–0

FOR MR. DAN AND UNCLE JOHN, THE STORYTELLERS;

FOR MAMA, THE HISTORIAN;

AND FOR DEARIE DADN, ALIAS POP, WHO WAS BOTH

Acknowledgment

The Chaneysville Incident has been some ten years in preparation. No project that continues for that length of time can properly be said to be the product of one person's imagination, or determination, or skill; certainly not of mine. I would therefore like to acknowledge the assistance that was given to me, at various times and in various ways, but I am not quite sure how many people. Their names, in no particular order, are: Lester V. Iames, Phyllis Johnson, Edward Frear, Nadia Kravchenko, Mara Pace Bannister, Lois Foell, Shelly Rice, Clydette Powell, Jane Vargo, Linda Venis, C. William Miller, Sheldon Brivic, Toby Olshin, Susan Edmiston, Pamela Walker, Thaddeus Kostrubala, Thomas Miller, Susan Ruehl, Justine Stillings, Deborah Kaplan, Muffy Siegel, Ellie Miller, Lou Ann Winegardner, Paul Schiffman, Denise Ozanne Hall, Doris Johnson, Judith Davies, Winona Garbrick, Edward Burlingame, Beatrice Rosenfeld, Linda Rubin, William Clark, David Watson, Eileen O'Neill, Dustie Gilman, Joseph Colp, Robert Tharp, Juanita Dennis, Richard Schmertzing, Mattie Jones, Oliver Franklin, John Wideman, Cheryl Gregory, Andrew Radolf, Spaid Gilman, Ann Lewis Kostrubala, George Jones, Wendy Clark, Laura Daly, Thomas Voss, Betsy Voss, Tina Nides, Jeanette Kraska.

My special thanks must go to Jonathan Dolger, who saw; Harvey Ginsberg, who focused; and Jake Ross, who made peace; to Tina Burr, who for some reason cared; to Carol Tracy, who was patient; to Wendy Weil, who, thank the Deity, did not *always* listen; to the Bedford County Heritage Commission, whose compilation of historical facts and reissuance of earlier works made critical research possible; to Harriette M. Bradley, who freely shared her knowledge; and to Temple University, whose Faculty Summer Research Fellowship made funds available at a critical time. Thanks to all of them, and to those my exhausted memory has omitted.

DB

THE

Chaneysville Incident

197903032330

(Saturday)

SOMETIMES YOU CAN HEAR THE WIRE, hear it reaching out across the miles; whining with its own weight, crying from the cold, panting at the distance, humming with the phantom sounds of someone else's conversation. You cannot always hear it—only sometimes; when the night is deep and the room is dark and the sound of the phone's ringing has come slicing through uneasy sleep; when you are lying there, shivering, with the cold plastic of the receiver pressed tight against your ear. Then, as the rasping of your breathing fades and the hammering of your heartbeat slows, you can hear the wire: whining, crying, panting, humming, moaning like a live thing.

"John?" she said. She had said it before, just after she had finished giving me the message, but then I had said nothing, had not even grunted in response, so now her voice had a little bite in it: "John, did you hear me?"

"I heard you," I said. I let it go at that, and lay there, listening to the wire.

"Well," she said finally. She wouldn't say any more than that; I knew that.

"If he's all that sick, he ought to be in the hospital."

1

"Then you come take him. The man is asking for *you*, John; are you coming or not?"

I listened to the wire.

"John." A real bite in it this time.

"Tell him I'll be there in the morning," I said.

"You can tell him yourself," she said. "I'm not going over there."

"Who's seen him, then?" I said, but she had already hung up.

But I did not hang up. Not right away. Instead I lay there, shivering, and listened to the wire.

Judith woke while I was making coffee. She had slept through the noise I had made showering and shaving and packing—she would sleep through Doomsday unless Gabriel's trumpet were accompanied by the smell of brewing coffee. She came into the kitchen rubbing sleep out of her eyes with both fists. Her robe hung open, exposing a flannel nightgown worn and ragged enough to reveal a flash of breast. She pushed a chair away from the table with a petulant thrust of hip, sat down in it, and dropped her hands, pulling her robe closed with one, reaching for the mug of coffee I had poured for her with the other. She gulped the coffee straight and hot. I sat down across from her, creamed my own coffee, sipped it. I had made it strong, to keep me awake. I hated the taste of it.

"Phone," Judith said. That's how she talks when she is not quite awake: one-word sentences, and God help you if you can't figure out what she means.

"The telephone is popularly believed to have been invented by Alexander Graham Bell, a Scotsman who had emigrated to Canada. Actually there is some doubt about the priority of invention—several people were experimenting with similar devices. Bell first managed to transmit an identifiable sound, the twanging of a clock spring, sometime during 1876, and first transmitted a complete sentence on March 10, 1876. He registered patents in 1876 and 1877."

Judith took another gulp of her coffee and looked at me, squinting slightly.

"The development of the telephone system in both the United States and Great Britain was delayed because of the number of competing companies which set up systems that were both limited and

2

incompatible. This situation was resolved in England by the gradual nationalization of the system, and in America by the licensing of a monopoly, which operates under close government scrutiny. This indicates a difference in patterns of economic thought in the two countries, which still obtains."

She just looked at me.

"The development of the telephone system was greatly speeded by the invention of the electromechanical selector switch, by Almon B. Strowger, a Kansas City undertaker, in 1899."

"John," she said.

"I didn't mean to wake you up."

"If you didn't want to wake me up you would have made instant."

I sighed. "Jack's sick. Should be in the hospital, won't go. Wants me." I realized suddenly I was talking like Judith when she is not quite awake.

"Jack?" she said. "The old man with the stories?"

"The old man with the stories."

"So he's really there."

I looked at her. "Of course he's there. Where did you think he was—in Florida for the winter?"

"I thought he was somebody you made up."

"I don't make things up," I said.

"Relax, John," she said. "It's just that the way you talked about him, he was sort of a legend. I would have thought he was indestructible. Or a lie."

"Yeah," I said, "that's him: an old, indestructible lie. Who won't go to the hospital." I started to take another sip of my coffee, but I remembered the rest room on the bus, and thought better of it.

"John?" she said.

"What?"

"Do you have to go?"

"He asked for me," I said.

She looked at me steadily and didn't say a word.

"Yes," I said. "I have to go."

I got up then, and went into the living room and opened up the cabinet where we keep the liquor. There wasn't much in there: a bottle of Dry Sack and a bottle of brandy that Judith insisted we keep for company even though Judith didn't drink and we never enter-

3

tained. Once there would have been a solid supply of bourbon, 101 proof Wild Turkey, but the stockpile was down to a single bottle that had been there so long it was dusty. I took the bottle out and wiped the dust away.

I heard her moving, leaving the kitchen and coming up behind me. She didn't say anything.

I reached into the back of the cabinet and felt around until I found the flask, a lovely thing of antique pewter, a gift to me from myself. It was dusty too.

"Do you want to talk about it?" she said.

"What's there to talk about?" I said. I filled the flask.

"Well," she said, "I just thought there might be something on your mind."

"What would make you think that?" I said.

"You want me to be a bitch," she said. "You want me to say something about starting to drink again. . . ."

"I never stopped," I said.

"Not officially. But you haven't been doing as much of it. And you want me to say something nasty about you starting again. But I won't."

"I thought you just did," I said.

She didn't say anything.

"It gets cold out there in those mountains," I said. I turned around and looked at her. "You don't understand how cold it gets."

She opened her mouth to say something, then thought better of it. I put the flask in my hip pocket.

"We could talk about it," she said. "About whatever it is that's bothering you."

"There's nothing bothering me," I said, "except being up at midnight with no bed in sight." I looked at my watch. "And it's time to go, anyway." I turned away from her and went to the closet to get my coat. She followed me.

"Someday," she said, "you're going to talk to me. And when you do I'm going to listen to you. I'm going to listen to you so Goddamn hard it's going to hurt."

I didn't say anything; I just got out my heavy coat and made sure I had my fleece-lined gloves and a woolen scarf and a knitted wool watch cap stuffed into the pockets.

"John?" she said.

4

"Yeah?"

"Would you like me to come with you?"

"What about the hospital?" I said.

"I'll get somebody to cover for me. God knows, there are enough people who owe me. I'll come tomorrow after—"

"No," I said.

She didn't say anything.

I turned around and looked at her. "You don't understand," I said. "It's not just like visiting friends. . . . I can't explain."

"Forget it," she said.

"Look," I said. "If you want to help, just call the department for me. Tell them . . . tell them it's a family illness. They can get anybody to do the Colonial History lecture—it's not until Wednesday. The Civil War seminar can take care of itself."

"All right," she said. "How long . . . I guess you don't know." Suddenly there was a lot of concern in her voice, which told me I must be looking and acting pretty bad. Judith is a psychiatrist; she's seen a lot of troubled people, and she never wastes undue concern on cases that aren't critical.

I smiled at her. It was a good smile, full of teeth; it would have fooled most people. "Now, dear," I said, "I'm just takin' a little run up the country, seein' a sick friend. Now, as every student of marital infidelity knows, a sick friend is just a tired euphemism for a willing wench. Seeing as we're not what you call legally espoused, it isn't precisely adultery, but—"

Judith said something highly unprintable and spun me around and wrapped her arms around me. I felt the shape of her body fitting the shape of mine like a template. Her hand moved over my clothes, finding the space between my shirt buttons and sliding through until it found the place at the base of my belly that somehow never seemed to get enough warmth. I let her hand rest there for a moment, and then I stepped away from her and turned and held her as tightly as I could, my nose buried in her hair, my hands feeling out the shape of her back. Then my hands stopped moving and we just stood there, very still, so still that I could feel her heart beating, slowly, rhythmically, steadily. And then I felt my own heartbeat steady. I pulled my face from her hair and kissed her. She stepped back and, with her head down, fastened the zipper of my coat.

"Stay warm," she said.

5

The key to the understanding of any society lies in the observation and analysis of the insignificant and the mundane. For one of the primary functions of societal institutions is to conceal the basic nature of the society, so that the individuals that make up the power structure can pursue the business of consolidating and increasing their power untroubled by the minor carpings of a dissatisfied peasantry. Societal institutions act as fig leaves for each other's nakedness—the Church justifies the actions of the State, the State the teachings of the School, the School the principles of the Economy, the Economy the pronouncements of the Church. Truly efficient societies conceal the true nature of the operations, motivations, and goals of all but the most minor institutions, some even managing to control the appearances of the local parish, courthouse, board of education, and chamber of commerce. But even the most efficient society loses control at some point; no society, for example, is so efficient that it can disguise the nature of its sanitary facilities. And so, when seeking to understand the culture or the history of a people, do not look at the precepts of the religion, the form of the government, the curricula of the schools, or the operations of businesses; flush the johns.

America is a classed society, regardless of the naive beliefs of deluded egalitarians, the frenzied efforts of misguided liberals, the grand pronouncements of brain-damaged politicians. If you doubt it, consider the sanitary facilities employed in America's three modes of public long-distance transportation: airplanes, trains, and buses.

America's airports are built of plastic and aluminum. They gleam in the sun at noon, glow, at night, with fluorescent illumination. They are reached most conveniently by private autos, taxicabs, and "limousines." In the airport there are many facilities for the convenience of the traveler; for example, there are usually several bars which serve good bourbon. The planes themselves are well maintained, and are staffed by highly paid professional people, pilots ("captains") chosen for their experience and reliability, hostesses chosen for their pleasantness and attractiveness. There are usually two classes of accommodation; in one both food and liquor are free, in the other the food is complimentary and alcohol can be obtained at a reasonable cost. The companies that operate airplanes are known by names that reek

6

of cosmopolitan concerns: American, National, United, Trans World, Pan American. The average domestic fare is on the close order of two hundred dollars, and the preferred mode of payment is via "prestige" credit card—American Express, Diners Club, in a pinch Carte Blanche. The sanitary accommodations, both in the airport and on board the plane, are almost invariably clean. Soap, towels, and toilet paper are freely available; on board the plane, the complimentary offerings often extend to aftershave lotion and feminine protection. Most significantly, the faucets turn. The sinks drain. The johns flush. And if they do not, they are speedily repaired.

America's train stations are built of granite and brick, smoked and corroded from the pollution in city air. Their dim, cavernous hallways sigh of bygone splendor. They straddle that ancient boundary of social class—the legendary "tracks." They are reached with equal convenience by private auto and public transport. There is rarely more than the minimum number of facilities for the traveler; rarely, for example, more than one bar, and that one oriented towards the commuter trade—the bar bourbon is of the cheaper sort. The trains are frequently ill-maintained. The operator ("engineer") wears a flannel or work shirt, in contrast to the airline pilot's quasi-military uniform, and the attendants, who take tickets rather than provide service, are most often elderly gentlemen; the overall aesthetic effect is somewhat less pleasing than that presented by an airline hostess. There is class-differentiated accommodation, but the actual difference is somewhat questionable; meals and liquor, when available at all, must be purchased in both classes. There is now only one passenger train company, really a gray government agency with a name dreamed up by some bureaucrat's child, too young or too stupid to know the proper spelling of the word "track." Before the government took over the passenger trains the names of the companies sang of regionalism; instead of a United or a National there was a New York Central and a Pennsylvania, and in lieu of a Trans World or a Pan American there was a Southern and a Baltimore & Ohio. The average railroad fare is on the close order of sixty dollars, and payment is often made in cash. When credit cards are used they are often bank cards (which allow time payments) as opposed to prestige cards (which do not). The sanitary accommodations associated with rail travel are somewhat less civilized than those associated with travel by air. In the station there is usually only one central rest room for each

7

sex, that one poorly attended. The items freely provided for use are the bare essentials in theory and often less than that in fact—the wise traveler checks for towels before he wets his hands. Perhaps fifty percent of the johns are operable at any one time; the others are clogged with excrement and cigarette butts. Repairs are delayed more often than expedited. Recent environmental concerns have favorably altered the conditions in the on-board sanitary accommodations; the newer trains have flush toilets modeled after those on planes. Still, until quite recently—within the last decade in fact—the accepted mode of getting rid of human waste was to eject it through a pipe at the bottom of the car, where it fell to the ground and lay exposed until natural decomposition could eliminate it.

America's bus stations tend to lurk in the section of town in which pornographic materials are most easily obtained. Like airports, they are built of plastic, but it is plastic of a decidedly flimsier sort. They are reached most easily by public transportation or "gypsy" cab; except in largest cities and smallest towns, ordinary taxis shun them. The facilities for traveler convenience are virtually nonexistent; in lieu of a bar there is a lunch counter, which (if one can attract the wandering attention of the attendant, who is usually of the gender of an airline hostess and the appearance of a train conductor) will offer up a buffet of *hot dog au grease* and sugar-water on the rocks. The buses are at times in good repair, at times not, but always uncomfortable. The drivers look like retired sparring partners of heavyweights who never have been and never will be ranked contenders. There is a single class of accommodation—fourth. *Nothing* is served on board; a sign in the on-board rest room cautions against drinking the water. The names of the bus companies sing of locality (White River, Hudson Valley), private ownership (Martz, Bollman), and dogs. The average fare is on the close order of twenty-five dollars; the maximum one-way fare to the most distant portion of the United States is only eighty dollars. The preferred mode of payment is cash; if, as with the larger bus lines, credit cards are acceptable, they are bank cards, never prestige cards. The sanitary accommodations are much in keeping with the rest of the scene. Inside the station, the rest rooms are of a most doubtful nature; usually they are wholly or partially closed for repairs that are so long delayed and so temporary in effect that they seem mythical. The on-board accommodation is hardly better. The john, which is not even supposed to flush, is merely a seat atop a square metal holding tank; below it the curious—or perhaps "sick" is a better adjective—traveler may observe the wastes of previous users swimming blissfully about like so many tropical fish.

The various degrees of civilization represented by the sanitary accommodations inevitably reflect class status that the society at large assigns to the passengers. It is no accident, then, that airline patrons are usually employed, well-dressed, and white, while train passengers (excepting the commuter) are more likely to have lower incomes, cheaper clothing, and darker skin. A randomly selected bus passenger, at least in common belief and easily observable fact, is, far more than the patrons of planes or trains, likely to be: un-, partially, or marginally employed; un-, partially, or cheaply dressed; in- or partially solvent; in- or partially sane; non- or partially white.

The Greyhound bus station that serves Philadelphia sits in the center of town, a prematurely deteriorating, fortunately subterranean structure which cannot escape its surroundings—the skin flicks down the street, the bowling alley on one side, the Burger King on the other. I emerged from the subway a block and a half from the station, ran the gauntlet of improbable offers from gypsy cab drivers, winos, and whores, entered the station, and stood in line to buy a ticket to a town that existed as only a dot—if that—on most maps, a town noted for its wealth of motel rooms.

Originally it was the crossing of two major Indian trails, one running north and south, the other east and west; the Indians, it appears, had not lived in the area, but like later whites, had used it for overnight rest—a sort of redman's Ramada. One group of these transient Indians, probably Cherokees, who made some kind of permanent residence in the area around the English colony at Jamestown, evidently had rather a malicious sense of humor; they whispered rumors of the lodes of silver to be found near the crossing of the great Indian trails. These whisperings reached the ears of an explorer, one Captain Thomas Powell, who accordingly, and no doubt to the great amusement of the Indians, fitted out an expedition.

And so, sometime in the year of our Lord 1625, Captain Thomas Powell of Virginia became the first white man to set foot in what would later become the County. Navigating by the North Star, he made his way north, discovering a stream of exceptionally sweet water, which is now called Little Sweet Root Creek, and a convergence

9

of three streams, which formed what is now called Town Creek. He found no silver, however, and so turned back before reaching the site of the present Town, and made a report so indifferent as to discourage exploration for some time. However, over a century later, in 1728, his grandson, Joseph, entered the region Captain Thomas had explored, leading a party of twelve men. They settled along the streams Captain Thomas had discovered, and evidently prospered—one man, Joseph Johnson, died in 1731, but the second of the party to die, Richard Iiames, lasted until January 26, 1758, a full thirty years after the first settlement. Powell, later joined by his brother George, did not fancy the farming life, and so, in 1737, became the first of several white men to build a trading post to do business with the Indians. Unfortunately, because Captain Thomas had never really reached the crossing point of the great Indian trails, the Powell trading post was built on Little Sweet Root Creek, which then, as now, was something of a backwater. Had this not been the case, the Town might have been named, originally, Powell. But it was not. The honor fell to a man named Robert Ray, who is believed to have built a post about 1751. The town that grew there originally carried the name Raystown.

There is some doubt about the accuracy of the claim that it was Ray's trading post that formed the nucleus of the Town. Other local features which bear his name (Ray's Cove, Ray's Hill) are located many miles away, and the spelling of the name in some documents is odd (Reas'). One historian reports that the actual nuclear establishment was a tavern, and another claims it was operated by John, not Robert, Ray. Such is history.

In any event, the name was legitimized by 1757, when Governor Denny of Pennsylvania ordered Lieutenant Colonel John Armstrong to encamp three hundred men near "Ray's Town" and from thence to do battle with the Indians. The matter dropped for lack of funding and, it appears, for lack of Indians. However, in the next year the English General John Forbes, who had been charged with retaking Fort Dusquesne (later Fort Pitt) from the French and Indians, used Raystown as a rendezvous point for 5,850 mixed troops and 1,000 wagoneers. The advance elements of this party, which included at least a hundred British troops, eighty "southern Indians"—basically Cherokees—who were allies of the British, and one hundred "Provincial" soldiers (the number a conservative estimate, as one hundred were reported "down with the flux"), built a fort at Raystown, which was completed by August 16, some six weeks after its start. The fort continued as a mustering point of the campaign.

The Town grew in importance through peacetime as well. In 1771 there was sufficient political power to have the entire area split off as a separate county, with Raystown as its seat. The name of the County was chosen in acknowledgment of political realities in England. The Town changed its name to match. Some sixteen years later, the political power of the Town and the County was such as to cause the construction of a road into the western reaches of the state. The surveys for the "Great Western Road" established that the Town was located "19 miles and 290 perches north of Mason and Dixon's Line."

The importance of the Town and the County to the early development of America was acknowledged by no less a historian than Frederick Jackson Turner, author of the controversial "Frontier Hypothesis," who pronounced it a watermark of westward expansion. However, both Town and County were of relatively minor importance during the War of Independence. Some three hundred men were mustered locally, but the local gunsmith was charged with providing only twenty-five muskets, and the commissioner's clerk reported that he was running behind schedule. In light of this and the fact that the fort had fallen into ruin, it is probably fortunate that the locale saw little rebellious activity.

However, during the Whiskey Rebellion (c. 1791–94), such activity was much the norm. For although the locals were not as involved with whiskey production as were farmers further west (who were farther from market and therefore more cognizant of the fact that a horse can carry only four bushels of grain but twenty-four bushels' worth of distilled grain products, and who were as a result far more sensitive to the limitation of commercial freedom implied by a federal tax on spirits), the County register of 1792 listed forty-two still-owners operating fifty-five stills; while they were perhaps not involved with the tarring and feathering of government revenue collectors, they were certainly sympathetic to the rebels and antipathetic to the federal troops, commanded by General Henry "Light-Horse Harry" Lee (father of Robert E.) who came to put down the rebellion. It is possibly for this reason that President Washington chose to come into the field and take personal command of the troops, making his

11

headquarters in the Town, thereby guarding the rear of the army with his personal prestige. Evidently the stratagem worked—the locals did not harry the flanks of the army, and a hotel, which later became a bakery, was named after Washington, He did not, however, sleep there, but made his headquarters at the home of Colonel Espy, a prominent local, a few doors away. In later years, the Espy House housed the local draft board.

In other national conflicts, the County and the Town did their part, sending several companies to the War of 1812, and a full company of eighty volunteers, along with many regular recruits, to the Mexican War in 1846. The volunteer company, the "Independent Greys," was mustered in the regiment that stormed Chapultepec, but the implied gallantry is somewhat misleading, as thirty of the eighty were "detailed, temporarily, on some other duty." Since "nearly half" of the thirty died (two of them from "diarrhea"), the fifty are to be congratulated on their discretion.

The County's participation in the Civil War is somewhat ambiguous. Without a doubt, many men served gallantly on the Union side. Equally undoubtedly, a large number, many from the southern part of the County, where the descendants of Powell and his party of Virginia settlers peopled a section now known as Southampton Township, served the Confederacy with equal gallantry.

Through the early and middle nineteenth century, the County knew some prominence due to a group of mineral springs which formed the basis for a resort industry attracting some of the richest and most powerful men in America. In the later portion of the century, however, both Town and County fell from grace. The decline of roads as principal means of transport injured the economy greatly. The Pennsylvania Railroad built its line thirty-nine miles to the north, through Altoona. The Baltimore & Ohio built its line thirty-five miles to the south, through Cumberland, Maryland. The South Penn Railroad, brainchild of William H. Vanderbilt and Andrew Carnegie, would have passed through the Town, but due to political and economical maneuverings, and the intervention of J. P. Morgan, work on the South Penn Railroad—otherwise known as "Vanderbilt's Folly"—ended on September 12, 1885. Even though some revival was occasioned by the use of the South Penn route for the building of the Pennsylvania Turnpike, which began half a century later, this was offset by the connection of a southern highway, Interstate Route 70, with the Turnpike at a point sixteen miles east of the Town.

Now the county seat and watermark of westward expansion is a town served by only two local buses a day. If you're in too much of a hurry to wait for one, you can buy a ticket and take your chances on begging or bribing the driver of an express bus to make a brief unscheduled stop on the 'pike, and walk four miles from there. I was in a hurry. I took my chances. The ticket cost eighteen bucks and change.

Three and a half hours later my bus was boring up a moonlit slab of highway, the snarl of the exhaust bouncing off the walls of rock that towered on either side of the road. Except for the bus, the Turnpike was empty; four barren lanes, the concrete white like adhesive tape applied to the wounds the machines had slashed into the mountains. The bus moved swiftly, slamming on the downgrades, swaying on the turns. The driver was good and he knew the road; we were ahead of schedule, and long ago we had reached the point where the hills were familiar to me, even with just the moonlight to see by. Not that I needed to see them; I, too, knew the road, could pinpoint my location by the sways and the bumps. I knew that in a minute the driver would downshift and we would crawl up a long hill, and the road would be straight as an arrow from bottom to top, then twist away suddenly to the right. I knew that at the crest, just before the twist, there would be a massive gray boulder with names and dates scrawled on it, a cheap monument to the local consciousness: DAVID LOVES ANNIE; CLASS OF '61; MARGO AND DANNY; BEAT THE BISONS; DEEP IN YOUR HEART YOU KNOW HE'S RIGHT; SCALP THE WARRIORS; NIXON THIS TIME. After that the road would twist and turn and rise and fall like a wounded snake for eighteen miles, and then I would be there, or as close as this bus would take me.

And so I settled myself in my seat and took another pull on my flask and looked out the window at the mountainsides black with pine, and thought about how strange home is: a place to which you belong and which belongs to you even if you do not particularly like it or want it, a place you cannot escape, no matter how far you go or how furiously you run; about how strange it feels to be going back to that place and, even if you do not like it, even if you hate it, to get a tiny flush of excitement when you reach the point where you can look out the window and know, without thinking, where you are; when the bends in the road have meaning, and every hill a name.

A truck swung around the turn ahead of us, its running lights dancing briefly in the darkness, the sound of its diesel penetrating the bus, audible over the rumble of the bus engine, and I thought of the nights when I would lie in bed, listening to the trucks on the 'pike grinding on the grades, bellowing like disgruntled beasts, and promise myself that someday I would go where they were going: away. Bill had done that too, had lain and listened to the trucks. He had told me— but not until years later—how he had lain there, night after night, chanting softly the names of far-off cities to the eerie accompaniment of the whine of truck tires. I had done the same, in my own way: I would start with the next town to the east or the west along the 'pike and move on, saying the names of the exits one by one, as if I were moving by them. Once I even reached New Jersey before I fell asleep. And I remembered thinking, when Bill told me of his game and I told him of mine, that his was so much better; that he had visited and re-visited Paris, Hong Kong, Tokyo, Peking, while I was struggling to get out of the state. Later, I had wondered if it would be that way all our lives, he flying from place to place while I crawled, making local stops. I had watched with some curiosity to see if it would work out that way, and to some extent it had; he flew to Vietnam and never came back, and while I had taken a few leaps, I had ended up in Philadelphia. And now I was coming back, passing little towns, know-ing their improbable names—Bloserville, Heberlig, Dry Run, Burnt Cabins, Wells Tannery, Defiance, Claylick, Plum Run, Buffalo Mills, Dott. The bus was an express, nonstop between Philly and Pitts-burgh, but I was making local stops.

The truck vanished behind us, leaving an afterimage on my eyes, and the bus rolled down into a valley and across a bridge. The stream below it was called Brush Creek, and this time of year it would be low. The logs would stick out from the banks and gouge gurgling hol-lows in the sluggish water. Half a mile upstream, near the hulk of a dead hickory, was the place where, surprising no one so much as my-self, I had caught my first catfish. Old Jack had helped me bait the hook, had shown me how to get the fish off it. And then he had taken his knife and shown me how to scale the fish and gut it, and we had built a fire and fried the fish in bacon grease in a black iron skillet he had packed along. It was a lot of trouble to go to and it could not have been much of a meal for him—it wasn't much of a fish—but he said there was something special about a boy's first catfish, no matter how small it was.

Then the bus was moving along the southern slope of a mountain—raw rock on one side, empty space on the other. I was almost there. I emptied the flask, capped it, put it in my pocket. I pulled my pack towards me, tightened the laces, checked the knots. Then I stood up and made my way towards the front. Five minutes later I stood by the side of the road, shivering in the sharp, clear mountain cold, and watched as the bus roared away into the darkness. And then I began to walk.

In the pink and eerie light of false dawn I stood and looked up at it: an array of houses spread out along four streets called, starting at the lowermost, Railroad, Union, Lincoln, and Grant, connected at the eastern end by a slightly larger one grandly and ridiculously named Vondersmith Avenue. The streets were only vaguely parallel; the houses were not much better. They were oddly shaped, so tall and thin that it seemed their foundations were too small to support their height and, more often than not, leaning dangerously to confirm the impression. Most were of wood, and had often been patched, with corrugated metal and plywood and tar paper. Paths led from their back doors to yards where clotheslines sagged. Smoke rose from their rough brick chimneys and drifted down the slope, bringing to me the odor not of fuel oil but of kerosene and pine wood and coal and, mingled with it, the faint effluvium of outhouses. At the center of it all stood a small church made of whitewashed logs. That was it. The place locally termed Niggers Nob and Boogie Bend and Spade Hollow and, more officially, since the appellation came from a former town engineer, Jigtown: the Hill.

I shrugged to resettle the pack on my shoulders and started up, thinking, as I did so, about the countless times I had made that climb, happy to be doing it, knowing it was the final effort before food, or drink, or bed, or just refuge from whatever it was that I needed to hide from. More than once I had reached the foot of the Hill on the dead run, pursued by white boys from the town, shouting names and curses; I would make the climb imagining that all the house windows

15

were eyes staring at me; that they knew, somehow, that that day someone had called me a name or threatened me, and I had done nothing besides close my eyes and ears, trying to pretend it was not happening.

But now I was a man, and the windows were only windows; the only effect they had was to make me wonder what was happening behind them. At one time I would have known with virtual certainty. Behind the windows of that house, the one with the siding of red shingle molded to look like brick, Joseph "Uncle Bunk" Clay would have been shaving, the muscles of his arms looking strong and youthful, his dark brown skin smooth and tight against the pure white of his athletic shirt. The steam would have been rising from the enamel basin before him as he wiped vestiges of white lather from his face with a creamy towel, and he would move with surprising agility for his fifty-odd years as he began to put on his bellboy's uniform. Aunt Emma Hawley would have been making sour milk biscuits. She had been making them exactly the same way every morning for forty years; Mr. Hawley insisted on having his breakfast biscuits. That was the weather-beaten house at the far end of Railroad Street, the one with the low shed next to it, in which three generations of Hawleys had tended store, one of the few places in the world where you could still buy a bottle of Moxie. A little way up the slope would have been the meticulously tended home of Aunt Lydia Pettigrew. Behind its shining clean windows Aunt Lydia would have been tenderly feeding the most bloodthirsty pack of mongrels north of Meridian, Mississippi. Aunt Lydia had kept the dogs since the state had taken her last two foster children, Daniel and Francis, away from her, and she was the only person who could come near those dogs without being torn to bits, for good reason—she had spoiled them by feeding them nothing but ground round steak, with Almond Joy candy bars for dessert. At the very bottom of the Hill, and way off to the left, two little girls would have been playing in front of a ramshackle house. The girls, Cara and Mara, and the house belonged to Miss Linda Jamison. It sat where it sat to spare visitors the necessity of climbing the Hill, of venturing any farther onto it than necessary. Inside it, Miss Linda would have been sleeping, exhausted from her night of entertaining a few "good friends" from the town. At the top of the Hill was the house Moses Washington had built. Behind its windows no one would have been stirring; Moses Washington had left his wife and children "comfortable," which meant that his wife could support the family on the money she made as a lawyer's secretary, and did not have to get up before seven. And on the far side of the Hill, where, quite literally, the sun didn't shine, and where the houses—only one now—had no windows, Old Jack Crawley would have been "doing his mornings" in the old battered outhouse down the slope from the spring where he drew his water.

I knew nothing about the Hill any longer, I had made it my business not to know. But now suddenly, inexplicably, I was curious, and so I thought for a moment, pulling half-remembered facts from the back of my mind—scraps of information—and made extrapolations. Uncle Bunk, his arms permanently bowed from sixty years of suitcases, trunks, train cases, hatboxes, golf bags, et cetera, now spent his hours playing checkers by the stove. There was usually no one there for him to play with, so he moved for both sides. Aunt Emma Hawley still made biscuits. She had seen no need to stop making them when Mr. Hawley died, and so she kept on making them and fed them to the chickens—she couldn't stand sour milk biscuits. The gleaming white paint and meticulously applied green trim on Aunt Lydia's house was flaking and spotted, for Aunt Lydia was no longer around to hire the workmen for shrewdly low wages and watch them like a hawk; she had been found lying on her spotless kitchen floor surrounded by her sleek murderous mongrels, who steadfastly protected her even after she had been dead for two days—from malnutrition. Miss Linda Jamison's house looked little different, but now it was just a hulk. She and her girls had moved to better quarters a few blocks from the center of town; Miss Linda's "good friends" had grown too old to walk so far, and their sons, who were "good friends" of Miss Linda's girls, did not like to walk at all, and the cars were . . . conspicuous. There would be fewer sleepers in Moses Washington's fieldstone house; the sons had gone away. And Old Jack Crawley was sick.

I reached the top and stood looking at Moses Washington's house. The walls were rock-and-mortar. The style of masonry was uneven, the lower, earliest-laid courses being of dressed stone, the upper two thirds or three fourths being of fieldstone. Despite the fact that all the stones were more or less triangular—the rocks in the lower courses having been trimmed to that shape, the ones in the upper courses having been, apparently, selected for it—the change in style from ashlar to rubble was apparent and abrupt and, in fact, quite ugly. The question of why the mason had changed styles had never been answered—my own early theory, that Moses Washington had wanted triangular rocks (the why of that being still another question) and it had been quicker and easier to find them than to cut them, proved erroneous—for the simple reason that the mason had been Moses Washington himself, and no one had ever been able to figure out why Moses Washington did anything; no one even knew where and when he had learned masonry. And given the ugliness of the house, one could say he never had.

Certainly he had laid his own ideas on top of any formal knowledge he might have possessed. The mortar, for example, was cooked limestone, the sort of cementing agent that Henri Christophe of Haiti had used to build the famed Citadel. But where Christophe was rumored to have thickened his mortar with the blood of goats, Moses Washington had used portland cement—although it was rumored, too, that the bones of more than one of Moses Washington's enemies might be discovered beneath the foundation.

The dressed stone had come from the foundation of the house itself. The rest of it had been dug out of the foundations of houses that lurked in the underbrush on the far side of the Hill, hauled over by Moses Washington and Jack Crawley and Uncle Josh "Snakebelly" White during one of the most murderous Augusts the County had ever seen. It would have been sensible to wait for cooler weather, but Moses Washington had a schedule, and the schedule said move the stone in August, so he had. That was how Moses Washington was. The only times he had backed off from anything was in order to get up speed. Laws local, state, federal, military, and possibly international had not stopped him, threats of incarceration and/or bodily harm had not stopped him; the weather was not about to. Jack Crawley and Josh White had helped him because they had always helped him. The three of them had run together for forty years, hunting and fishing and drinking and generally scandalizing the County. They had run together through—or perhaps "over" is a better word—Prohibition, and neither the Volstead Act nor the relative fortune that Moses Washington had made because of it changed anything. They had run together through the Depression, and that just made them worse; some of the market for Moses Washington's home brew dried up, and the three of them were forced to consume large quantities in order to keep the prices from falling due to oversupply. They had done a heroic job. When World War II had begun they had tried to enlist together, even though Josh White, the youngest of them, was fifty. They still tell the story on the Hill about how the three of them had stormed the old Espy House, drunk as lords, demanding to be signed up, threatening to take the place apart if they weren't. Uncle Josh and Old Jack actually did tear the place up, scattering files and file clerks, until they passed out. Moses Washington, seeming suddenly sober, had waited until the dust had settled, and then had taken the director of enlistment aside and spoken to him for a while, and nobody knows exactly what was said, but the next time anyone heard of Moses Washington he was a noncommissioned officer in the Army of the United States, and the next time they heard of him he was in Italy, and then they heard no more until he came back from the war with medals and ribbons bearing witness to his valor and discharge papers certifying his total insanity. This, it was rumored, was because he had tried to shoot one of the white Southern officers that were invariably placed in charge of black combat units. It was a rumor that nobody believed, since the last time Moses Washington missed something he was aiming at was a matter not of record but of legend, and it was widely suspected that the charge of attempted murder was really the result of the workings of Moses Washington's bizarre sense of humor. But as the days following his return from the war passed, it became evident that he was, if not actually crazy, certainly *changed*. He did not go back to his work, which, for as long as most people could remember, had been supplying the half of the County that drank with corn liquor. He gave that up, and he gave up drinking whiskey himself. He gave up cards. And he more or less gave up hunting—he still went out, but he went without a gun; no one, as usual, knew why, and no one was fool enough to ask.

Those changes, fundamental as they seemed, still might have been explained adequately by a simpler theory than insanity, but the rest could not. Moses Washington was seen to enter the church occasionally, although never during an official service; he was fond of attending choir practice, and he took over the job of keeping the sanctuary clean. He was seen to spend time in conversation with whatever minister the Central Jurisdiction of the Methodist Episcopal Church saw fit to send—it was suggested that he was the main reason that none of them lasted more than two years. Not that he was sectarian;

rumor had it that, especially during the winter months, he would prowl the countryside for miles around, and in the dead of night, appear at a parsonage and roust the preacher out of bed for far-reaching theological discussions.

But all that came after the biggest event; in 1946 he shocked everyone by asking for the hand of Miss Yvette Franklin Stanton, whose father had been a professor at Howard University before retiring to a neat house at the far side of town—away from the "other ones," as the Professor put it—in order to drink the local mineral water, which, the Professor maintained, had not lost any of its curative powers since the days when President James Buchanan had partaken of it. Miss Stanton was a spinster at thirty-one not because she was ugly, but because she had somewhat haughtily refused to become involved with any of the young men from the Hill, although, unlike the Professor, she was active in the Hill's affairs. The people called it uppitiness, the rejected suitors something else, but they all nearly fainted when Miss Stanton accepted not only a ruffian, but the Ruffian of Ruffians, even if he did appear to have settled down some.

Moses Washington and Miss Stanton were married in 1946, but the marriage was not consummated for a solid year, while Moses Washington enlisted the help of Josh White, and Old Jack Crawley, and built the house. The three of them lived in it while they built it, raising the walls around them, constructing the roof over them, and, if rumor has it correctly, adding numerous four-letter words to the English language while doing it. When it was finished, Jack Crawley and Josh White went back to their battered cabins on the far side and Moses Washington moved his wife in. Mrs. Washington did not approve of drinking in any form, or of cussing, or of Old Jack and Uncle Josh, for that matter, and so Uncle Josh never again set foot in the house he had helped to build; even during Moses Washington's funeral he, along with Old Jack Crawley, stood outside on the porch. And Old Jack had only entered it once more, on the afternoon of that day, when he had come looking for Moses Washington's elder son.

It was hotter than hell on the day they buried Moses Washington. All the men said so, muttering it softly, after making sure that neither their wives nor the preacher was in earshot. It was just barely hyperbole; it was the dry part of August and air that had been baked on the Great Plains hung unmoving over the mountains, heavy with tan dust that made a haze like smoke on the mountaintops and the trees gray like powdered wigs. There were nearly a hundred people at the funeral; everyone on the Hill who was both old enough to respect death and young enough to walk to meet it, and more than a few people who had left the Hill, and even one man who was white. They stood out behind Moses Washington's house—among his effects had been found a letter giving strict instructions about his burial, and the specifications pointedly excluded the church—while the sunlight came slamming down out of a too-blue sky, listening to the preacher deliver a eulogy that tried very hard to give the impression that Moses Washington had been deacon rather than doubter, bishop rather than bootlegger, and it must have occurred to everyone that the minister's designation of heaven as the destination of the soul of the deceased ran directly counter to the message from Mother Nature. Finally the minister finished, and the pallbearers present raised the coffin and carried it up the slope to the back door and through the house and out the front; that was easier than fighting around the corner of the house, where the slope was abrupt. When they had carried it out to the front porch, Old Jack Crawley and Uncle Josh White took up their part of the burden, and the boxed remains of Moses Washington moved across the brow of the Hill, the pallbearers sweating and grunting, the minister following, the too-long cuffs of his baggy black pants dragging in the dirt.

I moved along behind the minister, my mother's hand on my shoulder guiding and pushing me at the same time, my head shielded from the sun by the hat she had made by knotting the corners of a handkerchief. Behind us came the procession, moving slowly, a spiritual rising above it as if it were not a group of people but one giant organ. I wondered how they could sing in the dust and the heat; it could not have been easy. But they did sing, and the song that Moses Washington had called for rose like the dust itself. It was a tune I knew—Moses Washington had hummed it for as long as I could remember—but I had never before heard the words. Now they rose, languid and mournful: *And before I'll be a slave I'll be buried in my grave, and go home to my Lord, and be free.*

We reached the graveyard and stood watching while the minister prayed over the coffin, and then as it was lowered, in the old way, as Moses Washington had stipulated: six strong men slowly, solemnly paying out the rope. The undertaker, a greasy-headed black man who, as Moses Washington had demanded, had been imported from forty miles away, viewed the process with thinly concealed disgust; he would have preferred, no doubt, a gentle mechanical cranking, with the coffin dropping slowly and smoothly as if it were being lowered by the Hand of God. The men stood silently, the women were crying softly—all except for my mother, who remained brisk, efficient, and dry-eyed throughout. We dropped the ritual spades of earth on the coffin, and then we turned away and went back across the Hill. The pallbearers stood awkwardly for a moment, and then Old Jack and Josh White disappeared into the woods and the other four were free to join the rest of the people, who came crowding into the house to present their final comfort to the bereaved family and to consume the contents of the covered dishes they had brought to the house in the days since the word of Moses Washington's death had come rushing up the slope like a grass fire.

In the depths of the house, the heat was even worse: like oil, stubbornly refusing to circulate despite the almost frantic motion of two dozen paper fans thoughtfully donated by the Mordecai D. Johnson Funeral Home of Altoona, Pa., and expertly wielded by the ladies of the Women's Home and Foreign Missionary Society—middle-aged women of various shapes, sizes, and shades, who spoke often simultaneously but rarely unanimously. Many of the people left quickly, knowing that although the heat was everywhere they could at least escape the odor of dying flowers mingled with two dozen variations on the theme of cheap perfume that hung in Moses Washington's house like a fog. Those who remained had "duty" to do, or nowhere else to go. The minister stayed for reasons known only to himself; it would have been expected for most people, but Moses Washington had not been most people, and the church was abundantly represented by the WH&FMS. My grandfather, the Professor, stayed too, a thin frail man with pale liver-spotted hands who sat holding a glass of iced tea with fresh mint crushed into it, occasionally raising the glass to lips that reached out to take it like the mouth of a trout taking a lure. He did a manful job of looking mournful, but in moments of inattention a look of relief would spread across his face; there had been no love lost between him and his son-in-law, who had more than once suggested that the lightness of his skin and the manumission papers that he proudly displayed were both the result of a series of miscegenetic liaisons in which his female forebears had been ready, willing, and possibly even eager partners. They stayed, though they could have left. The rest of us had no choice; we lived there.

Bill was there, sitting on the couch, the soft pillows rising around him, seeming to swallow him. He was lonely and confused, and he had rejected every offer of food and drink. I sat in the far corner, gnawing on a turkey sandwich that had been prepared for me by one of the WH&FMS ladies. I was their darling, because I accepted their overtures. Periodically one of them would swoop down upon me and clutch me to her ample bosom and call me a poor orphan. I accepted everything and smiled and was quiet. They thought I was being brave, but I was not. I just did not know how to act. I had no idea how I should feel, what I should do. I knew what I wanted, though: I wanted them all to go away and leave me alone. Because something had happened and I knew it was something important, but I did not really know what it was. And so I wanted to sit and figure out the what of it, so that I could begin to figure out the why of it. Then I would understand it. And then I could begin to figure out what I needed to do— laugh, cry, hate, whatever—so that I could go about more pressing business. I did not think about it in those terms then, of course—I was only nine years old—but I knew it. And I knew that until I had time to think alone I would not do any of the laughing or the crying or the hating, because I simply would not know what to do.

And then Old Jack came. It was as if a boulder dropped into a pool; the silence had that same hollow sound to it that water makes as it swallows a stone. He stepped into the middle of the room and looked around, swaying drunkenly, blinking like some weird sleepy reptile. There was a collective gasp throughout the room. Old Mrs. Turner, who was noted for seeing signs and omens in nearly everything—she claimed to have foreseen Moses Washington's death in the actions of a flock of birds—stood up and raised her hands above her head and began to wail, her voice rising from a low, barely audible whisper to a keening that was painful to the ear. I heard a rush of feet as my mother came in from the kitchen.

Old Jack took another step forward, his eyes searching. They came to rest on me. "Mose tole me," he said. "Tole me to come for this here boy. An' I come." The statement must have stunned everybody, for no one moved when he advanced upon me.

I stood there, unable either to flee or to pretend to fight as he came towards me, bending, his face coming down at me with the speed, it seemed, of an express train. His eyes were bloodshot, his breath warm and sour. I could see the blemishes in his skin, see where the dirt was ground into the folds and wrinkles, see all the little irregularities around his eyes and lips. But my eyes fastened on an uneven wart that lay just beside his low, flat nose. "Come with me," he said. He reached out for me.

Suddenly my limbs were free from paralysis, and I let go with what must have been my first accurate punch: a short, chopping overhand right that landed squarely on Old Jack's wart. He howled and jumped back, and with that the spell was broken. The people in the room rushed forward and grasped him. "Get that . . . *man* out of here!" my mother ordered, and they hustled him out the door, trying to be gentle despite the fact that he was fighting like a wildcat, and shouting drunkenly about Moses Washington's last will. They maneuvered him across the porch and onto the street, where they released him. He fell to the ground and remained there, on all fours, his head hanging, his tongue lolling. Then he raised his head and his eyes met mine, and we stayed like that for a moment. And then I had felt my mother's hands on my shoulders, pulling me back inside.

As I had stood looking and thinking, the fatigue had come on me with a rush, all the force of the sleepless night and long walk. I felt the growing of old tensions, a sudden chill at the base of my belly. I tried to ignore it as I watched as morning chinned itself over the mountains. The sky was clear but the air seemed moist, and the sun was a deep red ball. I thought of the ancient adage "Red sky at night, sailors delight; red sky at morning, sailors take warning," and wondered exactly how old it was, knowing that it was common when Shakespeare wrote, in *Venus and Adonis:* "a red morn, that ever yet betoken'd/Wreck to the seaman, tempest to the field," having its origins probably before the year of our Lord 1, for in the sixteenth chapter of the Gospel according to Matthew, Jesus of Nazareth, when asked to provide a sign from heaven, said: "When it is evening, ye say, It will be fair weather: for the sky is red. And in the morning, It will be foul weather to day: for the sky is red and lowring," an event reported differently in the twelfth chapter of the Gospel according to Luke, which records Jesus as saying: "When ye see a cloud rise out of the west, straightway ye say, There cometh a shower; and so it is. And when ye see the south wind blow, ye say, There will be heat; and it cometh to pass," and thinking that the weather patterns of ancient Israel were almost directly opposite to those of the present-day Alleghenies . . . and then realizing what that red sky might mean, for him and for me, and I turned and left the porch.

The street ended at the stone walkway Moses Washington had built leading to his porch, evolving into a path of dirt. I reached the crown of the Hill and moved along the ridge while the light strengthened behind me. And then the path turned away to the north, and I followed it, dipping down into the shadow of the Hill. Here the path was cushioned by dead rusty pine needles, and in the eroded hollows on the downhill side of big gray boulders snow lay in unhealthy-looking, black-flecked lumps.

The path dropped steeply for thirty yards—so steeply that the branches of the trees near it had long ago been torn away by hands grasping for a hold—then it turned and ran along the hillside, dropping slowly while the land fell away sharply on the right hand. The going was easy there, except for the tendency to drift downhill off the path and into the tangles of brier and Spanish nettle that choked the spaces between the pines. As I corrected for the drift I remembered how, as a child, I had had to fight to stay on the track, walking, it seemed then, sideways in order to achieve a straight course. Once I had feared far more than brier; by the time I made my first trip no one lived on the far side of the Hill but Josh White and Old Jack, and either one of them was enough to make even my unimaginative mind dance with visions of the boogeyman.

Uncle Josh White had earned his more uncomplimentary nickname by being pale and dank-looking, with mangy yellowish hair and almost pink eyes. Since "albino" was not a term that was taught in the local elementary school, the suspicion that the children of the Hill, and of the Town too, often whispered—that "Snakebelly" White had been dead for some years—was allayed only by his actual demise and amazingly opulent burial; where the money had come from was a minor mystery, as nobody had ever thought "Snakebelly" White cared enough about tomorrow to take out burial insurance. To make matters more frightening, Uncle Josh White did not talk. Oh, he *could* talk, and if you followed him for hours you might actually hear him utter a word or two as he bought blackstrap or snuff or some other staple. But apart from those two or three words, Uncle Josh said nothing to anybody besides Old Jack Crawley and Moses Washington, and when he spoke to them it was on the other side of the Hill.

Old Jack was the opposite; he was dark, his skin the color of pine bark, his eyes blacker and beadier than those of the snakes he was rumored to keep as pets. His clothes were dark too; his pants were baggy gray-black things that had once been of a lighter color, perhaps, but which had gone too many years without washing to ever regain a fairer shade. In summer the top of Old Jack's union suit served for a shirt, and although it was cleaner than his pants, it suffered from drippings of coffee and dribbles of tobacco juice that had miraculously escaped absorption in the hairs of his grizzled chin. Sweat had made the union suit's underarms dark—there it matched the unholy color of the dark dirty suspenders that held up the dark dirty pants. The women of the Hill maintained that Old Jack owned only one set of underwear and one pair of pants, which he never took off, but that was a slander; he had two of each. He did have only one pair of shoes, old high-topped work shoes with studs instead of eyelets and rawhide thongs in place of laces, and they were stained with kerosene and soot and blood from his hunting. At most times Old Jack's overall darkness was augmented by random smears of shoe polish, black and brown and oxblood, for every morning he took up his station at the Alliquippa Hotel on Pitt Street, at the foot of the elevated shoeshine stand with its raised brass footrests and high-backed chairs.

The stand was the Town's official unofficial meeting place; for years the mayors and the judges and the lawyers and the Courthouse officers and the prominent businessmen had come there in the morning to read and comment on the news in the *Gazette,* and to do a little political horse trading: a man who had political aspirations would appear early and stay late into the morning; you could tell the candidates long before they announced it by looking to see who had the shiniest shoes. Over a hundred-odd years, more decisions had been handed down from that shoeshine bench than from the one in the Courthouse itself. And for the larger part of those years, Old Jack Crawley had moved among the decision-makers, slapping polish, making jokes, pocketing tips, and—although it was only a rumor—disposing of a good bit of Moses Washington's high-octane moonshine. What effect he had had on policy was not known; it occurred to only a few that he might have had any at all. Unlike Uncle Josh, Old Jack did talk. Constantly. His patter was a bizarre mishmash of aphorism and jive, witticism and wisecrack. He had "once heard" almost everything: that willow bark cured headaches; that milk was bad for babies; that whiskey, taken in seemly moderation, aided the digestion, prolonged life, and cleared the wandering minds of older folk. He spun out endless webs of tales that were either true or so blatantly false as to seem true, and he would, at the drop of a two-second silence, hold forth at some length on every subject from the weather to the state of the Union. But when evening came he would pack up his brushes and move like a tiny dark shadow through the town, heading for the Hill. He would not go up the Avenue but would take the old path at the far end, climbing up past the graveyard where the black people were buried, then crossing through the trees that crowned the Hill until he met the path that led to the far side. And, so the stories went, once he took the first few steps on that path he changed. Because the far side of the Hill was *different*. The far side was guarded by ghosts. Adults laughed about all that. But they never went beyond the crown of the Hill. Children dared each other to take the first few steps, to go and bring back a rock or a bit of brush from beyond the point where the path made its first precipitous drop and vanished into the undergrowth; those with imagination and bravery—like Bill—would go far enough not to be seen, wait awhile, then come back, claiming to have discovered . . . almost anything. I never did that; I had no imagination, and before I ever mustered sufficient courage my life changed: Moses Washington went hunting and came home dead, and Old Jack Crawley came for me.

I had awakened in the night. I had been bathed and soothed and fed and put to bed like a baby and, exhausted, I had slept through the heat of the afternoon and the cool of the evening. Now darkness lay on the mountains, and the blaze of daylight heat was a barely recalled flame. Air that was almost cold poured through the window beside my bed, and gusts of wind billowed the curtains and slammed insects against the screen. For a long time I lay there in the darkness, listening to Bill's light snores coming from across the room, wondering what it was that Old Jack had wanted. I tried to reason it out, but I could not. And then I realized why it was that he had frightened me, had frightened everybody: none of them knew what he had wanted. Whatever had frightened them, it had been something they were only guessing at. For some reason, that seemed *wrong* to me; or not wrong—pointless. And then it came to me: I would go now and find

Old Jack, go and find him and ask him what he wanted.

And so I slipped out of bed, being careful not to let the mattress creak—my mother claimed to be a light sleeper, but it had always seemed to me that she never slept at all. I found my sneakers beside the bed, moved carefully across the floor to where my pants hung on a peg. Carrying shoes and pants. I made my way to the window. It took me only a moment to slip through it onto the porch roof, then to put the screen back in place. I sat on the roof and slipped my pants on over my pajama bottoms, pulled my sneakers on. Then I made the drop to the ground. It was a lot farther than I had thought, and I landed hard, my knees jarring up into my chin. I tasted blood silvery in my mouth but I did not cry out, I just climbed to my feet and stood hauling air into my lungs and looking around.

I had never been out in the darkness like that before, without someone there to guide me and hold my hand. But I wasn't afraid, and I moved away from the house and stood at the top of the Avenue looking down. The Hill was dark. In the Town the streetlights were pale yellow, spaced like markers. I turned and started up the slope, finding the path with no difficulty; it was easy to see by the light of the full moon, which hung silver white in the sky. I moved confidently in that light for the first few yards, but then the path took its first big drop, and the moon vanished behind the Hill, and the trees closed over me. I lost my footing and my courage at the same time; as I tried to turn back I found myself slipping and sliding, all out of control, my arms windmilling as I fought for balance. I fell and rolled, it seemed, forever, finally coming to a stop against a pine tree. I was hurt and scratched, but too stunned to cry. I just lay there, with pine needles and pebbles digging into my back, listening to the night.

I had never done that before. I had heard the sounds—there was nothing new in the chirpings of crickets or the musical croakings of spring frogs—but I had never lain in the darkness listening to them. Suddenly I forgot my scratches. I listened to the faint rustlings in the underbrush, the creakings of the trees moving in the wind, the calling of nightbirds at whose names I could not guess. It was pleasant, and the world seemed a warm and friendly place. I got to my feet and regained the path, and moved ahead, feeling for the path with the toe of my sneaker.

The path was clear but the hillside dropped away; I had to fight to stay on course, to avoid being dragged off into the underbrush by the force of gravity. I began to be really frightened, recalling the stories about how once Old Jack and Snakebelly White reached the far side of the Hill they became something other than human. Boogeymen. But I thought it out, and reasoned that if being there changed them, then it ought to change me too. Now *I* was a boogeyman, and it would serve everybody well to stay out of my way. I moved on steadily for a few hundred yards, and then the path went diving almost straight down the slope again, twisting and turning between trees and boulders, but always heading down. I went with it, but more carefully this time, lowering my body to the point where I was almost sitting in the dirt and sliding. On either side of me the underbrush rose in purplish-black billows, and honeysuckle vines crawled over the trees and rocks like snakes. In a few more yards I came out of the trees into a clearing. By then my eyes had adjusted; I could see a little. What I saw was the outline of a cabin made of weatherbeaten wood and bejeweled with softly glimmering patches made of flattened tin cans. I knew it was Old Jack's house; I did not know how I knew, but I knew. Somehow I found the courage to move forward, but I was not without wariness; I got down on my hands and knees and crept forward as quietly as I could, hoping to detect the boogeyman before he detected me. It took me so long to reach the cabin I lost track of time. When I did reach it I crept around it, looking for a window to peer through and finding none. In a sudden burst of courage I got to my feet and moved to the door and reached up for the knob, but found instead a latch string. Then the unfamiliarity, the strangeness of it hit me. The night grew darker and suddenly silent. I trembled. I backed away, my eyes fixed on the door. I turned to run. And found myself staring at the boogeyman himself, holding a shotgun pointed at my head. "God, boy," the boogeyman said, "you near to got your head blowed off. If you're gonna sneak, for Ned's sake, *sneak!*"

The shack looked much as it always had: an improbably ugly structure leaning defiantly against the pull of gravity and the weight of time, the boards of weird grayish-green from the effects of weather. Once, when they had come to take the census, they had asked me (nobody, not even a representative of the federal government, was going to go over there to find out if Old Jack had an indoor bathroom, and I was the only person who would know) whether the house was deteriorating, dilapidated, or unfit for human habitation. (The census-taker had paused for a moment, trying to figure out a way to explain the terms to a twelve-year-old, who, presumably, did not understand them.) It had been a hard question, and I had said finally that it was dilapidated, an evaluation I happened on by elimination: the house could not be unfit for human habitation since Old Jack, who, I knew by then, was thoroughly human, lived there quite happily; nor could it be deteriorating—it had gone to ruin long before I was born. The census-taker had shaken her head and made clucking sounds, but that I really did not understand; Old Jack's house seemed fine to me. Then an outhouse was still an adventure, and so was getting water from the spring and transporting it in a galvanized bucket. Although I had never tried it, I imagined that bathing—if you ever did—in a big tin tub was the acme of bliss.

But my perceptions had changed over the years; now the shack looked as if it might be unfit for human habitation. And not only the shack, but the land around it; the whole scene, ravaged by winter, treated harshly by the morning light, foretold disaster. There was no grass to soften the impression as there was in the summer, no flowers blooming in the three old coal scuttles that he used for planters. The woodpile was depleted and the logs that remained were washed-out looking, the sharp browns of bark and pulp bleached an unholy gray. Down the slope the outhouse sagged, and the vines that covered it were brown and limp. The scene depressed me—it spoke of decay. Of death. I wondered how much of that had to do with the fact that the man who for years had made it all go, who had added life and force and interest to it, was not moving through it, might not be moving at all. There was no sign of him, not even smoke from the chimney. And so I hurried, breaking into a run as soon as I reached level ground, pounding towards the door. I slowed as I reached it, pausing for a moment to get my breath back, taking time to get a smile on my face. I knocked. And then I waited.

He had left me standing in the open doorway while he went to light the lamp, and waited there while I looked around, letting me take my time. After a few minutes he came toward me and placed his hand on my shoulder. "You pack a pretty good wallop for a youngster," he said.

It took me a while to figure out that he was talking about my hitting him, but once I had I felt a flush of a curiously mixed emotion: embarrassment at the praise, fear at the thought of reprisal, pride at my sudden capacity for violence. "I'm sorry," I said. "I hope I didn't hurt you."

"Hurt," he roared. "Hell, you damn near kilt me. But you ain't got no need to be sorry. If you hadda kilt me it woulda served me right—I didn't have no business comin' up there like that, stickin' ma face up in yours. It was the wrong way to go about things. I always was like that, get the idea 'bout what oughta be done, an' then haul off an' do it jest backwards. Your daddy now, he always thought things out, knowed what he wanted to do *an'* what was the right way to go about it. He—" He stopped, looked at me. "Damn, I guess I'm doin' it again. I hadn't oughta be speakin' a your daddy now."

"I don't mind," I said.

He must have heard indifference, or something, in my voice. "You don't care if he's gone, do you?"

I didn't say anything.

"It ain't nothin' to be ashamed of," he said. "Can't nobody make you feel somethin' you don't feel, an' there ain't no point in tryin' to pretend you feel it. Hell, I bet you didn't even like him."

I didn't say anything.

"Me," he said, "I guess you could say I loved him. He saved my life moren one time. But I'll tell you the truth—way Moses went about things, he was like to save your butt by kickin' you in it to get you movin' in the right direction. You mighta loved him for it later on, but right off you wasn't likely to be too damn grateful."

He had been hypnotizing me. He must have been, for somehow I found that I had left the door and was standing in the middle of the cabin, near an odd slate-topped table, and the door was shut behind me. I looked around for some other way out; there wasn't any. I started to edge back towards the door.

"Don't jest stand there, boy," he snapped. "Siddown."

I had to decide then whether to break for the door or not. There was no question about what I *wanted* to do, but my mother had told me to obey the commands of adults without question; besides, I was curious. So I moved forward towards a handmade hickory chair that butted up against the table. I pulled it out and got up on it, to sit with my legs dangling.

Meanwhile Old Jack had been busy, stirring up the stove, setting a kettle over an open hole. "You drink, boy?"

"Sure," I said. "Everybody drinks."

"Damn, son," he said. "I don't mean buttermilk an' root beer, I mean do you drink whiskey?"

"Oh, no," I said.

He peered at me. "Why the hell don't you?"

"Why, because it's bad."

"What's so bad about it?"

"Well . . . it's bad for you, that's all. It makes you do bad things. And it makes you sick. And . . ." I trailed off; I couldn't remember any more of the reasons they had always given for avoiding Demon Rum.

He shook his head. "You been talkin' to them Christians too much," he said. "Hell, boy, you could say all those things about women. Bet you them old biddies didn't tell you that, did they?"

"No," I admitted.

"You don't mess around with women, do you?"

"No," I almost shouted, even though I didn't know what he meant, precisely.

"That's good," he said. "Women's got their uses, but you're too young to 'preciate 'em. You stay clear of 'em for a good while yet. And stay clear a girls. I know, kissin' girls is fun, but you get to like the taste, an' you keep on likin' it you don't notice when they stop bein' girls an' start bein' women, an' women do more harm to a man than whiskey ever did. But I bet you don't even like the taste of whiskey."

"I . . . don't know," I said. "I never tasted whiskey."

"What?" He was shocked. "You ain't never tasted whiskey? You mean to tell me your daddy never even give you a taste?"

"He didn't drink whiskey," I snapped.

"Lord," Old Jack said. He left the stove and came over to the table. "Boy," he said, "how old are you?"

"Nine," I said. "Almost ten."

"Then it's time you learned the truth about a few things. An' the first thing you better learn is that your daddy drank enough whiskey in his time to float a battleship, an' he *made* enough to float the whole damn Navy. And the second thing you better learn is that you're damn lucky he did, because otherwise you wouldn't be eatin' tomorrow, 'less it was by some white man's handout." He glared at me for a minute, and then turned and stomped back to the stove, stood with his back to me. "He cooked the meanest moonshine a man could ever hope to taste. And he tasted. And I tasted it with him. Folks said a lot of things about that, but when he done somethin' for 'em, you didn't never see 'em turnin' the kindness away." He whirled then and looked at me hard. "You go over to that Sunday school an' let them holy-butted biddies tell you how bad whiskey is, but let me tell you somethin': they never give back a penny a what he put into the collection plate. I don't know why the hell he done it, but he did. He'd sneak in there durin' the week an' leave money for Sunday. They'd find it. They'd know where it come from. But they'd keep it. An' then whatever dumb-butted preacher they had over there would stand up on Sunday an' talk about how bad whiskey was, an' take his damn five dollars an' go home. Livin' on whiskey money. An' I'll tell you somethin' else they ain't told you: that Jesus Christ they pray to was a moonshiner Hisself; He turned water straight into wine. An', like Mose useta say, he didn't pay no damn tax on it neither." He came away from the stove then, and set a steaming cup in front of me. "That there's a toddy," he said. "Some folks makes 'em fancy. I make 'em the way Mose taught me, with hot water and honey. An' whiskey. Right now, yours ain't got no whiskey in it. I'll put some in if you want it. But you gotta make up your own mind." He stood there, patient and unmoving, while I made up my mind.

"He really drank whiskey?" I said finally.

"Indeed he did."

"I'll take some."

He nodded, went back to the stove, and returned with another cup and a bottle. "This ain't your daddy's whiskey," he said. "I ain't got much a that left, an' it packs a kick. This here's good enough for now." He reached out and dribbled some whiskey into my cup. Cheap bourbon, but the smell of the steam that rose to my nose was wonderful. "Stir, it with your finger," he said, "an' take care you don't burn yourself."

I did as he said, burned myself anyway, but didn't say anything. Then I cautiously raised the cup to my lips and tasted. It was mostly water, but I could taste the whiskey, and in a minute I could feel the warmth growing in my stomach.

"It's good," I said.

"Course it's good," Old Jack said. "Hell, why you think them Christians don't want nobody to drink it?"

We sat there for a while, drinking the toddies. I found myself getting sleepy, but I struggled to keep my eyes open. Presently he got up and mixed another toddy for each of us. By the time I was half-way through it, the room was starting to swim, and the heat from the stove was becoming thick.

"He liked you," Old Jack said suddenly.

"What?" I said.

"Your daddy. He liked you. He was proud a you. An' he was worried about you. That was jest about the last thing he said to me; probly the last thing he said to anybody." He took a sip from his cup. "He come over here with a jug; guess that's the last jug a Moses Washington Black Lightning left. He come in here an' we talked for a while. He was talkin' about you. Said you was too much your mama's child. Said he was worried you was gonna end up bein' a preacher or a sissy or somethin', on account a the way that woman carried on around you, fussin' with your clothes an' fixin' you food an' things that a man oughta be able to do for hisself. Said he wasn't worried about your brother, there wasn't enough woman in him for it to be dangerous. But you was different. He said there was a lot a woman in you. He didn't mean nothin' bad by that—jest meant that you was the kind that trusted people. Kind that believed there was always gonna be somebody to help you get through things. It ain't jest women that thinks that way—there's a lotta panty-waisted fellas runnin' around these days, get into trouble an' all they know to do is to pray to Jesus or the government—but women's the only ones that can afford it, on accounta they know that there's gonna be a man around somewheres to haul their wagon outa the mud, and that when the whistle blows they get first crack at the lifeboats. I ain't actually sayin' it's wrong for a man to believe that, but it's damn dangerous. On accounta he can't afford it. A man can't carry hisself, folks laugh at him. The women won't have nothin' to do with him. 'Cause what they want is a man that can haul their wagon outa the mud.

"Anyways, that was what your daddy was afraid was gonna happen: you'd spend so much time with women that the woman would come out in you and you'd end up rubbin' your hands an' cryin' 'stead a doin' what needed to be done. He was afraid your mama would do for you so much you wasn't never gonna be able to do for yourself, wasn't gonna end up fit for nothin' 'cept gettin' turned over to another woman an' goin' to work for a white man, an' end up the kinda fool that can't go to sleep lessen he knows 'xactly where he's gonna get his pussy an' his next pay. An' he said that was all right for some, but not for you, on accounta you was special. That's what he said. Special. Said you had a lot a woman in you, but you had one hell of a lot a man in you to go with it. He told me some a the things you done, things he was real proud of. You know what they was?"

"No," I said, wondering how Moses Washington had seen me doing anything, since I had learned early on that the best way to get along with him was to stay pretty much out of sight.

"He told me 'bout them books you read. Told me how you go down there to the library an' steal the ones they say you ain't old enough to read, an' how if you get one an' you start it, then you by God finish it, even if you don't know what the hell it's all about, an' how you read 'em over an' over until you think you do. He liked that. Told me how when your brother give you a lickin' you wouldn't say nothin' to nobody, you'd jest wait till didn't nobody think you was mad anymore, an' then you'd clobber that boy good. He liked that; he surely did. Course he did say he had to whup you for doin' your clobberin' with that there ax handle, but he didn't mind you gettin' the idea. Not at all. He liked all that. Course he jest about had to, on accounta that was jest the way he was." He smiled at me. "You know what he said he liked best about you?"

"No," I said.

"He said he liked the way you hated him."

I didn't say anything.

"He didn't mind; most folks hated him. I hated him some myself. He was a real hateable man. He wanted things his way all the time, an' if he didn't get what he wanted, he took it. He wasn't kind to people 'less it suited him; all he cared about was what got him where he wanted to go. He didn't give a good God damn about anybody in the world. Oh, he cared, but you knowed that if it come down to a question a him or you, it woulda been you, an' he mighta been sorry, but that was all. Matter a fact, the only time I ever seen him do anything to make me think he cared much about anybody was when he come over here an' ast me to take care a you if anything was to happen to him, to make sure you learned how to be a man. What he said was,

35

says, 'Jack, if anything happens to me, you take that boy an' teach him to hunt, an' teach him to fish, an' drink whiskey an' cuss. Teach him to track.' That's what he said. An' then the damn fool went out huntin' groundhog."

He paused, and I looked at him and saw the lamplight reflected in his eyes—they were glistening. "Hell," he said finally, "you gotta be mighty hungry to eat a groundhog. Meat's greasy an' stringy an' tough all at the same time. Seems to me if a man was gonna get kilt out huntin', the least thing he could do was to be huntin' somethin' worth huntin'. I recall a time when Moses Washington woulda rather drunk warm water than be huntin' a groundhog. Matter a fact, I don't recall him ever huntin' no groundhog before. An' I don't guess he's gonna be doin' it again. The damn fool." He rose then, and went to the stove and mixed himself another toddy. The smell of it reached me, and I knew he was making it stronger this time. He drank it down in a few gulps without coming back to the table, without even turning around, and then he mixed another, just as strong.

"You don't mind me talkin' 'bout your daddy the way I do?" he said.

"No," I said.

"Well," he said, "that's good. An' I don't guess it changes nothin' to speak of him. Everybody else is. They *been* speakin' of him. Most folks, they gotta be dead an' gone 'fore there's a chance anybody'll talk about 'em. Not Mose. They was probly talkin' about Moses Washington 'fore he was ever born. Wasn't nobody that knowed nothin' about him, though. I knowed some. Josh knowed a bit, but he wasn't the kind a man that set too much store by where a man come from, or where he went when he was outa sight. An' he's dead anyways. But not knowin' facts don't stop folks talkin'; hell, it just sets 'em goin'. Most folks'd a hell of a lot rather listen to rumors than go around the corner to see what's what. And Mose helped 'em right along. He let 'em talk, an' if they was to ast him a question—an' there wasn't many that had the nerve—he'd just smile an' let 'em think what they wanted. Pretty soon you couldn't go anywheres in the County without everybody knowed his name, an' who run with him, an' three or four stories about what we done. Wasn't half of it true. Fact is, you found out somethin' about Moses Washington, you knowed for sure either he wanted you to find it out jest 'xactly the way you done it, or it was a lie. An' most times, it was both." He

36

stopped then, sipped at the toddy, and looked at me hard. It frightened me, and I stirred uneasily and looked over my shoulder towards the door.

"You goin' somewheres?" he said.

"Well..." I said.

"You scared a the boogeyman?"

It must have been the lateness of the hour, making me cranky, or perhaps it was the whiskey. "Don't you make fun of me," I said.

His eyes grew wide for a moment, and then he nodded his head. "I'm sorry, son," he said. "I forgot you was Mose's boy. You want some more?" He gestured with the bottle.

"No," I said.

"Hell, son, I said I was sorry. Now, when a man apologizes, you either take his hand or you let him be, but you don't sit around takin' little bites out a him all day long; that's what women does. Now, you want some more or not?"

"I'll take a little."

He nodded, took my cup, and mixed the toddy. His hand was a little unsteady; he put in more whiskey than he should have. But I didn't notice it. All I knew was that the taste was strong and sweet and good, and that the warmth of it moved through me like joy. I sipped with abandon, and put the cup down. He watched me, then came, bringing his own cup, and sat down across from me.

"You wanna know how I met your daddy?" he said.

I looked at him, or tried to; my eyes wouldn't focus right, and all I could see was a dark face swimming in the darkness somewhere beyond the lamp's glow.

"Do you?" he said. "You want a story?"

"Yes," I said. "Yes, please."

"Then fetch me the candle," he said. "It's there, by the door."

He nodded to show me the direction, and I clambered down from the chair and felt my way through the darkness. I found the candle, a brand-new one, on a small shelf next to a flat, round coffee can.

"Bring the matches too," he said. "There, in the can. Can't have light without strikin' fire."

I took the candle and the can and brought them back to the table, moving slowly, unsure of my footing. He took them from me, opened the can, extracted a match. I stood beside him while he struck it, feeling the acid fumes tickle my nose. He lit the candle and extin-

37

guished the match, then he held the candle sideways, over the table. I watched, fascinated, as the melted wax formed a pool on the slate. When he judged it big enough he set the candle in the pool, held it while the wax hardened. We waited then, while the flame steadied, the light from the candle added to that from the lamp making the room seem almost too bright. He leaned over then and blew out the lamp, and the light faded.

"Put the matches back," he said. "Always put things back where you found 'em so you'll know where they are when you need 'em again."

There was no answer. The clouds of condensation blossomed in front of my face. I waited, listening. I could hear the sound of my own breathing, the pounding of blood in my ears. I wanted to push the door open and just go in, but you do not do that to a man, not even to save his life. And so I waited, and waited, and raised my hand to knock again. Then I heard the sound coming from behind the weather-ravished door: a long, racking cough. I shoved the door open and stepped inside. "Jack?" I said, as the door swung to behind me.

He coughed again. His breath came in harsh asthmatic whistles, and after each exhalation I could hear the squeaky sucking sounds of mucus shifting in his chest. Pneumonia. But I didn't mind; at least he was breathing. I moved towards where he lay and looked down, although I knew I could not see him. I could smell him, though. He stank of urine and feces and unhealthy perspiration. "Jack," I said stupidly, "you all right?"

He chuckled, the same deep, throaty chuckle he had always had, and my heart lifted. But then the chuckle ended in a cough, not a rumbling cough, but a high, deep, tight one. I shuddered at the sound of it, for I knew what it was like to lie in a bed feeling the vise closing down on your chest, knew that he would be feeling no relief, just a harsh burning every time he tried to clear his lungs. I waited silently until he stopped coughing, feeling the pain as if it were in my own chest, wishing that my feeling it would somehow make it less for him, knowing it would not.

He stopped coughing. I could hear his mouth working as he got up some spit and swallowed it to soothe his throat. "Hey," he said finally, "if it ain't the Perfessor. What brings you up this way?" His voice was a croak, but I could hear the bitterness in it; it had been a long time.

I didn't say anything.

"It does me good to see you, Johnny," he said, finally.

"It does me good to see you," I said. I reached out through the darkness, but I stopped myself before I touched him; he would not want that, not now, when it would feel like the touch of a nurse. He would rather die than have that.

197903040700

(Sunday)

"IT'S TIME YOU LEARNED HOW TO BUILD A FIRE," he had said, his voice sounding softer and more resonant than it did at other times. I said nothing. For I had learned that when he spoke in that voice, it was a time not for talking but for listening.

"Fire's the most important thing in the world. You know why?"

"No," I said. My voice was different too, softer and quieter, almost like a whisper.

He had paused to spit tobacco juice in a dark arc that ended, sizzling, in the campfire. "There's four things a man needs," he said. "He needs air an' he needs land an' he needs water an' he needs sun. Ain't nothin' else he needs, or could need, or want, or, anyways, oughta want, that don't come from those four. You understand that?"

I thought about it, trying to think of something that did not come from them. He waited patiently while I thought; it was one of the things I loved about him: he always gave me time to think. "Almost," I said. "He needs air to breathe and he needs water to drink. I don't know about the ground."

"He needs somethin' to stand on," he said. "A man can't stand on air an' he can't stand on water. He needs a place to stand."

I nodded.

"An' what about the sun?"

I hesitated. "I don't know," I said. "I thought heat and I thought light, but you said—"

"Power," he said. "The sun is power. The sun is what makes everything else happen. When the sun is weak the water turns to ice an' the ground is hard as nails an' the air ain't fit to breathe."

"I understand," I said.

"Good. Now, them's the four things a man needs, but he don't need them on accounta he's a man, he needs 'em on accounta he's an animal. An' if he stops when he's got 'em, he won't never be nothin' but an animal. He won't be a man. He won't be a man on accounta he can't make none a them things. So he ain't got no say. If he don't have no say over the things he needs to live, he ain't got no say over whether he lives at all, an' if he ain't got no say over that, he ain't no man. A man has to have say. You understand that?"

"Yes," I said.

"That's what it's all about. Everything a man does, that makes any kinda sense, anyways, is on accounta he wants some say. That's why he builds a fence around his land, an' digs in the ground an' plants in rows; so every time he looks at that piece a ground he'll know, maybe he didn't make it, but he had some say. That's why he builds a dam or a bridge an' digs a channel for the water in a crick; so every time he stops the water or goes over it or sees it goin' where he wants, 'stead a where it went before, he'll know, maybe he can't make water, but he can have some say. That's why he fears the wind, why when it's dark an' the wind blows you feel that little shiver up your back—on accounta there ain't no way a man can have no say over the air. You understand that?"

"Yes," I said.

"He can't have no say over the sun, either. An' the truth is, the little bit a say he's got over ground an' water don't mean much. On accounta the winds come an' the sun burns an' the floods come an' wash the ground away—that can happen anytime. An' even if it don't, havin' that little piece a say over a piece a ground or a stretch a water is 'most like havin' no kinda say at all. On accounta soon as you build your fences an' plow your land an' put in your crop, you gotta stay an' wait for harvest. You got say over the land, but it has say over you. Same with water. An' a man that spends his time just tryin' to have say over them things, he ain't much of a man. That's how come it useta be women that put in crops, an' women that went to get the water. So them things ain't all that important when you get right down to it. Fire is. You see why?"

"No," I said, feeling uneasy, because I didn't understand.

"It gives a man say. Gives him *final* say. It lets him destroy. Lets him destroy anything. There ain't nothin' in the world that won't burn or melt or change some way if you get it hot enough, if you got enough fire. An' when the fire's gone, there ain't nothin' left, for nobody. If a man comes to take your house, you can burn it, an' he can't have it. You can burn your crops. You do the same to his. You can get things right down to where they was to start with, down to ground an' air an' water an' sun. Now, that ain't much say, an' it ain't the best kinda say, but it's bettern havin' no say at all. Because a man with no say is an animal. So a man has to be able to make a fire, has to know how to make it in the wind an' the rain an' the dark. When he can do that, he can have some say."

I nodded.

"We'll start tomorrow mornin'," he said. "We'll start in the stove, where it's easy. Then we'll go on. 'Fore we're done, you'll know how to make a fire anyplace, anytime. Then you'll have say."

"Will that make me a man?" I said.

"No," he had said. "Nothin' *makes* you a man. It means you can be a man. If you decide you want to."

The cabin had closed in around me. The darkness hung there, pushed back only a little way by the light of the lantern, and in the darkness, at the very limits of my vision, lurked the walls. I could not see them, but I knew they were there; I could hear them. They took the sounds of our past breathing—his an uneven wheezing, mine a series of short, hard inhalations and exhalations, too rapid and too shallow by half— and sent them back to merge with the sounds of our present breathing. The result was something more than an echo, something less than a clear reverberation, a dark and clotted sound that grew and grew and grew until I could not listen to it and I could not ignore it; until I could not do anything but accept it and try to keep my mind on what I was doing: making a fire.

I had made the preparations slowly and carefully, because I knew neither of us could afford to be long without heat. I had started with the stove, clearing the grate with an iron poker, then sliding the box of ashes out and carrying them outside and spreading them along the path. Then I had cut wood, chunks of hardwood for lasting heat, slabs of pine for faster burning, strips of kindling. And then I had prepared the tinder, twisting sheets of old newspaper into tight wands.

Now I laid the tinder in the firebox, keeping it an open, crisscross pattern. On top of it I built a fragile edifice of kindling and small pieces of wood. Then I went to the shelf and got the old, rusted coffee can in which he had always kept his matches. I found it there, in precisely the same spot it had always occupied, and as I pried the lid off with fingers turned to ice I wondered how many days' worth of minutes he had saved in all the years of putting the can back, and how much longer it would make any difference. But I put the can back on the shelf before I lit my fire. The smell of phosphorus burnt my nostrils as I maneuvered the match into the stove. I watched as the fire caught the dry newspaper and began to devour the records of the goings on in the County three months back, and I wondered if some unimaginative scholar in some unimaginable future would have given his eyeteeth for the very bit of newspaper I had burned. Historians think that way, losing sleep over documents that they deem precious, but which, in the evaluation of people who have reason to know, are most useful as tinder, or mattress stuffing, or papier-mâché. I was burning sacred primary source material; but it was heat that mattered right then, not history.

He coughed again, and I slid the lid back on the stove to make sure no smoke leaked out. He was asleep, if you could call it sleep; the pain of each breath was written on his face, and it could not have been normal sleep, or the pain would have awakened him. I turned away, lifted the lamp, and examined his shelves. There was nothing much there. He had not canned as much as he usually did. Still, there were mason jars of beans and corn and carrots, two or three of peaches and pears, one of applesauce, a couple of venison. Enough for a stew; I wouldn't have to climb the slope to get food. I put the lantern down and checked the fire. The flame was catching the larger wood, and the metal of the stove itself was beginning to groan with the agony of uneven expansion. I slid a few larger pieces of pine into the blaze and closed the stove again, adjusted the drafts, then got the two water pails from the packing crate on which they stood, and went out.

The sky was fully light now, and the woods were silent. I moved through the underbrush, making little noise. He had taught me how to move like that, swiftly and silently, taking me to the pine woods, heading off in what seemed to me a random direction but which never was, eventually leaving me stumbling along trying to keep up and be quiet at the same time and failing miserably at both. Inevitably I would lose him, and would stand in the midst of the forest, dark trees rising on either side, listening to the pounding of my heart as I realized that I was alone on the far side of the Hill. It was then, at those times, that I learned the most. Not woodcraft, really. Or perhaps a true form of woodcraft: to bring my breathing under control; to still my own fear; to be methodical; to accept my limitations and compensate. I could not move quietly, but I could stand quietly and watch and listen, and when he came back for me, as he always did, I could sense him. I learned to reconstruct the man from the subtle whisper of cloth on cloth, the tiny clink of a buckle. And then I would turn in the right direction and find, as often as not, that my eyes had grown used to the dimness, that I could actually see him, and I would say to him, my voice quiet with triumph, "If you're gonna sneak, for Ned's sake, *sneak*."

That had been early on. In time I had learned how to move in near-silence, although I never attained the total quiet and ghostly grace that accompanied his movements. One day he had looked at me thoughtfully and said, "You hunt jest like your daddy done. Could be, if you was to put the time on it, you could be as good as him." He paused. "Mebbe better."

"Not better," I said.

He looked at me and shrugged. "What the hell. Ain't no man the best there is at everything, not even Mose, an' he come as close to bein' the best at anything worth worryin' about as any man I ever knowed. There was even some things Mose just couldn't do. It took Mose a damn long time to figure out how to die, for one thing. He tried to kill hisself in more different ways than any man I ever knowed. He didn't call it that, he called it havin' a good time, but tryin' to kill hisself was what it was. When they come an' told me he was dead, all I could think was, damn, Mose finely got the hang of it." He had been gazing off into space, but suddenly he became aware of me. "You mind me talkin' about your daddy that way?"

I shrugged. "You knew him better than I did."

"You want I should to stop?"

"No," I had said. "I want to hear."

44

That was the way it had been then; I always wanted to hear about Moses Washington, about what he had said and what he had done, about the adventures that had taken him, and Old Jack Crawley, and Uncle Josh White, tearing across the mountains pursued by lawmen and irate fathers and angry farmers. About the time Moses Washington had somehow managed to get a contract to supply the detachment of soldiers that was stationed in the Town during the First World War—God knows why—with "drinking water" and had instead delivered seven wagonloads of second-rate moonshine for which the government unquestioningly paid; about the time he had convinced the local sheriff that three Revenue agents were Southern moonshiners intent on expanding operations and got them run out of town; about the time he had kept Old Jack Crawley out of shotgun matrimony by loudly proclaiming that the child was his—which could have been true—and that he wanted to marry the girl and give the child a name—which was certainly not true—but she swore she would rather mother a bastard than marry a son of a bitch; about the time he had faced a three-hundred-pound farmer who was armed with a double-barreled shotgun and intent to do bodily harm and had reduced him to tears and apoplexy simply by repeating every threat the man made as a question while grinning like an idiot; about the time he had been hailed as a hero because he had gone up onto a burning mountain and rescued a group of high school boys who had been pressed into service to fight the fire and who had somehow got cut off—that was the official version; the true story, according to Old Jack, was that Moses Washington had had a cache of his best up on that mountain, and had agreed to lead the boys to safety only on condition that they carry the whiskey down. The stories were endless, and I had never tired of them, at least not for years. No; I had never tired of them. But somewhere along the line it had occurred to me that the stories were not just stories. They were something else: clues. The stories had changed then, it seemed. And Moses Washington, a decade dead by that time, had changed. And I had changed. And none of the changes had been for the better.

He had not been to the spring in a long while. The soft earth at the edge of the water was printed by the feet of small animals, the hooves of a pair of deer, but bore no track of man. He had not cleaned the spring in a long time, either. The bottom of it was littered with water-logged leaves, and I knew that below them would be a film of mud. That would make the dipping difficult. But I had no choice; I knelt down and slowly and gently maneuvered the edge of a bucket into the water, not pushing it too deeply, trying to let the water move without setting up a current. He had taught me how to do that, how to dip clean water from a shallow, leaf-choked spring. It was not an easy thing to learn; it required strength and patience and practice, and it had taken me years to really learn to do it right, for the very simple reason that each time I had failed, I had had to wait for the detritus to settle before I could try again. He had watched me do it, sitting silent and unperturbed, correcting my mistakes in a soft voice: I had got excited, I had got rushed, I had moved too quick, I had moved too jerky, I must wait there, quietly, until the dirt had settled, and then I must try again. Because someday it would be important that I do it right and do it right the first time. And now the day had come. And I was nervous, and frightened, not sure I remembered how to do it, not sure at all.

But I did remember. Something in me did, and I was calm and patient when I needed to be, and I was strong and steady when I needed to be, and I filled the buckets without disturbing the mess that cluttered the bottom.

I stood up then, feeling satisfaction at having done something so simple, and looked around at the mountains, trying to remember the days when this was exactly what I had wanted out of life: to get up in the morning and build a fire and go to the spring and pay a visit to the privy, and then cook my breakfast. But it was not that way now; now I stood in the shadow of the Hill and looked down the slope towards the gray, unsturdy-looking outhouse and almost dreaded the time when I would have to use it. But then I stopped daydreaming and paid more attention to the land that lay beyond the privy, and what I saw frightened me.

I was standing in the shadow, but there, on down the slope, I could see the sunlight. And it was weak sunlight, without warmth and without force, not at all the way it should have been on a clear March morning. I looked up at the sky. The clouds were low and gray, drifting almost imperceptibly northward. The air was wet and heavy. Snow. It was going to snow. Not one of those benign snows that lay light on the ground; it would be a blizzard. I knew how it would go;

for as long as I could remember, for as long as anybody could remember, the pattern of the blizzards had been the same. First the slow drifting of cloud cover, coming in from the south, pushed by the south wind. The cloud could build for hours or days, perhaps losing a little moisture in snow or freezing rain, but staying, until the storm center drifted far enough northward and drove the winds hard against the mountains. Then the snow would fall, fast and furious. That was the first phase. How long it would last no one could say. But sooner or later the matronly south wind would tuck up her skirts, go scuttling off across the mountains, taking the clouds with her. Then there would be calm, and clearing skies; the second phase. It might last a night or a week. But sooner or later it would end. And then the witch wind, the west wind, cold and sterile, would come slicing across the mountains, making a weird, oddly pitched, indescribable sound, ripping the snow from the ridges and making it go boiling down into the valleys to build impassable drifts. That was the third phase. It could last, it seemed, forever. I would have to get out of there before that happened; I would have to get him out of there before the snow fell deeply, or I wouldn't get him out of there at all.

I picked up the buckets and went up the path as quickly as I could. When I reached the door I stopped and waited a minute, catching my breath. Then I nudged the door open with my foot and went inside.

The cabin seemed almost warm now. It wasn't really, but the fire had made some difference; the chill was off the air and his breathing seemed less labored. I closed the door quickly to keep the heat inside, and then I stood there for a minute while my eyes adjusted to the dimness. As I stood I grew more calm, more sensible. My run up the hill, I realized, had been silly. Because there was no real hurry. The snow would not fall all at once, and even if it did there would be no rushing; there would never be any rushing Old Jack.

So, when my eyes adjusted, I took the buckets over and filled the reservoir on the stove; I would need hot water before the reservoir would supply it, but eventually it would raise the humidity and make his breathing easier. Then I added some hardwood to the pine that was burning in the stove—I needed even heat now; steady heat. Then I put some water in the kettle and set it to boil.

I opened my pack then, and took out some of the supplies I had brought: every vitamin we had had in the house; the penicillin Judith

47

kept around, defying her own best medical advice; aspirin. I laid it out on the table.

The kettle was almost ready to boil by then, and I made a quick search for his shelves. I found his cups, two of them, enameled metal. His honey supply was low, and what was there was so clotted by the cold that it would not have poured inside an hour. He had a little sugar, though. And he had plenty of whiskey, fifteen bottles of the stuff. Store-bought, he would have called it, implying that it was not good. And he would have been right; it was terrible stuff, as cheap as dirt and as harsh as kerosene, but it had alcohol in it and it would taste all right mixed with sugar and water. It would taste a lot better than nothing.

I mixed two toddies, using the recipe he had taught me: four fingers of whiskey, and if you have no honey, three thumbloads of sugar, and when the water boils, pour it slow till the fumes rise and make your mouth water. That had been on a winter night, when the winds had brought wet, sleety rain, and I had arrived on his doorstep soaked and shivering. He had instructed me to take off my clothes, had hung them close to the stove, and by the time the toddy was ready the aroma of wet, steamy clothes had pervaded the air. I had grown to really love the taste of whiskey that night, while he had spun some improbable tale into the fetid air. Standing there waiting for the water to boil, I tried to remember what the story had been about.

But I couldn't. There had been too many stories, told over too many years, too many years ago; they all blurred together in my mind. I wondered if they would be blurred in his. And then I began to think about what a man's dying really means: his story is lost. Bits and pieces of it remain, but they are all secondhand tales and hearsay, or cold official records that preserve the facts and spoil the truth; the sum is like a writer's complete works with crucial numbers missing: the works of Macaulay minus the essay on Milton; the Complete Henry Hallam without *The Constitutional History*. The missing volumes are often not the most important, but they are the stuff of background, the material of understanding, the real power of history. The gaps in the stories of the famous are filled eventually; overfilled. Funeral eulogies become laudatory biography, which becomes critical biography, which becomes history, which means everyone will know the facts even if no one knows the truth. But the gaps in the stories of the unknown are never filled, never can be filled, for they are larger than data, larger than deduction, larger than induction. Sometimes an attempt is made to fill them; some poor unimaginative fool, calling himself a historian but really only a frustrated novelist, comes along and tries to put it all together. And fails. And so, like a poor cook trying to salvage a culinary disaster, he peppers his report with deceptive phrases—"it appears" and "it would seem" when he is fairly sure but has no evidence, "clearly" and "almost certainly" when he has no idea at all, and salts it with obscure references and then he pretends (to no one in particular because no one in particular usually cares) that the seasoned mess is chateaubriand instead of turkey hash.

The water boiled then, and I filled his cup and set the kettle on the back of the stove. I stirred his toddy and carried it to him.

"Jack?" I said. I waited. His breathing changed ever so slightly. I leaned over and waved the cup under his nose. He stirred.

"Johnny?" he said, without opening his eyes.

"It ain't George Washington."

He smiled, opened his eyes. "I dreamed you was here."

"Wasn't dreamin'," I said. "I got here at just after daybreak."

He nodded, seemingly exhausted by the effort of moving his head.

"I'll be all right now," he said. "It's mornin'. I'll be all right till midnight. It's them small hours I can't abide no more."

"You ain't been eatin' right," I said. "That's all. You can't hardly expect to go runnin' around half the night if you ain't eatin' right."

"Hell, Johnny, I ain't been doin' nothin' right. I got this cough an' the bastard won't let go. Started coughin' blood, losin' weight, got so I could hardly stand up long enough to piss."

"You gotta eat," I said. "That's all you need. I'll make some stew."

"That stew'll probably kill me. You recall the time—" He coughed then, grabbing awkwardly for a stained rag beside him. I could see the blood. I held his shoulders to steady him while he coughed, then turned away quickly so he would not be embarrassed as he cleaned himself as best he could, and so he would not see my face.

"All you need is a little hot food," I said, "and if you say one more word about my cookin' I'm gonna eat it all myself." I gave him the toddy, waited until I was sure he could hold the cup. "We're gonna have to do somethin' about that cough," I told him.

"More whiskey," he croaked.

"You need a doctor."

"Like hell I do. I ain't never needed no doctor. Last time I went to a doctor, I went on over to see Old Doc Martinson, an' that old quack thumped me an' pounded me an' stuck his finger up ma butt, an' then he charged me a dollar an' sent me up to that bastard Hawkin's drugstore with a perscription, an' Hawkin charged me fifty cents for a little bottle 'bout the size of a bean pod, an' when I ast him what was inside he told me a whole bunch a crap an' then let out that it was twenty percent alcohol, an' I says, damn, Hawkin, I can get twice this much 'shine for a quarter, an' that's gonna be a hunnert proof, an' that was the last time I ever had no truck with doctors, an' I'm too damn old to start now."

"You're too damn sick not to," I said.

He grunted, and sipped at his toddy, pretending at being silent. But I could see what had happened; the weakness had come across him, and he was trying to finish the toddy while he could still hold the cup himself. I hesitated, then reached out and took the cup away. "Don't drink that so fast," I said.

"I wasn't finished," he snapped. "Man gets a little under the weather, an' first thing you know some damn Methodist is runnin' to snatch his whiskey away." He dropped his hands to the cot. I pretended I had not seen them tremble.

"You drink this crap that fast, somebody's like to snatch your butt off an' you wouldn't even notice."

"May be, but he ain't like to live to tell the tale. Give me my whiskey back." He reached out for it, and his hands were steady again.

"All right," I said, "but you take it easy." I went back to the stove and mixed my own toddy, keeping my back to him. I heard him sigh once or twice, one soft click as the cup hit his teeth, but I did not help him.

"You can mix me another in a minute," he said finally.

I turned around and set my own toddy down. He was holding his cup out to me, his face a mask of effort. I took it quickly and went and filled it with water. Then I made up a dose, two of every pill that might do him some good, and took it all back to him.

"I don't want no damn pills," he said. But he took them almost eagerly, and swallowed all the water. I got him another cup, and he swallowed that too. Then I went and mixed him another toddy.

I left him while he drank it, and took up my own, and settled down in the chair that was closest to the door. My chair. I pretended I was not watching him, that I did not see him resting his cup on his chest after each sip. We didn't say anything; it took all his strength to drink, and I was lost in thought, thinking about that chair, how once when I had sat in it my legs would not reach the floor and I would sit there and swing them, extending my toes, trying to reach the ground, about the thrill I had known the first time I had managed to touch it, and had known that I was getting my growth, just as he had said I would. I closed my eyes and listened to the muted roar of the air in the flue, to the soft keening of the fire. I heard a slurp as he took the last sip, and I relaxed; even if he dropped the cup, or fell asleep, there was nothing to spill.

Presently his breathing evened and he began to snore, and I knew it was real sleep this time, not the exhausted unconsciousness. I felt better. I got up from the chair, my joints creaking as if I were as old as he, and concocted a stew of venison and beans and carrots in his old iron pot, and set it to simmer. I was hungry now, but I would wait. I mixed another toddy, my hand perhaps a shade too liberal in the darkness. I sat down again and drank.

"I recall the night I met him," he had said. "It musta been near fifty year ago now, but I recollect it clear. It was in the back room a Hawley's store, halfways through a Saturday night. Back in them days, there was always a card game at Hawley's on a Saturday. I 'member this here night I wasn't playin' on accounta the night 'fore that I took the train up to Sulphur Springs to see this gal, lived back in the mountains, and wouldn't nothin' satisfy her ceptin' I bring her on back into town to walk around awhile, an' I had to buy her dinner, an' then I had to take her on home again on the train, an' after I done all that, she wouldn't do nothin' 'sides kiss me. Plus which, I was clean outa money, an' I had to walk back down. It wasn't but eight mile, but I tell you, I never went to see that gal again—she was knock-kneed an' cross-eyed, anyways. Way I heard it, she ended up married to a fella that worked cook on the B&O. Light-skinned fella. She left on to everybody that he wasn't colored at all, he was an Eyetalian. Whatever he was, he ended up with that gal; an' welcome, far as I's concerned.

"So anyways, I wasn't playin' that night, on accounta not havin' any money. Josh was playin', though, you better believe that. Onliest thing he loved bettern whiskey an' women was cards. He had the best pack a coon dogs in the County, but you couldn't get him to run 'em if there was a card game goin' inside a twenty mile. I forget who all else was playin', bunch a the reglar fellas. They was playin' an' gettin' along, an' all the sudden in walks Mose.

"Course, didn't none of us know it was Mose; hadn't none of us never put eyes to him before. But that ain't to say we didn't know who Mose was. Pretty damn near the whole County knowed who he was, even if he wasn't nothin' but twenty, twenty-one year old. Hadn't nobody seen him, but they sure as taxes *heard* of him. Don't know 'xactly when it begun; somebody—an' didn't nobody recall who—come into town talkin' 'bout some young boy up in the mountains, callin' hisself Moses Washington an' makin' moonshine that was strongern horse piss an' smoothern a bunny's butt. There wasn't no Prohibition then—a man could drink 'thout the government blowin' snot in his jug—an' the truth was, the tax on liquor wasn't all that high, but there's lotsa folks 'round here that'd sooner sip on home brew than swim in store-bought. Anyways, this here boy was sposed to be makin' whiskey so fast he'da drowned hisself if it hadn'ta been that he was sellin' it fastern he was cookin' it. I tell you, the way they talked about this boy, they had him livin' up in some damn holla somewheres in some damn mansion with a whole stable a half-time hillbillies tendin' his fires an' cookin' his corn, while all he done was try an' keep the greenbacks from cuttin' off his air. That an' shoot government agents.

"That was how Mose's reputation really got goin'. A couple a government fellas come sniffin' an' they caught the tail end a some whispers about Mose, an' they followed them whispers up into the hills, an' that was all anybody ever heard of 'em. A couple other fellas come lookin' for the first two, an' they went up in the hills, an' didn't nobody see them no more, neither. Then four of 'em come, an' two of 'em went up in the hills, an' the other two waited in town. The two that went up never come down, an' the two that stayed in town disappeared too; didn't pay no hotel bill, didn't take no bags. Jest went. After that, didn't no more come. Now, lotta things coulda happened to them government fellas, but people bein' what they is, they'd a lot rather figure there was eight government men buried in the woods than anything else. I would maself.

"But anyways, whenever anybody said 'Moses Washington' you thought right away about dead-eye shootin' an' moonshine an' money. You sure as hell didn't think about bib overhauls an' no shirt an' hair with Spanish needle stickin' out an' no damn shoes, which was what Mose was wearin', an' a old gunnysack, which is what he was carryin'. An' you sure didn't think about Hawley's back room, which was where he showed up, I s'pose on accounta when folks heard about one man doin' all that, didn't nobody think he was gonna turn out to be colored. I know I didn't.

"It didn't bother nobody that he was a stranger; there was always a lot a strange colored folks runnin' around in the summer. White folks'd come to stay out to the Springs or Chalybeate, to take the water cure—how them damn fools could figure splashin' around in a bunch a cold water that didn't even taste good was a cure for somethin' I'll be damn if I know—an' they'd bring a maid an' a man—that's what they'd call it, though from my experience, them fellas wasn't close to bein' men an' them gals sure wasn't maids; if they was when they got here, they sure as hell wasn't when they left—to dress the ladies an' tend the horses an' all that. We'd get some colored ones up to Hawley's, but they was generally too foxy to get clean plucked. But we didn't figure Mose for one a them; not the way he was lookin'. So what we figured was, he was one a them boys useta come in from down South to work on some white man's farm. The white folks around here wasn't fools, an' they knowed they could get away with payin' them fellas damn near nothin', so there was always a few around. Sooner or later they'd end up in town with a little bit a money in their pockets, an' sooner or later they'd end up on the Hill, since that was about the only place for a colored man to go, an' if it was Saturday, they generally ended up in Hawley's back room gettin' plucked cleanern a pullet. So we took one look at Mose an' figured here was one a them hayseeds, so dumb he didn't know to comb his hair. Only question was, did he have any money?

"So we all waited. Fellas that was playin' kept on, didn't even look up at him, although I swear I seen Josh's mouth water. Josh had been winnin' but he quit; all the usual tough stuff—an' them boys could get tough over cards—went right out the window. They didn't even bluff; soon as them boys smelled easy meat they got polite as a colored Methodist at a white man's prayer meetin'. Rest of us jest nodded to Mose polite like an' kept on watchin' the game.

53

"Mose, he seen how nice an' clean they was playin', an' he decided he was gonna set down an' clean up, so he steps up an' says maybe he'd set in for a hand or two, if that was all right with the gentlemen that was playin'. That's just the way he said it too, gentlemen, an' if anybody had a notion that Mose was from around here, that cleaned it out: that bunch a boys was noted as the sneakiest rascals north a the County Jail—an' wouldn't anybody that knowed 'em called 'em gentlemen.

"Course, they couldn't jest leave the man set down; he mighta cottoned on too quick. So Josh, he looks Mose up an' down, an' he says, 'Well, sir, I don't know. Me an' the boys, we been playin' together for a long time, an' we got ourselves a real nice friendly game.' Mose says he didn't mean to be bustin' in or nothin', but he was jest as friendly as anybody. Well, they hemmed an' hawed around for a while an' finely they said he could set down, but he had to understand there wasn't no dirty talk allowed. Mose said he didn't never talk dirty. They said if he had a pistol, he'd have to leave it with Old Man Hawley. Mose said he didn't have no pistol. So they said did he have a knife. Mose says yes, he did have an old jackknife. 'No knives,' Josh says, an' they made Mose give his jackknife to Hawley, which had to be the funniest damn thing, since hadn't none a them fellas gone nowheres without a knife, 'cept jail, since Hector was a pup. An' they wasn't no jackknives, neither. Funny thing was, with them bein' so cagey 'bout gettin' his fangs pulled, they didn't think maybe he had a shotgun down in that there gunnysack. Leastways, they didn't think it then.

"Anyways, they fixed him up with a chair to sit on an' a tin can to spit in an' a tin cup to drink from, an' they ast him did he want a little snort. Which he took. An' every one a them rapscallions breathed a whole lot easier when he did, 'cause they was countin' on picklin' him on the way to pluckin' him, so's to have him so scratchy by the time they was through he wouldn't be able to do nothin' about it. So they waited till he'd drunk it down an' they poured him some more, an' then they dealt out the cards an' proceeded to lose.

"Most a the time them boys could make cards do anything. You'd tell 'em to take a pack an' make the ace a spades jump out an' sing 'The Battle Hymn a the Republic' an' he'd jest ast you did you want it on the long edge or the short edge, an' how many times through did you want it sung? Usually the fella that won was jest the best cheater. I recall one time Charlie DeCharmes was fixin' to knife Josh on accounta he claimed Josh was cheatin', an' everybody was tryin' to stop him by sayin' how did he know Josh was cheatin', an' Charlie says, 'The sonofabitch had to be cheatin' 'cause he's showin' four of a kind an' I know I didn't deal him nothin' but two pair.' But right now they was losin'. Mose was rakin' in the money. I mean *rakin'* it in. Every time he won he'd let out a yell like an Indian an' you could see clear back to his tonsils an' smell the manure on his breath. Only time he didn't win was when he had the deal. An' he looked so happy, I tell you, I quit bein' mad at that gal for usin' up all my money an' keepin' me from gettin' in on the pluckin', an' I started feelin' sorry for him. They waited till he had hisself a goodly pile an' that there tin cup had been filled an' emptied so damn many times it was startin' to wear thin an' then, little by little, they started takin' his money away.

"It was beautiful the way they done it. There was four of 'em playin' 'sides Mose. When it started out, he was winnin' four hands outa five, an' then it cut back so he was winnin' three out a five, but the two he was losin' was big ones, an' he was definitely comin' up on the short end. On top a everything, he played the dumbest poker I ever seen. He'd bet big when he had a good hand, an' he wouldn't even try to bluff; it was like he was payin' to lose. After about two hours they had all the money back that they'd lost to him, an' then Josh goes into his act.

" 'Brothers,' he says, 'it appears to me that we're all jest about even, an' maybe this here is a nice friendly time to call this nice friendly game over. Ain't nobody won moren he oughta, an' ain't nobody lost moren he can afford. I suggest we all head home.' Which was pure horse manure, 'cause it wasn't but maybe midnight an' that back room didn't hardly come awake 'fore then. But Josh, he acted like he meant it, an' he started pickin' up his money.

"Mose looks around an' he says, 'Well, gentlemen, I wanna thank y'all for a fine evenin', but to tell you the honest truth, it do seem a little short. Now, if you folks wants to go on home, why, good night to you; but if there's one or two that wants to stay an' play a few more hands, I'd be pleased to keep 'em company.' So they hemmed an' they hawed awhile, an' when the dust had done settled every damn one a them was stayin'. Mose says he appreciates 'em all stayin' jest to keep a stranger company, an' says he wants to offer 'em some a his hospitality, which, he says, was home-grown but tasty, an' he reaches down to his gunnysack an' hauls out a jug an' pours 'em all a goodly-sized toot, an' they all drinks together, an' he fills the cups up again, an' they starts in to play.

"Well, I'd seen it happen many a time, an' moren oncet I was in the middle of it myself, but I got to swear it was mighty impressin' the way they took that man's money away. They sucked it up like babies on boobies. Matter a fact, it seemed to me that they was cleanin' him out too fast, makin' it too plain, you know. So I tried to catch Josh's eye, give him a look to make him ease off a bit. But then I seen it wasn't none a his doin'; Mose was playin' so bad they didn't *have* to cheat—'cept maybe a little here an' there. The pile a money that had started out in front a Mose jest drained away like water outen a busted dam, but he kept on smilin' an' bettin' like a Goddamn fool. He was tryin' to fill straights, or draw flushes, or some damn thing, all the time. Well, anyways, in a hour or so it was all gone.

"Well, Josh, he calls a halt, says he needs some air, an' he gets up an' goes out onto the porch, an' then he give me the eye when he goes past, so I waited a spell an' then I followed him on out there. He looks at me an' he says, 'Jack, somethin' stinks like a dead catfish on a pile a cow poop on a summer day. I ain't never seen nobody lose money like that an' grin about it.' Well, I said I could see his point, but I didn't see no way it could be anything 'cept a crazy man losin' money, which they do all the time; there wasn't nothin' tricky happenin' I could see. So we had a chaw an' went on back inside.

"Hadn't nothin' changed in there. Mose was still settin' grinnin' away an' passin' his jug around. Since they wasn't playin' I got me a snort of it, an' I mean to tell you, it was the sweetest taste I'd ever had. I took another swalla an' rolled it around in ma mouth, tastin' it real good, an' right then was when I caught on. Only I didn't really catch on. Sometimes, you know, Johnny, you'll get yourself an idea way back in the back a your head an' it's like you're lightin' up a coal fire; maybe there's a blaze when you set fire to the kindlin', but that dies, an' the fire jest sets in there, an' it's all black, an' you might even think the fire's done gone out, but when you reach in there with the poker an' lift up a chunk a the coal the flame jumps right out at you an' gives your whiskers a good singein'. That's the way it was. The idea sprung up, but I didn't even notice it, hardly. I jest started feelin' mighty uneasy.

" 'Long 'bout then the game got started up again. Josh said how sorry he was to see Mose losin' all that money, an' Mose said, why hell, that wasn't so bad, an' got some more outa his gunnysack.

"Right then was when Josh quit smellin' catfish or cow poop or anything at all 'cept money; Josh looked at that money on the table an' he started to thinkin' 'bout how much more might be down there in that there gunnysack, an' his eyes went all glinty an' red, an' you could hear the greedy growin'.

"It didn't take no time for Josh to get the deal. The fellas that had it 'fore him knowed what was happenin'—we all knowed what Josh got like when he sniffed corn an' coin at the same time—an' they was so busy gettin' the hands over so they could get outen his way that I know for a fact one of 'em folded his cards while he was holdin' a full house, 'cause he was settin right in front a me an' I seen it. Soon as Josh had the deal one a the other fellas stood up an' said to deal him out.

"Josh didn't care. He was busy. One minute them cards was jest settin' there in his hands an' the next they was jest about flyin'. The room got so quiet all you could hear was the cards rufflin' an' folks breathin'. Josh finished up his fancy shufflin' an' Mose cut the cards. Josh dealt 'em out. I knowed he was cheatin', an' I knowed jest 'xactly what he done. He'd give Mose a bad hand, a hand anybody in his right mind woulda folded on, an' if he folded, well, fine. But if he played it, Josh'd give him jest enough on the draw to turn that dead hand into a live one. It always made 'em stay an' play. They took that little piece a luck as a sign that God was on their side. Folks is stupid; God don't go to poker games.

"The cards was out there, layin' on the table, an' the lamplight glinted off the back of 'em. Nobody picked nothin' up. They jest looked. Finely one a the boys that was still in the game picks up the jug to take a swig, only it's all gone. But Mose jest laughs an' reaches down into his gunnysack an' hauls up another one an' says there's more where that come from. An' right then that little ole coal fire in the back a ma head caught a draft an' started spittin' flames, an' I took a good long look at Mose, an' this time I had enough sense to see past them bib overhauls to the way he held hisself an' the look in his eye, an' I says to maself, sweet merciful Lord, these boys is settin' here with that crazy moonshinin' boy that done kilt eight men we know of, an' God knows how many we don't, an' they're playin' cards

57

with him an' *cheatin'*. I tell you, I hadn't never believed what they said about blood runnin' cold, but there was ice in ma veins that night. I tried to catch Josh's eye, I swear to God I tried, but he had his brain screwed to that pile a money an' there wasn't nothin' gonna unscrew it. But I tried so hard I did catch somebody's eye: Mose's. He looked right at me an' there jest wasn't no way in the world for me to hide what I knowed an' what I was thinkin', an' I can't say for sure, but I wouldn't be surprised if there wasn't a little spit sneakin' outa the corner a ma mouth. But Mose, he jest grinned at me, an' winked, an' picked his cards up and got on with the game.

"An' let me tell you, that game was gettin' on. The money was goin' into the pot so fast it left holes in the air. Every one a them fellas was bettin' like there wasn't no tomorrow, an' I suspected then that if Mose'd cottoned on to what they was at, there was likely not to be. They went around an' around, an' everybody was raisin'. The bet come to Josh an' he raised it fifty, an' I says to maself, Josh's done it now; the sonofabitch is gonna call 'em an' be mighty surprised to find out his full house don't beat four aces an' a king, an' all hell's gonna bust aloose. I give Josh one last look, but he wasn't noticin'; his eyes was all glazed over an' he was sweatin' like a fountain. Wouldn'ta made no difference if I coulda warned him; the bet was down.

"Mose took his time. He looked at his cards an' he looked at the pot, an' then he looked at Josh an' looked at his cards again. Finely he smiles an' reaches out an' picks up the jug an' takes a long swalla. Then he looks at the other two fellas an' says, 'You boys like this here whiskey?' They look at each other an' shrugs an' says yes, they allowed as how it was pretty fair whiskey. Josh was gettin' antsy, an' he says to Mose, 'This here's a card game, not a whiskey judgin'. Play or fold.' Mose jest smiles an' says that fifty was a mighty hefty raise, an' bein' as it was a friendly game an' all, he jest wanted to think on it a minute. Then he looks back at the other two an' says, 'I'm pleased y'all like this here whiskey. I made it ma own self. Up in the mountains. Ain't 'xactly *legal,* but it sure do beat workin' for a livin'.' Then he grinned at 'em, a big, wide, flashy grin, an' the two of 'em started to catch on. Mose waits till he's sure they got it all—an' it wasn't hard to tell, they turned all ashy—then he sees Josh an' raises *him* fifty. Them other two boys jest about busted theyselves foldin'.

"But Josh, he didn't notice a thing wrong; he jest looked at 'em like they was crazy, then he settled back, figurin' he was gonna take all Mose's money all by hisself. I could almost see him calculatin' jest how far he was gonna be able to go, an' it never oncet occurred to him that he'd already gone too far by about six mile. Or maybe six feet is a more accrate way to put it. I looked at Mose, an' he was settin' there jest as cool as could be, wasn't even lookin' at his cards, or at Josh, he was jest starin' up at the ceilin' an' smilin' a little.

"After a while Josh made up his mind how he was gonna play it an' reaches for his money. But Mose stops him. 'You like that there whiskey too, Mr. White?' Mose says. Josh says, 'It's fine, but we're playin' cards here, not talkin' whiskey.' Mose grins at him. 'I know that, Mr. White,' he says, 'I know that. I jest thought I'd mention this here: that likker is so smooth it has a way a sneakin' right on by folks that don't see how strong it is. See, most folks, they think it's plain old country white lightnin'. But it ain't. No, sir. This here is a special ressipy handed down from ma old granddaddy, an' what it is, it's *Black* Lightnin'. He called it that on accounta it was made by a colored man, an' a colored man's whiskey is mighty special.'

"Well, you couldn't say the man wasn't given no warnin'. But Josh, he jest sniffs an' I swear, 'stead a foldin' like a man that knowed what he was up against, he reaches down an' shoves another fifty into the pot, an' I thought, sweet Jesus, the crazy fool's callin' the man. But Josh was even craziern I thought, 'cause he says, 'I'll see your fifty an' raise you,' an' he shoves another fifty in.

"Now, by this time everybody else knowed who Mose was, an' was figurin' which way to duck when the poop started flyin'. But Mose jest looks at Josh an' shakes his head real slow an' sad like, an' then he says, 'I hate to do this here. I really do. Tell me, Mr. White, you happen to be a married man?' Josh stares at him. 'Married? What the hell's that got to do with a card game?' Mose grins an' says, 'I was jest wonderin' if you had anybody that was countin' on you for their keep.' 'Hell, no,' Josh says. 'No wife?' says Mose. 'No widowed mother? No crippled-up father? No woman? No gang a little bastards that calls you Daddy?' Josh was fit to be tied. 'Hell, no,' he says. He leans across the table an' he gets his face as close as he can to Mose's face, an' he says, 'Now, for the last Goddamn time, you quit this cacklin' an' you bet or fold, mister—' An' that took the wind outa his little speech some, 'cause they'd been so busy figurin' out how to take Mose's money away they hadn't even stopped to ast his name. But Mose took him off the hook. He grins real wide an' he says, 'The name is Washington, Mr. White, Moses Washington. An' I promise you I'll be bettin' in a minute here.' An' with that he made a show a studyin' his cards.

"Not that Josh was noticin'. He was too busy chokin'. He choked for 'bout ten seconds, bein' real quiet about it, but chokin' all the same. But I'll say this for him: he set there. Never moved a muscle. There was sweat on his forehead but his hands was steady as rocks. After a while Mose looks up an' says, 'You sure you ain't got nobody dependin' on you, Mr. White?' Josh looks at him, knowin' it was a way out. 'No, sir, Mr. Washington,' he says, 'there ain't nobody.' An' I tell you, Josh could be mighty greedy, an' sometimes he was meanern hell, but right then I was proud a him, 'cause he sure wasn't no coward. Course, he was still gonna get his butt kilt. 'Nobody?' Mose says. 'Not even a dog?' Well, everybody in the County knowed 'bout Josh's dogs. But Josh says, 'I got a couple dogs. But that ain't got nothin' to do with this here poker game.' An' he looked Mose right straight in the eye. 'Yes, sir,' Mose says, 'yes, sir, you're right about that. But I must say, knowin' there ain't nobody dependin' on you makes it a lot easier for me to do what I guess I got to do.' An' everybody was expectin' him to pull a shotgun outa that sack, on accounta he *had* to know the man was cheatin'. But maybe he wasn't sure, on accounta what he done was to push more money into the pot an' say, 'I call.'

"An' then, let me tell you, we was lookin' for hideyholes for real, on accounta when Josh showed his royal flush or whatever, Mose wasn't gonna have no more doubts an' there was gonna be murder done for sure. Josh, he give this look, real slow an' funny, an' he went to go an' turn his cards over. But Mose stops him an' says, 'You sure you ain't got nobody—' 'Nobody, Goddamnit,' Josh says. Mose grins. 'Well, in that case, I think I'll try an' take all your money. I'll raise you fifty.' An' jest like that, Josh was off the hook; all he had to do was fold. But did he fold? Hell, no. The damn fool saw Mose's fifty an' raised him fifty more.

"Mose was shocked. We was *all* shocked. I do believe Josh was a little shocked hisself; ain't every day a man watches hisself commit suicide. An' then Mose started to laugh. It was the craziest Goddamn laugh I ever heard; sounded like a cross 'tween a church choir an' a screech owl. He about fell off his chair laughin'. But he was laughin' alone, I'll tell you that. Finely he settles an' says, 'I guess we'll have to play it your way, Mr. White. Dealer's choice after all.' An' he puts in another fifty an' calls.

"I guess it was 'bout then that Josh come to his senses. But it was too late. He set there for a second, knowin' he'd give up his chances a livin', an' then he grins an' shrugs, an' turns his cards over. It wasn't as bad as it coulda been—just a full house, queens an' jacks. But it was gonna be enough. 'Umph,' Mose says, 'that's a good hand, Mr. White, a mighty good hand. You deal out real good hands. Seems you dealt me out a good one too.' An' he turns it over. I didn't bother lookin' at it, I was lookin' at Josh to see if he was gonna make a play. An' I b'lieve he was fixin' to, only I seen his eyes bug out. He was starin' at Mose's cards, an' that made me stare at 'em too, an' God damn if Mose wasn't showin' four deuces. An' then he starts to laughin', an' in between chuckles he was sayin', 'Yes, sir, Mr. White, we gonna play it your way.'

"Well, it took maybe half a minute 'fore folks could say anything, an' for the whole half a minute the only thing you could hear was Mose laughin' an' Josh makin' these funny little sounds that I can't even begin to explain. An' then Josh jest got up an' walked out, an' everybody followed him out to the main room, where they could talk free without worryin' maybe Mose was gonna blow their heads off. But I stayed. After a while Mose quits laughin' an' he looks at me an' says, 'I seen me some crazy folks in ma time, but that boy is one a the craziest.' Well, I don't know what come over me. I thought about it a lot since. Maybe I didn't like what he'd done to Josh. It was hard to say who was right, who was wrong, but it was jest right there on the borderline 'tween fun an' mean, an' that there is a line I like to stay way on the fun side of by a goodly ways. So when he said that I says, 'I believe they got their share a crazy colored men up there in them hills, an' I ain't sure but that the ones we got down here ain't a better breed.'

"Mose didn't say nothin'. Not for a long time. It give ma anger a chance to cool some, an' I was surely wishin' I hadn't stayed behind to step in the dog dirt like I done. Finely Mose reaches out an' takes his jug an' takes a long pull, an' then he sets it down. Then he looks at me. 'I ain't sure yours is *better*,' he says. 'I ain't sure that, as a genral thing, yours is any good at all. But some of 'em is pretty damn fine.' An' he gets up an' gathers up his gunnysack an' starts countin' money outa what's on the table. Musta been twenty dollars on the table, but he didn't take but five or six. Then he heads for the door. 'Hey,' I says, 'ain't you gonna take the rest a this here money?' He jest grins an' says, 'Why, what for? It was jest a friendly game.' An' that was the last anybody seen of him for quite a spell."

We had dreamed away the day, he in delirium, I in reverie. From time to time he wakened to cough, from time to time I stirred to put more wood on the fire. The stove's mechanical clankings disappeared; what was left was a soft, eerie, almost undiscernible squeaky hissing hum, the sound of a drawn-out kiss. I drifted, recalling another time when I had sipped whiskey and listened to a fire's keening.

My eleventh birthday. A night in summer, the air warm enough, but tinged with the chill that always haunts the mountains. There was a strong wind aloft; the clouds were strung out like great hurrying ghosts.

We had been camped in the lee of a giant boulder, near a minor stream called Nigger Hollow Run, waiting for Uncle Josh White's dogs to catch the trail of some unfortunate raccoon. Uncle Josh himself sat stoically beyond the range of the firelight, pulling steadily at a bottle of Four Roses. Old Jack sat closer to the flames, sipping a toddy from a tin cup. I sat beside him, sipping from a tin cup of my own. Uncle Josh, as usual, was as silent as the tomb. Old Jack, as usual, was talking, but softly; he was telling a tale. I could not really hear him; I had had three or four toddies by that time, and all I could really do was to sit and hold the warm cup clutched against my belly, watching the flames dance against the backdrop of the night. His words came to me only in bits and snatches, but I had not needed to hear more; I knew the tale. He had told me the story twenty times by then, but he had only needed to tell me once, for at that first telling he had said that it was a tale that Moses Washington had liked to tell, over and over again. And so I could sit by the campfire, hearing the words with only half my mind, filling in the details on my own, telling myself the story of a dozen slaves who had come north on the Underground Railroad, fleeing whatever horrors were behind them, and who had got lost just north of the Mason-Dixon Line, somewhere in the lower reaches of the County, and who, when they could no longer elude the men who trailed them with dogs and horses and ropes and chains, had begged to be killed rather than be taken back to bondage. But that night had been different; he had added something new. His voice had come clearly to me, coming, it had seemed, out of the flames: "Some say they give up. Some say they quit. White folks say it mostly, though I've heard some colored say it too. Bunch a sorry niggers, they say, too scared to fight, too scared to run, too scared to face slav'ry, too scared even to kill their own selves; couldn't even get away that way, lessen a white man done it for 'em. An' maybe that's the truth of it, though it seems to me you don't want to be judgin' folks too quick, or too hard. Maybe you can do it if you're white, but it strikes me a colored man oughta understand what it coulda been like, white folks all around you, an' no place to turn. But judgin' don't matter when you get to the bottom of it, on accounta don't nobody know what happened down there in the South County, or when, or even 'xactly where. I doubt the killin' part of it myself. On accounta they ain't dead. They're still here. Still runnin' from them dogs an' whatnot. I know, on accounta I heard 'em. I ain't never heard 'em that often—maybe five, six times in ma whole life. Funny times. I never heard 'em anytime when there wasn't snow on the ground, for instance. An' I ain't never heard 'em when I was listenin' for 'em special. Now I think on it, I only ever heard 'em when I was on the trail a somethin' else, an' I'd be listenin' for whatever I was after, jest settin' there lettin' the sound come to me, an' then I'd hear 'em. Wouldn't be no big noise. Wouldn't be nothin' like them sounds them dumb-butted white folks, don't know a ghost from a bed sheet, is all the time tellin' you ghosts make. On accounta they ain't ghosts; they ain't dead. They're jest runnin' along. An' the sound you hear is the sound of 'em pantin'. First time I heard 'em, I recall I was caught out in a storm, up along Barefoot Run. I thought I had time to make a kill an' get on back, but the wind shifted on me an'..."

Then he had called to me, his voice cracking, and I had risen from the chair and gone to him, had touched his forehead. The flesh had seemed hot enough to burn.

Later, I fed him stew, and then I filled his chipped enamel basin and had washed him as best I could, trying to be gentle with him despite the rough rag and lye soap I had to use, despite the embarrassed looks he gave me. Then I helped him use the old enamel chamber pot, hating what it did to him to be so helpless, hating the process, hating myself for hating it. I had escaped outside to empty the pot, and had found the ground covered with snow, the air clotted with flakes. And so I had turned and gone back inside, to tell him we had to go.

"No," he said. "No, Goddamnit. No."

"Jack . . ."

"I said no."

"You need a doctor," I said. "You need a hospital. That cough sounds like your guts are comin' out."

"I feel fine."

"You look like hell."

"I ain't never been pretty."

I turned away then and went to the stove. I started to put more wood in, but I realized that would be a step towards giving in. "Jack," I said. "You can't stay here."

"Hell I can't. I stayed here for fifty years. If I got sick, I took care a myself. I didn't need no hospital then, I don't need one now. Don't nobody do nothin' in the hospital 'cept die."

"It's startin' to snow," I told him. I let it go at that; he would know what it meant.

"You had to go out there to find that out? I could smell it." He started to cough again. I stepped across and stood above him while he coughed. He looked up at me over the rag he held clamped to his mouth, his eyes wide and guilty, as if he were a little boy who was being naughty. When he had finished I moved to clean the mucus from his face before he could even begin to do it for himself. And when it was over, when he lay back panting for breath, I took the rag away from him and went and threw it into the gathering darkness and the accumulating snow. Then I washed my hands. I did not look at him.

"Johnny," he said, "they'll kill me."

I spun around to face him. "God*damn*it, Jack, they don't kill people. They take care of 'em."

"White people, maybe."

"Jack, things have changed a little—"

"Listen to him: 'Things have changed.' I spent the best part a my life tryin' to teach you up from down an' left from sideways, an' now you come tryin' to tell me that things have changed to the point where they give a good Goddamn about what happens to a colored man." He was silent for a moment, and I thought he was getting ready to cough again, but he wasn't; he was thinking. "Johnny, sit down there." I hesitated. "Go on," he said. I shrugged, pulled out my chair, sat. "Do you recall when you got your hair cut the first time?"

"What does that—"

"Do you recall it? I don't mean when your mama first took the shears to you; I mean when you went to the barber the first time?"

"Sure," I said.

"What happened?"

"What do you mean, what happened? We went to the barber an' he cut my hair. You took me."

"Where'd we go?"

"Altoona. What—"

"An' after that first time, where'd you get your hair cut?"

"Everett. Jack, you know that as well as—"

"Well, now, as I recollect it, Altoona's pert near forty mile off, an' Evert's eight. An' this here is the county seat. You mean to tell me there wasn't no barbershops in the county seat?"

I didn't say anything.

"You know why you didn't go to none a them barbershops, Johnny? I'll tell you why. On accounta every colored man in this town knowed that if he was to walk in an' set down they'd tell him they didn't know how to cut a colored man's hair. Wasn't that they didn't *want* to, now; it was just that they didn't know how. An' a course it wasn't their fault that they didn't learn, on accounta after the third or fourth colored man come out 'thout gettin' his hair cut, didn't no more go in. Well, we coulda done a lotta things; if we'da been like some these folks nowadays, we'da probly burnt them barbershops to the ground. Maybe we shoulda. Folks now probly think we didn't even think about it, but we did. But then that didn't seem to make no sense. So what we done, Johnny, was we worked it out like it was some kinda ceremony down to the Legion—just like that, on accounta it was Bunk that thought it up, an' Bunk surely loves his Legion ceremonies. We kept it secret; wasn't moren ten, twelve of us knowed. What we done was to keep a real close watch on the young boys—wasn't never that many—an' soon as a colored boy looked like he was gettin' tall enough to go to his first real barber, we'd get together an' scratch up some way to carry him over the mountain to Altoona, so's he could get his hair cut by a colored man. After that, the white fella down to Evert was good enough; an' he sure as hell was smartern the barbers around here; a head a nappy hair didn't slow him down one bit. Now, we done that so you young boys wouldn't have to set there an' hear some damn peckerwood tell you that you was such a strange kinda animal that the same pair a scissors that cut a white man's hair wouldn't make a dent in yours. We didn't want you to have to hear that; figured you'd hear somethin' like it soon enough. Mose said we was all crazy. Said there wasn't no use puttin' it off. Said what we was doin' was lettin' boys go along thinkin' the world was one way when it wasn't, that this here town was one way when it was just about as near to the other as it could be. An' I think now maybe he was right; we shoulda let you find out. We shoulda let you bleed the same damn way we did every damn day; maybe then you wouldn't be tryin' to tell me I oughta go runnin' to the hospital jest to hear some white man tell me he don't know where a colored man's gizzard is at."

I shifted uncomfortably in the chair. I wanted to argue, but I couldn't. Because things that I had never really understood were suddenly coming clear: the time when Bill and I had decided that the river wasn't good enough for us and had scraped together the nickels and dimes with which to pay the admission to the Town's one swimming pool, and had set out to walk the three or four miles to get there, but had never made it because we had come across Uncle Bunk (who hadn't taken a day off in twenty years that anybody could recollect, but who for some reason had that day), who had asked us where we were going and, when we told him, had proceeded to tell us about the eye-burning chemicals in pool water, and to point out that we could swim in the river for free and buy sodas with the money. Or another time: when, after a football game, I had been heading for one of the high school hangouts, a coffee shop on Juliana Street, and Old Jack had appeared as if by magic, and had asked me to help him with some odd or end, and had kept me with him by spinning out one of his long, involved tales—which had more attraction for me than any milk shake—and by the time we were finished, the time for milk shakes was past. Eventually, of course, we had come to know that we were not welcome at the swimming pool or in that particular coffee shop, but by then we had been scarred by so many of the little assumptions and presumptions that go with dormant racism or well-meaning liberalism that a little overt segregation was almost a relief.

Old Jack watched me, his black eyes sharp. "There," he said.

"You see? An' you want me to go over there an' trust them people. Like hell I will. I ain't sayin' they'd kill me, now, but they sure as hell would let me die. Wouldn't be the first time it happened, neither. Lord knows, your mama, she's anxious to think well a white folks, but even she'll tell you 'bout what happened to one a them big-time colored Methodist bishops, took sick an' they put him in a white folks' hospital an' before they could turn around them white folks had just like forgot to give him what he was supposed to be gettin' an' he up an' died."

"That was down South," I said weakly.

He stared at me. Shook his head. Struggled to sit up. I moved to help him. "Lemme be," he snapped. I sat back and watched as he fought his way up and then turned so that he could lean against the wall. "Plague take it, Johnny," he said. "I know you think I'm dyin', an' maybe I was, but now I don't dare, 'cause if your daddy heard that, he's gonna be settin' up to chase my tail from one end a hell to t'other. An' when he catches me, he's gonna say, 'Jack, I told you to teach my boy, an' you taught him to trail a deer an' drink whiskey, but you let him grow to man size still thinkin' that you can draw a line an' put somethin' on one side without it sneaks over to t'other side by an' by. You let him grow up thinkin' the whole world changes on account of somebody draws a mark on a map, or passes a law. You let him grow up thinkin' like a white man, an' a dumb white man at that.' God*damn*it, Johnny, you may a been to college, but you don't know nothin'; you don't know where you growed up at."

I looked at him, trying to think of something I could say that would have enough truth in it to make him seem wrong. But there wasn't anything.

"Johnny," he said. "I ain't no fool. I know I ain't doin' too good. I knowed it for a while. An' I knowed I needed help—that's why I called for you. On accounta, if somebody has to see me like this, I wouldn't want it to be nobody but you. . . ."

"Jack," I said. "Jack. You can't just lay here an'—just lay here because you don't want anybody to see you sick."

"I know that too," he said. "But it don't make no difference. On accounta they get me over there they'll kill me. On accounta they don't know what I need. They'll take away my whiskey an'—"

"I'll bring you whiskey," I said. "I'll bring you anything you need. . . ."

"What I need don't travel."

"What you need is help," I said. "Their kind of help."

He didn't say anything.

"Look," I said. "I'll stay with you. Right there. I won't go anywhere. I'll watch every move they make, make sure they do everything right."

He smiled sadly, shook his head.

"Why not? What's wrong with that?"

"Nothin'," he said. "Nothin's wrong with it. It's a fine idea. Only you can't do it."

"Why can't I?"

"Because you can't. You'd have to set up day an' night. It'd be just like waitin' for a buck on a game trail. . . ."

"I can do that," I said. "You know I can."

"I know you done it. I know you know how. But you'd forget somethin'."

I turned away from him then, and busied myself putting wood in the stove. When I turned around again he was looking at me, his eyes half closed.

"You don't think I'd forget anything," I said. "You think I've already forgotten it."

He didn't say anything.

"Why?" I said. "Why do you think that?"

"Why? On accounta it's true. I can see it in you, the way you move. You useta move strong an' easy. You still got the strength, I guess, but you ain't used it. You ain't kept up with it. That's what comes a city livin'. . . ."

"Oh, hogwash," I said.

"Hogwash, nothin'," he said. "I know what I'm sayin'. Your blood's got thin from livin' inside a houses all the time, with no time in the woods. You walk funny; that's on accounta your feet is all flattened out from standin' around on cement all the time. You set in a chair like it's home. I don't know what's at the bottom of it. Maybe you ain't been eatin' enough fresh-kilt meat, or you been drinkin' watered whiskey, or you been messin' with the wrong kind of women. . . ." He stopped. I hadn't said anything, but he must have seen something in my face. "That's it, ain't it," he said. "It's a woman."

I didn't say anything.

"I wondered if that was it," he said. "It happens to men sometimes. They find a woman an' they start in to changin'. If she's a bad

68

woman they change on accounta she makes 'em, but if they're any kinda man at all they get tired a that, an' they end up walkin' free, lessen of course they don't get kilt first. That ain't so bad. But if it's a good woman, that's dangerous. On accounta she don't try to change a man, she jest makes him think he oughta change. Makes changin' his ways seem . . . sensible. That's the dangerous kind. Which kind is yours?"

"She's the . . . dangerous kind," I said.

"You love her?"

I didn't say anything.

"Well," he said. "It ain't no sickness. But it does make a man weak. Not in every way, but in a lotta ways. Anyways, you can see why . . ." He stopped.

"Why you can't trust me to watch out for you," I said.

"Yeah," he said.

"No," I said. "No, I don't see. You're tellin' me that Moses Washington got weak on accounta my mother. . . ."

" 'Deed he did. He put down his gun an' he put down his whiskey an' he went over there an' lived butt-to-belly with them Methodists, an' when he tried to take his gun up again he ended up killin' hisself. I call that weak."

I didn't say anything.

"Johnny," he said. "You started trustin' white people, ain't you?"

"Hell, no," I said.

"Yes you have. You want to take me over there to 'em on accounta you started trustin' 'em."

"No," I said.

"It looks that way," he said.

"It ain't that way," I said.

He was quiet for a moment. Then he said, "This woman a yours. She's a white woman, ain't she?"

I just looked at him. Then I got out of there, and went to stand in the falling snow.

"Why don't you ever talk about home?" Judith had said. It had been a night in late fall, the moon full and milk white, the naked tree branches, shaken by the cold wind, clattering against each other like

69

dry bones. We were going west on Pine Street, a quiet street, far from the cars and the people. We moved slowly, despite the cold, our arms around each other, keeping each other warm.

"There's not much to talk about," I said. "It's a one-horse town on the road to no place. They've got five traffic lights now. It used to be four, but they had to put one in to control the traffic on the detour while they built the bypass; now there's nobody to stop at any of them."

"Well, what about the *history?*"

I hadn't answered her. I had shivered a little in the cold, but I hadn't answered her.

"Oh, hell," she said. "I don't care about any of it, really. It's just that you don't *talk* to me."

"I talk all the time," I said.

"Yeah," she said. "About the Ottoman Empire or European nationalism. But you never talk about anything that has to do with you."

"That *is* what has to do with me," I said. "I'm a historian."

"That's what you hide behind. All the Goddamn time. Quotes and anecdotes. Humorous little lectures guaranteed to make you the wittiest fellow at any cocktail party. Only I'm not a cocktail party."

"What do you want to know?" I said.

She stopped suddenly and whirled, spinning out from inside the circle of my arm. "What do I want to know? I don't want to *know* anything. I just want you to talk to me. I just want you to tell me things. I just want you to *want* to tell me things."

"What things?"

"*Jesus!* I don't know. How am I supposed to know? I want you to tell me what you want to tell me."

"I do," I said.

"Yeah. Nothing." She turned and started to walk again. She crossed her arms in front of her, hugging herself against the wind. I went with her, trailing her slightly.

"John," she said, clenching her teeth against the cold. "Usually when two people, a man and a woman, spend as much time together as we do, there is some kind of . . . basis for that. Trust, I guess. Sharing. Something between them. I don't know what there is between us."

We stopped at Forty-second Street to let a trolley rattle past. Judith took a deep breath. "John, a man asked me to go out with him today."

I didn't say anything. We crossed the street, moved on half a block to the building in which she lived. There was a low wrought-iron gate across the walk that led up from the street. It had come unlatched and swung in the wind, making tiny little metallic screeches, fingernails on a blackboard. She took her arm from around me and turned to face me. I let my arm drop away from her. "You ought to oil that gate," I said.

"Did you hear what I said?"

"You haven't said anything yet."

"I said a man asked me to go out with him. He's an attractive man. An intelligent man. I like him. I told him no."

"Look," I said, "I never asked you to—"

"Shut up," she said. "I know you didn't ask, and if you had I would have told you that who I see is my decision, not yours. And that isn't the point. The point is I tried to tell him about you and it just sounded . . . silly. Oh, not to him; he just heard what I was saying, that there was a man I had known for six months that I was spending a lot of time with and that I thought maybe I was in love with. And he went away thinking all kinds of things were happening between us that just *aren't*. And it bothers me that they aren't. You think I'm talking about sex, but I'm not. Oh, I think it's pretty damned odd that we haven't ever gone to bed together, but it's even odder that I've never seen your apartment. After six months I've never seen where you *live*."

She looked at my face, searching it with her eyes, waiting for me to say something, but I didn't have anything to say. Finally she looked away.

"I guess what I'm trying to say, John, is that there are some things I can do without and there are other things I can't do without. I can do without sex, I guess, but I can't do without learning about you, and who you are and what you want. I can't do without love."

"I see," I said. "Well, let me tell you something: the things I don't talk about I don't talk about because I don't like to talk about them. I don't like to think about them. And I'll be damned if I'm going to wring my guts out to get some blood on the floor so you can feel loved."

I glared at her. I couldn't see her eyes, because the wind caught

71

her hair and blew it across them, but I could see her lips tremble for a moment before she turned and went up the walk towards the door. I didn't move. She pulled it open, stepped into the foyer, and let it swing behind her without looking back. It was a heavy door, and it made a solid bang as it hit the jamb. I stood there looking at it. Then I reached down and pushed the gate open and went up the walk.

She had not gone beyond the foyer. She was huddled in the corner, crying. She looked up when I came in, her eyes wide, saying nothing. I put my hands on her shoulders and pulled her to me, and she came into my arms easily, but stood stiffly, her arms still crossed across her breasts. I turned her and pulled her with me out into the night.

We went silently through deserted streets, my hand on her arm, squeezing, holding her so tightly it would have hurt her had it not been for the thickness of her coat. She stumbled a little from time to time, but I kept her moving. We crossed more streetcar tracks, breasted the wind that whistled up along the wall of the old cemetery on Woodland Avenue. I turned her into my dark street, pulling her along, up the steps of my building. She waited silently, shivering a little, as I fumbled with the keys, then followed me inside and climbed the stairs unaided. Our footfalls sounded in the dark stairwell, sounded but did not echo; the soft, rotting wood of the stairs absorbed the vibrations and hushed them. At the end of the stairway, five flights up, I fumbled with the keys again, and opened my door. I stepped inside and went to the center of my room, my hand reaching up to find the chain. My hand brushed the naked light bulb; I remember thinking how cold it was.

By the time the light was on she was inside, leaning against the wall beside the door, her arms again crossed before her. I went and closed the door, locked the locks. She didn't move. She had stopped crying.

I went to the sink, put water in the kettle, set it on the hot plate. I got down cups and put instant coffee into one, bourbon and sugar into the other. I heard her moving behind me; slow footsteps as she walked across the floor to the middle and stood beneath the light, scrapings as she turned, looking around at the books. I stood there, waiting for the water to boil. It took forever.

I heard a small clink of metal on glass and the light went out. It was not dark; the moonlight came in through the dormer. I heard her moving again, towards the window. The kettle whistled and I poured the water by the glow of the burner. When I turned she was standing looking out at the cemetery. The waving branches of the tree outside the window cast weird shadows across her face. I held the cup out to her and she took it without looking at me. I sipped the toddy, warming myself with it. She held her cup in both hands, then raised it and drank the coffee down in slow, steady gulps, not lowering the cup until she was done.

I started to speak to her, but I didn't know what to say. She looked at me then, for a moment, then turned away and went to sit on the cot. I heard the metal frame creak, then the rasp of leather as she slipped out of her coat. I stood for a moment sipping the toddy, then turned to look at her. She was sitting on the edge of the cot, her hands beside her. Her face was pale and white in the moonlight. I swallowed the last of the toddy.

"You want more coffee?" I said.

She shook her head. I went to the hot plate and made another toddy. I made it strong and I made it large. I carried it back and sat beside her, drinking.

"I shouldn't have done that to you," she said, "and I shouldn't *be* doing it. I should take you or let you go, but I shouldn't threaten you with it."

"It's all right," I said.

"Yeah," she said. "It's all right. Because that's what you expected. You didn't trust me, and I just finished proving you were right not to."

I didn't say anything.

"What I want to know," she said, "is why you don't trust me."

"I trust you," I said. "I trust you as much as I've ever trusted anybody."

"As much," she repeated. "Damn it, John, what are you afraid of?"

I tried to think of something to tell her. There wasn't anything she would understand.

"Oh," she said suddenly. "Am I dumb," she said. "Stupid. I was thinking all the time there was something wrong with you. But it's me, isn't it? I've got this horrible skin disease. I'm white." She shook her head and gave a short laugh. "That's it, isn't it?"

"Yes," I said. "That's it exactly. Only you don't understand what it means."

"Then tell me."

73

"I can't," I said.

"Try," she said.

"I can't."

She moved then, slipping closer to me, reaching out and taking the cup from my hand. She unbuttoned my coat, lowered her head and rested it against my chest. And then I felt her hand moving at the buckle of my belt. I found I could move then, and I tried to stop her, but she slapped my hand away impatiently, then slipped her hand inside my waistband and let it rest there, cupping my belly. Her fingers moved gently, in slow circles.

"I'm listening," she said.

And then I knew what I would have to tell her. "I want to tell you," I said, "what I did when my brother died." I stopped, took a deep breath. "I got the news on the telephone. My mother called. She said, 'Your brother got himself killed over there. The funeral's tomorrow.' Then she hung up."

Her hand stopped moving. "Just like that?" she said.

"Yeah," I said. "Just like that."

"But . . . isn't that a little quick? I mean, they'd have to fly the body . . ."

"Oh, she'd known about it for days. She didn't call until the body was back, until all the arrangements were made."

Her hand moved again, softly, encouragingly.

"I went in and took a shower."

She didn't say anything, but her hand kept moving, slowly, gently. But I felt no warmer.

"I had a date, you see. A special date, with a very special girl. It had taken me months to work up to asking her out, and I was scared to death of her, and I was scared of going out with her.

"So I took a shower and got dressed and went and picked her up. We went downtown for dinner. A place on Sansom Street, called 1907. That was the address. We sat in the first booth on the left. We had drinks. She drank Manhattans. I drank Scotch then, Ambassador Deluxe. She had two, I had four. We talked about politics. She was still upset because McCarthy had folded. We had dinner. Broiled lobster, baked potato, salad. She had bleu cheese, I had oil and vinegar. Then we had dessert: cheesecake and coffee. We talked about her family. Then we had more drinks. She had a Rusty Nail. I had another Scotch. We talked about relationships. I paid the bill; it was fifty dollars, I left a ten-dollar tip. After that I had fifty cents, which was exactly what we needed for the bus.

"We went back to her place. She made coffee, put on a record, Simon and Garfunkel. 'Bridge Over Troubled Waters.' We talked some more, and then we started to make out. It got heavy. Then she said she really liked me and she wanted to see me again, but it was too soon for her. So I went home and took a shower and then hitched home to my brother's funeral.

"It was a great funeral. The mayor was there. The town council. The lieutenant governor. All the boys who had played on the football team with him were there, arguing about who were going to be pall-bearers. The TV people came from everywhere. Newspapers. They had speeches and then they made more speeches. They had ten different eulogies. And then they left. We got to bury him in private. You see"—I looked at her—"in my home town, white people and black people aren't buried together. It isn't anything official, like down South. It's just the way things are done. I expect that if somebody black wanted to be put away in a white cemetery, nobody would say a thing. But the practice is we have our place and they have their places. And our place is a little shabby. No gardener, no graveled walks. And none of those big people wanted to go over to Mount Ross and get their shoes muddy. So we got to bury him in private. After that I borrowed some money and caught a bus back. I went to see the girl. And I raped her." I lay there then, in the darkness, listening to her breathing. It was ragged. "You're probably wondering why I wanted to tell you all that," I said finally.

"Yes," she said.

"It was because of the girl," I said. "Something about her. She was white."

She didn't say anything.

"It was wrong, what I did," I said. "I don't know how badly I hurt her; I don't mean physically. I still feel guilty about it. But deep down inside I understand what happened; I looked at her and saw white. . . ."

"I think that's sick," she said.

"I don't care what you think," I said.

"And you think it makes sense to blame white people, just because they're white. . . ."

"Yes," I said. "I do. Things have happened and it's somebody's fault, and it sure as hell wasn't ours." I had waited for her to move, to get up and leave, or at least to say something, but she had not. She had just stayed like that, holding me.

Night was falling with the snow, and a cold, wet wind came whipping out of the south. I could not see the snow very well in the growing darkness, but I could hear it crunch beneath my feet when I moved. In an hour, perhaps two, the path up the slope would be a sheet of cold, gritty snow. The tree branches beside it would be coated with slick. I might be able to make the climb. He would not. And I would not be able to make it with him. There was a way to keep the path open; each winter—until this one—he had strung ropes along the path at the spots where the incline became too precipitous for easy passage. I could go up and do that now, and perhaps then we could make it out if we had to; if I could find the eyebolts in the darkness, if the snow did not get too deep, if the air did not get so cold that it would sear his wounded lungs beyond bearing. Or I could prepare for a siege: chop more wood, fill the buckets, wet down the dirt floor around the stove, close the damper, and pray that the night would not get as cold as I feared, that the fire would not burn through the aged grate, and most fervently of all, that he would not get worse. Logic gave a clear answer—go up at once—and a sensible alternative—rope the path and try again to convince him. But logic had nothing to do with it. And so I went back inside and got the buckets and filled them; got the sledge and the wedges and split logs and carried the wood inside and stacked it carefully along the wall, hoping that would keep the wind out; opened the last jars of venison and built another stew and set it to simmer. When I was finished I put the kettle on and mixed two more toddies. He watched me, his eyes steady and unblinking. He said nothing; the only sounds he made came from the wheezing in his lungs. I took him his toddy. "You rope the path?" he asked.

I shook my head.

He nodded, accepted the cup, settled back. "You don't understand, do you?"

"I understand," I said.

197903042100

(Sunday)

LATER THAT NIGHT, when the fire was roaring in the chimney and the cold came slicing through the cabin's walls, Old Jack taught me another lesson: if you would bend a man, abandon all the usual means. Do not bother with psychology or diplomacy or even war; if you would bend a man, not just influence him or sway him or even convince him but *bend* him, do it with ritual. For even if he claims to have no belief, no religion, no adherence to any formal or informal order of service, there is, somewhere within him, a hidden agenda. And he will respond to it without hesitation, without thought, almost without knowledge, certainly without will. All you need to do is to guess the beginning of it. With me, Old Jack did not even have to guess—he knew. He had created it.

And so, when the meal was finished and the dishes washed, when the fire was stoked and the mugs of warmed and sweetened whiskey were in our hands, he did not hesitate; he did not even ask. He just said: "You want a story."

No, I did not want a story. I wanted to sit and drink hot whiskey and pray that we would make it through the night, and later fall into a drugged and dreamless sleep. And so I did not give him the response he wanted; I did not give him a response at all.

But he spoke as though I had: "Then fetch the candle."

I didn't move. I just sat there with the cup held tight against my belly, trying to keep the cold at bay. For a while we struggled, and then I knew that I would win, even if he was a weak old man. I must have relaxed a little then, and he must have sensed it. Because he said:

"Bring the matches too. Can't have light without strikin' fire." And I found myself moving, getting up and going to the shelf, taking down the candle and the matches, the motions so familiar they were almost painful. But when I came back to the table it changed. Because he was lying on his cot, not sitting in his chair. And so it was not precisely the same as it had been, not precisely as he would have had it. Now it was I who struck the match and lit the wick and set the candle in a pool of wax, a prisoner of its own substance, I who blew the lamp out. And so it might have been all right. But then he said:

"Put the matches back." He did not need to say the rest of it.

"Time was," he said, "when folks figured I was one a the orneriest bastards alive. An' they figgered Josh was another. Tell the truth, I suspect as how we was; we was pert near as ornery as Mose.

"Now, could be you don't know what I'm sayin' when I say we was ornery. You probly think bein' ornery is jest like bein' mean, or stubborn, an' that's on account a you found out about it from lookin' in some damn book. Well, bein' ornery is bein' stubborn, an' it is bein' mean, but that ain't the best part of it. What ornery comes down to is how you act 'roun' white folks. Now, I recall old Charlie DeCharmes, don't know if you recollect him, but if Charlie wasn't mean an' stubborn, I don't know who was. Nasty too. You coulda said to him, Charlie, we got us a barrel a whiskey an' a pot a venison stew, come on an' help us do it in, an' you had a good chance a comin' away without him. But if you was to say to him, Charlie, we're goin' down here to the field an' beat the livin' daylights outa each other with two-by-fours jest for the pure pain of it, why, you'd be lucky if he didn't get there ahead a you an' start in an' beat hell outa his ownself. He was married to a girl from down McConnellsburg way, an' folks down there couldn't understand why didn't nobody up here try to stop him from beatin' on her all the time, but the way we figured it, she musta knowed what she was gettin' into when she married him, on accounta the night she met him he was poundin' the hell outa three fellas down to Hawley's. She knowed Charlie was mean; *everybody* knowed Charlie was mean. But every mornin' 'cept Sunday he went to work down to Heckerman's, an' he always got there on time. When he went to town he always put on a necktie, an' he always called the white folks mister an' ma'am. He was meanern a snake an' nastiern garlicky milk, but he weren't ornery.

"Me and Josh, we didn't beat on nobody much; there was more times than not that we'd go outa our way to steer clear of a fight, lessen there was whiskey or money in question. But we was ornery. Me, why, I'd been knowed to make fun a white folks right to their faces, which was ornery. I'd been knowed to come right out an' tell 'em to buy their butt a ticket on the express train to hell, which was surely ornery. An' Josh? He went so far beyond that . . . Well, lemme tell you, what he done ain't the kinda thing folks is gonna quit talkin' about, an' it ain't the kinda thing folks is gonna still be talkin' about, neither; it's the kinda thing they won't ever talk about at all.

"It first come out one Saturday night, when we was all settin' around to Hawley's, which me an' Josh an' Mose done jest for the company, seein' as what we was drinkin' was Mose's whiskey marked up to make a profit for Hawley. Only Josh wasn't there that night, which wasn't hardly usual; only time Josh missed a Saturday night at Hawley's was when we was all three off somewheres. So as you might expect, somebody sooner or later wanted to know where he was, an' somebody else said they seen him ridin' down the Springs Road, an' swore he was wearin' a suit. Now, everybody knowed better. I questioned the fella perty close—I forget now who it was 'xactly, but I made him get mighty particular 'bout what he seen, an' what he only thought he seen, an' what he only wisht he seen. An' what it come down to was, he seen somebody *looked* like Josh ridin' hard down the Springs Road. An' soon as I got him to stop bein' so sure, I was perty certain it wasn't Josh, an' I said so. Mose, he shook his head. 'Jack,' he says, 'you shoulda been a white man. Fella come along an' says he seen somethin' an' you hound him till he admits it might not a been that he saw, only somethin' that looks jest like it, an' from there you say he couldn'ta seen what he said he seen.'

"'Well, damn,' I says. 'There's a big diff—' But 'fore I could say much, in through the door comes Josh hisself, and he was dressed in

overhauls jest like always. 'There,' I says, 'ya see?' 'See what?' Mose
says. He looks at Josh an' says to him, 'What the hell was you doin'
on the Springs Road in a suit?' 'Who, me?' Josh says. 'I wasn't on no
Springs Road, an' I don't have no suit.' Mose looks at him real close,
an' he wrinkles his nose up a couple a times. 'You lyin',' he says. 'I
ain't,' says Josh. 'You is,' says Mose. 'You callin' me a liar?' Josh says.
Well, the whole place got real quiet; folks was figurin' out how to get a
bet down an' get out the way at the same time. Woulda been a fair
fight—Mose had the muscle, but Josh was fastern a blue racer—but
it never come off, on accounta Mose says, 'No, I ain't callin' you a liar.
Way I figure it,' he says, 'you jest forgot all 'bout buyin' a suit an'
borrowin' a horse an' ridin' down to wherever. Ain't your fault; fellas
forgets all the time, 'specially when they been sniffin' bay rum. You
know what I mean?' Well, I started sniffin' too, like I shoulda been all
along, an' I was startin' to see what Mose meant when I seen that
Josh knowed what he meant. You could tell sure, 'cause Josh, bein' so
damn white an' all, Josh could blush. An' he was blushin' then.
Looked like a cross 'tween a raspberry an' a McIntosh.

   "'Goddamn!' I says. 'This nigger's in love.' Mose looks at me an'
grins. 'Damn, Jack,' he says, 'you ain't so dumb after all.' But Josh
wasn't havin' none a that. 'Naw,' he says, 'naw, he ain't dumb. He's
jest a damn fool that don't know his butt from a bung hole.' But I
knowed I was on the right track, an' Mose did too. 'I don't know,
Josh,' Mose says. 'Jack seems to be perty sure you been out cattin'
around. . . .' 'Nawsir,' I says. 'He ain't been cattin' no place. We ain't
talkin' 'bout pussy-snatchin'. This here is *love* we're talkin' about.'
Mose shook his head—Josh was jest too busy splutterin' an' blushin'
to say anythin'—an' he says, 'Now, how you know all that, Jack? I
can't see it.' Well, he was lyin'; half the time Mose acted dumb, but
you didn't need to know him too well to know he was always one step
ahead a you, sometimes two, an' half the time he was leadin' you by
the nose. But he liked to let things come out their own way. So I went
straight on. 'Well,' I says, 'he done shaved on Saturday afternoon, an'
that means women is in there somewheres.' Mose nods. 'An',' I says,
'he was wearin' a suit. . . .' 'Hold up there,' Mose says. 'I thought you
didn't believe that.' 'I didn't,' I says. 'Reason I didn't was that it
woulda been mighty strange. But when you got a woman stuck in the
middle of somethin', actin' mighty strange is reglar.' Mose considers
that for a minute, an' then he says, 'Good point. Continue, sir, if you

please.' Sounded jest like a white man. Jest 'bout everybody there started grinnin', 'cause they seen Mose's 'white man' act before. As for me, I knowed how to play too.

" 'Certainly, Mr. Washington,' I says. 'Well,' I says, 'we're sure about the woman. We're sure about the suit, on accounta women makes strange things reglar, an' if that ain't enough, you can take a whiff a Mr. White an' you'll sniff the stink a bay rum, which sure as hell ain't no more reglarn a suit, an' if one unreglar thing is goin' on, then why not another one?' 'Indeed,' Mose says. 'Continue, sir.' An' I was glad to keep goin' too, on accounta I was havin' a real good time turnin' Josh into a cherry. Every time I'd say somethin' else, he'd turn red someplace else. By that time I had his face red an' his neck red. So I pulled up ma socks an' went to work on the backs of his hands.

" 'Certainly, sir,' I says. 'Now, this here woman must be a mighty special woman. Man don't put on a suit an' stinkwater jest to lay out in the brier patch with some country girl. She's so special, Mr. White is in love with her. He *respects* her.' 'An' how do you know that, Mr. Crawley?' says Mose. 'Well, my dear Mr. Washington,' I says, 'it ain't but midnight, which is jest about the time willin' women is crawlin' out their windows, or leastways throwin' up the sashes, an' Mr. White is here among us, which means the lady is not willin', on accounta if she was, Mr. White would be elsewhere. On the other hand, he didn't come in cussin' an' swearin' an' goin' on 'bout bitches what gets a man to dress up an' put on stinkwater an' gets his nose open an' then don't wanna do nothin' 'cept sit on a porch swing an' hold hands. An' that must mean that Mr. White don't mind jest settin' on a porch swing an' holdin' hands. An' *that* means he's in love.'

"Now, about this time Josh was 'bout the shade of a barn door, an' I was ready to ease up some. But Mose, he looks at me an' he says, 'Well, I'll tell you, Jack, you reason that there out jest like a white man. Onliest problem with it is you left out one thing: man said he seen Josh here headin' down the Springs Road, an' that road don't go nowheres but south, an' as I know don't nobody know bettern you, there ain't nary a colored family that way 'fore you get clean to Cumberland. An' lessen Josh done stole hisself somebody's racehorse, ain't no way he could get clean to Cumberland an' back in that little piece a time, let alone doin' any courtin'. So I wisht you'd think like a white man a while more an' tell me jest 'xactly who this lady is.' Well, he surely had a point, an' I knowed he did, an' if I hadn't a knowed it I woulda been able to figure it out pert quick by the way old Josh jest quieted down an' looked at me. Quit blushin', quit chompin' at the bit; he jest looked, 'sif to say, there, you smart-butted bastard, let's us see who gonna be laughin' at who in 'bout three minutes. Everybody else was lookin' at me too, seein' what I was gonna do. An' I didn't know, but I did know if I didn't do somethin' I was gonna look like God's own fool, an' the only thing I could figure was to make a joke outa it, so I says, 'Thinkin' like a white man, the answer's clearern air: Josh's been a courtin' a white woman.'

"Well, nobody said nothin' for a second, an' then for 'bout five minutes you couldn't hear nothin' but folks laughin'. Hawley was laughin'. Charlie DeCharmes was laughin' fit to bust his gut. Mose, he was damn near rollin' on the floor. Me, I was perty happy gettin' outa that little tight spot I'd jawed ma way into, an' I was laughin' perty good for a minute. But then I looked at Josh, an' I seen somethin' knocked the chuckle clean outa me: Josh, he wasn't laughin' at all. He wasn't even smilin'. He was lookin' at 'em all laughin', lookin' real hard. An' then he spun around on his heel an' stomped out. The rest of 'em was so damn busy laughin' they didn't even know he was gone. But I knowed, an' it didn't take a whole lotta figurin' to see that there wasn't nothin' good gonna come of it.

"Well, the next day, I went huntin' him. It took me a load a huntin', too. It was sundown 'fore I come on him, settin' on a rock by the side a the road, up on Blackoak Ridge, watchin' the sun go down. I come up on him from behind an' he didn't even hear me come; he was that far gone with starin'. So I walked right up behind him—didn't try to be quiet, but it didn't make no difference—an' I grabbed his arms real tight. Had to do that; you don't walk up on a man like that an' say somethin'—it's a fast way to get your head took off. So I grabbed him, an' I swear to God he didn't hardly notice that. He just turns an' looks up at me an' grins. Dumbest damn grin I ever seen. I left him go. 'Lissen here,' I says. 'I come lookin' for you to tell you I didn't mean to ram them spurs in like I done—' Now, usually Josh woulda made you beg him to leave you apologize, but this time he jest waved it off. 'Why, Jack,' he says, 'that wasn't nothin'.' An' he goes right back to lookin' at the sunset. 'Naw,' I says, 'I don't think there was no harm done; wouldn't nobody believe it 'cept me.' That there got his attention. 'What?' he says. 'What the hell you sayin'?' I jest

shrugged at him. 'I ain't sayin' nothin' 'cept that your secret's safe.'
'Ain't no secret,' Josh says. 'Ain't gonna be for long,' I says, 'if you
keep on settin' out in the middle of a Goddamn field in plain sight a
the main road, moonin' over a sunset. Everybody gonna know what
you doin'.' 'Damn if they are,' says Josh. 'Damn if they ain't,' says I.
'Hell, you act like you the first sorry soul ever fell in love. I'll lay you
five to one you an' this girl decided you was gonna watch the damn
sun go down every night an' think sweet thoughts an' . . .' I let up
there, 'cause he was turnin' so red I figured he was gonna bust somethin'. So I says, 'Josh,' I says, 'lemme tell you somethin'.' I says, 'You
recall when I was all het up 'bout that Berry girl, one lives out near
Pleasantville? The one you an' Mose kept actin' like you was sniffin'
around jest to get me goin'? You remember all that, Josh? Well, I'm
gonna tell you what me an' that girl useta do. We went to town one
day an' we bought us each a colored candle. Blue ones. An' every
night at eight o'clock, she'd be in her house an' I'd be wherever I was,
an' we'd light up them candles an' stare at 'em an' think 'bout each
other jest as hard as we could. So you go back to your sunset, 'fore it's
all gone.'

"Well, I moved off a ways an' waited there till the last piece a
pink was gone outa the sky. Wasn't bored waitin'. I had me a couple
things to think about. First thing was that Berry girl. Lord, she was
somethin'! Long strong legs an' eyes like gooseberries an' skin that
felt like hot whiskey on a raw throat, an' that damn candle-starin'
was damn near as good as bein' right inside her, an' I swear to God I
mighta married her if it hadn't been for the fact that I went out there
one day an' seen where she had a yellow candle an' a green candle an'
a red candle right upside the blue one, an' every one a them others
was shorter. But she was still somethin'. But then I started thinkin'
'bout what was sure to happen when the word got out. An' that's what
I was thinkin' 'bout when the sky got dark an' Josh stood up an'
shook hisself like a hound dog comin' outa a crick, an' come over to
me.

" 'I guess,' he says, 'if I'da knowed how you was feelin', I
wouldn'ta give you such a hard time 'bout that Berry girl.' An' then
he told me the whole damned story: how he was drivin' down to the
railway depot in Cumberland to pick up a load a stuff for some white
man, an' how he saw this girl walkin' along the road, an' he offered
her a ride, even though she was white an' it was the middle a the

South County, on accounta she smiled at him jest like he was anybody else, an' how she talked to him jest like a woman oughta talk to
a man, how she wasn't puttin' herself above him. An' he told me how
he quit hurryin' the horses along, jest so he could stretch out talkin'
to her. An' he told me how he finely drove her right up to her door an'
she ast him to get down an' have a taste a cider, an' how he done it,
an' how she poured it for him an' set with him at the table, an' how
that girl had walked him out to the wagon an' told him how much she
had liked talkin' to him, an' how much she had always dreamed about
talkin' to somebody the way they talked to each other, an' that she
hoped he'd come back. He told me how he kissed her, with his heart
beatin' hell outa his chest half from excitement an' half from fear. An'
he told me how he whipped them horses over them mountains, half
the time thinkin' like a colored man that jest finished kissin' a white
girl, wonderin' if maybe hadn't somebody seen it, or if maybe it
wasn't some kinda trap, an' the other half thinkin' like a man oughta
think about a woman, never mind what color she was. He told me he
knowed that last didn't make no sense, on accounta he knowed he
was down there in the South County, an' headin' into what useta be
slave territory, an' he knowed he shoulda been hatin' jest as hard as
he could, but all it took was a glass a cider an' a young girl's kiss, an'
he was ready to forget everything he knowed. He told me all that, an'
I listened to him. An' when he was done tellin' me we went over an'
got on the road an' walked on back. An' we never spoke of any of it
again. Not never.

"Well, if it hadda been up to me, wouldn't nobody a spoke about
it, on accounta this wasn't jest a little piece a trouble Josh was fixin'
to get hisself into. An' it was surely the wrong time to do it—I don't
guess there's ever been a right one, but this surely was the wrong one.
Folks don't recall too good anymore, or they don't want to, but 'round
here the Klu Klux Klan was a perty big thing. Jest about then the Re-
publicans an' the Klan was the big parties, an' the Klan managed to
elect the sheriff. So if it hadda been up to me the whole thing woulda
stayed mighty quiet. But it wasn't up to me. The word got out some-
ways. An' once it was out, wasn't no question how it spread; them
biddies up to the church done it. Them bitches'd spread anything
'ceptin' their legs for their husbands. I swear, you want to keep
somethin' quiet, the onliest way to do it is to pass a law against sewin'

84

circles an' tea parties. Better yet, get rid a the women. Anyways, they spread it.

"Truth was, when it come out it wasn't all that bad. They thought Josh was foolin' with some piece a white trash, which scandalized the women, but hell, none a us woulda give a damn, an' sure wasn't nobody tellin' the white folks, so when I heard that story, I done all I could to keep folks thinkin' it; tole 'em the truth. Said Josh wasn't cattin' around, he'd found hisself a white girl that had a good family an' went to church an' didn't have no mustache nor harelip nor gimp leg or nothin' an' she loved him. Well, didn't nobody believe it, an' I figured if the truth ever did come out they still wouldn't believe it. Only problem was Mose. He was liable to catch on to the truth. An' that was gonna be trouble, 'cause Mose didn't have no love for white folks. He'd sell to 'em, an' he'd buy from 'em when he had to, an' he'd talk to 'em if there wasn't no way around it, but he sure as hell wasn't goin' to think too much a Josh fallin' in love with one of 'em. But as it turned out, what Josh was up to was so far offa Mose's line a thinkin' he couldn't even guess at it. An' I sure as hell didn't want to tell him. But the time come when I had to.

"Way it fell out was like this. The whole thing went on clean through the summer. The talk was gettin' louder an' Josh was gettin' moonier. Mostly he wasn't around. When he was, he'd show up down to Hawley's an' lose his money an' grin like a fool. He'd carry Mose's 'shine aroun' an' deliver it an' never take a taste. Three different times I knowed about, gals he'd been carryin' on with up the country someplace come a huntin' for him, so fired up they come up the Hill walkin' bowlegged, an' they left the same way—he wouldn't have nothin' to do with 'em. It was sad. Went on like that through the hot months, into the fall. Then things got a little easier. The talk started to die down a little bit—some girl's belly started to show 'fore they got her to the altar, an' them biddies had that to go on about—an' I figgered maybe it was gonna turn out okay, Josh'd come to his senses 'fore the dam busted loose. But jest about the time the first frost hit the ground he come to see me, an' when he tole me why he come, I knowed that dam was gonna be bustin' mighty quick, an' it wasn't no millpond it was holdin' back, it was a Goddamned cesspool.

"He come in the mornin' an' we set out there underneath the oak tree drinkin' spring water an' eatin' cold chicken by way a breakfast, an' he told me how what he'd been doin' was goin' down there to the South County to work for that girl's daddy, helpin' in the fields an' forkin' manure an' I don't know what all, jest so's he'd have a chance to see her, an' how they'd had their chances, but they hadn't done nothin' but talk, she jest loved to talk, an' he didn't want nothin' else from her, on accounta there'd be time enough for that. That there made me set up, on accounta I could see it comin' but I couldn't believe it. So I left him tell me about how he'd spent three months stayin' away from other women an' cleanin' everything he owned, an' cleanin' up his mind—gettin' hisself worthy, was the way he put it— an' then he'd gone down there one night an' asted that girl to marry him, an' how she said she would, an' how he figured that maybe, since her daddy had seen how he could work, an' had always treated him fair, maybe it would be all right with him. An' how he was fixin' to go down there an ast the man if he could marry his daughter.

"I tell you, Johnny, I jest set there. Finely I says to him—an' I knowed I was walkin' on marshy ground, but the way I seen it, he was fixin' to go marchin' over quicksand—'Josh, does this girl know you ain't as white as you look?' But he didn't get all huffy like he usually done whenever somebody made mention of the fact that he wasn't 'xactly what you'd call dark-skinned. He said, yeah, she knew; matter of fact, that was jest about the first thing she ast him, on accounta he looked colored, 'cept for his skin. So I says to him, 'You mean you let her talk to you like that? Like you was some kinda funny-lookin' animal?' An' he says, 'It wasn't like that. She was jest . . . curious.' Well, I knowed then he was too far gone for me to hope to talk sense into him, but I knowed I had to try, so I said to him, 'Josh, I don't know. I ain't said nothin' 'bout none a this, mostly on accounta so far as I can see it ain't done nobody no harm, 'ceptin' a couple country girls. But what you're talkin' about now . . .' He held up his hand an' says, 'I know what I'm sayin'.' I looked at him, an' I says, 'I ain't sure you do. You're settin' there happiern a pig in a garbage pile on accounta you love the girl an' the girl loves you, an' you think maybe her daddy ain't gonna get too upset at the thought of a colored man for a son-in-law an' pickaninnies for grandchildren. You figure you found somebody white that's worth takin' serious. Well, maybe you have. Maybe that girl ain't never gonna look at you an' think nigger, an' maybe her family ain't neither. But you talkin' 'bout the South County, an' you an' me both know ain't nothin' good come outa the South County—'

'I know that,' he says, 'I been knowin' it. An' I tell you, Jack, it ain't too much different from the North County.' Well, he had a point there, but not much a one, an' I says, 'North, south, east, west, any way from Sunday. What you think is gonna happen when the neighbors find out?' He was quiet there for a minute; he hadn't taken that into account. 'Well,' he says finely, 'maybe we'll have to move away.' 'Yeah,' I says. 'Take her away from the folks she loves. She's gonna end up hatin' you, for sure. She will think nigger, for sure. An' where you gonna go? East? West? North? Clear to Goddamn Canada? Same damn story. Colored man an' a white woman, an' sooner or later somebody's gonna say somethin', an' it'll set her to thinkin'. Or maybe you'll have babies by that time; somebody'll say somethin' to them. An' you know you—you can't let nothin' like that go by 'thout you say somethin' too, an' that's jest how the end's gonna start.' He thought about that for a while, an' then he looks at me an' says, 'I'll tell you, Jack, from the day I was born I hated everything white, jest on accounta I couldn't see good an' didn't look right. An' you know how folks has treated me over the years. Well, I got even now, 'cause if there's one thing I can sure do, it's pass for white.'

"I jest set there. I couldn't say nothin'. I couldn't even think. What the man was talkin' 'bout doin' jest plain turned ma stomach. Finely I said, 'If this girl's so good, how come you don't get her to pass for colored?' He jest looked at me; he couldn't even begin to see what I was gettin' at. 'Damnit,' I says, 'you listen to me—' An' he put up his hand again an' stopped me. 'Jack,' he says, 'I made up ma mind. I'm gonna go down there an' get this thing set up decent an' formal an' proper, an' when we get that done good an' right we'll set down an' we'll figure out what to do about the rest of it.' An' he got up an' walked away.

"Well, I set there a long time, thinkin' 'bout how you could grow up right 'side a man an' not know a damn thing about what made him do what he done, an' how any way you cut it, Josh had a right to go to hell any damn way he wanted. By the time I got done thinkin' 'bout that, it was time to go to work. So I did.

"Shined me quite a few shoes that day; it was the dusty time a the year an' fellas'd come down from the courthouse three an' four times a day, jest to get the dust knocked off. There was a lot more of 'em than usual too, on accounta the boots was in town. The reglar fellas, see, the judge an' the sheriff an' the county commissioners an' the lawyers an' whatnot, them was what I called the shoes, on accounta that's what they wore. They was always around, on accounta most of 'em had offices in the courthouse or on the Square, or somewheres. But what I called the boots—on accounta that's what *they* wore—didn't have no offices. They was the ones that went out to the townships an' made sure things got done the way the shoes wanted 'em done. Some of 'em was around as much as the shoes was—a couple of 'em hung around the Alliquippa, settin' up in the lobby, an' every oncet in a while somebody'd come in an' give 'em somethin' to take to somebody else, if you get ma meanin'—but most of 'em stayed clear a town, lessen there was somethin' goin' on. But I knowed 'em all anyways, on accounta I might forget a face, but I don't never forget a pair a shoes. Or a pair a boots.

"So between the shoes gettin' dust knocked off 'em an' the boots—which was there, I figgered, on accounta elections was comin' up—there was a lot more shinin' to do, an' that was fine with me, on accounta there ain't nothin' like workin' hard an' steady to make your mind work. An' I needed to work mine. On accounta oncet I quit thinkin' 'bout stoppin' Josh I started thinkin' 'bout the South County.

"I knowed the South County. I had reason to know it. If there was anyplace in this whole part a the country a colored man would want to steer clear of, the South County was it. All them folks down there had come up from Maryland an' Virginia, an' some of 'em didn't know the Civil War was over, or, leastways, didn't know which side won. Anyways, I was thinkin' maybe I oughta get maself together an' go on down there with Josh. An' I was thinkin', too, that maybe I ought to let Mose in on what was goin' on, 'cause sure God if there was gonna be any kinda trouble, we was gonna need Mose. But on the other hand, I more or less give Josh ma word that I wasn't gonna say nothin' to nobody, least of all Mose. So I polished an' I pondered. Wasn't payin' too much attention to what them fellas was sayin'; most times it didn't amount to a hill a beans anyways, an' when it did, I usually knowed it 'fore they did. But 'long 'bout one o'clock, one a the fools that worked in some damn office or other, shufflin' papers in between takin' bribes, come over an' set his butt up there an' tells me to shine, but 'fore I can get started good he leans over an' gives me that fishy-eyeball look white folks toss at you when they're tryin' to act dangerous. I can't recall his name now; I do recollect that he bought his shoes outa the Montgomery Ward catalog, an' his heels was always run over, an' I recall he was so damn stupid they caught him takin' bribes. Now I think on it, he mighta been so damn dumb he wasn't takin' bribes, so the rest a them crooks had to make it look like he was, jest to get shut a him. Anyways, he leans over an' he says to me, 'Jack,' he says, 'I want you to know you're a good fella. You're a credit to your race.' Well, I thanked him kindly an' kept on shinin'; when they start with that it's best to jest ignore 'em; they don't mean no harm. But he wasn't through. 'Jack,' he says, 'I want you to know some folks come to me today, astin' 'bout you. Seems they heard some colored boy was nosin' 'round with a young lady down in Southampton.' *That* made me stop polishin'. But I managed to play dumb. 'Southampton?' I says. 'Why, I wouldn't be seein' no gal down there. Ain't a colored family—' 'I said a young *lady*, Jack,' he says. 'Well, like I was sayin' . . . Oh,' I says. Like I jest caught on. 'Well, you ain't got to worry none, Jack,' he says. 'I told them folks that you was too much a credit to your race to be actin' that way towards a young lady. Now ain't that the truth?' Well, I was about ready to fall offa ma stool, but leastways I could keep ma head down an' shine, so I says, 'Yes, sir, that surely is the truth.' He says, 'Well, I'm glad to hear it. On accounta these folks was mighty upset. Bad enough, boy even thinkin' 'bout interferin' with a young lady, but the way they tell it, he's been bein' perty slick, goin' down there to Southampton an' actin' like he was workin' for the young lady's father, an' then hangin' 'round down there, tryin' to talk that young lady into doin' unspeakable things. You wouldn't know any niggers that slick, would you, Jack?' Well, there was enough trouble brewin' 'thout me startin' a pot, but I wasn't about to take that crap from nobody. So I put the polish down an' I stood up an' I looked him right in the eye an' I said, 'Mister, I don't *know* no niggers.' Well, he faded clean to pale white, jest like a catfish's belly. That's when white folks scare me; when they gets that fishbelly white color. Unpredictable as a copperhead, an' could be the bite's poison too; I couldn't say. But he got up an' he didn't say a damn thing. He jest looked at me, 'sif to say, If I had me a book, your name would sure God be in it, an' then he went away.

"Well, in a way it was good that it happened like it done, on accounta it settled ma mind on jest about everything. So as soon as I could get outa there I set out lookin' for Mose.

"Now, Mose wasn't the easiest fella to find, 'specially that time a year. What he'd be was holed up somewheres cleanin' his equipment so he'd be ready when they harvested the corn, or he'd be trampin' over half the County lookin' for God knows what. He done that all the time. I don't know why; he already knowed the County bettern God knowed Creation. Anyways, you couldn't find him if he was holed up; places where he kept his worms an' his kettles an' whatnot was the closest-kept secret this side a Eleanor Roosevelt's underwear. You couldn't track him if he was explorin'; wasn't a man alive could track Mose 'thout a bloodhound, an' maybe not then. But what we done a long time 'fore all this was to set up a couple signs; I had ma signs an' Mose had his an' Josh had his. So the first thing I done was to head for a old hollow tree about two mile northwest, out towards Wolfsburg, an' when I got there I felt around inside it for a while an' come up with an acorn. Which meant that he wasn't holed up—in which case he wouldn'ta left nothin' an' ma butt woulda been busted—an' that he had headed south from there. Which may not sound like a whole lotta help, but if you know where a man started an' which direction he headed in, you oughta be able to find him 'thout too much trouble. So I found me a creek, an' I followed that upstream—which was what Mose woulda done jest in case somebody decided to track him with some dogs—lookin' for high ground, an' when I found some I headed south again, right up over Kintons Knob.

"I was halfways to Manns Choice when I heard him comin'. He was singin'. He always done that. May sound strange for a man to take all that trouble hidin' his trail from dogs that ain't even there an' then go around makin' noise like that, but Mose claimed that it didn't make no difference, on accounta what he sung was spirituals an' couldn't nobody but colored folks hear 'em, an' even they couldn't hear 'em too far. Well, he musta been right, 'cause I could hear him comin'—well, more like I could feel him, on accounta his voice was so low—an' it wasn't moren five seconds later that I seen him. I tell you, it was always a sight to see Mose movin' through the woods. You'd see him in town, or even up to Hawley's, an' you'd start to think maybe he wasn't so much, nothin' moren any other man. But you see him in the woods, movin' along over dry leaves without makin' a sound, movin' in big long strides that done to distance what a flame does to wax, you'd jest about want to head for town an' streetlights an' sidewalks 'cause you'd know you never had no more business in the woods than a catfish in a foot race.

"I stopped an' he come up to me. Says, 'Hey, Jack, what you doin' out here with your pants wet?' I still hadn't dried off from wadin' in that damn creek. 'I been pissin' in 'em,' I says, 'an' you gonna be pissin' in yours when you hear what I got to say. Siddown.' An' he done it, an' I told it all to him. Well, not all of it. I didn't tell him about the sunset-starin' an' whatnot, on accounta he wouldn'ta understood it; Mose wasn't never crazy enough over a woman to do anything like that. He had a hard enough time understandin' it as it was.

" 'Damnation,' he says when I'd done finished tellin' him. Says, 'I can't see why a man'd want to go an' get messed up with a white woman for.' 'Hell,' I says. 'You can't see what a man'd want to get messed up with any kinda woman for. But this here ain't no time to be gettin' into that. This here's the time to be catchin' up to Josh.' Well, he seen the sense a that, even if he didn't see the sense a nothin' else, an' we set out.

"Well, it was 'bout four o'clock when we got back; Mose coulda made it faster, I imagine, but I held him back a bit. So we was too late. When we come up the Hill—we come up the back way, a course—we could jest about smell the fact that old Josh'd already lit out; you could hear his dogs a yippin' an' yappin' like they only done when they'd got fed recent an' knowed they wasn't gonna get left out to run nothin'. But we stopped by Josh's place anyways, jest to make sure. Well, he was gone, all right, an' it didn't look like he'd done changed his mind about what he was gonna do—you could see where he'd took a bath an' shaved, an' his overhauls was hung up on a nail, so he musta been wearin' that suit didn't nobody believe he owned. Mose looked the place over for a minute or two an' then he looks at me. 'I ain't never seen this fool this neat,' he says. 'Me neither,' I says. 'This place don't smell a nothin' 'sides pine tar soap,' he says. 'Surely don't,' I says. 'He ain't had a woman in here, 'cause you can't smell that,' he says. 'Surely can't,' I says. He shook his head. 'You mean to tell me some little old pasty woman can do all that to a man?' 'Mose,' I says, 'I think what's important here is that she's a woman. Now, we know white men ain't worth dog dung, but it strikes me that *any* kinda woman is a mighty powerful thing to fool with.' Mose shook his head again an' went outside. I knowed where he was goin', so I jest waited. He come back in about a minute. 'Sonofabitch,' he says. 'The sonofabitch limed his sonofabitchin' outhouse!' You could tell he was struck with it. 'Hell,' he says, 'maybe he is fool enough to go down there an' ast a white man can he marry his daughter.' 'Well, damn,' I says, 'I tole you that. Tole you he was fixin' to get his butt busted.' Mose looks at me real sharp. *'His* butt? *Your* butt. Every black butt this side a Pittsburgh. You think they gonna let it go at his butt? Why, the first damn thing them white folks is gonna get to thinkin' is if one nigger can quit sneakin' in the back winda an' start knockin' at the front door, we all gonna be linin' up on the porch. What you think they gonna do?'

"Well, Mose may not a been the smartest fella when it come to men an' women, but he sure knowed a good bit about politics. I tell you, I had never even thought that far, but I seen he was dead right. I heard 'bout the riots they had right down in Philadelphia an' out there to St. Louis maybe two, three years before this all went on. Way I heard it, that St. Louis thing started on accounta some little boy went swimmin' in the white folks' water, an' they throwed rocks at him till he drowned, an' if they done that to a little boy that went swimmin' in the wrong swimmin' hole, I hated to think what they was gonna do to a full-growed man that started tryin' to marry some-body's white daughter. So I thought about that for a half a second, an' then I says, 'Well, we best not be settin' 'round here talkin' about outhouses, then. We best find that fool an' pound some sense into his head.' Mose nods. 'Yeah,' he says, 'only we gonna have a damn hard time, seein' as the way I judge it he's got about a half-hour lead, an' he's gonna be on horseback.' I thought hard, an' then I says, 'Would be, 'ceptin' he's gonna be ridin' slow, on accounta the road'll be dusty an' he won't wanna mess up his suit. An' we can borrow a horse from Hawley. An' you know every shortcut for thirty miles, so we shouldn't have no problem.' 'Well,' says Mose, 'we do got one. We don't know where he's goin'.'

"Which was true. So there we was; half an hour behind already, an' we didn't even know where the finish line was. All I could do was stand there. 'Come on,' Mose says, an' he starts out the door. 'Come on where?' I says. 'Well, hell, Jack,' he says, 'we know he's headed south. We'll head that way an' maybe we'll get an idea.'

"So we lit out. Went chargin' down to Hawley's, but he wasn't there, so we jest told his missus we was borrowin' the horse. Turned out he took the horse with him. So we hotfooted it down the west side a the Hill, headin' for the swingin' bridge into town—that was stand-in' then—so's we could hit the Springs Road, but then, jest like Mose said, an idea hit me. Well, all it was was me recallin' what that white fella had said 'bout Southampton Township; but I guess you could call it an idea. Anyways, I jest says, 'We go east,' an' Mose didn't even bother to say what the hell or give me a funny look; he jest swung off an' we went hightailin' it down towards the Narrows. I tried to get up enough breath to tell him what was happenin', but he waved me off. I was grateful for it too, on accounta travelin' with Mose on foot was somethin' that took all the breath you could spare, leastways till you caught your second wind. So I didn't try to explain nothin' else, I jest kept movin', an' pretty soon it come to me what we was doin': we was trailin'. Not trackin', now; trailin'. Anybody that's spent jest a little bit a time in the woods knows there's a world a difference. Maybe you got a pack a dogs, an' they'll all take after a bear, an' every one of 'em will head off one way, followin' the scent. Trackin'. But there'll be one old hound—mostly it's an old hound, though I seen a couple pups that could do it—an' he'll circle around an' whine an' sniff an' whine some more, an' then he'll take off in some damnfool direction that don't make no sense. He won't act like he's got a scent, on accounta he don't; he'll jest act like he knowed right where he was goin', an' jest what he was doin'. An' if you're out for the exercise, you follow the pack, but if you want bear meat, you follow that hound, on accounta what he done is put hisself right into that old bear's head. Started thinkin' jest like him. Knows where that bear is goin' an' what he's gonna do, jest as soon as the bear knows.

"Now, Mose, he wasn't no fool. He knowed I'd knowed Josh a sight longern him, an' he knowed we was still a sight closer, an' he figured I knowed, jest *knowed*, what the man'd do. An' I started to tell him he was wrong, but then I says to maself, Jack, maybe you do know. So I forgot about where I was goin'; I jest let the spirit move me, so to speak, an' old Mose come whippin' along beside me, never sayin' a word, never astin' a question. We was trailin'.

"An' we was movin' too, I mean to tell you. We covered some ground in the next hour or so. 'Bout a mile, mile an' a half down, we cut off from the river an' headed south on that road, runs down that side a the mountain, down towards Charlesville, an' we went on down there lickety-split. Might not a been too hard on Mose, but it was a pace that shoulda been gettin' to me. Only it wasn't, on accounta I had that knowin' feelin'. I seen old hound dogs that'll go like that all night, long as they got a scent. An' I had it, so we kept on. Musta covered seven, eight mile in that hour, all told. But then the feelin' left me. Jest like that, an' soon as it did, the strength went outa me too, an' I stopped dead.

"Or anyways, I tried to. Mose wouldn't let me. We dropped back to walk, but he made me keep movin'. He knowed jest what had happened, too. 'Lost it?' he says. I was too outa breath to do nothin' but nod. An' then, 'thout knowin' why, I looked up in the sky, an' I seen the sun.

"I stopped dead in ma tracks. I says, 'Mose, if you was to want to get up on top a mountain to watch the sun go down, which one would you pick?' Well, I think that shook his faith, a little bit anyways, on accounta he says, 'Jest what the hell would I be wantin' to watch the sun go down for?' Well, I didn't want to tell him. I didn't know *how* to tell him. So I says, 'Look, you're on your way to see this fella about marryin' his daughter, an' you figure seein' as he's white an' you're colored it might be the last damn sunset you're ever gonna see, so you want to get a good long look, an' the fella you got to see is down in Southampton Township.' Mose shook his head. 'Well,' he says, 'if I had me a horse, an' I was comin' down this way—' I stopped him there, on accounta the fella that said he seen Josh said he seen him on the Springs Road. 'Naw,' I says, 'you're comin' down—' 'The Springs Road,' Mose says. An' I knowed I didn't have to say no more. 'Yeah,' Mose says, an' he was starin' up at the sky, which was a mite dangerous on accounta we was pacin' along perty good again. 'I come down the Springs Road. Reason I'm on the Springs Road is so won't nobody know where I'm headed—' 'An' on accounta you couldn't borrow no horse from Hawley an' the onliest other place for a colored man to get one is to pay Les down to the Springs for one a them ridin'-stable nags.' 'Uh huh,' Mose says. 'So it takes me a while to get down there an' pay Les his dime an' ride out—' 'Saddle up an' ride out, on accounta Les ain't gonna be saddlin' up no horse for no damn dime.' 'Uh huh, an' I ride on down the valley as fast as I can go—' 'No, not that fast, on accounta it's dusty an' I'm wearin' ma suit.' 'Uh huh, an' I get to Patience an' cut off an' head up over the mountain, then I come down through Rainsburg an' head up over the mountain again, an' jest about sundown . . .' An' he looked at me an' I looked at him, 'cause now we knowed where Josh was gonna be. He was either gonna be goin' so slow he'd be on Evitts Mountain, west a Rainsburg, or he was gonna be pushin' to get to the top a Tussey Mountain, east a Rainsburg, an' all we had to do was get up on that east mountain 'fore

94

the sun was clean down, an' either we'd catch him or we'd be ahead of him. So we lit out.

"Now, I don't recall too much more 'bout that part of it, mainly on accounta the fact that Mose wasn't 'xactly human when it come to coverin' ground in a hurry. I seen him run moren one dog into the ground, an' there was stories that he'd outdistanced a pair of fellas that was after him on horseback. You may not believe it, but I sure as hell do, on accounta that night was like the Goddamn trottin' races at the county fair, so far as I'm concerned. I won't say the trees went flyin' by, but there sure wasn't no time to be carvin' your name into the bark. An' I know we passed up moren one farmer's wagon. Don't know how many; couldn't count an' move at the same time. But it was a lot. An' jest 'bout the time the sun started touchin' the tree-tops, we seen some smudges a smoke an' 'fore we knowed it we was in Rainsburg. Wasn't much of a town—still ain't. Couple houses, a gen-ral store, an' a couple churches. Well, for a small town there was a goodly amount of commotion goin' on; bunch a farmers at the store, settin', but we didn't have no time to stop an' pass the time a day. We jest hightailed it to the south end a town, an' we cut up over the ridge, an' we had to slow down, but we made the best time we could, an' even Mose was puffin' a shade when we hit the top. Me, I was damn near dead. An' I damn near died for real when we got there, 'cause the sun was gone, an' so was Josh. There was enough light for us to find the place where Josh'd tied the horse.

"We headed off again; there was a chance we might catch him 'fore he got to the fork in the road at the bottom of the mountain. We mighta too, if it hadn't been so damn dark an' that road hadn't been so damn windy. Time we got to the bottom I felt like I jest come through a prizefight with three dozen pine trees. So we sat at the bottom an' caught our breath; wasn't nothin' more to do till the moon come up.

"Soon as we caught our breath Mose says, 'I don't like this. I don't like all them farmers back there, an' I don't like all them wagons on the road.' Well, I told him I didn't like it neither, but I had worse things to worry about. 'Like what?' he says. 'Well, for one thing,' I says, 'you an' me figured out somethin' that ain't gonna make us too damn comfortable is likely to happen if we don't catch up to Josh.' 'Yeah,' says Mose. 'Now, jest what do you think that might be?' Well, I hadn't really thought 'bout *'xactly* what it might be, an' I said so. 'Well,' Mose says, 'jest 'xactly what you think is gonna make us any more uncomfortable than a bunch a redneck farmers with shotguns in their hands an' likker in their guts, 'cept maybe a bunch a redneck farmers with shotguns an' full a whiskey that's got wind of a colored boy tryin' to marry up with a white girl?'

"Well, then it hit me. An' I was jest about to start gettin' religion real quick when two things happened, right at the same time. First thing was, the moon come pokin' over Warrior Ridge; a big, full or-angey moon, looked like it was swole up like a blood blister. Second was, we heard harness jinglin' an' hoofbeats comin' from up the mountain, on the road we jest come down. Lots a harness. Lots a hoofbeats. An' voices, the way drunk men sound when they think they're bein' sneaky. I looked at Mose, an' I swear to Jesus, it was the onliest time up till then I ever seen that man scared. Wasn't scared when that damnfool Langford Beegle hired us to kill a bear for him an' didn't bother to tell us he'd winged the sonofabitch already, so when we got there the bear come chargin' out of a thicket maddern Joseph after Mary said she was interfered with by an angel. Wasn't scared when the sheriff took his money an' then tried to kill us an' take the whiskey. But he was scared that night, let me tell you. Me, I wasn't scared, I was pure terrified. An' I looked at him an' he looked at me, an' the same damn thought come to us both at the same damn time: headin' for trouble like we knowed we was, an' hadn't neither one of us thought to bring a gun. All we had was Mose's huntin' knife.

"Course, even if we hada had a gun, we wasn't gonna do nothin' right then, 'cept what we did, which was slink off into the woods aside of the road, an' set there, waitin' for 'em to come past, hopin' to God they wouldn't see us, or smell the fear comin' offa us, which was a damn sight more likely. 'Jesus, Mose,' I says, 'I hope they ain't got dogs.' 'Dogs?' Mose says. 'What the hell would they want dogs for?' 'Why, to try . . .' an' I stopped. 'Cause I seen somethin'. They wasn't gonna need no dogs, 'cause they knowed where Josh was goin' even if we didn't. All we had to do was follow 'em. 'Mose,' I says, 'Mose, all we got to do—' 'Is follow 'em. Yeah, I know that. But since you're so smart, what the hell we gonna do after we follow 'em?' Well, I didn't have the answer to that one, an' it didn't matter anyways, on ac-counta they was damn near on top a us by then.

"They come by us, ridin' slow. I wanted to be 'bout six miles away, downwind, but where we was 'bout four feet from the edge a the road, sucked up right to a birch log. We couldn't half breathe. What we could do was watch, an' what we seen was 'bout thirty old white farmers with faces that looked like somebody shoulda made shoes outa 'em. They was likkered—they was *well* likkered—you could smell it. But you couldn't see it in their faces. Those faces was set. An' they set in their saddles, them that had saddles to set in, straightern hell. Every one of 'em had a shotgun or a rifle. An' I could moren see 'em. I could smell 'em—smell the whiskey an' the horses an' the sweat an' all that, but mostly I could smell the angry. Maybe you don't think angry has a smell, but it does. Smells just like hot iron, only it's jest a shade softern that, jest a touch more fleshy. In a funny way, it's like a woman's smell. A woman, first thing, when she's fresh an' young, she smells sweet an' tangy. You can let her be for a while, couple years, maybe, an' she's still got that sweetness, maybe a little more salt to her, but that don't hurt. But you let her set for too long 'thout touchin' her an' it all turns sour. Not lemon sour; rotten sour, like the way milk tastes if you take it atop a maple syrup. An' that's what happens to the angry smell. An' that's what'd happened down there, 'cause the angry I was smellin' was an old-smellin' angry, an' I knowed soon as I smelled it somebody was gonna die that night.

"We waited till they passed, then we straightened up a shade. I looked at Mose, an' Mose looked at me, an' I knowed he'd been sniffin' the angry same as I done. But there wasn't nothin' to do 'cept light out after 'em, so I stood. Or I tried to; jest 'bout the time I got to ma knees, Mose hauls me back down. I wasn't fool enough to say nothin'; I jest looked around till I seen what he seen. An' presently I did. They had a rear guard; one fella on horseback, with canvas tied 'round his horseshoes so's they wouldn't make no noise. He had hisself a shotgun, jest like the rest. But that wasn't all. He was all dressed up, wearin' a hood, made outa some kinda white cloth, came to a point at the top an' hung clean down to his chest, an' a kinda sheet over the rest of him that hung down to his knees. He rode by slow an' quiet. An' we watched him till he was near outa sight, then we crawled out onto the road an' set off after him.

"We didn't have to worry 'bout him seein' us. Fool runs around in a white sheet on a moonlit night is gonna stay in sight to you a damn sight longer than you're gonna stay in sight to him. What we had to worry 'bout was stayin' outa earshot. So we couldn't talk. An' that was a problem, on accounta I wanted to tell Mose somethin'.

Which was that I knowed who that last fella was. Could tell him by his boots. Pair I shined damn near every day for years. Belonged to Parker Adams. Parker, he'd been round the courthouse longern the man on the monument. You wanted somethin' done, you went to see Parker, an' Parker knowed who to talk to, an' he'd talk to 'em, an' he'd tell you yes or no, an' how much it was gonna cost. Parker took the money, an' I guess if any of it had ever come out, it woulda been Parker that went to jail, only none of it never did. Thing was, Parker wasn't no free lance. He done what he done on accounta it worked both ways, an' come election time he was right out there twistin' arms for the party. I wouldn't say they owned him, but wasn't no question a whose side he was on, an' who he took orders from. Which jest let you know 'xactly how far the whole thing had gone. 'Cause havin' Parker Adams there, dressed up in a sheet, was 'bout the same thing as havin' a speech by the mayor, an' the Presbyterian preacher handy to lead the prayer. Whatever they was gonna do to Josh, it wasn't gonna be no lynchin'. It was gonna be damn near as official as the Fourth of July.

"So we followed quiet. We knowed how to do that, an' you can bet we never done it no better. 'Bout two miles from the forks, or maybe it's closer to three, we come up to Chaneysville, which ain't much of a town, but there was likely to be somebody to see us, an' maybe call out or somethin', an' tip off Parker. Thing was, we couldn't take a chance on goin' around, on accounta the road splits off three different ways that I know of, an' maybe a couple more. So I was worryin', but it turned out that town was shut down tightern I don't know what. All the porches was empty an' all the curtains was drawn, an' there wasn't no lights showin' behind 'em. Wasn't nobody in that town takin' a chance on seein' something they wasn't wanted to see. Which was fine, since it meant they wasn't gonna be seein' us.

"Parker took the left-hand fork, or maybe it was the middle one, I don't recall too good, but anyways we followed him down the road an' past a few farmhouses, an' up over a couple hills, an' we was gettin' a little tired on accounta we couldn't hardly breathe right for fear a makin' noise, but we stuck to him. Had to. An' finely he stopped.

"I don't know how close he come to spottin' us. He jest stopped dead an' whirled that horse around an' looked over his backtrail, an' wasn't time for us to take cover; wasn't time for us to do nothin' 'cept freeze an' hope to God that whatever was behind us was dark enough to keep us hid. I swear I don't know how it was he didn't see us. But he didn't, 'cause after a long minute he turned off on a lane, an' that was that.

"I wanted to set there for a second an' shake, but we didn't have no time. Mose lit off through the woods fastern a scalded hound dog, an' I knowed he musta knowed a shortcut, so I jest tucked in close to Mose's butt an' kept ma head down, an' we went tearin' through them woods for maybe a quarter mile, an' then we come out into some old loggin' road, wasn't much moren a track but it was a hell of a lot clearer than the woods, an' we started runnin'. I don't know how we managed it—ma feet was 'bout ready to pack up any second, but I'll tell you, I knowed how bad things was gonna get an' a set of blistered-up toes was hardly gonna be the worst of it. So we run, an' about ten minutes later that track widened up a bit, an' Mose quit runnin' an' took to the woods again an' circled us around, an' we busted up onto some open fields, a pasture, a couple cornfields, an' then we slipped into a little ring a woods, an' come up back of a farmhouse.

"'Zis it?' I says. 'Better be,' Mose says. 'We beat 'em?' I says. 'How the hell do I know?' says Mose. Well, I didn't see nobody. The house was jest a big old two-story white farmhouse, with white curtains in the windows with yellow lamplight comin' through, an' a old glider swing on the porch. There was a front yard an' a back yard an' a barn an' a outhouse an' what looked like mighta been a separate stable. There was a faint odor a hog, but the pens musta been a good ways off 'cause I couldn't see no hogs or hear 'em grunt. What it all come down to was a perty picture of a country farmhouse, an' not a livin' soul in it.

"Mose waved his hand an' we backed outa there a ways. 'Whad we back out for?' I says. 'We busted our guts gettin' down here 'fore them peckerwoods, an' we ain't 'xactly got time to spare.' 'Yeah,' Mose says. 'We ain't got a lotta things. We ain't got no guns an' we ain't got no horse an' we ain't got the love a nobody this side a hell, so we sure God better have ourselves a plan.' Well, that's the way Mose was. 'Mose,' I says, 'this here ain't the kinda thing you want to go make a prayer meetin' outa. All we got to do is nip up to the back door there an' knock an' get in an' get Josh out, an' hightail it 'fore them bastards get here.' Mose shook his head. 'Jack, you ain't thought it—' 'Mose,' I says, 'I ain't got to think nothin' through, an' if I do, I'll do it when I has to. Now, I know you ain't really got that much love for Josh, or nobody else for that matter, but he's like a brother to me, so you all jest set on your butt here an' plan, an' when I bring him back you tell us both about it.'

"Now, maybe I wasn't as careful as Mose, but I wasn't no hot-headed fool. I took a good look around 'fore I done nothin', an' I waited two seconds while the moon went behind a cloud, but once it did I didn't waste no time with sneakin' an' crawlin'. I busted right outa cover an' hightailed it across the back yard, prayin' whatever dog them folks had wouldn't start in to barkin'. I come up to the back door an' opened her up an' went in. Wasn't no time to be polite—if them farmers rode up I sure God didn't want to be outside.

"Soon as I come in I could see 'em settin' there, 'round the table. Josh was there, an' an old rawboned-lookin' fella had to be the father, an' two big dumb-lookin' country boys had to be the brothers. Wasn't no woman in sight.

"I hadn't made a whole lotta noise, an' I guess I come in so fast they didn't have no time to do nothin' about what I did make, so I took 'em all by surprise. I says, ' 'xcuse me, gentlemen, I hate to bust up the meetin', but I got some business to discuss with Mr. White here,' an' I jest reached right over an' grabbed old Josh by the shoulder an' tried to jest haul him away. An' when I pulled him he come all right, but the chair came with him. On accounta he was tied to it. Whole thing fell on the floor an' there he was, layin' on his side, lookin' up at me with his eyes widern the sky. I looked at him for a second, an' then I looked up an' I seen three pistols pointed at me, an' jest like I told Mose, I thought it through when I had to. An' then I put ma hands up, real slow.

"The old man looks at me an' he grins real wide, an' I could see where his teeth was goin' green. 'Why, boys,' he says, 'I guess we went to a whole lotta trouble for nothin'. We wouldn'ta had to work on this one so hard if we'da knowed these fools was jest gonna come droppin' by.' The two boys laughed real good at that one. Real deep belly laughs; went 'Wheeyoo, wheeyoo.' 'That's enough now,' the old man says, an' the two of 'em shut up 'sif they was switched. He waves the gun at me, an' he nods toward the chair. 'Siddown, boy.' I sat. 'Merle,' he says, 'Merle, you come 'round behind me now an' go over there an' tie him up.' One a them fools come around, an' I damn near seen ma chance, 'cause he started to cut in 'tween us, but at the last minute he recollected what the old man told him ten seconds back an' went be-

hind. He come around an' rummaged around in a cupboard for a
while, with his behind stickin' up in the air, lookin' like a mountain
covered over with denim. After a while he backs outa the cupboard.
'Pa,' he says, 'we done used up all the rope on that un there,' an' he
gives a nod at Josh, who was still layin' there on the floor. The other
lunk hadn't said nothin' up till then, but he chimes in on that, an' he
says, 'That's right, Pa, we used her all up on this un here,' an' jest in
case Pa didn't know which un where he was talkin' about, he fetched
poor Josh a kick in the kidneys. I was lookin' right at him when it
landed, an' it wasn't no love tap, neither, but Josh didn't show it. His
eyes was blank, an' he hardly even winced. Well, up till then I hadn't
really been thinkin'. But lookin' at Josh, seein' him hardly even wince
when that dumb ox kicked him, well, I did start thinkin' 'bout how in
hell we was gonna get outa there. An' the first thing I seen was we
wasn't gonna get outa there. I had maybe an outside chance, 'cause I
wasn't tied yet, an' with three of 'em there they was gonna have to be
mighty careful how they fired them pistols, an' if Josh coulda maybe
kicked one in the shins or somethin' to give me half a second's start,
well, maybe I coulda made it. An' if I coulda got clear, maybe me an'
Mose together could do somethin'. But none a that looked likely, on
accounta Josh wasn't gonna be kickin' nobody to give nobody else
half a second's nothin'. It didn't take much figurin' to know what had
happened. His mind was ruint. On accounta he figgered out—too
late, jest like I figgered out too late—that that girl had been settin'
him up all along. Maybe he even figgered out that there was folks
comin' to lynch him. An' if he figgered that far, he was surely gonna
have figgered that when he swung she was gonna be right there,
watchin' an' grinnin' an' fixin' to go gushy in her bloomers when he
started jerkin' around. Anyways, I knowed I couldn't 'xpect no help
from Josh. Meanwhile, Pa was tellin' the second one to take it easy,
he didn't want Josh to die 'fore they was ready. 'Wayne,' he says, 'you
go on out to the spring porch an' see if there ain't none a that there
chain left hangin'.' 'Hey, Pa,' the first one says, 'there's a whole heap
more rope out in the barn.' 'I know that, Merle,' the old man says,
'but I don't want nobody outside jest now.' Well, it turned out there
was some chain, an' the two of 'em, Merle an' Wayne, they chained
me to the chair, an' the old man never once took his eyes off me, so I
didn't have a chance to do nothin'. When they was done, Wayne says,
'Pa, we finished on this un here,' an' he slaps me upside the head jest

so's there wasn't no mistake. 'You want I should set that un there on his feet?' 'You do that, Wayne,' the old man says, 'but stay outa ma line a fire. This un looks like he's got some run in him.' Wayne looks at me. 'This un here?' he says, an' he went to give me another crack. Onliest thing I could move was ma head, but I twisted around an' took the slap flush on the mouth, an' I got a mouthful a finger an' bit as hard as I could an' twisted ma head as sharp as I could, an' I heard the bone go snap jest 'fore Wayne started bellerin'. Sounded awful. An' it was an awful sight, let me tell you, a two-hundred-an'-fifty-pound farm boy starin' down at his pinkie finger that was pointin' south when the rest a his fingers was pointin' east, cryin' like a baby. The old man jest shook his head. 'Yeah, Wayne,' he says, 'that un there.'

"Well, I can't say what they mighta done to me—I suspect as how that wasn't ma smartest move—but they never got the chance, on accounta there come a knock on the front door. The old man told Merle to set Josh an' me aloose from the chairs, which he done, an' they herded us both down the hallway towards the parlor. Josh jest walked along, calm as you please, lookin' dead. I suspect it wouldn'ta mattered if they hadn'ta tied his hands. It was harder for me; them chains was the heaviest damn things you can imagine. They wasn't even tied to me, jest wrapped around, an' it woulda been easiern hell to whip 'em off if it hadn'ta been for the fact that ma arms was inside next to ma chest. There wasn't nothin' I could do, so I jest clanked along.

"Jest 'fore we got to the door I heard a sound. Funny sound. Like a dog makes when you hit it all the time. I stopped an' I turned around an' looked, an' then I seen her. The girl. She was standin' up to the top a the steps, lookin' down at us. She was a little bit of a thing, with long dark hair an' skin the color a snow an' these big black eyes; I could see 'em starin' at us. She was dressed all in white, in a dress that went clear to the floor, an' the wall behind her was white, an' there wasn't no light up there to speak of, so all you could see was the hair an' the eyes an' the size of her. But you could hear her voice; that was the sound.

"Well, the old man looked up at her an' he says, 'Clydette, I told you to get outa sight an' stay outa sight.' But she didn't pay him no attention. She says, 'Joshua? Joshua?' I looked at Josh, but it was like he didn't hear her. I didn't blame him for not turnin' his head, I wouldn'ta turned my head for her no more neither, but it was like he didn't even hear her. But the old man heard her, an' went flyin' up them steps and fetched her a good clean slap an' knocked her sprawlin'. Then he come back, an' him an' Wayne an' Merle hauled us out inta the yard.

"They was waitin' out in the yard, all them farmers an' Parker Adams in his sheet, laid out in a half circle. They was all carryin' torches, an' the whole yard was lit up brightern day. Soon as they seen Josh, the whole bunch of 'em left out a roar like a mangled she-bear, an' for the first time it come to me jest how bad it was. I had perty much figured out I was gonna die, but I'd been too close to that too many times to let it spook me. But hearin' that roar, I got to thinkin' 'bout what they might do to me 'forehand, things that, well, once they happen to a man, he'd jest as soon die, an' if you come along an' save his life afterwards, it ain't no kindness.

"Well, Parker waited till they quieted down, an' then he waved his hand an' some a them farmers come up on the porch an' laid hold a Josh. Then Merle gives me a shove an' I come out in the torchlight. I seen old Parker give a start, 'cause I knowed he recognized me. 'What the hell you got there, Mr. McElfish?' he says. Only he made his voice all high an' whispery, an' it come to me that didn't nobody else there know 'xactly who he was. 'Don't rightly know,' the old man says. 'He come bustin' into the party so's me an' the boys give him these chains for a door prize. Figger he must be hooked up with that un there. But I don't see it matters none; a nigger's a nigger, an' if you gonna have a lynchin', two's as good as one.' 'Maybe,' says Parker, 'but these two runs with a third one, an' if they're both here, third one can't be far off. You, Jack,' he says, 'where's Moses at?' I give ma voice a good shake, on accounta I seen a chance an' I wanted Parker to think I was scaredern I was, an' I says, 'He was right here, but he went to get the sheriff, an' when they get here you gonna be in some kinda trouble, an' if I was you I'd turn tail an' head back to Maryland fast as I could.' I wanted old Parker to get it in his head that I didn't know who he was. Only it damn near backfired. 'Mr. McElfish,' Parker says in that high whispery voice, 'you told this man where I was from?' 'No, sir,' says the old man. 'He musta been listenin' for a while 'fore he come bustin' in.' So I was safe; Parker musta let on to 'em he was from Maryland, which made all kindsa sense. ''Sides,' the old man says, 'we gonna kill him anyways, so it don't make no diff—'

'Listen here, McElfish,' Parker says. 'You bear in mind who's runnin' this lynchin'. Now, maybe we'll kill 'em both, an' maybe we'll let this one watch so he can go back an' tell the rest. I ain't decided.' Well, jest about then Wayne perks up a little, an' he says, 'If we only gonna lynch that un there, kin we mess this un here up a little 'fore we leave him go?' Parker looks at him. 'McElfish,' he says, 'you shut this lump of pork fat up 'fore I decide to lynch him too.' 'Shup, Wayne,' the old man says, an' Wayne shut up.

"They put us up in front of a bunch of 'em an' they made us march. Josh coulda run, maybe, but he looked deadern a two-day-old catfish, an' I wasn't gonna get too far wearin' eighty pounds a chain. So we jest walked along, me keepin' ma eyes peeled for a sign a Mose. I figgered he had to be doin' somethin', an' I knowed it wasn't goin' for no sheriff. But he didn't show hisself, an' nothin' happened. So all I could do was march.

"Well, they took us back down the lane to the main road, an' they marched us south for maybe a mile or so. It musta been a sight: two colored men walkin' along with ropes around their necks like they was dogs an' thirty men with guns on horseback an' wagons, an' what all. I got to thinkin' it musta looked jest like somebody goin' huntin'. We was the dogs an' they was the hunters, an' the onliest thing we needed was a coon, only we was the coons, an' they sure as damnit was gonna tree us, or one of us anyways, an' that got all mixed up in ma head, an' I started to laugh, real soft like, an' the chains started to clinkin' a little when ma chest moved, not much, jest a little *clink, clink, clink,* an' that was funny too, an' I started laughin' a little more, an' I marched right along while we turned off the main road an' went up over a hill, chucklin' an' clinkin', an' I mighta turned right into the jolliest bastard in hell if it wasn't for the fact that when we got to the other side a that hill there was a clearin' an' 'leven more fellas in sheets an' a big oak tree an' underneath of it a pile a wood, an' it come to me that when I said lynch I thought about hangin', but didn't everybody think that way, some thought about burnin'. An' I stopped chucklin'. I'm shamed to say it, but when them chains stopped clinkin' I heard a funny sound, like hoofbeats far off. An' Wayne, he sings out, 'Looky, Pa, looky, that un there wet hisself.' An' I looked down an' I seen he was right. But I couldn't feel it. Even when I seen it, I couldn't feel it.

"But nobody was payin' no attention. The 'leven sheets come

trottin' up an' the farmers come up closer with the torches, an' they looked us over. Didn't say nothin'; didn't nobody say nothin'. It was so quiet all you could hear was a horse snort now an' again. They jest set there lookin'. After a minute Parker come up an' nods to the other sheets, an' they nodded to him, an' one of 'em says, 'Where'd *he* come from?' Said it in that same high whispery voice, so's wouldn't nobody know him. But I knowed him. I knowed 'em all. Knowed 'em by their boots. I'd shined every damn pair, that very day. Parker tole 'em how I'd come into the party, an' then he tole 'em how Mose was goin' to get the sheriff, an' they all chuckled a little, an' I knowed why: if he *hadda* gone to get the sheriff, you coulda bet dollars to double eagles there was least two deputies that wasn't gonna be handy. But after they was done chucklin' they stirred a little like they was uneasy. An' I seen why, right away: they wasn't sure they could kill me. If Josh was to disappear wouldn't nobody much know, or care. Me, I was another matter. Folks would miss me. An' somebody was maybe gonna look for me. An' the only way they was gonna be able to make folks stop lookin' was by tellin' 'em the truth, or somethin' like it, an' that wasn't gonna go down too easy. On accounta folks is funny; they'll get off their porches an' pull the shades an' keep their eyes screwed shut, but sometimes if you tell 'em what it is they ain't seein', they take notice.

"Well, Parker an' the rest a them sheets trotted aside to try an' figger out what to do. Me, I was feelin' mighty guilty, on accounta Josh was gonna die, an' I was feelin' good knowin' that I maybe wasn't. An' that's the way it was lookin', 'cause when the conference was over they hauled me over to the edge of the clearin' an' chained me to a tree an' they set Wayne to keep an eye on me, an' then they dismounted an' set about lynchin' Josh.

"It's funny how you see things. Why, a day before all that, if you was to a tole me I could set there an' watch the Klan lynch ma best friend an' not feel a thing, I woulda laughed in your face. But the truth is I can get more riled about it layin' here than I was then. It was jest like watchin' somebody butcher a hog. First they pulled his clothes off him—coat, vest, tie, shirt, pants, long johns, everything— an' they tossed the free end of a rope over the limb a that oak tree an' looped the noose end 'round below his armpits, an' they hoisted him up. Then Parker commenced to make some kinda speech. I couldn't hear what he was sayin' but I knowed what he was gettin' at, on accounta he kept pointin' to Josh's privates an' every time he done it them farmers would grumble. An' then he pulled out a knife an' held it right upside Josh's parts, an' they left out a roar. But Josh didn't. He jest hung there. An' that started gettin' to 'em; I guess it don't make no sense to lynch a man that don't pay you no mind. So Parker said somethin', an' one of them farmers went to his horse an' come back with a whip. I guess they figured to get old Josh's attention.

"They sure as hell had Wayne's. He could barely keep his eyes off 'em while they was uncoilin' that whip an' gettin' people moved around to give the sheet that had it enough room to swing. He started closer an' closer so's he could get a good look at what was goin' on. Matter a fact, one a the sheets seen how far from me Wayne was gettin' to be, an' he come over to take care a that. That was what I figgered, anyways. Only when that sheet came up to Wayne, he walked right on by him. Or looked to. Then he stopped an' turned, an' went back t'other way. An' I couldn't figger what *that* was all about, until all the sudden Wayne goes 'Wheeyoo,' real soft like, an' falls on his face. The sheet kept right on walkin'. It was too dark for me to see the boots, but it wasn't too dark for me to count, an' when he got back to the middle a the clearin' there was thirteen sheets there.

"I didn't waste no time.

"They hadn't bothered to chain me good, jest wrapped 'bout eighty pounds a chain round me an' a tree. So I wriggled around as much as I dared, made a little noise, but there wasn't nobody near enough to hear 'sides Wayne, an' I was perty certain Wayne wasn't listenin'. I twisted an' turned, an' I bruised maself on that chain, but I was gettin' a little play when they started in to whippin' Josh.

"The first crack made me jerk ma head up. Now, you gotta understand, that there wasn't no ridin' crop. It was a bullwhip. If it'd been me I woulda screamed when the first one caught me, but Josh didn't make a sound. The sheet that was whippin' him started windin' up for another go; they was set on gettin' sound outa Josh. Only you don't bullwhip a man too long—it ain't sound that comes out; it's his guts to come out. I had to do somethin' fast. All I could think about was Wayne's pistol. I wanted that pistol so bad I could taste it. An' I started twistin' harder, an' pert soon I could see ma way out. I needed to give three good jerks, that was all. Trouble was, I was gonna have to make noise, lotsa noise. But if they heard that there chain clinkin', that was gonna be the end of everything. So I had to time it. I jest hoped Josh could take three more cracks.

"The second one come. Whip went slappin' through the air an' I twisted them chains. They give a little. Not enough. Josh, he didn't give at all. He jest swung there, his face jest as blank as a whitewashed board.

"The third one come. I got so close to bein' aloose I coulda cried. Close, but close ain't there. Josh still wasn't sayin' nothin'. I could see blood startin' to drip on the wood underneath him, but he didn't make a sound, he jest swung back an' forth like a scarecrow in the wind.

"The fourth one come. I got it that time, an' I left them chains fall easy as I could, an' I dropped an' scooted across the ground to where good old Wayne was layin' in the dust. It took a minute to work his pistol out from under him, but 'fore they was ready to give Josh another crack I was lined up. I waited. Sights was lined up perfect. That sheet wound up an' let the whip go, an' jest about the time it was halfways to Josh I squeezed that trigger jest as gentle as I could. I was aimin' for the chest but the slug dropped moren I'd figgered an' took the bastard in the hip. Blowed him halfways into the woods. Well, they stood there for a second, like they didn't know what the hell happened. I lined up on Parker. Coulda taken a closer shot, but I couldn't be sure about 'xactly who the others was, you see. Well, I was hurried an' the shot went high, but that second shot sure attracted some attention. One a them sheets looks over an' shouts, 'The nigger's loose,' an' one a the other sheets shouts, 'You all get him, I'll watch this sonofabitch.' An' then they come.

"Those bastards was stupid. Farmers can't do nothin' in the woods at night, an' them sheets was even worse—they was all the time gettin' their hems caught. I backed away real fast, an' soon as I was in the woods I left off the other three shots in the pistol to slow 'em down, an' then I lit out. I coulda got shed of 'em in two or three minutes, but I pulled 'em along for a good ten, lettin' 'em catch sight a me—they couldn't read sign worth a damn—takin' 'em uphill all the damn time so they'd wind theyselves good. After about a mile an' a half a dodgin' tree trunks an' playin' peekaboo, I cut back downhill an' left 'em play tag with theyselves.

"By the time I got back to the clearin', Mose had got his knife outa Wayne an' had Josh cut down from the tree an' tied onto a horse. Josh wasn't blank-lookin' no more. I guess that whip had cut loose a lotta things. He jest set there, cryin' like I ain't never seen a man cry. I don't know if it was the pain or the fear or the way that girl done him, but he wasn't good for nothin'. Soon as I was on horseback—Mose had picked out three good ones, an' run off the other horses—we rode out.

"We rode as hard as we could, but we couldn't make no time on accounta we couldn't keep Josh in the saddle. He wouldn't hold on. He wouldn't do nothin', 'cept cry. I wasn't too happy with him, but Mose was downright disgusted, an' he commenced to cussin' Josh three ways from Sunday. 'Damnit,' Mose says, 'we go through hell an' high water to rescue his pasty hind end an' all he wants to do is cry. Goddamn you, you mutilated sonofabitch, if you don't quit that cryin' an' start to ridin' I'm gonna lynch you ma own self.' 'Mose,' I says, 'go easy on him.' 'Easy, hell,' Mose says. 'You think them bastards are gonna go easy on us when they catch up? Which they gonna be doin' perty quick if we don't start ridin' hard. We got maybe ten minutes start in a two-hour ride outa this damn place, an' God knows what kinda fancy steppin' when we get back to someplace where we can hide, an' we can't do none a that with a Goddamn dead man to cart around.' He reins in right there an' he says, 'Now, Josh, you listen to me. I know you been through a lot, but I swear 'fore God if you don't straighten yourself up an' start ridin' I'm gonna leave you here an' leave the bastards lynch you. I ain't entirely sure you ain't got it comin'.'

"Well, he was right in a way, an' he was wrong in a way, but 'fore I could say nothin' Josh looks up an' says, 'Leave me. I don't give a damn.' Mose jest stared at him. Then he says, 'All right. I got a life, an' I aim to keep it. Come on, Jack.'

"I says, 'Now wait a minute. Let me talk to him. Looka here, Josh,' I says, 'I know how you feel. I swear I do. But you dyin' ain't the way to do things. Why, what you oughta do is go back there an' take that bitch out in the woods an' beat her till there's no tomorrow. Kill her if you want to, I'll help you. But lettin' 'em kill you, that don't make no sense. That's what they wanted to begin with.'

"Mose looks at me an' he looks at Josh. ' 'Zat it? 'Zat all?' 'What you mean, 'zat all?' I says. 'The man was in love with that girl. He worked honest labor all damn summer jest to stay close to her. He give up other women to stay clean for her. He was fixin' to marry her. He trusted her. He was ready to pass for white, for *white,* so's he could be with her. Then she turns around an' tries to get him kilt, an' then you come along an' say 'zat all? Yeah, that's all. Damn near all there is, anywhere. But what the hell would you know about that? You don't love nobody. You don't trust nobody. You don't give up nothin' for nobody. Well, maybe he was wrong, an' maybe he shoulda knowed better, an' maybe I think he's a damn fool too, but I tell you, I can't be real certain that if I was in his shoes I'd be too wild about stayin' alive maself. Now you ride on if you want. I'm gonna stay here an' talk to him, an' if I have to leave him, I swear, I'm gonna kill me a white girl.'

"Well, Mose, he looks at me, an' he shakes his head, an' he says, 'Jack, I swear, you as simple-minded as this here fool. Where you think I got this here sheet?' I couldn't think a nothin' to say, on accounta I didn't know where he got that sheet. So he told us. Told us how he'd gone on in that house, lookin' for a sheet, an' found that girl all beat an' bloodied, an' how she claimed she didn't have nothin' to do with it, that they musta been watchin' her an' Josh all along, an' waitin' for the right time, an' when they was ready they wanted her to tell 'em when he was comin' down to see her, an' she seen they didn't have nothin' good in mind, so they beat her an' made her tell, an' then they beat her again when they caught her tryin' to make some kinda signal to warn Josh off, an' how she begged him to save Josh somehow, an' give him the sheet, an' told him where they was takin' us.

"Well, I'll tell you, sometimes I useta get a little hot with Mose, on accounta the way he could lie easiern most folks breathe, but I was glad he could make stuff up that quick right then—or maybe he didn't have to make it up, maybe that was the guff she give him when he went in there to steal that sheet, to keep him from killin' her right then. I don't know. All I know is, Josh was whipped enough to believe it, an' he started ridin' better.

"Mose knowed a trail that ran along the top a Polish Mountain, an' we followed it almost to Evert. I was all for comin' on into town, but Mose kept sayin' he wasn't satisfied as to what was happenin'. I says to him, 'We know what's happenin', on accounta we jest finished puttin' a stop to it,' but Mose wouldn't listen. We finely holed up way up near dumb-butted town Mose called Oppenheimer. I hadn't never heard of it. It was a Godforsaken place to hole up, too; dry as dust, not a stream for miles. But Mose knowed a spring, an' he knowed a

109

cave, an' it turned out he had some food cached up there, an' bandages an' some horse liniment, an' we cleaned Josh's back up an' bandaged him, an' then we ate an' then we had some whiskey, an' by the time the sun come up we was feelin' pretty good, most ways. 'Cept I could see that Josh wasn't comin' around the way he shoulda. He didn't say mucha anything. I knowed what it was, too; he finely seen through the lyin' Mose'd been doin' about that girl. I tried to tell Mose that, but he wouldn't listen. He jest wanted to go on an' on about politics, an' what them sheets was hopin' to accomplish by lynchin' Josh. I swear, Mose could make things about ten times as confusin' as they neeeded to be. An' I told him that. Said, 'Hell, Mose, we know what they was tryin' to accomplish.' 'Yeah,' Mose says, 'but why?'

"'Why?' I says. 'Hell, why ain't even a question. They done it on accounta white folks ain't noted for feelin' kindly towards colored folks, that's why. They're doin' the same damn thing all over the country all the damn time.' Well, Mose says, 'I know that, Jack. But there's more to why than jest that. There's "Why here?" an' there's "Why now?" an' there's—' 'Yeah,' I says, 'I know you know all the letters in the whatchemacallit, but I don't give a damn.' Well, he says, 'Jack, don'tcha see, we gotta figger out them whys so we can figger out who done it an' then begin to do somethin' about 'em. We can't jest go in there an' start beatin' on everybody white.' Well, I said, I didn't see why we couldn't, it sounded like they wasn't too particular about which nigger they started in on, but anyways, I already knowed who they was. An' I told 'em how I knowed, an' I told him who they was. An' Mose got real thoughtful.

"Well, we holed up that day an' the next, which was Sunday. Josh got so's he could move around pretty good, but his mind jest wasn't there. He still wasn't talkin'. Jest set there, sippin' whiskey, sayin' nothin'. By Sunday night, I was beginnin' to think we was gonna have to shoot him, like you do a horse with a busted leg—he was that bad. Finely Mose sets down with him an' he says, 'Lookahere, Josh,' he says, 'we had about enough a this moonin' around. If you worryin' about that girl—' 'Hell with her,' Josh says, an' I begun to think that maybe that there whippin' was a good thing some ways; it got some sense in his head anyways. 'All right,' Mose says, 'hell with her. I ain't got no time to be huntin' down women anyways; we got twelve men to lay for.' Well, there he was, lyin' again, but I didn't

110

mind it this time, neither, on accounta I seen that he was tryin' to get Josh's juices flowin'. Course there wasn't no way we was gonna ambush them twelve without causin' a whole lot a stir, but maybe we coulda done one or two, which mighta been enough to get Josh back whatever it was he left down there in the South County. So I says, 'That's right, Josh, we got twelve sheets that needs to be taken to the scrub board an' hung out to dry. An' if that ain't enough, we can go get that farmer an' the one fool son he's got left—' Well, to tell you the truth, I was beginnin' to warm to the idea. But Josh cut me off right there. 'Leave it be,' he says. That was all he said. But he said it in a voice that was lowern a mole's belly an' deadern Thursday night. An' that took the starch right outa me. An' I left it be.

"I left it be the next day when I come on in an' took to shinin' shoes. I shined every pair a shoes in the courthouse. An' I shined every pair a boots that was down there in Southampton—'cept one. Story was a tree fell an' busted up that one's hip. They told me that. Othern that, didn't nobody say nothin'. I didn't neither. I left it be.

"Next day Josh come on into town an' went down to Hawkin's an' bought hisself some Mail Pouch an' walked around town half the day, chewin' tobacco an' spittin' juice on the sidewalk, jest like Mose told him to do. Didn't nobody say nothin' to him; they was leavin' it be.

"An' the next day Mose come down, leadin' two horses an' ridin' the third, an' he hitched 'em to the post in front a the courthouse. Half the Town seen him doin' it but didn't nobody say nothin', an' an hour later them horses was gone, an' didn't nobody say nothin' 'bout that, neither. They left it be.

"That's the way it was. They left it all be. Course, Josh, he wasn't never the same. I don't think he ever did say moren three words at a time to anybody again. He'd walk aroun' town silent as the grave. He'd go into Hawkin's an' half the time he'd say what he wanted, an' the rest a the time he'd jest point. I guess he was so mad he didn't want to start talkin', 'fraid it would all come out. He left it be, too.

"But somebody didn't leave it be, on accounta every month or so something bad would happen to one a them sheets. One went blind from drinkin' leaded shine. One fell in a ditch an' broke his leg an' caught pneumonia an' died. 'Nother one's wife left him. On like that. Jest bad news. Not too much at any one time, but steady; somethin' got every one of 'em. An' inside a 'bout three years wasn't none of 'em

111

around here no more. Some moved on. 'Bout half was dead. Somebody didn't leave it be. . . ."

And then he started to cough. Long, racking coughs, as if he had been holding it all in while he told the tale, and now it had to come out. When he was finished the rag was bloody and his body was shaking with chills. I blew the candle out, got up and lit the lamp. When the light was steady I busied myself with stoking the fire and stirring the grate, with making the hot gases roar in the flue. I boiled water and made him a strong toddy. He could barely drink it but I got it down him, along with more of the penicillin. He swallowed and coughed. When the toddy was gone I let him lie back. He lay perfectly straight on the cot, but the chills made him shiver. He tried to talk. "Hush now," I said.

I sat up through the night. I fed the fire and drank hot whiskey and tried to stay awake. He slept a sleep that was closer to coma, from time to time rousing to something close to consciousness to call a name or mumble bits of tales. The stories were breaking up inside him; he coughed out fragments. I listened to him, sitting by the roaring stove, sipping whiskey and feeding the fire.

197903051900

(Monday)

THE COFFEE WAS WEAK. I had made it that way on purpose; I needed the warmth of it and I needed to stay awake, but I needed to be calm too, and so I had made an insipid brew, lower in caffeine, as a compromise. Drinking coffee was itself a compromise. Because what I really wanted was a toddy. But I was going to call Judith, and if I had a toddy she would know. She would not say anything, but she would know. So I had made some coffee and sat there, sipping it. It was doing me no good at all. The only thing it did for me was to remind me of Judith.

It was seven o'clock; she should be coming home from the hospital now, unless some emergency had delayed her. I could see her fighting her way off the Spruce Street bus, and then wearily walking the block and a half to the apartment. The elevator would not be working, and she would curse it and—because I had told her once it was wrong to curse the instrument and not the author—the name of Otis, the foul terms coming lightly tripping off her one-of-the-finest-families-in-Virginia tongue as if she had been raised at a truck stop and not on Axe Trail Road. After the first distinct outburst she would mutter and mumble the words as she plodded up the three flights of stairs, hauling with her a battered briefcase that bulged with work:

case files to review, articles to read, drafts of monographs to revise, books to review for one professional journal or another. Reaching the landing, she would set the briefcase down with a thump loud enough to waken the dead, open her purse and unerringly select the right key, unlock the door and push it open with a foot so small and dainty it seemed more suited to ballet slippers than to the "sensible" shoes she wore. Letting the door slam shut behind her, she would drop the briefcase on the sofa and head for the kitchen to brew coffee so strong it could lift the pot. She would sip the first cup while she watched the *CBS Evening News*—she never really believed anything unless she heard it from Walter. After that she would change into her leotard and do her exercises. Then she would draw a hot tub and soak in it while she sipped another cup and read a file or two and listened to something on the stereo; she preferred something breezy and contemporary.

The coffee reminded me of all that, and of the way I was, after three long years, just beginning to fit into it: that I never carried a briefcase, never carried papers at all, if I could help it, preferring to write my articles in my head and dictate them; that I never complained about the elevator because I never expected that it would work; that I never used street language, for to me it was and always would be a tongue as foreign as French or German; that I never got the right key on the first try, not even after three years; that I winced every time she banged the door; but that now I joined her in the coffee when once I had sipped hot toddies instead; that I would watch Cronkite more out of a desire to be with her than out of concern for current events, since it seemed to me that trying to evaluate the significance of news hot off the wire is a lot less useful and almost as dangerous as speculating as to whether the woman into whose lap you have just dropped your lasagna is destined to be your partner for life; that I would watch her as she exercised, thinking that the exercises were fairly useless—I preferred to get mine through long midnight walks—but that hers was the most lovely and graceful body in the world, the exercises the most erotic movements I had ever seen; that I would listen to the music—when I chose it it was something dark and complicated, Sibelius or Mahler or Holst—reading something obscure while she soaked, waiting until I heard the sounds of splashing and then going in to have a towel waiting for her when she emerged, pink and dripping, from the tub. I would dry her carefully and slowly, just to have an excuse to hold her, then we would go into the bedroom and lie together for a while and talk. Not about anything much. She would tell me something strange a patient had done or said. I would offer a small tidbit, one of those fascinating, offbeat, seemingly useless facts that historians are forever discovering. Sometimes it would end there, and sometimes we would make love. When we did that in the evenings it was always a special thing, an expression, almost, of a desire to save the later time, the final going to bed, for tired kisses and chaste hugging. And when the sharing, whatever its shape, was done, we would stretch, and I would massage the spot just inside her left shoulder blade that seemed to always be a little sore, and we would get up and decide what to do about dinner.

I should have made the coffee stronger, or have had none at all: strong coffee would have made me feel closer to her, and none might have let me think of something else, but the weak brew simply made me understand how far I was from her; how far I was from anything.

I had brought him out at first light, as soon as I could see my way through the pines. I came out of the cabin, shaking with sleep and cold, and found that there would be no problem with the footing. For sometime during the night the storm had stalled; and now it hung there, caught in its opening phase. The clouds boiled aimlessly in the sky, the wind blew fitfully; the snow had stopped; the path had not become impassable. It made me want to laugh, and I did laugh, sending the sound out to die without echo in the brooding pines. Then I went back in and stirred up the fire and set the place to rights, washing the pots and pans and cups and bowls and spoons and placing them where he had always placed them. I put out the fire, and dressed him in his clean clothes. I put on my coat, and got him into his coat, and I carried him out.

I cradled him carefully as I carried him, protecting his arms and legs from collisions. It would have been a far easier proposition had I slung him over my shoulder, but I could not do that. And so the trip was difficult; I slipped to my knees countless times, and twice I fell heavily, twisting to take the impact on my back so as to spare him. I cried when my foot slipped and his shoulder struck a boulder; cried and told him I was sorry.

I brought him down the path and into the house that he had not entered in twenty years, and I set him in my mother's parlor, in the chair that she reserved for the most favored of guests—the preacher and the presiding elder and, on one infamous occasion, one of Bill's teachers—plumping up a feather pillow and placing it so that his head would not loll and cause a crick in his neck. I placed his hands on the chair arms. I straightened his shoulders. I lifted his feet and placed them on a hassock. Then I went into the kitchen and made two cups of instant coffee, brought them back and sat down on the floor beside him, holding my mug in both hands to absorb as much of the warmth as I could.

I sat there for a long time, sipping the coffee and listening to the sounds the house made—the creakings and the groanings of wood and rock shifting under the strain and cold, the high whining that the stove clock made when the gears got cold—and thinking about the countless little bits of lore he had imparted to me over the years, the trout and bass and catfish caught and cleaned and fried in sizzling bacon grease in black cast-iron skillets, the tender meat of young rabbit caught with handmade traps to avoid the necessity of digging shot out of the tender haunches, of the stories, told around a fire or in the darkness of the cabin. I finished my coffee, reached up and took the other cup and drank his coffee too.

That was how she found us. She didn't say anything, she simply went to summon the coroner, acting as if getting up in the morning to find your sole surviving son sitting in the parlor in company with a stiffening corpse was an everyday occurrence. I didn't say anything, either.

They came in a jeep since even the light snow had muddied the streets of the Hill, making it impossible for them to bring the dead wagon. They were soft-spoken and polite and did not laugh even though they were forced to drive away with him sitting up in the back seat, because rigor mortis had stiffened him.

When he was gone I went into the kitchen and sat down at the table. She was cooking eggs and bacon, wearing an old flannel house-coat over flannel pajamas, the sleeves of both pulled up and tied with remnants of cloth to keep them out of the range of the grease. The sound of the frying was almost musical, the smell warm and rich and enticing, and it was almost as it had been years before, beginning just after Moses Washington died, when I would rise with the dawn and come creeping down to the kitchen to sit at the table reading some book that I had probably read five or six times before, and an hour or so later, she would come down and we would talk as she would fry the bacon and crack the eggs and cook the oatmeal or the pancakes, and as I, feeling grownup and responsible, would slice the bread to make toast and siphon some cream off the top of the mason jar of raw milk fresh from Miss Minnie's cow, and then go get Bill out of bed. A short interlude—ten minutes, fifteen—but, repeated thousands of times, it had made us close. Now she fried the eggs and the bacon, but the bread was presliced and the milk pasteurized and homogenized, and there was no Bill upstairs to be dragged kicking and screaming out of bed. And we didn't talk at all until she gave me a cup of coffee and a plate of eggs and bacon and took her seat across from me with her own.

"It does me good to see you," she said then.

I sipped at the coffee. "Good coffee," I said.

"I don't know that the preacher's going to want to bury him from the church," she said. "Hard to heat that place, this kind of weather, and oil isn't cheap."

"I'll give him a check."

"Oh, there's no need for you to do that," she said. "I just mean that the preacher's a new man and all, and I'll just have to explain who . . ." She stopped when she saw me staring at her. "What?" she said.

"You just love arranging burials, don't you?" I said. Her jaw tightened. I sipped my coffee.

"Anyway," she said after a minute, "there's no need for you to pay for anything. I suspect the County'll pay for the funeral. They ought to. He never would take a penny from relief. Too proud. I'll say that for him, that man was proud."

"The only way they would pay is if he was on relief. Then he would have been a good darky, taking handouts from Massa. The way he was, the only way the County would pay to bury him is to have him hauled away in a garbage truck."

She was silent for a minute. Then she said, "He paid his insurance, you know that. I'll call the agent this morning. I can do it from work."

I stared at her again. "Why do you want to do it? You didn't give a damn about him when he was alive."

"He helped build the house I live in. He was my husband's friend. He was my son's friend. I didn't want to rub elbows with the man, and I won't say I'm going to cry a tear over his smelly carcass,

117

but I'm not so quick to forget I maybe owe him a thing or two."

I didn't say anything; I just looked at her.

She sighed. "You want more coffee?"

I nodded. She poured it, sugared it, added too much milk. That was the way she had done it the first time she had let me drink coffee. It had been a rather momentous morning; the two of us in the kitchen as always and then suddenly she, with no fanfare, with an almost elaborate casualness, putting a cup beside her mug and pouring it half full. She meant it as an entry into her world, and it might have worked had it not been for the fact that, long before, Old Jack had initiated me into manhood with a sip of a far more potent brew. But she did not know that, and it did not seem to me then that I had to choose one or the other, and so I sipped my coffee-milk elaborately, flaunting it in front of Bill, and floated off to school, swollen with my new status. Predictably, I stood up to some taunt and got into a fight, for once giving as good as I got. They called her to the school. She chastised me in the principal's office, while that gentleman looked on in stern satisfaction.

"You're going to be *persona non grata* if you keep up this fighting," she said. "Do you know what that means?"

"No," I mumbled.

"Speak up when you talk to me," she snapped. "And show some respect. Do you know what *persona non grata* means?"

"No, ma'am."

The principal leaned forward.

"It means that people don't want you. It means they won't talk to you or be with you. It means there won't be a soul you can trust. Folks won't have anything good to say about you."

The principal sat back, looking relieved; he hadn't known what it meant, either.

I had been staring at the floor, because it was impossible to look her in the eye when she spoke that way and looking anywhere else but down would have been a sign of impertinence. But her words kindled something inside me, and I raised my head and looked her straight in the eye. "Well, then, I guess I'm person-whatever-it-is already. Because that boy called me a nigger. So I might as well fight."

For a moment she stared at me, speechless, and then she brought her hand around in a long sweeping curve that ended just above my left ear. The room spun. My head rolled on my neck, swinging up towards the ceiling. Somehow I stayed on my feet, brought my head under control, forced my eyes to focus. She stood looking at me, waiting to see what I would do. I smiled at her. She hit me again. In the moment before the blow landed I saw the look on her face; it was cold, determined, almost murderous. And then the world spun. I literally saw stars. But I stayed on my feet, stumbling a little, yet somehow keeping my balance. I did not look at her face again; I kept my head down.

"He won't be gettin' into no more fights," I heard her say, through the slowly fading ringing in my ears. "If it's all right, I just take him on home and clean him up, send him back this afternoon."

"That's fine," the principal said.

She had turned to me, tugging at my collar points. "Let's get you home and clean you up."

"Yes, ma'am," I said.

We left the school and walked the half block to where she had parked the car. I got in and sat silently, staring straight ahead. I ached. They had been tough fights. She got in, started the engine. Then she turned to me. "John, don't you forget, don't ever forget, that white people are the ones that say what happens to you. Maybe it isn't right, but that's just exactly the way it is. And so long as you're going to their school, so long as they're teaching you what you need to learn, you have to be quiet, and careful, and respectful. Because you've got your head in the lion's mouth. You understand?"

"Yes, ma'am," I had said.

She rose from the table and took her mug to the far end of the kitchen and set it on the windowsill while she unshipped the iron and the board. She sipped absently at the coffee while she waited for the iron to heat. "It almost seems like I ought to be going up to shake your brother awake. That boy sure did love his sleep." She took a sip from her mug, then tested the iron with the moistened tips of her fingers. She pulled a blouse from the laundry basket by the door, spread it on the board, took another sip from the mug, set it down, and began to iron. She would, I knew, forget about the coffee. She always did. She would get engrossed in whatever it was and forget the half-full cup, and when she wanted more coffee, she would make a cup of instant, eventually leaving that one too somewhere half drunk. Hours, sometimes even days, later she would find a cup and take it up again, never minding the fact that the coffee was cold now. That's

119

what she was trying to do now—take it up and carry on like it was only cold coffee.

"Yeah," I said. "He sure did love his sleep."

She looked up at me, still ironing. "I . . . " she said, and stopped.

"You what?" I said, realizing my slip as soon as I said it: I had given her permission to say whatever it was that she was going to say.

"I always wish we could have talked more about your brother. About him dying." She did not look up. The iron moved slowly and evenly across the board.

"There wasn't anything to talk about. He died."

"And you still hate for it."

I saw the trap then. "Not now," I told her. "I'm tired now."

"Now is the only time. You'll be on that bus and we'll never talk. Because the only thing that brought you back here was that old man. You leave now and I'll never see you again."

I looked up at her. There wasn't any pleading or pain in her eyes, and the iron moved as evenly as ever: it had been only a statement of fact. "What," I said, "do you care?"

"You're my son. The only child I've got left."

"That's not my fault," I said.

"Meaning it's mine." She did not look up then, either.

"Not now," I said.

"Well, that is what you mean, isn't it?"

She was winning again, and I knew it, and I couldn't stop it. I couldn't keep myself from putting the coffee down and saying, "Fact: when he left me he had a thousand dollars and a bus ticket to Montreal. Fact: he came here in the dead of night to say goodbye to you. Fact: in the morning he was down there in town, and they were so good to him they let him enlist. Fact: he went off and died. Summary: he left me to live and he left you and died. Now, Mother, exactly what was it you wanted to talk about?"

"I guess I don't expect you to understand," she said. The iron moved over the cotton blouse in slow smooth even strokes.

"Well, that's just as well. Because I don't."

"And you don't want to."

"Not a whole hell of a lot, no."

"Don't you *talk* like that in my house," she snapped. "I raised you right; I raised you to show more respect. And let me tell you, what he wanted to do was *wrong*. Running away! That boy had a future,

120

and he was ready to throw it all away, running off to Canada. . . ."

"Good future he's got now."

"You don't know. There were good people in this town that wanted to see him do well. And he still had a chance. You don't know how I begged Mr. Scott. They were going to put that boy in jail. Son of mine in *jail*. So I begged him. Pleaded with him. And so they gave my boy a chance. . . ."

"Yeah," I said. "To die for them."

"To do right," she said. "To do his duty."

"The only thing I want to know," I said, "is did you talk him into giving up, or did you just turn him in?"

She was silent. And still. I waited, and presently I saw a curl of smoke rising from the blouse; her hand no longer moved the iron. I didn't say anything: I let it burn. After a moment she became aware of it. She moved slowly and deliberately, without haste or panic, lifting the iron and carrying the smoldering cloth to the sink, dousing it with water. She held the burnt blouse up to the light, looked at it. "I have to go to work," she said. She had put the blouse down and vanished up the back stairs. For a few minutes I had heard her rattling around up there. I listened to her footsteps moving across the floor as she went about the business of dressing. I listened carefully, waiting for her to go into her powder room, where she had always kept the keys to the car. Finally I heard her steps going in there, caught the faint jingle of keys. And then I knew that I had perhaps touched her just a little; I heard her come down the stairs at the front of the house. The front door slammed. The car started, idled for a moment, and then churned away, down the Hill.

I sat there for a minute or two, not doing anything, just sitting and looking out the kitchen window at the plot of dead earth that had been Bill's garden. Originally, it had been Moses Washington's private truck farm. At unspecified hours he would descend from the attic and go out there and tend the vegetables, and a lot of the time Bill and I would be pressed into service to stand around holding his hoe or his rake, or to pick rocks out of the soil, or to weed around the plants. Whatever it was, we had never done it quite right, and he had not been averse to telling us about it in no uncertain terms. The worst part of it had been that there was never any end in sight; the ordeal ended when Moses Washington grew tired, and he was tireless. So we had hated the garden, hated the vegetables that came from it. And the year after his death, as spring approached, I had found myself looking forward to a summer free of it. But Bill had not.

As soon as the snow had melted he began to prepare the ground, hauling manure in Moses Washington's old wheelbarrow, hoeing with his hoes, raking with his rakes. He begged or borrowed or stole his seed from God knows where. He planted and tended with a devotion that verged on obsession; he was nine years old and driven. Daniel and Francis laughed at him and called him "the farmer." The WH&FMS ladies had clucked their heads sadly and prayed for him, sharing the opinion, voiced by Aunt Lydia Pettigrew—who, despite being childless, understood children—that what he was doing was showing how much he missed his daddy. Even Old Jack, who had paid a call on the plot one afternoon when my mother was not around, and who had inspected the plants closely (which was something nobody else had bothered to do), had a reaction; he grinned. And wouldn't say why. And he was probably the only person who was not surprised when the plants matured into chrysanthemums and marigolds and violets; Bill had converted Moses Washington's truck farm into a flower garden. It was his kind of revenge, and he had exacted it in full every Saturday, by taking a bouquet of whatever happened to be blooming across the Hill to the cemetery and laying it on Moses Washington's grave.

I looked at the garden and wondered what he had thought when he did that, week after week, year after year, and, not for the first time, wondered if perhaps I was not wrong about his motives; if perhaps he really meant it as a tribute. But I couldn't afford to believe that he had been that good—I hated them enough already.

After a while I got up and went to the stove and poured the rest of the coffee into my cup. I had meant to sip it, but I found myself gulping it down, hot, black; felt it scalding down my gullet and slamming into my belly and turning my stomach sour. I turned the stove off then, and put the cup in the sink. I realized I was tired. But I was not ready to risk sleeping, or even to go upstairs in that house. Not yet. And so I went into the dining room.

Nobody knows where Moses Washington got the design for his house, although according to one apocryphal tale, Miss Winifred Brainard, the old-maid librarian, had looked up one day from the book she was checking for obscene language to find him standing over her waving a library card and demanding to see back numbers of

122

House Beautiful, whereupon she had fainted dead away. The story might have been true, but it was also true that Moses Washington got his design from no such magazine. Most likely he got it out of his head. The lower floor was a claustrophobe's dream: there were no less than seven exits. There was rampant duplication: two entrances to every room, making it possible to make a complete tour of either floor without backtracking; two fully equipped bathrooms, the first and second built on the Hill (also the last and next to last); two staircases, front and back—a schizophrenic could have lived in the place without ever having to face his alter ego. A paranoid would have found it equally comfortable, for although there were no hallways, and each room opened directly into the next, none of the doorways was in line with any of the others, and since none of the rooms was a simple rectangle, but rather a combination of rectangular shapes, there were nooks and crannies all over the place which you had to actually enter to see into.

Those who saw it interpreted it—if they got beyond simply thinking it was all very weird—as an egomaniacal expression by a sick personality. It was far from that. Moses Washington, for some reason known only to himself, after nearly forty years of telling society to go to hell, had decided to come down from the mountains and live in society; something had to contain him, to make it possible for other people to live with him, and for him to live with them. So he had built a house with lots of exits and plenty of places to hide, and he had reserved, for his own use, a place that had to be entered by a folding staircase that he could pull up after him. That he had surely needed. Because in the lower portion of the house he made the ultimate concession to society and to his wife: he had built a parlor and a dining room so that people from outside could be entertained.

They rarely had been. For while Moses Washington had made concessions for the comfort of guests, he had never gone out of his way to invite any, or to make those who were invited by his wife particularly welcome. And so during his lifetime the parlor knew no abundance of visitors, most potential callers having been discouraged by the story of how he, neatly dressed in pinstripe and tie, had joined his bride's first—and only—tea party, taking a seat in the fragile-looking Queen Anne chair that had been the pride of his wife's mother, his bulk threatening to turn it into kindling at any second, and sipping tea from one of his wife's frail china cups, the delicate arch of his pinkie seeming obscene. He had joined in the conversation—had taken it over, rather, since everybody else had ceased speaking as soon as he had come through the door—asking, in a polite, gentle, and totally inoffensive voice, the preacher's opinion of certain Christian assumptions concerning the afterlife. It had been obvious to all present—except the preacher—that the questions were stupid, offensive, and obscene, all the more so for coming out of the mouth of such a well-known heretic; as usual, Moses Washington was making fun, and those present had taken rapid and outraged leave, as angry over the fact that Moses Washington had not actually done anything as over what he *had* done. Finally, the only persons left in the parlor had been Moses Washington and the preacher—who had seemed curiously insensitive to his personal and professional humiliation—who now had their jackets off and their ties loosened and were engaged in spirited debate, the hostess having retired to an upstairs bedroom to cry her eyes out in frustration. The experience had totally befuddled the preacher, everybody agreed; nobody blamed him when, afterwards, he was heard to say that Moses Washington was, in terms of theological understanding, far more advanced than most of his parishioners. But at the next annual conference, they had had him moved.

Nobody much came visiting after that. In fact, the only times I could recall the parlor being used was during the infrequent visits of whatever minister the Central Jurisdiction of the Methodist Episcopal Church had seen fit to punish with an assignment to the Hill, and on the first Wednesday of every August, when the annual rotation made it my mother's turn to host the monthly meeting of the Women's Home and Foreign Missionary Society—obviously, nobody felt comfortable visiting in Moses Washington's house unless he was under the auspices of God Almighty. The preachers, at that, had always been a little frightened. The WH&FMS ladies, on the other hand, had been fearless, the courage no doubt born of their personal bulk and relatively formidable numbers. Moses Washington probably could have taken them, but it would have been a costly victory, and on the occasions of the meetings he had stayed not only away from the parlor but away from the house—from that side of the Hill, in fact.

But even the WH&FMS ladies did not go into the dining room, not even after Moses Washington was dead; when my mother served

124

food to them, or to other guests, she served it in the parlor, buffet style. Nobody, not even family members, had ever eaten a meal in Moses Washington's dining room.

Which is not to say it went unused. No space that fell inside my mother's orbit ever went unused, or, at least, unfilled. She regarded such space as territory ripe for conquest, and she proceeded to take it in the same way she conquered the minds of those who opposed her; she piled things in it. Anything. It didn't matter what, just so long as it wasn't anything big, anything anybody could reasonably object to. She would pile and pile, a little bit at a time, until one day there wasn't any space anymore, and the original shape of anything that had been there was lost under the piles. It was an effective technique, and over the years she had managed to pretty much conquer every clear space in the house. She had failed on only one occasion; then she had been piling things on the front stairs which led from Bill's and my bedroom down into the parlor. The assault had got pretty far advanced; Bill and I were small and able to slip through the space she left for a long time, and were motivated to do so as long as possible, to avoid Moses Washington. But eventually we had been forced to use the back stairs, and he had noticed the shift in the traffic pattern. I don't recall him asking a single question; probably he knew her well enough to figure out what was going on. Or perhaps he had just gone to look. At any rate, we had heard the sound and had come running just in time to see an avalanche of odds and ends of cloth and sewing patterns and three years' worth of David C. Cook Sunday School literature sliding down to drift on the parlor floor. We had peeked cautiously around the corner and seen him there, his face impassive, not a sound escaping his lips, his heavy shoes mopping up what was left of her occupying forces. And later we had seen her, just as silently, clearing the mess off the floor.

But perhaps that was not a real defeat. For while she had never again blocked a passageway in Moses Washington's house, he had pretty much tolerated her other occupations. He had said nothing at all that I could recall about the use to which she had put the dining room, which was to turn it into a family photo gallery.

My mother had an inordinate love of photographs. For years she put them everywhere, sticking them in the edges of windows and mirrors, pasting them to walls and taping them to doors the way some people hang up flypaper. Eventually she had tired of such a haphaz-

125

ard arrangement, and established the dining room as the Washington Gallery, collecting in it the pictures she believed were most representative of us all. I think that was her rationale. At any rate, she had selected the pictures, after lengthy and silent deliberation, and the representation seemed significant because, in the presence of such a wealth of material, it was so Spartan.

Moses Washington himself was there only three times. The first photograph was a formal portrait, perhaps the first picture ever taken of him, which dated from the time he had returned from the war. He wore his uniform, the decorations weighing down the material. The photographer had tried to make him seem humble and benign by having him pose with his hands resting on his thighs, but the strategy had failed: the left hand was beginning to curl into a fist, and despite the sepia tint and the fading print, the eyes shone out hard and dangerous. The second photograph was a wedding picture. In it he was dressed formally, white tie and tails, and a top hat. He stood rigidly beside my mother, his arm arched uncomfortably around her. She was smiling. He was not. The same arrogant eyes stared out from beneath the brim of the top hat, which he had somehow managed to sport at an angle like a Stetson.

The third photograph was the one that had always fascinated me. In it he was standing on a hillside, his feet and lower legs concealed in wild grass, his back to a low stone wall, behind which was a stand of leafless elms. He was dressed oddly for him, in a wide-lapeled coat and white shirt and sober tie, and pants that might have been the match of the coat—it was hard to tell and still harder for me to believe that he had ever voluntarily worn a black suit. And it certainly must have been voluntary, because in the picture there was nothing of the stiff, formal discomfort that showed in the others; he looked relaxed, calm, his eyes deceptively sane. And so I had wondered where the hillside was, and when the picture had been taken, and by whom. I had never found out; it was one of my earliest researches, and like the ones that followed, it had ended in dead-end confusion. I could tell from the way the shadows fell that the hillside was facing south, but that was all I could tell; I believed the hill was local, but it could have been any place that had a similar climate and geology—certainly it was not familiar to me. The photograph had appeared shortly before his death, and the paper was of a type that was in common use in the mid-fifties, but the negative could have been made at any time before then, and Moses Washington did not appear any older or younger in that photograph than he did in any of the others. I had at first believed that the key, not only to dating the picture but to finding out more about its background, was to discover who had taken it, but nobody knew anything about that. My mother claimed not that she had not taken the picture, but that, in fact, she had not even selected it; it had been something pressed upon her by Moses Washington. Old Jack also claimed ignorance, and even Uncle Josh, who grunted his answer in monosyllables, denied any knowledge. I had concluded that Moses Washington had, for some reason, decided he wanted a picture taken of himself, and had gone out and figured a way to take it himself. Further research revealed that the idea of a black thread device, which would have made such self-portraiture possible, dated back to at least 1878. And so my research had ended, as it always did, at a stone wall.

From looking at the gallery one would have suspected that my mother was a modest woman; she had placed only two depictions of herself on display. She smiled out from a small oval portrait that showed her sitting on an angle, shoulder dipped slightly forward in the old-fashioned style. Her face was unlined, youthful, beautiful. It was a graduation picture. She smiled out from the wedding picture, teeth flashing, face framed by the white veil. She looked a bit older there, a bit harder, but still young, still beautiful. But that was the end of it; it was as if she had given up having her picture taken on the day of her wedding. Or perhaps she had just stopped smiling. But I did not need a portrait; I knew what she had looked like. In the first few years after Moses Washington had died her body had thickened and softened, her breasts and thighs seeming to swell to form a warm safe nest for Bill and me. It was hard to imagine where the plumpness had come from: she never ate breakfast, although she prepared it for us, and she always skipped lunch so that she could get off work early and be there when we got home from school. She walked everywhere then, sometimes pulling us in a big stake wagon, to the river to wade on summer Saturday afternoons, or to the green on summer evenings when the local softball teams had fought it out for the greater glory of Calhoun's Atlantic or Deist Cleaners. But despite the skipped meals and the exercise, she got plump. I wondered about it even then, and I watched carefully to see what it was she ate, and once, only once, I saw her slipping down the back stairs in the dead of night, and I slipped down the front stairs and crept into the dining room and saw her take a quart of vanilla ice cream from the back of the freezer and sit at the table with a spoon poised, and sigh, and consume it all. Perhaps it had been the ice cream that had fattened her, although she would have had to eat it every night. Perhaps she did; perhaps it was a ritual born of sublimated sexuality, or just a simple indulgence. But whether it was the ice cream or not, *something* had plumped her, and although she had never really come to look fat, she did begin to look more like a member of the WH&FMS. But one day she had changed.

In later years I had looked back on that change in her, trying to find a cause for it. I never had. Not that her motivations were as unfathomable as those of Moses Washington. The difficulty was that there were so many possible motivations; it had been a year of change for her. The ancient lady who had been the legal secretary for the Scott law firm had a stroke. In her usual fashion and with no more fanfare than a subtle cough, my mother moved from her tiny desk in the front office, at which, ever since the third week after her husband's death, she had been answering the phones and typing nice neat copies of leases and wills and contracts, to the rather more elegant one in the middle office. There was never a formal promotion; in fact, as far as I had ever been able to figure out, neither old Judge Scott nor his son and partner, Randall, had ever told her to move. She just began to pile her papers in the middle office, and eventually the *fait accompli* was recognized, her salary was raised, and her working hours became more flexible and quite a bit longer. Not that that mattered; I was twelve then, and occupied after school with delivering papers and selling Burpee seeds. Bill was ten, and he had discovered football, wrestling, and baseball; he probably never even noticed that she was no longer waiting at the schoolhouse door. Not that she neglected us; breakfast was always prepared, lunches were always packed, dinners always hot and plentiful. She was with us almost as much as she had ever been, certainly as much as a mother needed to be with two young sons coming up on adolescence. But there were Saturday afternoons and evenings after supper when she would announce that she was going back to the office for a few hours, and disappear. There were rumors, of course—a woman did not disappear from the Hill, from anyplace in that town, for that matter, without there being some kind of talk. None of it was true; I knew because I had gone down after her and peeked through the back windows of the office, to see her poring over books and papers, making notes, checking references, and I had known that one day soon old Judge Scott or young Mr. Scott was going to need to know something and was going to be nonplussed by the speed with which his newly promoted secretary could have the reference available. Before they were done they would realize—because they would have been shown in ten thousand subtle ways—that they could not get along without her. And if they responded correctly, they would never find out that she could destroy them.

Perhaps that—growing sons, growing responsibility in another area—had motivated the weight loss. Or perhaps she had had an affair or two (although we had never seen evidence of it, and I secretly suspected that once a woman was married to Moses Washington, the thought of having another man would seem like the most boring notion this side of a baseball game in July). Or perhaps it had been the death of the Professor.

Bill had never liked the Professor, mostly because the old gentleman was given to making Bill stand beside him while he lectured interminably on the incompatibility of brain and brawn, implying, sometimes stating, that Bill's interest in athletics was sure indication that he was little better than an ape, certainly no better than a savage. I had hated him, mostly because he refused to let me read any of his books. His house was full of them. He had books that no local library or high school library, not in western Pennsylvania, was going to have. Books by black people. Books by Langston Hughes and Countee Cullen and William Melvin Kelly and Paul Laurence Dunbar and all the rest. He loved to take me into the library and point them out to me, taking them down and showing me that here was a first-edition copy of *Cane* by Jean Toomer, and that there was a copy of *The Souls of Black Folk* with a personal inscription from W. E. B. Du Bois, making sure I did not touch the pages, because I was, he said, too young to comprehend them. Even though I had, certainly to his knowledge, read and reread every book the County library had to offer. The thing that most outraged me was the fact that *he* didn't read them. He rarely even touched them. He had hired a woman to come in and dust them, a white woman; he had been particular about that. So I had hated him, hated him for every time he had taken me in there and tortured me. But when he did it I had never said anything but "Yes, Grandfather." Because I had known that sooner or

129

later I was going to find a way to get in there and steal a book and read it and put it back without his knowing, and do it again and again until I had read them all. But he died first. I had hoped he would leave me some of those books; not, perhaps, the signed first editions, but some of the more mundane volumes. But he left the lot to Howard University. And so when they had buried him neither Bill nor I had shed any tears; for me, dropping the ritual spade of earth on his coffin had been a pleasure tempered only by curiosity—he had been buried in his ancestral home in Virginia, and I had never before then seen red Piedmont earth.

But for my mother it must have been something different. For years she had been almost a wife to him, keeping his house in Washington while he taught his classes, acting as hostess for the parties he threw to drag in anybody who had a name and whose presence might serve to get his "soirees" mentioned in the Pittsburgh *Courier,* and then she had closed the house and helped him move to the town to which he, in the tradition of rich white families stretching back for two hundred years, had been coming each summer to drink the mineral water and bathe in the medicinal springs. (Evidently the Professor did not realize that hydrotherapy was out of style, or that Chalybeate Springs, one of the most famous medicinal spas, had become, instead of a retreat for Republican Presidents like Garfield and Hayes and Benjamin Harrison, a swimming pool that would not admit black people.) And then she had left him for Moses Washington, a man four years his junior, with four times his wealth, forty times his virility, and less than a fourth of his respectability. Over that decision there had been battles fought, and while my mother had won, as she always won, and Moses Washington had won as he always won, the old man had not been without his weapons and his tactics, and she must have borne scars. And probably she loved him. And so perhaps the weight loss had had something to do with his death.

But the odd part of it all was that her appetite, which had, to all appearances, vanished years before, improved just as all the other things were taking place; she had begun to eat and lose weight at the same time. She had always cooked good wholesome meals for us; now she began to eat them herself: big two-course breakfasts, pancakes and bacon-and-eggs; lunches of cold fried chicken; dinners of meat and potatoes and homemade bread, with pie and cake for dessert. Perhaps she gave up the ice cream; it must have been something, for

130

by the time Bill entered junior high school and began winning at every sport in sight she had shrunk back to the size she must have been when Moses Washington first saw her. And she had stayed that way, through all the years since. Her body had come to sag a bit, but mostly her aging showed only in her face, in jaws that came to be just slightly pouched, in lines that crept imperceptibly away from her eyes. And that, perhaps, was why there was no current picture of her there; none was needed.

The Professor was there, of course, but only once, in a pose that was more typically him than any other I could imagine: he was seated in front of a wall of books, at a table that was barren as the Dakota plains. The photograph was fairly recent, no more than twenty years old; my mother must have had it taken when she sensed that his years were drawing to a close. It was set in a gold-painted metal frame, covered with glass; just the way the Professor would have liked it.

Down in the lower-left-hand corner of the frame, in an ancient, tiny photograph, was my grandmother. It was impossible to really see her, to tell what she looked like; all I could see was that she had been a young girl when it was taken, her hair wrapped in braids around her head, her eyes dark little nuggets against the faded print.

And then there was me. I had always been bemused by the pictures that my mother had chosen to represent me. Some, of course, were inevitable: the ordered progression of school photographs, showing me changing, through predictable stages of plumpness and pimpledness, into a too-serious-looking "young man" with smooth-shaved cheeks and a part razored into hair trimmed so short as to be little more than a skullcap, thus concealing its natural kinkiness; the series of photos in which I was little more than a prop to the pose of a gaggle of buxom ladies who had sat in the living room praying while my mother had struggled upstairs to bring forth her firstborn at the relatively ripe age of thirty-three, and who had thereby earned the rights to a place in the photo gallery and the honorific "Aunt." But there were other pictures, odds and ends of photography that fit into no sequence and had no obvious *raison d'être:* pictures my mother thought were "me." The first showed me as a plump-legged toddler with a great mass of dark wavy curls—"good" hair that had delighted both my mother and the Professor until, when I was about eight, it had suddenly recalled itself and become properly kinky—and dressed

131

in white shoes, white socks, white bibbed shorts, and a white shirt. Another showed me, at about five, uniformed in a miniature sailor suit, accurate to the last detail, right down to a thirteen-button—scaled down to about a six-button—fly, a feature that had made it all but impossible for me to go to the bathroom without assistance. A third caught me as I came down the steps of the church, dressed in my seven-year-old's Sunday finery: a blousy, wide-sleeved white shirt, a red bow tie, and a pair of pleat-fronted black trousers held up with suspenders because I had been so thin that a belt slipped past my nonexistent hips. There were others, taken at different times and at different places, but they all had two things in common: in every one I was clad in one of the outfits my mother had made by improvising on a theme from a standard pattern bought at the dime store or culled from some magazine sold at the checkout counter at the A&P; and in every one of them the configuration of my face and body was precisely the same, my eyes flat and empty, directed straight at the camera, my mouth in a straight line, without a hint of curl in the lips, my body straight—head level, shoulders squared, hands flat against thighs, feet firmly planted and perfectly parallel, not a hint of a bend in either elbow or knee. It seemed an abnormal posture, and yet I looked calm and relaxed—I had, it seemed, learned the lesson that parents have been trying to teach their offspring for centuries: how to stand up tall and not fidget. But it was not a pose of obedience. Perhaps then I had thought it was. But now I could look at a fading image of myself, cloaked in one of my mother's costumes, and tell that, at age seven or five or two, I had been angry. No; furious.

That was the sum and essence of the official family portrait gallery: one hincty old man, one cipher of a wife, one dutiful—and probably resentful—daughter, one ex-moonshiner and murderer who had taken up philosophy, eccentricity, church-cleaning, marriage, and fatherhood as retirement avocations, and one furious child. There had been another child in the gallery, but he had not fitted in. He had declined to participate in the family's inter- and intra-necine emotional football games. His passion had been for real football games on crisp autumn days and for bringing ten-year-old Chevys down the dark winding road off Blackoak Ridge, with the gas pedal flat against the firewall and the brake drums glowing cherry red. He had liked milk shakes and hamburgers and french fries almost as well as normal food; he had been the first black in the history of the County to call and have a pizza delivered. He had somehow delved into the tortured family gene pool and come up with "normal" American interests, hopes, characteristics, abilities. Not the bad ones, not the conservatism, stodginess, stupidity, chauvinism, jingoism, and greed that have helped motivate the making of blots on our history. He had got the good things: the patience to invent vulcanized rubber; the self-confidence to launch the steamboat or buy Alaska; the determination to cross the Great Plains; the strength to give orders; the humility to take them; the loyalty to stay by his friends; the bravery to confront the clear and present dangers of the world. You could say he had been sane. Or he would have been, if it had not been for the fact that his skin was the color of Hershey's chocolate; given that fact, normality—or perhaps normalcy is a better word—was probably a distinctly higher order of insanity than that possessed by the rest of us. But at any rate, he did not belong among people who could take an event and swallow it and worry about it for years, hoping for a pearl but ending up with a tumor, and so she had taken the earliest opportunity to get his simple face out from among our tortured visages. She had done it with a speed too great to be termed deliberate: she had received the telegram and long before whatever had been scraped out of the body bag and smeared into a coffin had been delivered to a local undertaker (charges, FOB San Diego, plus domestic haulage, courtesy of the formerly segregated United States Marine Corps), long before she had informed me, she had taken the pictures—the school portraits, the pictures of him kneeling beneath a goalpost or crouched in a wrestler's stance, or swinging at a baseball, the snapshot of him dressed in his overalls and kneeling in the garden plot, the picture of him in the costume that he had worn in the Sunday school Christmas pageant (in which he, portraying the innkeeper, had explained the cold fact of no vacancy with such honesty and compassion that the Christmas story had taken on a much more complex meaning), the picture of him in his uniform with his PFC stripe, and the blurred Polaroid of him and his buddies standing mock guard over a grass hut with a Budweiser sign in the window—and she had put them, together with the telegram (which she had framed) and the other nonsense that surrounded his dying and burying, on a flag-draped table at the far end of the dining room. She had arranged lighting, two small spotlights, perpetually lit, and I was half surprised that she had never managed to hook up some kind of recorder to play

133

patriotic organ music. But even given her failure with sound effects, she deserved a lot of credit for having got him out of the family portrait gallery in the only decent way: she had got him killed and then she had enshrined him. She had kicked him upstairs.

It was all there now—pictures, telegram, the flag with which they had covered his casket, the notes of condolence from the local politicos, the congressman, the senators, the commandant, the President, the citation for conspicuous gallantry above and beyond the call of duty, the Medal of Honor itself. All the materials any historian worth his hire would need to write a glowing preface to the biography of a Great American, a war hero who had gone on to play professional sports, perhaps, and then run for Congress. . . . That was just one of those stories that would never be. But it was nice to think about what might have been, and so I stood there looking at his pictures until I couldn't stand any more, and then I went upstairs.

I went up the front stairs, the ones that Moses Washington had cleared with such silent fury. They were still clear and so I passed quickly up and into the bedroom Bill and I had shared until the day he, grinning proudly because he had just passed his driver's test, had driven me down to catch the bus so that I could go to college. That had been a special day for both of us; she had treated it as business as usual, getting up and making breakfast and going off to work, the fact that she went on foot so that we could use the car being her only acknowledgment of my departure.

Bill had helped me wrestle my suitcase and trunk down the stairs and load them into the car, and had driven me down to the Alliquippa, where I would catch the local bus. He had parked by the curb, not ten feet from Old Jack's shoeshine stand. I had got out of the car and gone over to talk.

But Old Jack was not talking to me. He had not spoken to me in three months, not since the night I had gone over to the far side to tell him that I had won a scholarship, that I was going away to college. He had said nothing for a long time, and then he had exploded. He had cursed me roundly, claiming that in all the years he had shown me things I had never learned anything, that I was going away to ruin my eyes and my brain with books. When that had failed to change my mind he had got up and made himself a toddy and sat down and drank it in stony silence, without even looking at me.

That was the last time I had gone to the far side. In truth, I had not missed it. I had been too busy, working at two different jobs, one as a busboy, one as a cook—the scholarship was generous but not lavish—and, in whatever time was left, trying to read the things that I believed, erroneously, my soon-to-be classmates would have cut their intellectual teeth on. Since then I had seen him, but I had said nothing to him; it was the way he wanted it. But now I was leaving, and I wanted to say goodbye. And so I had got out of the car and gone over to him.

He turned to me and smiled, and for a minute I thought that he was ready to forgive me. But then I noticed that the smile was too wide, showed too much tooth. "Yassuh," he said. "You want a shine, suh?" It was what he had always called his "white folks" voice.

"Jack," I said.

"Yassuh," he said. "That's ma name. You climb right on up here, young suh, an' I'll give you a shine that'll make them city boys set up an' take notice. You goin' off to be a white man, you best learn how white folks act."

"No," I said.

"Course," he said, "I 'spect you already know. I 'spect that woman's been teachin' you how to flip your coattails 'fore you set down like a Goddamned sissy. An' I bet you learned it real good; you always had a taste for that kinda thing, like a hound dog that's tasted chicken blood. Ain't good for nothin' after that. Don't want to hunt, jest wants to kill chickens."

I didn't say anything.

"I see you had your name in the paper," he said. "I seen the picture, an' I asted somebody, an' they told me what it said in there. You know somethin', Johnny—'scuse me, I mean Mistuh Washington, suh—these white folks, ones wouldn't give you the time a day last year? Now they think you're somethin'. Course, they ain't 'xactly sure *what,* an' I 'spect as how they're jest as pleased you ain't gonna be around here makin' 'em try an' figger out what, but they sure do think you're somethin'. Why, you know, the mayor hisself set up here an' tole me you was a credit to your race. Yes indeedy, that's jest 'xactly what he said. Course, I didn't correct him, an' tell him that you wasn't colored no more, on accounta you read enough a them damn books to turn your head clear white. . . ." And then he stopped. Because I had climbed up on the stand and sat on the bench and put my feet up on the supports.

He sat there on his stool looking up at me, his eyes soft and pained-looking. I nodded at my feet. He kept on looking at me. I nodded again, a short, quick nod, as cold and imperious as I could make it. He reached for the polish, taking up the can slowly, slowly dipping his hands into it, slowly bringing them out. He hesitated then, holding his polish-laden hands over my shoes, and he looked up at me. I nodded again. And then he shined my shoes.

When he was finished I got down and paid him, giving him a dollar and turning away before he could offer change. I went back to the car and sat there in silence. Bill didn't say anything either, not until the bus had come sighing in and we had got out and I had thoroughly annoyed the aging bus driver by insisting that it was his job to help me get the trunk into the luggage compartment, not Bill's. Then, after the driver had gone into the hotel to see if there were any packages, Bill looked at me and said, "I pity them."

"Pity who?" I said.

"Those people where you're going. I bet they took one look at that application and they saw all those nice tame things you did, and they looked at your picture and saw a neat, clean-cut colored boy, and that's what they think they're getting, a nice, gentle, shy Negro, won't be a bit of trouble. Only one day those people are gonna find out how dangerous it is to fool with somebody who doesn't know how to do anything but go for the throat."

I didn't say anything. But I looked at Old Jack, sitting on his stool, his hands still black with polish, still not looking at me but instead staring east, down Forbes Road, where the bus was going to go. I wanted to move then, wanted to go over and just speak to him, say I'm sorry, or I didn't mean it, or maybe just goodbye. But of course I didn't do that. And he would have been upset if I had; that was the kind of weak display reserved for women and preachers and piano teachers. And so I just stood there, watching him looking down the road I was going to travel, until the driver came out and took the one-way ticket I had purchased the day that they had informed me about the scholarship, and then I climbed on the bus. I had found a seat on the right-hand side, where I could see them, and as the bus pulled away I had waved my hand. But the angle was wrong. The glass was tinted. I doubt that either of them saw.

In the bedroom, my mother had pressed her attack in the usual manner, overrunning the bed that had been Bill's with six months' worth of issues of the local paper. But she had retreated in other quadrants; she had cleared off my bed and my dresser and, as I saw when I opened the closet, she had removed whatever trash she had piled in front of my old clothes. There were not many of them, but there were enough; I had never really moved out. Before Bill died I had lived there. After he was buried, I had never come back.

I closed the closet door and stripped off my clothes, becoming conscious for the first time of the smells that were attached to them: smoke, sweat, dying. Suddenly the aromas were not only noticeable but powerful, so powerful they made me feel sick. My skin was crawling suddenly, as if I were infested by some kind of bug, and I wanted to shower badly.

And so I went back into the bathroom and climbed into the stall and let the hot water cascade over me and wash away the stink, and then I dried myself and went and crawled beneath the sheets and closed my eyes. Thoughts did not come, but pictures did, little flashes across my mind: Old Jack's hands guiding mine as he taught me to aim a rifle; Bill's face twisted with effort as he tried to lift his barbells; my mother bent over her ancient black Singer sewing machine, the glow from the built-in light bouncing off the maple cabinet and reflecting off the maple-colored skin of her face, sparkling on the row of pins she held between her tightly compressed lips; the muscles of Moses Washington's back rippling as he swung the double-edged ax against the trunk of the oak tree that had had the poor judgment to grow where he wanted to walk; and, in a weird skein of imagining, a vision of myself seated at a table, beside a kerosene lamp, with an ancient-looking book in front of me. The scene was no mystery, although I had never looked at it from that vantage; I knew where it was. Above me. Upstairs. In the attic. The place Moses Washington had taken as his own.

The attic was reached by a trapdoor set into the ceiling in the far corner of the bedroom Moses Washington had kept for his own, sleeping there on occasions when he and his wife were not seeing eye to eye. It made sense to place the trapdoor there, since nobody went up into the attic except Moses Washington. Nobody would have been welcome. Nobody *wanted* to be welcome. Bill and I had often speculated about exactly what he did up there, but we weren't crazy enough to go and see, or even to ask, not even when we were very small. So all we ever knew was that every day he would climb up there and pull the staircase and the trapdoor up after him. You could hear him rattle around for a while, and then the floor would creak as he would settle down to do whatever it was he did. There was no set time for all this; sometimes he would not make the ascent until after dinner, and we would hear him moving around until we drifted off to sleep. There were times when I had wakened in the middle of the night and heard him pacing. He could go up after breakfast, and if he did we would very often not see him for the rest of the day. And if he did come down, it was well to be out of sight, because his actions were totally unpredictable. Usually he would pursue one of his insane projects, truck gardening or stonemasonry—he had, by the time he died, managed to build a stone wall around every tree and hedge in the back yard. But sometimes he would break even that bizarre pattern. Once he had descended and grabbed me by the hand and dragged me down the stairs and out the back door and on a long and exhausting and silent tour of the Hill, hauling me by the hand up one street and down another, again and again, for two solid hours, without saying a single word, and when he was finished with whatever it was he was doing he had picked me up and kissed me wetly, and there had been tears in his eyes. Another time, shortly before he died, he had come down slowly and heavily and had stood above me as I sat reading a book. I had tried to look up at him, but he had put his hand on my head and forced me to look at my book, and we had stayed like that, a tableau in tension, until, for reasons known only to him, he had let me go. I had turned to look at him then, and had found that I could not look away; his eyes met mine and held my gaze more firmly than his hands had held my head. We had stayed that way for a while, and then he had turned and gone back upstairs.

Those were not the only such occasions; far from it. For as time went by, it seemed that the occasions when he would come storming—or not always storming; sometimes he would come down slowly and thoughtfully—down from the attic and go out and do something aberrant and frightening became more and more frequent. In fact, it was probably not surprising that he had taken up his gun and gone out and covered twenty miles of countryside and still been wild and reckless enough to trip over a root or something and kill himself, because before he had done that he had been up there. At any rate, we knew that whatever he had been doing up there was bizarre and probably unfathomable and almost certainly crazy-making, and so the attic had remained pretty much a mystery until the day that I had decided that I was going to go up there and get one of Moses Washington's books.

It had been a day like this day, early in spring and a fresh snow on the ground, cold and nasty as only Appalachian spring days can be. I had been getting over one of my perennial bouts with the flu—I was still coughing up great vile clots of green mucus tinged with the blood from nosebleeds—but I was not hurting anywhere, and I only ran a fever in the afternoon. And so my mother had left a pitcher of water by the bed and a pot of soup on the stove and had gone to work. At noon, after I finished reading *Huckleberry Finn* for the ninth time, I had got out of bed and gone down and had my soup. I had felt quite well then—too well to go back to bed. So I washed my bowl and went wandering in a vague search for new reading material, although I had read everything in the house at least once, including my mother's Missionary Society magazines and the Sears, Roebuck catalog. But I looked anyway, and somehow, in the midst of that fruitless wandering, it came to me to go up into the attic and get one of Moses Washington's books.

I was thirteen then; Moses Washington had been dead for three years. Yet in all that time, I had not thought to venture up into his stronghold. Bill had; once the funeral was over he had made it his business, the first time my mother had turned her back, to take a flashlight and go exploring. He had come back to report, in tones of disappointment and disgust, that there was nothing up there but a mess of old papers and books. For him the matter had ended there, and for me it had too, although it shouldn't have—that "mess" of things to read should have put me in mind of Paradise, and knowing about it should have galvanized me into action. But for some reason—possibly because of my memories of the strange states in which Moses Washington had emerged from there—I had stayed away. My mother had stayed away too; she had pushed her pickets into every cranny of the lower part of the house, but she had not attempted to storm the high ground. Bill, in his exploration, had touched nothing. And so the attic was the same on the day I had determined to enter it as it had been on that bright hot August morning when Moses Washington had left it to go prowling through the South County, carrying a gun for the first time in a decade. And when I, armed with a flashlight, mounted the steep, folded-down stairway and emerged into the upper darkness, I was almost going back in time, and when I thumbed the switch on the flashlight and sent a cone of weak light on a handmade chair and a large, roughly carpentered table on which sat an open book and a kerosene lamp, I was looking at a perfect memory; dusty, but perfect. It was almost as if the chair, the table, the book, the lamp, the empty fireplace, were items under glass; they were the keys to a man's mind, laid bare to me, clues to a mystery, the answer to every question there. All I had to do was interpret them. It was the greatest thrill I had ever known.

I did not, of course, know what I was about. And so, without even suspecting the danger, I fell prey to one of the greatest fallacies that surrounds the study of the past: the notion that there is such a thing as a detached researcher, that it is possible to discover and analyze and interpret without getting caught up and swept away. I believed, being a naive thirteen-year-old, that I was going to climb up into that attic and look at a few heirlooms and some dusty mementos and figure Moses Washington out, and once that was done, I was going to climb back down and go on about my merry way, unaffected, unchanged, unharmed. And so I moved with an arrogance and fearlessness born of nothing but ignorance. But at least I realized that what I was looking at was perfect, and that anything I did, one false step, would destroy that perfection, would probably obscure whatever message might be in the scene.

And so I stood at the head of the stairway for many minutes, *looking* at it—fixing it in my mind—before I walked across the loosely laid floor of two-by-six planks to the table, and looked down at the book lying on it. It was a Bible. Beside the Bible stood the lamp, and I could see that there was still some kerosene pooled in the reservoir. Beside the lamp was a small box of matches. I looked at those things for a long time, trying to understand why the matches were there, in the open, not put away. For I knew the way in which those men's minds had worked: put things back when you are finished with them; put them in the same place every time, so that when you need them you won't have to guess or fumble or even think. And then I realized that I had made an incorrect assumption (although I did not think of it in those terms). I had assumed that I was stepping into the scene at the middle of a cycle, when in fact, I was stepping into the beginning of one. They were beside the lamp because that was where he would want them when he first came in—to light the lamp. *Then* he would put them somewhere out of the way. His last act before blowing out the lamp and leaving would have been to take them out again and place them where he could find them easily, in the dark. I stood there feeling the flush of pride and power that comes from having been able to figure something out; pride and a surge of confidence. And so I reached out with a steady hand and removed a match from the box and struck it, and then I lit the lamp. Then I reached out to drop the match into the can that I knew (because Old Jack's description of Moses Washington's ways had extended even to the way he snuffed matches) he would have kept there half full of sand.

But the can was not there. For a moment I was frantic, certain that I had moved wrongly, and had therefore forever lost my chance to understand. But then I saw it, on the left-hand side of the table, not the right. Which made sense, since Moses Washington had been left-handed. I dropped the match into it, and all my confidence returned, tempered with some reason. All I had to do, I thought, was to use my head, to think carefully, to use all of the things I knew, not just part of them. Then I would be all right. And so once again I moved, slipping into the chair and settling back, trying to sit as he had sat. It was uncomfortable for me, for he had built it for himself, for a man, not for a thirteen-year-old. I understood that, and I almost gloried in the discomfort, for the chair was like a print of his body; each part that pressed against my body was an expression of his. I sat there, my eyes closed, feeling the odd shape against me. And then I looked down at the Bible.

I opened the Bible at the place where it had been marked, the Book of Jeremiah. Part of the first chapter had been marked with pencil. I did not read it; I sat there and memorized it: "Then said I, Ah, Lord God! behold, I cannot speak: for I am a child. But the Lord said unto me, Say not, I am a child: for thou shalt go to all that I shall send thee, and whatsoever I command thee thou shalt speak."

I memorized it, and I puzzled over it, wondering why he had marked it, why he had been reading that at all. I was so busy with that that I almost missed the card that he had been using to mark his place, an ordinary plain white file card, but it was covered with writing in a small neat hand, writing that I knew was his from the way the letters were shaped, but which seemed to me to be terribly cramped and neat to be his. It was another Bible quotation, but one that was totally unfamiliar to me. Which was odd, since I had been required to memorize half of the Bible before I could read, and had read the whole thing several times in the years since. But I had never read this passage, had never even heard of the book from which it came. But I knew it was the Bible, from the way it sounded and from the manner in which he had identified it: 2 Esdras: xiv: 25. So I memorized that too: "I shall light a candle of understanding in thine heart, which shall not be put out. . . ." I wondered about that for a while, what Esdras was, why I had never heard of it.

But then my eyes drifted up from the page and I was, for the first time, looking into the recesses of the room, and what I was seeing was Bill's "mess" of books. Only his description had been misleading. There was no mess, no clutter, no haphazard piles threatening to slide and tumble. I should have known there would not be, should have known that Moses Washington would have never tolerated here the kind of disorder that most people permitted in their attics. Still, I could hardly have been prepared for what he had done, which was to set seven-foot-high shelves into the spaces between the joists and the rafters. Every one of those shelves was burdened with books: printed volumes, record books, loose-leaf binders, tracing books, sketch pads, ledgers, plat books, bound volumes of newspapers, and a seemingly endless array of notebooks of every size, shape, and color. The number of those books was unfathomable, but whatever it was, it was large. I had never realized the Moses Washington had loved books as much as I did: it was a side of him that it had never occurred to me existed, that I had never heard about. Knowing about it made me feel easier about my own passion. And, like mine, his had been a passion for using books, not just for owning them; every one of those books had been read, and reread. The colors of their bindings were faded, and any stamping on the spines had long since been worn away. And that made me realize that he would have had to know not only what was in those books, but exactly where they were on the shelves. He would have had to assign each one a place, and memorize that place, and put it back exactly in that place when he was done with it. There would have been no other way to refer to them. It did not occur to me that he would not refer to them; I knew instinctively that he had been researching something, that what had happened was not, as everybody thought, that Moses Washington had given up hunting, but rather that he had transferred his efforts to a different forest, to the pursuit of other game. Until the day he had, for some reason, gone back. . . . I sat there, reconstructing it: he lifting his eyes from the words of the Prophet, standing, stretching, taking the matches from their keeping place and laying them beside the lamp, ready for his return, leaning over and cupping his hand behind the lamp's chimney and blowing out the flame, taking— I stopped then. Because something was terribly wrong. It was not one of those seemingly odd configurations of data that it is the task of research to explain—not why had he not put the Bible back in its place, or whether it was significant that the Book was open to Jeremiah, not even why he had left his books and taken up his gun after ten long years. No; the problem was of that terrible basic variety that threatens the very possibility of meaningful research; the problem was an incongruity in the data itself: the problem was the matches.

They were ordinary kitchen matches—what the old folks call barn burners—and they were in an ordinary box, and they lay there exactly where I had put them after I had used them, without even thinking about it. Carelessly. It had been a mistake to do it that way, because I was not left-handed, and my casual replacement of the matches would have changed the picture. The matches should have been in the wrong place. But they were not. They were in exactly the same place as they had been when I had come in; available, easily available, to a right-handed person. *That* was what was wrong. I sat there in the attic, thinking furiously. Perhaps he had simply lit the lamp in a different way. But that would have meant the can was in the wrong place. . . . I sat there, staring at the box of matches, the confusion rising in me like a flooding tide, realizing how arrogant it had been for me to come in there like that, making judgments as to what made sense and what did not, how hopeless it was, how little I knew, how much I needed to know before I could hope to understand that place. And in the first act of sense I had probably ever performed, I had risen and blown out the flame and taken my flashlight and gotten myself out of there.

But I had found my reading; I had taken my Bible to bed with me, and by late afternoon I had been through Jeremiah three times and, not understanding why he had been reading it, had gone back to Genesis, and was well into the begats before the fever had come upon me.

That had been the beginning of a magic time. For that day, perhaps in the illogic of my fever, I had dedicated myself to the task of unraveling the whys and wherefores of Moses Washington. It was not as hubristic as it might sound; I was thirteen years old but I was not stupid—I knew that there was a great deal I needed to know before I would be ready to confront so great and absolute a mystery; my errors with the matches had convinced me of that. And so I had developed a plan, and I had followed it to the letter.

I had spent a month writing down in a loose-leaf notebook everything I knew about Moses Washington from my own observation and recollection. I had spent the next month writing down in a second notebook anything I could find out from other people, keeping those facts cataloged according to source. Then I had collected data from records—or I had tried to: there was practically nothing about Moses Washington written down anywhere in the County besides the recording of the deed to the property and the coroner's certification of his accidental death.

Then I had composed two lists of questions. One set I labeled preliminary questions: Where had Moses Washington come from? Why had he come to the County? Why had he stayed? Why had he been a moonshiner? Where and when had he learned to read? What had happened in the war to make him change? The second list was only two questions long; I labeled it final questions: What had he been researching up in the attic? Why, after a ten-year hiatus, had he taken up his gun?

And then I had turned aside from anything that had anything directly to do with Moses Washington. For the next two years I had contented myself with the task of learning what his world had been like. Two years I had recorded and cataloged every world event I could find. I had realized early on that the key to it all was chronology, a strict time-ordering of events, and so I had developed a system of color-coded index cards on which I recorded events, and which I ordered by carefully noting the time of their occurrence, the time dating expressed as a string of numbers, year, month (in two digits), date (in two digits), and time of day (in a twenty-four-hour military-style expression), followed by the day of the week.

That was how I learned history. That was where the magic came from. Because in preparing myself to track down Moses Washington, I had begun to perceive connections where others, it seemed, saw only unrelated facts, and I had begun to delight in exposing those connections to the unaware; I had learned how much fun it can be to shock with the truth. (I had once given the World History teacher, a good-hearted soul who moonlighted as a Lutheran minister, a bad case of indigestion when, in the middle of class, I suggested that the form of Luther's Theses had as much to do with his chronic constipation as with his complex theology.)

And then, after years of preparation, of reading history and theology and philosophy and anthropology and psychology and science, of cataloging events from the sublime to the ridiculous, I assembled my notebooks and my card files and pens and paper and, one morning at the beginning of summer, when my mother had gone to work, moved it all up into the attic.

For the rest of the vacation, I spent my days in the attic, among his books, filling in the gaps in my education, looking for clues as to what he had been. I worked nights as a busboy at a Howard Johnson's restaurant on the Turnpike; I slept—when I slept at all—between five-thirty, when my mother came home, and ten-thirty, when I had to leave for work. Bill thought I was crazy; I was not, I was simply driven. I did not lose weight. I did not get sick. I was happy.

And then, when fall had come and I had to go back to school, when I had to give up the night shift for part-time work between three and eleven, I had begun the final phases of my research. Each night I would open the trapdoor and creep up into the attic. I would light the lamp (I did not bother with the fireplace) and open one of my notebooks—I had a separate one for each of the preliminary questions—and I would write down potential answers, speculations, references, cross-references. When I was done I would begin to check out the speculation, eliminating impossibilities, assigning probabilities. I had done that for a year.

And then, in the beginning of the following year, my final year in high school, I had felt I was ready. I had begun at the beginning, reading over the dossier of Moses Washington that I had compiled, reading over the cards time and time and time again, etching the order of the world's events on my mind, looking over my own speculations and eliminations. And then I had begun to think.

I thought about it constantly throughout that fall and winter. It looked, I suppose, as though I were coming out of some kind of shell—I did not spend nearly so much time in the attic. But I could think anywhere, and I thought everywhere, daydreaming through school, it seemed, hunting, it appeared, almost by instinct—Old Jack had marveled at the sudden ease with which I tracked, and commended me for finally giving up trying to think my way to game and allowing myself to feel my way to it. But towards the end of the winter I had begun to go up into the attic again, to write again in notebooks, speculating now, not on the preliminary questions, but on the final ones, working now towards what I expected to be answers.

I do not know how I thought those answers would come. Perhaps in a blaze of light, or of heat. I don't know. I only know that gradually something had occurred to me that had never occurred to me before: the attic was cold.

At first I had not minded too much, but as the nights had worn on and each attempt to fit the facts together had failed, the attic had grown, it seemed, ever more drafty. At last I had had to risk building a fire in Moses Washington's fireplace. But that had not seemed to help. I had used the fires I built to heat water and mix toddies with the cheap liquor Old Jack was only too happy to supply—that had helped. But only for a while.

Because there had come a night when the snow had fallen heavy and deep and the air was so cold it burned the lungs, when the wind was coming from west, ripping clouds of snow from the mountaintops and singing its ineffable eerie song, when the fire had died in the grate and I knew it would do no good to rekindle it. Because I had sat there at that table, with the flame from the lamp flickering over the pages of notes that I had made, and had known that I had failed. Not just taken a wrong path, or run into a dead end in research. Failed. Completely. I had put the facts together, all of them, everything I could cull from those books and his notebooks and my notebooks: everything. I had put it together and I had studied it until I could command every fact, and then I had stepped back and looked at the whole and seen . . . nothing. Not a thing. Oh, I had seen the facts, there was no shortage of facts; but I could not discern the shape that they filled in. There were, it seemed, too many gaps. But what I had feared was that there were not too many gaps; only too many for me, my mind. For I simply could not imagine what I should see. Could not imagine what it was I was looking at part of. I had everything I needed, knowledge and time and even, by then, a measure of skill—I could follow a fact through shifts and twists of history, do it and love it. But I could not imagine. And if you cannot imagine, you can discover only cold facts, and more cold facts; you will never know the truth. I had seen the future stretching out before me, my life an end-less round of fact-gathering and reference-searching, my only discoveries silly little deductions, full of cold, incontrovertible logic, never any of the burning inductive leaps that take you from here to there and let you really *understand* anything. I had known that was how it would be, had known that if I could not look at the things Moses Washington was looking at and, at least, discover what it was he had been working on, then I could not do anything important at all. And so I had risen from the table and had set the room to rights, putting my notebook on the shelf next to all the other notebooks—his, mine—and extinguishing the lamp, and, leaving the matches in their keeping place, I crept down from there, going to lie in my bed, to shiver between icy sheets. I had not slept. I had lain in that half-sleep, half-trance state in which reality provides the impetus for bizarre driftings of mind, in which it is possible both to dream and to know you are dreaming, and to rest secure in the knowledge that all you have to do if the dreams get a bit too threatening is to decide to wake up. And so, when I had felt the dreams beginning, I had not tried to stop them, I had welcomed them, in fact, as a relief from the failure. But they were no relief. For in the first one I saw myself lying sick with fever, felt the burning of my own skin, hot as the fires of hell. And then my mother had come, as she often had when I was a child and feverish, with a chipped enameled basin of ice water and cloths. She bathed me with the cold water, and the burning went away. But she kept on bathing me, and the fever turned to chills. I had asked her to stop but she had kept on bathing me, and I realized that she was trying to kill me. I leaped up from the bed and evaded her grasping hands and ran out through the window. It was winter outside and the snow was deep, and my naked feet froze as soon as they touched it, but I ran on, the only idea in my mind being to get to the far side, to have a toddy and build a fire and get rid of that awful cold. I ran through the snow and I heard her running after me, heard her panting as she ran, and knew, because she was breathing so hard, that I could easily outdistance her, that I was safe. But when I reached the crest of the Hill I found that there was no path, but a giant gorge a hundred feet deep, with a stream of frothing white water echoing and booming at the bottom of it. I stopped and shivered, hearing the wind singing in the trees, hearing the panting and then the footsteps as she came up behind me. . . .

But when I turned it was not her, it was Old Jack. He asked me if I knew where I was and I started to say no, but then I realized I did know, and I started to say the Hill, but then I realized that was wrong, and then I knew where I was and I told him: the stream was Laurel Branch, and it ran south along the upper ridges of Tussey Mountain, a few miles north of the Line. He smiled, pleased, and said I deserved some comfort. I was wearing clothes and shoes now, and I did not feel as cold, and I felt even better when he built a fire and made us toddies. But before I could drink mine he looked at me and said, "He's down there," and waved his hand downslope, to the east. I saw tracks then, the spoor of a big buck, bigger than any I had ever seen, and so I picked up the shotgun and set off, tracking through the snow. At first the prints were clear, but then there began to be breaks in them, and I would have to stop and sight off into the distance to pick them up again. Then the prints vanished altogether, but I tracked on anyway, following the vague impression of what might have been a trail, the subliminal lingerings of scent, the almost invisible bendings of leaves. I felt good then; I was tracking better than I had ever tracked in my life. And suddenly I knew I had found him. I could not see him, but I could hear a hollow silent space in the woods, a little dead spot. I knew what caused it—all the other creatures, in his presence, were keeping quiet. And so I brought the shotgun to my shoulder and fired into the dead spot, and heard a sudden, dreadfully human cry of anguish and anger. I turned to look for Old Jack but I did not see him anywhere, and I ran forward and found the buck lying on the ground, blood dripping into the snow, and a set of prints leading away again into the snow.

I followed the prints, moving quickly because they were clear. In a few minutes I came to the edge of a clearing and saw a man in the center of it, naked to the waist, despite the driving snow and horrible cold, building a cairn of giant triangular boulders. I knew that it was Moses Washington. I watched him from cover, seeing the rippling of muscle as he lifted the massive rocks, hearing him grunt as he clumsied them into place. When he finished he stepped back and admired his handiwork, and then he brought up his foot and proceeded to kick the cairn apart, sending the rocks avalanching down in disarray. I said nothing, made no sound, gave no hint of my presence, but nevertheless, when the destruction was complete, he turned and looked at me and laughed, and then he vanished into the woods.

I went forward then, and put the gun down, and tried to lift one of the rocks. I found that it was not at all heavy. And so I began to rebuild the cairn. It was amazingly easy; all the stones fit together in a sensible and logical way, and in only a moment I had finished. But it did not look quite right. And then I realized that since the stones were all triangular, they would all fit together logically and easily, and so I took them down and put them up another way, and when done I took them down and put them up again. . . .

Then I had seen that it would go on like that. Then I had tried to wake. But I could not. Something had shackled me in the dreaming state, and I could not open my eyes. The escape for me had not been up into wakefulness but down into deeper slumber; not out of the dreams but into them. There, at the bottom of it all, there was only one dream. Not even a dream; just an all-encompassing sensation of icy coldness, and a visual image of total white. No sound. No smell. No feeling really; just the cold. That was the dream, the coldness and the whiteness growing to envelop me, like an avalanche of snow, deceptive in slow motion, covering me, smothering me. And I could not stop it. I could not free myself. I could not wake up. Not on that night. And not on any of the nights that followed. Of course, I would awaken, sooner or later. But never spontaneously, never of my own accord. Someone—or something—had to wake me. For years it had been Bill, coming across the room and touching me lightly and waiting until the cries had stopped, until my eyes were open, and then wordlessly going back to his bed. Then for years there had been no one, and I had acquired a reputation for brilliance simply because I would rather sit up late into the night studying than take the risk of going to sleep. When I had slept, when I had had to sleep, I had religiously set my alarm clock to awaken me at half-hour intervals, and had always found my lodgings near sources of sound—trolley car tracks, truck routes, anything that might provide occasional rescue. And then there had been Judith, who had said nothing when I had explained to her about the alarm clock and the dreams, but who had turned the clock off and slept with her hand on me, to feel the first shivering, and then, even though she was never fully awake herself, waking me and holding me and watching with a hurt, rejected look in her eyes when I would leave the bed and go and mix a toddy too strong and too hot and large enough to sedate a horse, saying nothing, but not understanding that even though I knew she was there to

149

awaken me, even though I had faith in her, I could never really trust her. Because some night she might not feel the shivering, and there would be nothing to wake me, and I would freeze.

That day nothing woke me. Not for long hours, not until I heard the sound of my mother returning. Then I came up out of sleep shivering, the springs beneath me squeaking with each spasm of my body. Eventually I got up and got into the shower, under water as hot as I could make it. Eventually I stopped shivering, and I got out and dried myself. Then I went back into the bedroom and dressed in clothes out of the dresser and the closet, some Bill's, some mine. And then I went down the back stairs into the kitchen.

"I made the calls," she said.

She did not look up from the counter, from the salad she was preparing. I didn't say anything, simply stood on the lowest step, looking at the condiments arrayed on the thin veneer of Formica she had had cemented over Moses Washington's maple countertop, noting them carefully, trying to figure out what kind of strange offensive she was mounting.

"John . . ."

"Thank you," I said.

"Reverend Williams said we can use the church."

"Thank him."

She looked up then, annoyed, a strand of hair falling free from the bun rolled at the nape of her neck. "Don't you want to know about the arrangements?"

I kept my eyes on the countertop, although I could feel hers on me. "Friends will be received at the E. F. Cohen Funeral Home from seven to nine tomorrow evening. Services will be held at two-thirty Wednesday at Mount Pisgah Methodist Church, with interment following at Mount Ross Cemetery. I leave anything out? Get anything wrong?"

She turned back to the salad. "Just the time," she said. "Funeral's at ten. Reverend Williams works the afternoon shift."

"Good," I said. "I can catch the afternoon bus."

She looked at me again then, and I met her eyes. "You can't stand to be around me a minute longer than you have to, can you?"

"I can't stand to be here *while* I have to," I said.

She looked back at the salad, went on a moment. Then she said,

"Well, then, I guess your mongrely friend oughta be mighty grateful to you for coming all this way for his funeral."

"I didn't come for his funeral," I said. "I came because he asked for me. I came because he was dying."

She didn't look up; she just moved her hands along in a cupping motion, gathering the salad together. "John," she said, "would you come if I asked for you?"

"Why?" I said. "Are you dying?"

She said nothing while she scooped the cut-up vegetables into a large wooden bowl. The bowl had been a birthday gift to her from Bill. It had been a project for a Boy Scout merit badge. He had spent hours on it, selecting the log, burning out the inside of it as the African natives had done to make canoes—although he had been taught it was a practice of the local Indians. I watched her use it and wondered what in the name of God she was playing at. She finished scooping and set the bowl aside, wiped her hands on the towel below the sink. Then suddenly she stopped, hands still on the towel, and looked out the window, down over the nearly dark hillside to the softly glowing lights of the town. "We're all dying," she said. "I was thinking that today. I remember we used to have a chain. Just like an old bucket brigade, only it was for news. Every woman would have two others to get word to, and each one of them would have two more. That was the old way. When I moved here it had been going on as long as Negroes had been living here. The thing that changed it was the telephone; folks started listening in on the party lines. You'd hear your ring, and soon as you picked up you'd hear the other phones, click, click, click, all down the line. When all the Negroes had telephones, or most did, well, the system just died. And then they brought in the dial phones, and you didn't know when your neighbor's phone was ringing anymore, and we needed that old way again. But it was too late then, we'd forgotten how to do it, and we had to get our news like everybody else, over the radio, or in the paper. Just like everybody else."

"Just like the white folks," I said. "I'd have thought that would please you."

"Yes," she said. "Yes, it did please me, while it was happening. Your father used to go down and watch them digging the holes for the poles to bring those phone lines up on the Hill here, and he'd get so mad. He'd come home mad. I'd say to him, 'Moses, that's progress.' And he'd say, ' 'Vette, that's white man's progress. It's colored man's death.' And I never knew what he meant, because when he passed, the phones weren't in yet, and everybody heard, and when your brother died, the whole County heard, but today, they said they couldn't run the announcement in the paper until day after tomorrow, and so I tried to get through to folks on the phone, and I thought to myself, there was a time you could have told everybody you needed to tell by talking to two people, but now you have to make twenty phone calls, and you have to look up the numbers in a book, and those poles marching up the Hill weren't progress, they were death. Just like Moses said."

I stared at her. Not because of what she was saying—she was perfectly capable of saying anything if she thought it would help her get what she wanted—but because she meant it. I could tell from her body; she had somehow drawn herself together, like a caterpillar near a flame.

"The Hill's dead, Johnny," she said. "I didn't mind making twenty phone calls. I minded that there were only twenty to make, and half of them were outside of town. You know, we don't even ring the church bell anymore—hardly anybody lives close enough to hear it. We don't have a Sunday school anymore, because there aren't any young children to come to it. There aren't enough people to have fights at quarterly conference. We wouldn't even have a preacher if Reverend Williams hadn't come to work at the shoe factory. There's not enough work for young people, and not enough young people, and they move away. . . ." She stopped suddenly, straightened, stepped away from the window, went to the stove and turned on the broiler. "Dinner'll be ready in a few minutes," she said. She went to the refrigerator and took out a jar of mayonnaise, came back to the counter and began to mix it into the salad.

I came the rest of the way down the steps and sat down at the table, watching her. I realized that I had not seen her in a long time; years. And that I had made a stupid assumption: that she would not have changed. In most ways she had not. And yet there was something different about her. I wondered what it could be, what could have caused it, what it would mean. I knew it would not mean that much; it couldn't because she was doing the same old things. Or had been. I watched her mix mayonnaise into the salad, knowing she

152

hated mayonnaise, knowing she knew I hated mayonnaise, and I wondered.

I was still wondering when she had set the meal before me: a slab of fresh prime round steak, broiled medium-well; a potato baked until the meat was soft and fleshy, with a pat of hand-churned butter inserted when the potato was not yet done, so that the flesh was a golden yellow throughout; a loaf of bread, fresh-baked, and beside it a pound chunk of the sweet butter, warmed until it was soft enough to spread. The salad was not as perfect as the rest, but Italian tomatoes, Bermuda onions, and romaine lettuce are not common to the northern Appalachian region in March; she had done well to find them at all, and they were, to be fair, fresh enough. It was a superb meal. The result of much effort and not inconsiderable expense, and a high degree of concern. It was an expression of something—of a desire for some kind of reconciliation, perhaps even of love. Or so one would have thought just from looking at it, without knowing the history of it. But I did know that history, and so I could recognize it as another one of her little stratagems, or part of one; an emotional pincers movement devised to encircle the unwary. Well, I was wary. But I did not know what the objective was.

"I hope you're hungry," she said, as she set the food before me. As she sat down across from me, behind a cheaper cut of meat, a smaller potato. Her voice seemed higher than usual. "Did you have anything to eat today?"

"No," I said. "I slept."

"Good," she said. "You're hungry then."

"I'm hungry," I said. Warily. She was planning something. And the meal was central to it; she wanted me to eat it. She seemed to want me to *like* it. I didn't understand it at all.

"Did you sleep well?"

"Fine," I said. "I slept just fine." I took a bite of the steak. It was tender and full of flavor, but it was done too well for me—I like mine rare. "How was work?"

"Real good. Busy, but not too busy. You know. Is your steak all right?"

"It's fine," I said.

153

"It's not too rare, is it?"

"No, it's fine."

"I could put it back in for a minute. . . ."

"It's fine. Perfect. Wonderful. Dandy. *Okay?*"

She didn't say anything, just looked hurt and chewed her food. I ate silently then too, chewing the steak, slicing at the potato, pecking cautiously at the salad, trying to get as little of the mayonnaise as possible, trying to figure it out. She had gone to a lot of trouble to prepare a favorite meal, and there had to be a reason, and it had to be a strange reason. Because it was not my favorite meal. It was Bill's.

"That's Hellman's on the salad," she said.

"I know," I said.

"John, I called the insurance. Or I tried to; the company's out of business."

"You tell Cohen not to worry about getting paid. I'll write him a check before I leave."

"You don't have to; Mr. Scott said he'd be happy to pay for it."

I looked up at her. "You know what to tell him about that."

"John, he only wants—"

"You know what to tell him about that."

"All he wants—"

"I don't give a damn what *he* wants. He turned Bill's funeral into a Goddamned three-ring circus, and he's not going to do it again. You tell him to take his money and use it for a suppository."

"How's your potato?" she said.

"What?"

"Your potato. It's not too firm, is it?"

"No," I said, "no, it's just perfect."

"Oh," she said, getting up suddenly. "I forgot." She went to the refrigerator, came back carrying a pint of sour cream. "Here," she said. She opened the container and put it before me, and then resumed her seat. "You have to bury things sometime, John," she said. "All right, you think what he did about Bill was wrong. He didn't think so. . . ."

"He still doesn't," I said.

"All right, maybe he doesn't. But that's not a reason to keep him from doing what *is* right."

"Nothing that bastard wants to do is right," I said. I sounded angry, and I was angry, but mostly I was confused. Because the moves

154

made perfect sense for her—a frontal attack with the steak and baked and tossed, and when the main source of resistance had been encountered, dig in and bring up the sour cream. What didn't make sense was the fact that it was Bill's meal, and she expected me to eat it and then give in to Scott.

"At least talk to him about it. Talk to him."

That was it.

"What the *hell* do I want to talk to Scott for?"

She didn't say anything; she just reached for the spoon and the sour cream and started to ladle it onto my potato. I reached out and stopped her. "I don't want any of that," I said.

"What?"

"I don't want any of that. I don't like sour cream."

"Why, John, you always loved sour—" She stopped. Looked at the sour cream, then at me.

"Oh, my God," she said.

And then I realized how simple the explanation was, how simple and how unthinkable: she had made a mistake. She had calculated her strategy perfectly, but she had made the wrong meal—or she had thought she was cooking for the wrong son. It was almost funny. I let go of her hand, watched it drop lifelessly to the table. "I *hate* sour cream," I told her. "I hate mayonnaise too."

Suddenly, for the first time I could recall, she looked old. Her cheeks formed little pouches, and her mouth seemed just a little loose. But she picked up the spoon. "Then I'll have some," she said.

"You hate sour cream too," I said.

But she paid no attention, and smeared it all over her potato. She took two bites, her eyes staring at me, hard and defiant. And then she stood up quickly and turned and mounted the stairs. I heard her steps as she walked into her bedroom, the creak of springs as she lay across the bed. And then there were smaller creaks; her body was shaking.

I listened to them for long minutes before I pushed the carcass of the meal away from me and mounted partway up the stairs. She heard me coming; the creakings stopped.

"All right," I said, keeping my voice soft, but knowing she would hear. "All right. I'll go and see the bastard." I had turned and gone back down the stairs then, to get out the pot and brew the coffee.

The average commentator on the manners, mores, politics, and structure of society is, as a rule, too easily confused by the trappings of power. He assumes, for example, that a man's influence is indicated by his position, or his wealth, or his connections in business, completely ignoring—or choosing to ignore, for reasons of hypocrisy or deception—the awesome effect of tennis and bridge partnerships, school groups, marriages, clandestine affairs, and the interpersonal bonds forged by mutual experience. He is even more confused by surface appearances that pertain to cities and towns. Importance is often confused with population or *de jure* factors. Washington, D.C., for example, is the capital of the United States, and many observers, especially foreign observers, have come to speak of America as "Washington," an error that may explain many a diplomatic gaffe. An observer who would know the true state of things must rely on more subtle indicators. He must look at the map, for example, and note that cartographers habitually build a dimension beyond latitude and longitude into their charts; they grade roads according to their surface and size, a fair indicator of importance of the towns which those roads connect. They also provide graphic indications of the size of cities, from large, sprawling masses for cities of size to tiny open circles for towns of none. (This is not a fact lost on those who inhabit truly minor towns—they speak continuously of getting their hamlet on the map.) But even these indirect indicators can lead one astray, and to truly judge the impact of a given area on a total society, one must look at the lines of communication: the number of major highways, the number and size of airports, the number of AM radio stations (FM stations, because of their frequency, being limited in range), the national circulation of the newspapers. Perhaps the best indicator of regional importance is provided by the telephone company: the greater the importance of a locale, the smaller the number of digits that are required to dial beyond it. From the city of New York, one can dial any point in the continental United States by using only ten digits. In the city of Philadelphia, which is of slightly lesser importance, one must prefix those ten digits with an additional "1." From the County, the process of dialing long distance is interminable. In order to call Judith I dialed area code and local number,

156

prefixing it all with a four-digit "direct distance dialing number," a total of fourteen digits. I reached a machine.

"This is Judith Powell. I'm not in at the moment. If this is a medical emergency, please dial—"

I hung up, then dialed my number and let it ring three times before hanging up. I glanced at my watch, and waited, shifting uneasily on the stool that sat in front of my mother's vanity table in what she called the "powder room" and what anybody else would have called a closet. The vanity was an ancient stand of some cheap wood, the top of it fringed with pleated cotton material in a nondescript print which hung to the floor. The top itself was a slab of wood covered over by a slab of glass made permanently greasy by nearly three decades' residue of Dixie Peach hair pomade. Sandwiched between, barely visible through the smeared glass, were pictures. Old pictures, tiny black-and-white things gone brown with age and dim with grease, dead images of dead people. Bill, dressed in white shorts, standing beside the stone barbecue pit Moses Washington had built in slow stages over a summer. The last summer. Bill and I had both hated that barbecue pit. It was, to us, a symbol of the total power of the adult over the child, of Moses Washington over all of us. We would be playing, or reading—I devouring a book while Bill gobbled up a comic which portrayed the latest adventures of Sergeant Rock and Easy Company—when suddenly Moses Washington would come storming down from the attic, angry beyond words, grasp us firmly by the scruff of the neck, and haul us out into the yard to help him—by watching, mostly—while he vented his fury by building an edifice of stone and mortar. He would, it seemed, invent tasks for us—finding the perfect triangular rock from the pile of triangular rocks that he had amassed, holding a trowel while he grunted it into place, searching amidst a mound of smaller stones for a pebble with which to shore it up. His face would be cloudy, clotted, and he would work with a sweating fury that would abate only as the rocks were hefted and placed and cemented. When the sweat poured off of him and he was quite calm, he would return to the attic, but we would know that he could emerge again at any moment. Two years after his death, while Bill tended the garden, I had puzzled out the formula for nitroglycerin, had rigged an electric detonator, and, luckily not killing myself with my own ignorance, I had blown that barbecue to kingdom come. One minute.

Another picture: Moses Washington dressed as he always dressed, bib overalls and a khaki work shirt, a squashed-down cap pulled down over one eye, leaning on a broom beside the church. I wondered when that one had been taken, exactly—after the job of church-cleaning had become indisputably his or earlier, while he and the WH&FMS had been contesting the point in a series of marathon battles that had culminated in his slinging a two-hundred-and-thirty-eight-pound matron through a stained-glass window, and then calmly sweeping up the glass. Two minutes.

And me. I was there too, in a pose for once truly natural: sitting in the big overstuffed chair beneath the floor lamp in the living room, dwarfed by the chair and the book that I held in both hands, propped on my knees. Three minutes.

I dialed the fourteen digits that would get my voice out of there. She answered on the first ring.

"You," she mumbled.

"In bed already?" I said.

" 'Mergency. Up late. John?"

"What?"

"I'm sorry."

"He was old," I said.

She didn't say anything.

"The funeral's Wednesday," I said. "I'll be back after that."

She didn't say anything, and I sat there listening to the sounds the telephone was making. I wished she would say something. She did finally.

"I could drive up there," she said.

"What about the hospital?" I said.

"I already told them I might need somebody to cover for me for a few days."

I didn't say anything.

"John?" she said.

"No."

She didn't say anything.

"The roads are bad," I said. "There was a snowstorm, and the roads are bad."

She didn't say anything.

"I thought they'd have to delay the funeral, but you know what

158

they're going to use to dig the grave? A ditchdigger. Same thing they use for sewer lines."

"I want to come," she said.

"I don't think that's a good idea," I said.

"On account of the roads?"

"On account of the roads."

She didn't say anything.

I waited her out, listening to the sighing wire.

"You don't want me there, do you?" she said.

I didn't say anything.

"I know it," she said. "I just want you to know I know it."

"All right," I said.

"I'm sorry," she said. "I shouldn't do this to you now. I'm sorry."

"Yeah," I said.

"I miss you," she said.

"I'll be back soon."

"John?"

"What?"

"Are you . . . Never mind."

"Am I drunk?"

"I know you're not drunk. You never get drunk."

"Am I drinking?"

She didn't say anything.

"Don't you know?" I said.

She didn't say anything for a minute. Then: "No," she said. "You're not drinking. Not yet."

"What I love about you is your faith," I said.

"Cut that out," she said. "You know I don't care if you drink."

"Oh, boy," I said.

"I care about what makes you do it," she said. "I care about what makes you need to do it."

"Reality makes me do it," I said. "Now let's drop it."

"If I were there," she said, "you wouldn't need it."

I didn't say anything.

"I just want you to be all right," she said. "I just want you to get through whatever it is that you're going through and be all right. Do that, will you?"

"Sure," I said.

She didn't say anything.

"I'm fine," I said.

"You don't sound right."

"I can't help the way I sound," I said.

"I wish you'd let me come," she said.

"I'll be back on Wednesday," I said.

"Please, John," she said.

"Let me be," I said.

She didn't say anything.

"I love you," I said.

"John, I'm worried about you. You don't sound—"

"I love you," I said.

She was silent, then she sighed. "I love you," she said, and hung up. I held the phone for a minute, keeping the connection open as long as I could. The line echoed and buzzed, and then there was a click and the dial tone came back; Ma Bell was getting impatient. I cradled the receiver. I looked at it for a while, wondering if I should call her back, wondering if it would make any difference. I decided it wouldn't. I stood up then, and turned out the light and went back towards the kitchen, to make a toddy. And it occurred to me that she did not understand—she thought that he was dead.

197903062300

(Tuesday)

IT WAS EVERYWHERE. It had sifted into every cranny, drifted into every crack. It lay thickly on the horizontal surfaces. It clung tenaciously to the vertical ones. It was a deep rich gray in color, with little iridescent highlights of turquoise and pink, like rat fur. It was ancient and implacable, deceptive and dead. It was remorseless; irresistible. And it was everywhere.

Once I would have hated it, for it would have been a reminder of my failure. But now it was different. Now I was not a naive boy struggling to give shape to amorphous data, hoping to discover what a legend had been up to, and, in my wildest fantasies, hoping to finish what he had begun, hoping, by doing so, to measure up. Now I was trained to order facts, to control data. And now I was a man, and I could take my own measure; a lesser one, perhaps, but my own. And now I knew that Moses Washington had had plans for me. More than plans; a will. I did not know yet what he had wanted me to do. I did not know if I could do it the way he would have wanted it done—I could not imagine how he would want it done. But this I did know: I was going to understand. He had left me the means for that. And if I found that even now I could not build up the truth out of facts, then I would have the means to tear away at the lies they told, to tear away

161

at them, to find my understanding that way. If I could not imagine, I could, by God, be ruthless. And if, in the end, I found that I still could not understand, there would still be something. Not the best of things, but something; if there was not going to be understanding for me, there could at least be revenge. Because he had left me more than books and papers; he had left me power.

And so I put aside the things I had brought with me and set about my business. By the light of the flashlight I laid a fire in Moses Washington's hearth and I filled the reservoir of the lamp. When that was done I extinguished the flashlight and took the matches from their keeping place and found my way across the floor. I knelt by the fireplace. I lit the match and thrust it in against the kindling. The wood was dry, and caught quickly; I knew in a moment the fire would not die. And so I rose and went to the table. I took up the cloth I had brought with me and sent it sweeping over the table and the chair. I struck a second match and lit the lamp and waited patiently as the glow from the flame spread out into the dark corners of the attic.

And then I laid out the tools of my trade: a fountain pen; a bottle of black india ink; a bundle of arrow-sharp pencils; a half-dozen yellow legal pads; stacks of three-by-five index cards, red, gold, blue and orange and white. And to that array I added the worn leather folio with the clasp of greened and ancient brass, the clasp broken and the flap therefore held down with a seal of candle wax.

I knew that folio. I had heard Old Jack talk about it, about how it was once the most feared artifact in the entire County. For in that worn leather folio Moses Washington had kept his records: the lists of names of those from whom he bought and to whom he sold, and how much, and at what price; the lists of those to whom he gave bribes, and precisely what services he exacted. And about how, before his carcass was even in the ground, they had come, the pale-skinned, pale-eyed men who had never before set foot on the Hill (except, of course, to visit Miss Linda Jamison), sniffing around like a pack of well-fed hounds, smiling, offering, bartering, bribing, begging, finally threatening. About how they had gone away finally, to sit in their book-lined studies and wood-paneled offices and sweat into their collars, praying to whatever gods white men have that it would never see the light of day. For none of them could have stood that, not in a county where a few South County preachers could stand before their congregations and say that betting on horses was the recreation of the

Devil, and the people would go to the polls to defeat a referendum to establish a racetrack that would have made property taxes a thing of the past. They may have been rednecks, but those people were not hypocrites: they did not hold with bribes, and they did not hold with drinking, and they believed it right and proper and Christian that the sons be held accountable for the sins of their fathers.

So the fear of those sons and those fathers must have been an exquisite fear, wondrous in all its facets. First, they would have to fear chance discovery by someone who was smart and avaricious and who would see the potential for profit that the folio represented. That was not much of a fear: they could all afford to pay; or at least, none of them could afford not to. More than that, they would have feared that the discoverer would not be smart enough to use the folio, but only stupid enough to talk about it, or that he would be righteous instead of avaricious. Either way, the end would be the same: exposure. But what really must have made them quake in their spit-shined oxfords was the thought that the folio wasn't lost at all; that Moses Washington had placed the material in the hands of someone he trusted, along with instructions to make it all public should he die under suspicious circumstances, and that that someone would decline to accept the verdict of coroner and sheriff—functionaries who could surely be counted on to say precisely what they were told to say— that his death had been an accident. In the weeks following the event they must have sweated long and hard, and I wondered idly if a survey of the political and business dealings of the County during that period might not have indicated a marked incidence of poor judgment, or if the doctors' records might not show a high number of wives and children who fell downstairs.

But the fear must have dissipated in time. They had no doubt reasoned—or rationalized—that if anybody were going to question the verdict of accidental death they would have already done so, and that if nobody could find any of Moses Washington's hideyholes in forty years, it was not terribly likely that somebody was suddenly going to do so now. They would have relaxed. But not entirely. No, they could have never relaxed entirely. For there was always the possibility of that chance discovery. Worse, there was the possibility that someone did have the folio, someone who would know how to use it, someone who would wait until one of them had taken a particularly righteous stand and then reveal to those sections of the County that still took their Bible literal and preferred their leaders clean and un-hypocritical that the man who stood before them with a Testament in one hand and a flag in the other had been not only drinking bootleg whiskey for years, but had been taking a dollar or two in tribute. And so the leaders would have had to tread softly, for any man they of-fended might be precisely the man who could bring their political house tumbling down around their ears. They would have had to be careful of everybody. For that man might have the folio. Or that man. Or that one over there.

And that man over there was a black man.

It could not have been better if he had planned the whole damned thing.

The funny thing was that it still frightened them, even though most of those whose names would have been on any such list were no longer wielding any kind of power. The thought of exposure still frightened them. And not only them—it frightened those around them, who had come to count on the status quo for . . . something. It frightened my mother. Frightened her beyond words. I had seen the fear when the Judge had dropped it in the center of his desk, the leather making a soft, flat slapping sound on the wood. She had stared at it for an instant, and then she had almost jumped out of the chair in which she had been sitting, and had backed away, so swiftly that it seemed she did not even use her legs—she just *went*. She might have kept on going right out the door, but there was another chair in her way, and it had caught her behind the knees and she sat down in it, hard.

I did not look at her; I was looking at the folio and, beside it, the Judge's hands, pale white and lifeless-looking, with the green-blue of the veins sharp lines that ran up and vanished beneath the slightly frayed edges of his perfectly starched cuffs.

"Your legacy, John," he said. Pronounced. He may have stepped down from the bench, but his voice was still a judge's voice; a voice that ordered, a voice that decreed. "Your legacy. If you acknowledge that you have come to call for it."

But I had not. I had not done anything of the kind. I had come tripping into the law offices of Scott and Scott with my heart set on a little innocent revenge, and nothing more. It had begun with an im-age that had come to me while I was shaving: Old Jack laughing at the thought of a whole bunch of respectable white men begging for the honor of paying to have his moldering carcass laid away in style. It had been such a good image that I had laughed aloud, and the plan had formed in my mind as I finished shaving and dressed in jeans and an old sweat shirt: not only would I allow Scott to talk me into letting him pay for the funeral; I would let him commit himself to the cost of coffin, casket, cemetery plot, headstone, footstone, and maybe even a historical marker to be placed over Old Jack's shoeshine stand. And then I would get him to corral all the courthouse crooks over whose shoes Old Jack had bent for all those years into getting their beloved oxfords muddy trooping up the Hill to attend the services. *And* the burial. The idea made me almost euphoric. I pulled on my old hunting boots and shrugged into the field jacket Bill had spirited away from the Marines, and went down the stairs, plotting strategy.

I stood on Moses Washington's porch and looked at the thick gray clouds that boiled around over the mountains to the south. The storm was still stalled; the snow that had fallen had turned to slush or, on the Hill, to mud. But the storm was still there, and even though the air was warm enough to melt the snow, it chilled me to the bone. I pulled the field jacket close around me and I went slogging down Vondersmith Avenue, the mud tearing at my shoes. I reached the bottom of the Hill and negotiated the deceptive little gully there, the one that made bringing a car off the Hill in foul weather an exercise of some difficulty and no little danger, for the walls of the warehouses—all unused now, but still standing—that lined the railroad tracks—also unused—loomed close on the other side of the cross street. The fact that nobody had ever piled into those walls was probably due solely to the fact that there had never been more than a dozen cars on the Hill at any one time. Of the total number—perhaps fifty over the years—only two had been new. The first of those had not been purchased until 1958, when, about a week after she buried her husband, Yvette Stanton Washington borrowed money from her father and bought a Chevrolet sedan. She probably did not need to borrow the money; Moses Washington had left a goodly supply, and the only reason I could ever see for her taking out the loan was that she wanted the car as quickly as possible. The speed with which she completed the transaction—she went to the bank in the late morning and bought the car in the early afternoon and by sundown she had got Simon Hawley to drive it up the Hill and park it beside Moses Washington's house—might lead one to infer that she felt some burning need for an automobile, but the fact that she let it sit there, unused, for the next three years, which was how long it took her to get around to learning how to drive, seems to introduce some doubt as to the accuracy of the inference. In fact, it is incorrect. It wasn't the car she needed; it was the keys.

She needed the keys because she had already got the telephone. They had installed it, in fact, that very morning, placing the receiver in her powder room. And that night, with the phone sitting there on the floor and the car sitting outside, doing the carpentry with a dogged competence, she had built a shelf with a small brass hook on the side and had secured the shelf to the wall of the powder room. She had placed the new telephone on the shelf, and she had hung the new car keys on the hook. The shelf, of course, was her idea of an altar to the memory of Moses Washington, who, despite the fact that he had put in indoor plumbing, and electric water heating, and an electric range, and a refrigerator, and even a wringer washer, had steadfastly, loudly, and, whenever she tried to insist, violently refused to install a telephone or buy a car.

I turned left and went quickly along Railroad Street, the mud falling from my shoes. I stumped along the pavement next to the deserted warehouses, reaching, in perhaps a quarter mile, the main north-south route. It was a federal highway, technically, but within the precincts of the Town it was called Richard Street, being named, as had most of the other streets in the old original Town, for a member of the family of William Penn.

That naming, no doubt, was a function of provincial sycophancy—certainly the Penn family had not had a whole lot to do with the Town. Certainly, too, they had not all been of much importance; I had never been able to find more than the sketchiest records of who Richard was and what, if anything, he had done. The street that bore his name was likewise of little importance; its function had once been to connect the trail that ran north to the western reaches of New York State with the road that General Braddock had cut to give access, along the Potomac, to the heartland of Virginia, and with the road to the west built by General Forbes, but in recent years a bypass had been built around the Town.

Forbes Road was not, in fact, the road built by Forbes, or even the route of it, but rather a sort of averaging out of several different wilderness and wagon roads that had been begun in the seventeenth

166

and eighteenth centuries, some abandoned for lack of interest or funds, or because of hostile Indians. The segment that connected the Town with Pittsburgh was commissioned in 1789 and was finished in time for Lee to march over it to put down the Whiskey Rebellion. But it wasn't terribly important otherwise, and so I continued on Richard, crossing the Town's main east-west street (which was named, of course, Penn Street), continuing on to the next corner. There Richard Street changed to the Springs Road and began its run to Maryland, after intersecting the second street named for a Penn.

John Penn, at least, was somebody. In fact, he was the lieutenant governor of the colony, and the last of the colony's owners to have say in its operations. He had been thrown out of office by the Revolution of 1776, and having determined to stay in the New World, he died in Philadelphia in 1795; not much of a record, but better than that of Richard.

On the corner of John and Richard streets stood the building that housed the local white Methodist Church. It was not the oldest Methodist organization in the County, by any means. A group of Methodists had come to Broad Top Township in 1787, no doubt to avail themselves of Pennsylvania's offer of religious toleration. Their leader had been a physician, one Jeremiah Duvall, who was, evidently, a shrewd businessman. At one point, for example, he purchased the County's first stableman—who, so local legend would have it, was once a celebrated savage chief—by trading for him with a steer. (The stableman, who eventually became free, married Mrs. Duvall's maid, Black Rachel, but the union was not a happy one, and ended in divorce.) Even that was not the earliest record of Methodism, for three years before Duvall arrived, in 1784, a Methodist minister named Thomas Leakins traveled a circuit that included Maryland, Virginia, and Southampton Township, in the South County. Leakins presided over the building of a no longer used but still extant log church at the northern end of Beans Cove, and eventually held services in the town of Chaneysville, at the home that, before his death in 1820, belonged to Joseph Powell, Jr., great-grandson of Thomas. The Methodist organization in the Town, by contrast, dated back to only 1816, the lot on which its building stood only to 1818 (when it had been purchased from a Dr. John Anderson, for seventy-five cents), and the building itself to only 1827. I had, nevertheless, spent many an hour in the graveyard beside the church, examining gravestones, for it was said that, because a separate organization for nonwhites had not been established until about 1845, there were black people buried in there. But I had never found evidence of any.

I turned west on John. I crossed Thomas Street—Thomas Penn had managed the Colony for nine years and then gone back to England—and came to Juliana.

Who Juliana Penn had been and what she had done were total mysteries to me. I supposed that, given the tenor of the times and her female sex, she had not been allowed to be or do much of anything. The street named for her was, in contrast, one of the most important in the Town. At its southern end was the Heights, where the most prominent families of the Town lived in their old Georgian houses. The mayor lived on the Heights. The judges lived there. The most prominent lawyers lived there. Doctors had rarely been permitted to buy there, because the lumpen elements, visiting the consulting rooms, would have spoiled the Heights' exclusivity, if only temporarily. In fact, it was something of a scandal when Lucian Maccabeus Scott had purchased his house. But they couldn't do anything about that.

To the north, Juliana Street ran through the business district—if the Town had had a Main Street it would have been Juliana—and eventually ended at the gates of the Fort, which had been rebuilt, in a burst of local pride, during the County Bicentennial in 1958. The construction methods used were supposed to be identical to those employed two centuries earlier, and the local men who volunteered their labor had all grown beards to be in keeping with the historical spirit of the project. Ten years later, of course, anyone who wore a beard was liable to verbal abuse, and in more than one case, physical assault, by some of those latter-day frontiersmen. The irony of that, of course, escaped the locals.

Juliana Street stopped at the Fort, because beyond the Fort was the Raystown Branch of the Juniata River. From time to time there had been talk of building a bridge—there had, in fact, been a bridge there, a swinging footbridge, now in disrepair—but the motion had always failed, perhaps because if Juliana Street went across the river it would have connected perfectly with Vondersmith Avenue. Or perhaps the irony of that, too, escaped them, and it really was a lack of funds that prevented the building of the bridge.

In any case, I did not go down Juliana to the Fort and the river. I went only as far as the point where Juliana met Penn Street, the point called, in much provincial correspondence, the Great Square.

The order of the provincial government which, in 1766, had decreed the survey that laid out the Town called for the planning of a "Commodious Square in the most convenient place." That was the Square. Until the mid-fifties it had been presided over by a granite soldier on a granite monument, who occupied the center of the intersection and created a traffic snarl. About the time of the Town's Bicentennial they moved him to one corner and put in a traffic light, which made the intersection more of an intersection, but, to my mind, relegated the Square to something less than the planners had had in mind. Still, the Square was the political heart of the Town, and, in fact, of the County. On the southwest corner stood the County Courthouse, a red brick structure that dated back to 1829. When I was young I had always thought it was a church, primarily because it had a steeple-like clock tower. (The clock had been purchased for two hundred and fifty dollars in 1857.) Given the way politics was carried on in the County, my childish supposition was either precisely accurate or dead wrong, depending on what your opinion was of organized religion.

The northeast corner was the churchyard of the Episcopalian Church. The lots had been reserved by John Penn as the site of an edifice of the Church of England (despite their advocacy of religious toleration, the Penns knew which side of the altar the power was on), but no church was built there until after the Civil War. Something had been there, though; the postwar excavation unearthed the remains of several bodies, no one knows of whom.

The northwest corner held the Old Man on the Monument and, set back a ways, the Lutheran Church, a relatively new building, constructed in 1872 to replace the original structure, built in 1849. Before that time that corner had been the site of the County Courthouse and Jail. That building was erected in 1774 or '75. It had always, it appears, proved inadequate as a courthouse (as, in fact, had the present one, where, until the mid-fifties, the lack of a sanitary accommodation for women had precluded female service on juries), but, by all accounts, it was more than adequate as a jail. One record, which dates back to 1884, declares that the structure was, for its incarceratory purposes, "pronounced, by those who saw the building years before its demolition, perfect." It is recorded that the jail provided classed

169

accommodations, varying according to the nature and severity of the crime. The debtors' prison is described as having had a "grated window," and there was a "cell for ordinary criminals." The turns of phrase might be taken to mean that the cell was windowless, but if this was true, one must wonder at the marvel of colonial invention which would allow for even less light in the third—or perhaps, given that it was a jail, first-class accommodation, which is described as a "dark dungeon for convicts." In any event, one suspects that the lightless "convicts" and "ordinary criminals" looked forward to coming out into the yard, even if they did have to look at the whipping post and the pillory. Despite its perfection, the jail was condemned in 1826. It was condemned again in 1833. Finally, in 1842, it was sold for ninety-three dollars and, presumably, razed. Now on the exact spot where it stood the old men sit on concrete benches, chewing tobacco and discussing the weather.

I sat with them awhile, not saying anything, just thinking about all that history, drowning my mind with the detail of that much of it to keep me from thinking about any more of it. But I knew the connections were there, even if I did not look at them.

Finally I rose, and when the courthouse clock bonged out half-past eleven and every businessman's mind would be turning to lunch, I was climbing the wooden stairs that led to the second story of the block of offices that occupied the remaining corner of the Square, where, for over a hundred years, the Town's most prominent lawyers had traditionally taken space. I put a scowl on my face and allowed my eyes to look just a little bit wild, and when I reached the door that bore the brass plaque saying SCOTT & SCOTT, I shoved it open so hard that it bounced off the wall.

The reception area was almost the same as it had been when my mother occupied it—a plain wooden table that was old enough to have been considered an antique, which held a black phone with several buttons and a small portable typewriter. The receptionist was nothing like my mother had been; she was small and young, with dishwater hair and a slightly reddened nose. I told her that Randall Scott wanted to see me.

She hesitated. "Do you have an appointment?"

I leaned across her desk, supporting myself on my fists, putting my face about three inches from hers. "I guess you didn't hear me; I said Scott wanted to see me. I don't want to see him. I don't give a good God damn if I ever see him again. And I don't have all day, either. So why don't you stop asking dumb questions and tell the man I'm here." She gaped at me—I could see her lip tremble—and I felt briefly sorry for her, briefly ashamed of myself. But I smiled at her anyway, and then I straightened up and took a few steps away and stared pointedly out the window at the old men sitting on the stone benches under the stony gaze of the old man on the monument.

"What—" she began.

I turned slowly and gave her a hard look.

"I'll tell him you're here," she said, and got up and came from behind the table, nearly stumbling over the phone cord in her haste. She went through the door to the inner offices. She closed it behind her.

I didn't mind that; I could deduce what would happen when she tried to explain to Scott's secretary that there was this ... *person* outside wanting to see him, and then, since she didn't know my name, trying to describe me without ever once using the word "black" or "Negro" or—as would probably be her impulse—"colored." She would have to do it that way, for Scott's secretary was one Yvette Stanton Washington, and white people who had the misfortune to find themselves in subordinate positions simply did not use that kind of terminology around her, not if they wanted to keep their hides intact. The lady had been trained in the South, and she was as deferential as she had to be around the upper crust, but she was sudden death on poor white trash. So I expected a slight delay, and then my mother charging out to deal with the problem of an ... informally dressed peasant who had the audacity to demand audience without benefit of appointment.

But it was Scott who came, hustling through the doorway, hand extended, teeth bared in a broad smile. "John," he said. "Good to see you. *Good* to see you. And good of you to come." He managed to sound as if he meant it.

I had not seen him in years, not since he had come to Bill's funeral, spouting patriotic platitudes like a Gatling gun and holding his prized daughter Mariam firmly by an oversexed elbow; he didn't trust her around Bill, even if he was dead. (I didn't blame him for that; I didn't trust her around Bill, either.) Then he had been a sort of blocky, paunchy fellow in the first flush of prosperous middle age, dressed in subdued shades of polyester, the bulk that had made him a star fullback in high school and a second-string guard at Penn State (he had never had enough speed to get outside, with or without the ball) turning inexorably to firm suet. He had been the quintessential home boy made good, vice-president of the Junior Chamber of Commerce and treasurer of the Lions Club, a man with all his lines of development mapped out. He would become the president of the Junior Chamber. He would gradually take more and more responsibility for the business of the law firm. He would stand at the church door and shake hands as an official greeter. His suet would soften. The pinkness of his skin would change to redness, perhaps even floridity. He would change his sports from hunting and tennis to fishing and golf, trade in his Buick for a Continental, his double knits for flannel, and begin to winter in Florida.

But he had fooled me. He had lost weight, a lot of it, and his clothes hung on him. Now he moved with a sort of deliberate dignity rather than with the popinjay bounce that had once told anyone who saw him that here was a small man trying to look important. I wondered at the reason for the change. Perhaps he had seen the same lines of development that I had seen and had not liked where they led. Or perhaps he had been sick. Probably the latter, because the changes did not seem positive. Before, at least, he had seemed healthy. Now his skin was an unholy gray. But even if all that had changed, his eyes had not. They were just as they had always been, chilly and distracted, icy and flat, gray as winter fog.

He pumped my hand. "We hear good things about you, John," he said.

"Who from?" I said.

His smile slipped for a moment, but he slapped it back. "Why, from your mother, of course. She's just proud as the dickens of you, John. And I know your granddad would be proud of you too. Two professors in three generations. Quite an accomplishment."

"Oh, hell, *Randall*," I said, putting a little push on the first name, "I don't know. Why, look at your family; two lawyers in *two* generations. Why, when my grandfather was getting his Ph.D., your grandfather was busting sod out in the North County. You're the ones with the accomplishment."

The grin didn't even slip. "Well, John, I guess we can both be proud. Now let's not stand out here. Come on into my office. Would you like some coffee? Betty, get us some coffee. How do you take—"

"I don't drink coffee," I said.

He looked at me blankly, then turned to the receptionist, but she had already gone scurrying away. Scott turned back to me. "Ten cups a day," he said, ruefully. "I'm supposed to cut down." He took hold of my elbow and ushered me through the door and down a short corridor past the closed door that, I knew, led to my mother's small office, and on into his own fluorescently lit little "environment."

"Have a chair, John," he said bouncily. "Have a chair." He indicated an uncomfortable ultramodernistic armchair, settled himself behind a plastic table of a desk that was loaded with phone, in-box, out-box, clock, desk calendar, pen set, frames holding pictures of wife and pictures of daughter, all sired by Du Pont out of Design Research, and with six or seven bulging file folders and stacks of loose papers.

Scott noticed the direction of my gaze. "I'm sorry about this *darned* clutter, John." He ran a finger around the inside of his collar, smiled ruefully. "Sometimes these litigations get so doggoned complicated that you have to go all the way back to the year one to figure out what's going on, let alone whose fault it is. You might not believe it, but this"—he slapped the pile of papers, sending a troupe of dust motes dancing upward—"is a simple piece of business that only goes back to a year or so before the war. And it still has all—"

"Which war?" I said.

"What? Oh. The Second World War."

"Oh," I said. "*That* war." He looked at me warily, and I tried to stop myself, to shut myself up. I had a strategy, and I wanted to stick to it. But I couldn't. The temptation was too strong, and the opening was there. "Well," I went on, "I'm glad you have these old cases laying around to keep you busy. Things must be pretty slow down at the draft board these days."

He looked at me with those flat gray eyes. There was no expression on his face, but his skin grew a little paler, just a little, and I could hear him suck his breath between his teeth. "Yes," he said finally. "Thank God all that's over. For good, I hope."

"For better, anyway," I said. And I would have let him go then. But he took it up.

"John . . . " He gave a little carefully calculated hesitation—I could almost hear him count the beats. "I want you to know this: I hated like the dickens to send boys off to fight. I hated to send your brother. It would have been hard not to send him—God knows he was a healthy specimen, and everybody knew it. And your mother's working here would have made everybody suspicious if we hadn't called him at all. But I would have gotten him out of it somehow, if only he had trusted me. But he insisted on taking matters into his own hands. He defied the law. Openly. This is not a liberal community, John, we both know that, and after he wrote that letter to the paper telling everybody he was running off to Canada—I never understood why he did that—"

"He said why," I said. "In the letter. 'I want others like me to know they have a choice.' That was the part they didn't print."

Scott looked at me blankly. "Well," he said, "maybe so. And maybe that's what he wanted. But that's not the way things work in the County, John. You know that. We like to do things . . . quietly. And after people learned that he had started to run to Canada . . . well, we did well just to keep him out of jail. By that time, going was the only chance he had to be able to come back here and live a normal life. And surely it was the only thing that would let your mother hold her head up. I think he realized that. I think that's why, in the end, he agreed to go quietly—"

He was interrupted by the girl bringing his coffee, in a bright red plastic cup that matched his flowerpots. "Judge Scott called, Mr. Scott," she said. She gave me a quick sideways glance. "About the—"

"I know what he called about," Scott snapped.

"Yes, sir. He said to tell you he'd be in about noon."

"Call him back," Scott said. "Right away. Tell him that it isn't necessary that he come in. Tell him I can handle everything. And here . . . " He swept the papers together into an untidy pile and shoved them into a large manila envelope, then loaded the folders and the envelope onto her thin arms, like cordword. "Take this and put it in my car." He fumbled in his pants pocket for the keys, laid them on top of the envelope. "Put it in the trunk."

"Yes, sir," she said, turning ponderously towards the door.

"And close the door, Betty."

"Yes, sir."

"And hold all my calls."

"Yes, sir."

We watched as she somehow maneuvered through the door and managed to close it with her foot without dropping a file or even the keys. When it was done, Scott leaned back and sighed. "Now, John," he said. "I know this isn't the best of times for you. Your mother's told me how close you were to Jack, and I understand how you might feel ... resentful about somebody ... well, helping out. But you have to understand, John, that old man was an institution in this community. We all loved him. And maybe you want to be responsible, but ..." He looked to see how he was getting across. I gave him nothing but a stony glare. "Look, John. I guess you know my father hasn't been well these last few years. He's not *sick,* but you know how people are when they're getting on. It's a terrible thing to watch a man you've loved and respected just slowly deteriorate—"

"I *know,*" I said. "It must be terrible for you."

"Yes, John, it is, especially—"

"Especially the drooling."

He gave me a sharp look. "The what?"

"The drooling," I said. "That's what would get to me. I mean, the incontinence isn't really so bad. If you have to take them out, you can always put them in diapers and rubber pants and nobody will notice a thing—expect for the smell, of course, and people are usually too polite to mention *that.* But there's just no way to cover up the drooling."

Scott was suddenly paler, and it seemed that there was a flicker of green in the flat gray of his eyes, but otherwise he didn't react. He was starting to puzzle me. "Well, John," he said, "I thank God things aren't like that. It's just that he's a little forgetful. Doesn't have a real grasp of reality sometimes. It's partly that his mind isn't as it once was, and partly that times have just ... passed him by a little. There isn't much you can do about it, except try to understand. But what I was getting at was this: whenever something happens to him I want to be the one to handle it. So I know how you feel about letting people help with Jack. But you know, John, I've come to realize that for me to try to do everything just isn't right. It's draining, of course, but basically it just isn't fair. There's my wife, for example. She loves Dad as much as I do and she wants to be involved with seeing to his needs. And then there's Mariam—"

"Ah, yes," I said. "How is good old Mariam?" I realized that I was losing it. I had just about had him and now I was letting him get away, and I wanted to stop myself, but there was something else going on, something I didn't have control over.

175

"She's fine, John, fine. Now, about Jack—"

I should have let him go on. I tried to. But there was something inside me, some part of me that just wouldn't let it be. It was almost as if I were watching someone else who looked just like me sit there and say: "You know, Randall, I often think about Mariam, being the same age as Bill and all. The reason I think about it is, if Mariam had been a boy, they could have been real good friends, up to a point. They could have played ball together. Maybe even hunted together, although Bill never did care too much for hunting. Who knows? They might have joined up together. Maybe been in the same outfit. Why, maybe one of those boys he brought out of that ambush would have been Mariam. Or maybe they would have done it together, maybe Mariam would have gotten a medal too. Maybe they'd have stepped on the same Goddamned land mine—that would have been integration with a bang."

I wanted to stop then, but I couldn't. Scott just sat there looking—not reacting at all, just looking.

"Well," I said, "all that's just speculation. Unlikely too. You being on the draft board and all, I guess Mariam wouldn't have been in anybody's outfit. She'd have been 4-F. A quiet 4-F. People still would have had something to say about it, I bet. A lot of people don't know how things are done in this County, including most of the folks that live in it. So all things considered, I guess it's just as well you never had a son. And Mariam's a fine-looking girl—I'm sure she's roped herself a man and settled down. . . ." I stopped. Scott was reacting. He looked uncomfortable, and turned visibly paler.

"Why, yes, John," he said. "She seems quite happy."

"Really? Well, that's fine." I should have let him go then. But I smelled blood. "Tell me, Randall," I said, "how long have they been married?"

He didn't say anything.

"Good Lord!" I said. "Randall, you don't mean . . ." I shook my head sadly. "And she was such a *nice* girl too. But it's a new day. Any children?"

He just looked at me.

"No? Well, don't let it worry you, Randall. Mariam's a healthy girl. I'm sure she'll present you with a grandson before too long. A man ought to have a grandson. Especially if he can't have a son."

Scott's eyes weren't flat anymore; they were sharp and icy. And his flesh was so pale I could see the hair follicles showing blue against it, even after his close shave. It was Old Jack's "fishbelly" look, and it was every bit as scary as he had said it was. But when Scott spoke, his voice was still calm and even, if a bit forced. "You're right about that, John. I just hope she marries first." He managed a chuckle. "I guess I'm a little conventional about such things. But as I was saying . . ." and he went on, pressing his argument. But I wasn't listening; something was wrong. Terribly wrong. I had come to play a little vengeful game—not a deadly game, or even an important one, just a little exercise in exacting payment—and like a fool I had let old angers and festered bitterness carry me beyond the boundaries of even a radical strategy; beyond the limits, even, of good taste. That meant that I was losing control of myself. But the frightening thing was that even though I had lost control I had not lost my game. That was perhaps a matter of luck. But I thought not; I had just never been that lucky. No, it was simply that my little game did not matter, for somewhere there was a larger game in progress. Perhaps it was Scott's, perhaps not. In any case, it had hidden players, unknown rules, and no discernible objective.

". . . what professors make," Scott was saying, "but I don't imagine it leaves you with money to throw away . . ."

I didn't like it.

". . . be willing to cover all expenses. . . .?

Whichever way it was, I didn't like it.

". . . realize what Jack meant to this town. Now, I can't guarantee it personally, but I'm sure the Town Council . . ."

Suddenly I recalled one of Old Jack's interminable hunting tales, this one about stalking a bear through the North County woods for a night and a day and another night, only to turn, on the dawn of the second day, and see the bear circling in from the rear.

". . . suitable inscription. Anything you'd feel appropriate. Now, what do you say to that?"

"Why?" I said.

"What?"

"Why. Basic question. Why do you want to do all this?"

"Well, I thought I just explained . . ."

"You explained all the wonderful things you were going to pay for, and you explained why I should let you, but you never said why you wanted to do them in the first place."

He didn't answer right away. He thought a minute, then made a sucking sound with tongue and teeth. "Isn't it enough that I want to?"

"Woulda been," I said. "Twenty years ago everybody would have been just thrilled at the charity. But some of us have learned to be a little more . . . careful now." I looked at him hard. "What's in it for *you*, Randall? And don't give me crap about civic duty."

He looked at me for a minute, then shook his head. He stood up and came from behind the desk and went to look out the window. His fingers toyed idly with the plastic rod that controlled the blinds, opening and closing the slats, making bars of darkness alternately widen and narrow on his face. He sighed deeply. "These are hard times. First, I suppose, it was the deaths of the Kennedys. Then Vietnam. Then Watergate. Next? God knows. A man gets tired speculating. I guess we've all grown a little cynical. I know I have. I guess it's too much to expect that younger people would not have grown even more cynical." He sighed again, and turned to face me. "I don't blame you, John. I don't. And I'm not offended; I know you feel you have reason not to believe me; perhaps you do. You feel that I treated your brother badly, that I was . . . involved in his death. I believe I was doing my duty as a duly appointed public official. I may have been wrong. But I was trying to do the right thing; it was a dirty, tawdry, confusing little war, and the only clearly honorable course of action was obedience. Or maybe I'm just 'copping out' on that. But I say this, and I want you to believe it. . . ." He turned quickly and fixed me with his gaze. "I have come to understand and value and *cherish* the contribution that col . . . Afro-Americans have made to this country, this state, this County, this Town. And what I want to do now is just a small step towards demonstrating that understanding."

That made me feel a lot better. I smiled at him. "Not bad, Randall. Not bad at all. For a while there you actually had me worried. Silly me, I forgot it was an election year. But I didn't know the opposition was that strong."

"I'm not running for anything," he snapped.

"Of course you aren't. You guys never are. But just in case you find yourself giving that little speech to some collection of dumb niggers somewhere, remember it's 'black' this season. Afro-American was so damn cumbersome even Whitney Young couldn't say it."

Scott sighed.

"Oh, it's all right, Randall. Don't worry. You can buy the funeral. The plaque too. Any nigger who's fool enough to vote Republican on account of a couple of slabs of rock and a piece of brass probably votes that way anyway on account of he thinks Mr. Lincoln freed the slaves."

He looked at me, and I found myself feeling uneasy again, because he looked positively *grateful.* "John, I—" he began, but the buzzing of the phone interrupted him. He stopped and gave me an apologetic, man-to-man smile. "I'm sorry, John. This must be important. It had better be. Excuse me, please." And he actually waited until I had nodded before he picked up the phone. "Betty, I told you . . . I see." He glanced at me, then away. "Well, tell him I'm in conference. . . . He *what?* . . . How . . . Never mind." He looked at me, shook his head. "All right, Betty, thank you. Tell him Dr. Washington and I will be in in a moment." He hung up and gave me a rueful look. "John, I'm sorry. My father has decided to come in today. There's really nothing for him to do, but he likes to feel needed, and when he does come in we try to . . . keep him busy." He smiled. "Well, it seems that he found out you were here and he's heard your mother rave about you, and he'd like to see you. If it's a bother, I'll make some excuse."

And I was back to being puzzled. Something was still wrong. But I wasn't going to find out what it was trading insults with Scott. "Not at all, Randall, not at all. I think it's wonderful that you let the useless old fart think he's still worth something. I'll be glad to humor him. So long as he doesn't start to drool."

His eyes were angry again, but he stayed polite. "Thank you, John. You're very kind. Now, I don't want you to take up all your time with this; you don't have to stay more than a minute. This way."

He led me out the door and on down the corridor, past the entrance to a spacious and crammed library, to a set of double doors. He knocked twice and pulled them open.

The room was large, subdued, solid, rich . . . deep. There was no way to compare it with Scott's office; there was simply no comparison. The air itself was different; it seemed thicker, almost as if it were dust-laden. But it was impossible to be sure, for the sunlight was blocked out by heavy drapes; the only light came from an odd ugly Edwardian floor lamp that sat in a far corner and from a simpler green-shaded lamp which sat on the desk. The desk itself was old—

not an antique, just an old oak desk that had been made with care and kept with love. There were nicks and scores in the wood, but years of oil and tender rubbing had healed the wounds, until now they were only fading keloid scars. Behind it sat the Judge.

I had seen him before, of course. Many times. Even if he had not been my mother's employer, I would have known him. It would have been impossible to grow up in that town and not know him. He was a local legend, a regional projection of an American political phenomenon, the local boy who had risen by means both fair and foul to become a minor dictator, loved by some, hated by many, feared—and, if the truth were to be told, needed—by all. He had been born of Scotch-Irish yeomen who had farmed land near Mount Dallas, an area noted for its independent peasant stock, but which was neatly owned and handily dominated by the Hartley family, whose history included having come over on the *Hyder Ali,* the French bottom which had brought to America the final version of the peace treaty between England and the Colonies, and having quartered President Washington when he had come west to supervise the putting down of the Whiskey Rebellion. By the time the Judge was born, the Hartleys were firmly ensconced as local aristocracy, having purchased the farm at Mount Dallas from the original peasant settlers, and were doing a formidable business in freight and iron. There had been, so the tales would have it, a constant friction between the Norman-English Hartleys and the Scotch-Irish peasants; not a feud exactly, but . . . at one point three of the younger Hartley boys had been found beaten senseless in a ditch, and before the day was done the Judge had left the local schoolhouse, where he seemed to be perpetually assigned to the fourth grade, and had started walking east. In two days he crossed a hundred miles of mountains and made it to the state capital. He was thirteen.

For the next five years he ran "errands" for the state legislators, making himself indispensable and acquiring the reputation of performing delicate tasks with great success, total discretion, and no comeback. He could have stayed there forever, a sort of backwoods Bobby Baker, but he was also a restless young man, and he left Harrisburg in 1914, took passage for France, and was a veteran of the trenches long before Pershing and the AEF came into the Line. He was decorated several times and probably would have risen rapidly through the ranks had it not been for his propensity towards brawling; he was demoted twice and he was scheduled for court-martial on charges of striking an officer—of beating him bloody, in fact—when a wisp of gas weakened his lungs and left him open and vulnerable to the influenza that killed more soldiers than the gas and bombs and bullets combined. He spent a year on his back in hospitals. That was where—so he claimed in his frequent speeches—he changed. Saw the same light that had blinded Saul of Tarsus. Lost his fascination with flesh and the Devil, and the terrible anger that had made him hate instead of love. It was there, he said, that he read his first book, the New Testament, of course, and read it in French too, thereby acquiring a skill, a language, and a faith, all at one time. When he was discharged he thought to enter the ministry, but, he admitted candidly, while he was no longer preoccupied by the pleasures of the flesh, he was much too fond of them to be an effective pastor. And so he returned to the state capital and spoke to his old cronies, and somehow, without benefit of high school diploma or money for tuition, managed to be admitted to Dickinson College. That, he always claimed, was the only favor he ever took from his old friends and employers, the politicians. For the next five years he turned his back on pleasure, living on study and scraps, graduating at the end of it with a Phi Beta Kappa key, a bachelor's in Latin, and a degree in law. And then he came home, walking in order to keep the few dollars he had saved to rent a decrepit office at the east end of town.

There he hung up a shingle that he whittled himself, and set about getting a meager living and a prodigious reputation by successfully defending the poorest, orneriest, and guiltiest-looking defendants he could find, North County poachers and South County chicken stealers and renegades from every point of the compass, and by bringing suit against the powers-that-were on behalf of any small farmer or businessman who could make him believe in the rightness of the case. At the same time he was winning the love of the local church groups by telling the story of his miraculous conversion and by staunchly and publicly embracing the cause of temperance and Prohibition. By 1926 he had forged a political coalition composed of conservative church congregations, yeoman farmers, and small businessmen, and backed by the muscles of some of the most violent rascals in the Alleghenies. He threatened to upset the reigning Republican order at the ballot box, and to make it stick, if it came to that, in the street. The powers-that-be were worried. Not just about farmers

181

and chicken stealers and a scrawny Irishman who quoted Blackstone, Shakespeare, and Moses with equal facility; news had reached them of goings on in the backwoods of Louisiana, of a man named Huey Pierce Long. Popular revolt seemed to be all the rage.

But the local powers had never desired to be fashionable, and so, long before the elections, they went to the Judge and sat down to haggle. According to Old Jack—who had been privy to much of the informal chawing over of policy—they hadn't expected the negotiations to take long. The Judge held all the cards, they knew that. All they wanted to know was, what did he want?

In the end, the Judge surprised everybody. He could have taken *de facto* control of the Town and most of the County, and gotten God knows how much financial leverage, and, if he had wanted that, been well on his way to the governor's chair. But he settled for a few insignificant-seeming reforms in the local tax structure, and some minor adjustments in the zoning ordinances, and a few actual zoning changes in remote regions, including Mount Dallas, and the right to appoint a few unimportant men to a few unimportant patronage jobs. The price was so cheap the powers-that-were fell all over themselves giving in. They went away talking about what a fool he was, and once the word of the bargain got out, the general opinion was that he was worse than that. Then, a few months later, it was announced that the Judge was engaged to a cousin of the Hartley family, one noted more for her crazy liberal notions and her literary pretensions than for her congeniality, and the wiser heads nodded sagely. Probably, so the speculation ran, the betrothal was part of the political agreement; it was hard to imagine that the Hartleys would have permitted such a *mésalliance* otherwise. (The opinion was confirmed when the Hartleys gave the Scotts a fairly substantial plot of land east of the Narrows as a wedding present, and defused the explosion that was almost triggered by the Scotts' purchase of a house on the Heights.)

But while the wags called it politics and the romantics called it love, the people whose cause the Judge had championed—the farmers and the poachers and the two-bit rednecks from Helixville and Chaneysville and Artemis and Yellow Creek—called it a betrayal, and they turned away from him. One story had it that an old farmer had passed the Judge on the street and spat at his feet.

But the Judge did not seem to mind. On the contrary, he seemed to thrive on the sudden isolation. He devoted his time to supervising the planting of his land and making other land deals here and there, always for property that nobody much could see the use of. He accepted and diligently pursued the cases of those who were humble enough to come to him. He made more speeches to church groups. He supervised the restoration of his house. He doted on his wife and dandled his newborn son on his knee. His opponents called it acknowledging defeat. His former supporters called it quitting. Those few who still supported him said he was only resting before pursuing the fight. None of them understood that he had won.

The victory became apparent when the WPA began to bring sewerage and water and roads and bridges to areas that had been previously known only to the most desperate of farmers and the most enterprising of hunters—and perhaps a moonshiner or two. "Useless" lands became prime building sites, and the Judge's insignificant-seeming concessions gave him the power to zone and control. He even had some say as to setting the priorities of the WPA. In a few short years more than one farmer had discovered that his back woodlot or worst cornfield had virtually turned into gold—or would have, if anybody had had any money. A few speculators did, and the land was bought at prices then thought to be outrageous.

By 1936 the Judge had regained all the power and prestige that he had ever had, and the powers-that-were suddenly realized that what they had thought was a cheap victory was in fact a very expensive defeat. There were talks of a new compromise, and it was desperate talk, for now the Judge not only had power, he had money. There would be no compromise. And if anybody thought there might have been, the publication of Mrs. Scott's novel, a thinly disguised *roman à clef* which aired the dirty linen of half the County's aristocracy and made only slightly vague reference to the dinginess of the long johns of the other half, corrected the impression. In the 1938 elections the Judge backed two candidates. Both won. After that his hand was never seen; he endorsed nobody, contributed to no campaign, gave no speeches except the perennial ones to church groups, attended no dinners. He simply ran the County. The aristocracy had to be content with still owning most of it.

By 1946 even that was slipping away from them. The GI's were coming home, the ambitious young sons of farmers armed with the confidence that comes from years of war and ultimate survival. They had educational opportunities and financial leverage courtesy of the

GI Bill, and the potential gold in all those woodlots and cornfields became real. The farmers who had had the foresight and the liquidity not to sell out early made money. The speculators made money. Anybody in the County who had clear title to an acre made money.

The Judge, it seemed, owned three parcels that just accidentally lay to the south, west, and east of town. Exactly where the money to buy two of them had come from, no one knew. It was certain that the cash had not come from his in-laws (although the third parcel, the one to the east, had been his wife's dowry). Perhaps the money came from the sales of Mrs. Scott's novel. At any rate, the Judge went into the housing business, providing land and capital to erect three large "editions." He invested the profits outside the County. By 1955 he owned nothing but common shares of GM, Ford, and AT&T, and preferred shares in two little-known companies, Sperry Gyroscope and Xerox.

But the population boom that had made him rich had eroded his base of power; the newcomers owed their allegiance to new industries—trucking companies, a shoe factory, a metalworking plant. Now it was the old power structure that bided its time, forging an alliance with the new industrial middle class just as the Judge had once forged his with an agrarian one. They waited for the Judge's inevitable decline, waited to drag him down and chew him up and spit him out and nail what was left of his hide to the barn door. But they had underestimated him. After delivering a record number of votes to the gubernatorial campaign of David Lawrence, votes that no Democrat had any right to expect from that county, the Judge went to work and parlayed the rest of his power into state jobs for his most loyal supporters and a seat on the State Superior Court for himself, thereby achieving immunity to the local vicissitudes.

Once on the bench, he had shown himself to be more than just another country lawyer. His decisions were rarely questioned, and never overturned on points of law. His opinions were cogently expressed, written in the kind of language that had once distinguished the writing of law as a genre of literature. He had more than once been mentioned for a seat on the Supreme Court. But he had had no love for Richard Nixon, had given what support he could to Nelson Rockefeller. By the time that could be rewarded, it was too late for him. Still, even without the final achievement, the Judge's career was something people write books about, certainly something that was repeated, time and time again, in Sunday schools and in elementary school rooms, albeit in a slightly edited version.

The man I saw before me seemed likewise an edited version. He had always been a thin man, but one of solid, imposing physical presence. Now he was an old man. Frail. Slight. With watery blue eyes and limp hair so white it was nearly blue, and liver-spotted skin drawn tight over thin bones. He wore a venerable three-piece suit of black wool gone shiny and a little green, a white shirt with a narrow collar, a faintly clocked four-in-hand. The only things about him that could have been called a hint of color were those watery eyes and the gleaming gold of the watch chain that drooped over his nonexistent belly, supporting an old half hunter and the Phi Beta Kappa key.

He saw me and rose; Scott moved to help him. But the Judge was not as frail as he looked—at any rate, he was too agile and quick for Scott, and was around the desk and holding my hand in a firm grip and my eyes with clear gaze before Scott could clamp the protective and restraining hand on his elbow. "Dad," Scott said, "this is Dr.—"

"I know who he is, Randall," the Judge snapped, without taking his eyes from mine. He looked at me hard, pumped my hand hard, released it, and stepped away. The effort made him puff a little, and his breath came to me, carrying the sweet smell of bourbon. "It's a pleasure to meet you, sir," he said. "Will you sit?"

"Dad, John and I—"

"Will you sit, sir?" the Judge repeated.

"Thank you," I said.

The Judge indicated one of two high-backed leather chairs that sat before the desk, then returned to his own chair, with Scott, a hand still clutching his elbow, trying to keep up. The Judge paid no attention until Scott caught his thigh on the corner of the desk and gasped in pain. "Be careful, Randall," the Judge said mildly. Scott let go of the elbow and went to a chair in a corner, hobbling slightly.

The Judge looked at me, not saying anything for a few moments, letting his eyes rove over me. "You bear a great resemblance to your father," he said. "Did you know that?"

"No," I said.

"Well, you do. Consider that a judicial opinion." He smiled slightly, but he did not really mean the joke—his eyes did not smile. "When he was young, of course; maybe thirty. And you're about that . . ."

"I'm thirty-one," I said.

"Yes. And your brother . . ."

"My brother would have been twenty-nine."

"If he hadn't been killed," the Judge said.

I didn't say anything.

"A sad thing."

"A wonderful thing," I said. "Greater love hath no man than he lay down his life for his friends. He was privileged not only to save his comrades, but to die in the service of his country, and in the cause of freedom."

"That's absolutely right," Scott said.

"Don't be an ass, Randall," the Judge said. "He was quoting the speech you made at the boy's funeral." He looked at me. "You don't feel that way at all, do you?"

"No," I said.

He smiled slightly. "I thought not. You're a historian, they tell me." He looked at me, but I gave him no confirmation. "I've delved into history," he said. "I never studied it, but I delved into it. Enough to know that it was not a subject that appealed to me. There were too many differences of opinion, too many gaps, too many hidden motivations, too many coincidences. And no rules. I found it frustrating. Don't you?"

"At times," I said.

"But you keep on."

"Yes."

"Searching for truth?"

"Trying to find out where the lies are."

The judge smiled, for real this time. "A worthy ambition," he said. "I imagine you've found this region a treasure trove of material. The history of this County alone . . ."

"I don't do regional history," I said.

He looked at me sharply.

"I specialize in the study of atrocities."

"I don't quite understand."

"History is just one long string of atrocities," I said. "You could say history is atrocious. The best way to find out what they did is to find out where they hid the bodies."

He didn't say anything.

"The best part," I said, "is that I don't have to worry about finding material. Bodies are always turning up."

186

The Judge sighed heavily. "Yes," he said. "I suppose they are." He paused. "Well, it's not like that in this County. We mark our graves with great care. It's the skeletons we try to hide."

"Dad . . ." Scott said.

"What? Yes, of course. Randall, I know you're busy. If you need to get back to something, you just go ahead."

"Thanks, Dad. John and I were discussing paying for John Crawley's funeral; there are a few more arrangement to be made."

"Well, fine, Randall. John . . . May I call you John?"

"Yes," I said.

"Fine. You'll want us to spare no ex—"

"*Dad*, we've already straightened all of this out."

"Then go take care of it, Randall. You can make the arrangements. That's what you're paid for. But there's more to it, and it's past time we attended to it."

"Dad . . ." Scott stood up and looked at me uneasily, while he shifted nervously from foot to foot, looking for all the world like a little boy who has to go to the bathroom but is embarrassed to say so. "Dad . . . I think we'd better talk about this."

"We shall, Randall," the Judge said. He reached out with one liver-spotted hand and picked up his phone. "Mrs. Washington? Yes. Would you step in here, please?" He put the phone down, looked up at Scott. "What *is* it, Randall?"

Scott looked at me, closed his eyes, and sat down again. "Nothing," he said.

We waited a moment in silence, Scott seeming to shrink into himself, the Judge looking stern, while I tried desperately to figure out what was happening. In a moment the door opened and my mother came in, moving briskly and efficiently. She held a steno book in one hand and three perfectly sharpened pencils in the other. She came quickly across the room, slipped gracefully onto a straight-backed chair at the corner of the Judge's desk, crossed her legs, opened her book, and waited. Her eyes were on the Judge; she did not even glance at Scott. And she had not seen me.

"It's time we made the final disposition of your husband's will," the Judge said.

I could not see her face, but I saw her back stiffen, saw her head turn ever so slightly as she gave Scott a quick glance.

"Dad—" Scott began again.

The Judge raised his hand. "I know, Randall, I know; under the terms of the will the trusteeship can be passed on. But I'm the executor. And I don't know how long I'm going to last. And . . . circumstances have affected a good many of the provisions. The younger son is dead. Jack Crawley is dead. And John"—he nodded at me—"is here."

She turned then, and saw me. The expression on her face shocked me. I had never seen my mother look guilty or ashamed or afraid. And now she looked all three at once. "John," she said.

"Good afternoon," I said. It sounded stupid. But it was all I could think of to say. Things were beyond anything that I understood. Scott was desperately uneasy and my mother was guilty and ashamed and the Judge seemed . . . unerring.

"We are all here now, at last," the Judge said. His voice was low, clear but somehow rhythmic, almost as if he were reading some ritualized form from a judicial bench. I looked at him. His eyes were clear and bright. He, at least, seemed at ease, seemed to know what was happening.

"In the last Will of Moses Washington, deceased, the power was given to the executor of the estate to relinquish his control of all trusts and settle them on the parties designated in the document in the manner therein prescribed. The executor, who is I, was charged with following a particular form in exercising that option. One condition of that form was that all parties concerned be either present or deceased. A second condition was that those present be under no duress. If either of you wishes to leave, you may do so." He paused, looked at me, then at my mother.

"I want to leave," Scott said. "This is wrong, the time isn't—"

"Be quiet, Randall," the Judge said. "You are not a principal." He looked at the two of us once again. "I take it you choose to remain."

"Yvette," Scott said.

The Judge glanced at him, then looked at my mother. "Mrs. Washington," he said, "will you stay?"

"What the hell is going on here?" I said.

"Will you stay, Mrs. Washington?" the Judge said.

Her head was down. "Yes," she said, mumbling. Then she brought her head up. "Yes." Clear this time. Almost harsh. She looked at Scott. "Yes." She twisted in her chair and looked at me. "I'm sorry, Johnny," she said. And then she turned back and opened her steno book. She raised a pencil and began to move it across the page in staccato jerks, taking dictation although not a word was being said. Eventually she stopped, looked at the Judge expectantly.

"You have all that, Mrs. Washington?" the Judge said.

"Yes," she said.

"Excellent," the Judge said. He cleared his throat. "The conditions of the form having been met, we may proceed with the reading of the Will." He paused. "Off the record, please, Mrs. Washington. John, I think you should understand that wills are not usually 'read.' That's the stuff of murder mysteries. But your father specified that his be read in the hearing of all heirs and principals at such time as the trusts were to be ended. Now, I have it in my mind that he didn't know what he was letting you in for—letting everybody in for. Your father was the kind of man who said what he wanted done and expected it to be done, but he didn't understand the complexities of the law. He didn't hold with complexities. He was a Gordian knot man. I suspect he'd approve of what I'm going to suggest: you can have a copy of the Will and the trust instruments and read them when you want, and if you have any questions, I'll be glad to answer them, and for now I'll just give you the outline in laymen's prose. But if you insist, I'll read the damned thing." He looked at me.

"What does the Will say?"

"That it's to be read."

There was no question in my mind that it should be done the way Moses Washington had wanted it done. But suddenly I was tired of him; tired of the man who never erred, whose foresight was right up there with that of God, Jeane Dixon, and Jimmy the Greek.

"Summarize it," I said.

The Judge nodded. "In theory," he said, "the matter is not complicated. About a month before his death Moses Washington came to me and asked me to set up several trusts. When he died, they were to be administered according to the instructions he left in his Will." He paused for a moment, and I listened to the sounds of his breathing and the faint scratching as my mother's hand moved across the steno pad. When the scratching stopped, the Judge continued. "There were four individual trusts, each supported by an endowment, and a simple fund, which is to be used to pay for funerals for Yvette Stanton Washington, William Washington, Peter John Crawley, and Joshua White. That fund will, of course, continue until your mother's death."

He paused. "It always seemed odd to me that there was no provision made for your funeral, John. In fact, there is no mention in the document of the possibility of your death. . . . Well. Do you understand about the endowments?"

"No," I said. I did, of course. But I needed time, because there was something else I didn't understand: why I hadn't known anything about any of this.

"Well, let me go on a bit, and perhaps it will make sense. The first endowment, in the amount of fifty thousand dollars, was to be held in trust for William Washington, until he reached the age of twenty-one, at which time it was to become his. Until that time, the interest, and if necessary the principal, was to be used to pay any taxes and assessments made against the real property that was also left to William Washington, if those expenses were not offset by rental income.

"The provision was made that, should William Washington die before reaching twenty-one, both the endowment and the real property were to become yours, subject to other provisions I'll get to in a moment." He paused. "This is hard to explain. . . ."

"I'm with you," I said.

"Fine," he said. "The second endowment was set up in a slightly different way. The amount was the same, fifty thousand dollars, and it was to be held in trust for you, until you reached age eighteen. The difference was that before you could take possession of it, and of the real property associated with it, you had to agree also to accept certain other items. Which I'll get to." He looked at me.

"Get on with it," I said.

"Yes," he said. "The third endowment was quite different. It was for one hundred thousand dollars, and it was to be used to pay taxes and assessments, insurance, and upkeep on a house on three lots on Vondersmith Avenue, which is, of course, the house your mother currently occupies. I might as well digress here and tell you that that is the only real participation your mother had in the will. Her income was provided for through insurance policies, which your father evidently purchased at the time of their marriage. According to the Will she was to have the use of the house, expense free, until either her death or remarriage, at which time the liquid funds were to be merged with the endowment held for you, and the real property was

190

to be merged with that held in trust for your brother. Essentially, if she remarried, she could have continued to live in the house so long as William was under twenty-one, or agreed to allow her to do so. Now, that brings us to the real property. . . ."

"Wait," I said. My voice surprised me. I had expected it to be excited, or outraged, or incredulous. Instead it was calm, almost flat. As if it were doing nothing more than discussing the shopping list with Judith, deciding whether to buy asparagus or broccoli. "Wait," I said again. "You're telling me that . . . Moses Washington owned the Hill."

"That's right," the Judge said. "I happen to know he bought it in 1946. He had held an option on it for some years. He could have sold that option for a lot of money. He took the land." He looked at me quizzically. "How did you know . . ."

"That's the way he would set it up. She gets the house as long as she needs it, and then the whole Hill becomes a single parcel . . ."

"Well," he said, "not the whole Hill . . ."

"No," I said. "No, of course not. He'd split it in two. He'd leave Bill this side. And me the far side."

He was staring at me.

"That's right, isn't it?"

"Yes," the Judge said. "Essentially. Although your real property includes several other small parcels of land scattered around the County. I'm not sure what they were. I imagine they had something to do with his . . . business."

"Great," I said. "He made Bill the biggest slumlord this side of Pittsburgh, and he turned me into a moonshiner."

Nobody said anything then; we sat there and listened to the sounds my mother made, taking shorthand.

"Does she *have* to do that?" I said.

"It's one of the provisions of the Will," he said. "All right, Mrs. Washington?"

"Yes," she said. Her voice was strained. I realized that she had known about the Will—nobody had had to tell her to take it all down.

"That's pretty much all of it, in terms of property. There were strictures and provisions, most of which do not apply any longer. You were not to be permitted to make any alteration in the property on the Hill, for example, until both Joshua White and John Crawley were deceased. But one proviso does apply: you were not to take possession of your portion of the estate until such time as you came to call for it."

He paused again. My mother's hand went scratch-scratching across the paper. I could hear that, and his breathing, which was slightly ragged, and Scott's breathing, which seemed even more ragged. And I could hear my own. "You understand, John, that I do not have the power to end the trust. You still have to call for the property, of your own initiative."

"I understand," I said.

He waited again, while my mother caught up, and I listened to the breathing again. But it was different now: the Judge's breathing seemed easier, calmer than it had been; now it was Scott's breath that came harshly, Scott who breathed with his mouth slightly open. I twisted slightly in order to look at him; his face was composed, and he sat with his legs crossed in a pose of seeming calm. But I knew by his breathing, and by the desperate light in his eyes.

"Those trusts and their endowments comprise the major financial portions of the estate," the Judge said. "It is, of course, yours now. One fund has become rather depleted, since the Hill no longer brings in the income it once did, but the financial portion of the estate is intact. . . ."

He paused again, waiting. We all listened to my mother's pencil on the paper. When she stopped, the Judge took a deep breath. "The financial portion," he repeated, "is intact, and it is yours whenever you choose to call for it. However, there is another proviso: when you do so you must also take possession of the nonfinancial portions of the estate." He stopped, looked at me expectantly.

Suddenly the room was quiet. My mother had stopped taking down the Judge's words, and the scratching sound of pencil on paper had cut off abruptly. And everyone in that room except me was holding his breath.

"What happens," I said, "if I never call for the property?" As soon as I said the words, the silence was gone; they were all breathing again, not easily and deeply, but breathing.

"If you don't call, the trusts continue."

"Perpetually?" I said.

The Judge hesitated. "I'm not sure. I think your father was certain you would call. But if you do not, I suspect the courts would simply direct that the trusts be continued, and that suitable disposition be made of the . . . other materials. But that would not happen until you were deceased; until then, you might call at any time."

"I see," I said. "And you would continue as executor?"

"I or the firm."

"Randall," I said.

"Yes, Randall."

"Humph," I said. "So my choice is to either become a slumlord or let good old Randall bide his time until you die and then start squeezing the last drop of blood out of a bunch of lame old ladies and half-blind old men."

"John," Scott said, "I know you don't trust me, but I wouldn't do that."

"You *can't* do that," the Judge said. "The Will's instructions are quite specific and the restrictions on the trustee are clear. For one thing, the rents are pegged at the level they occupied when your father died, so long as the same tenants are in occupation."

"Glad to know you're so restrained, Randall," I said. "Not to mention magnanimous."

Scott didn't say anything; he looked slightly murderous, but he didn't say anything.

"Do you have any further questions, John?" the Judge said.

I had a few. I wanted to know what those other parcels of land were. I wanted to know what those "nonfinancial portions" of Moses Washington's estate were. I wanted to know how I was supposed to come calling for anything without knowing there was anything to call for. But I knew better than to ask any of those questions; any historian who was worth his footnotes would know that. For any complex issue is surrounded by a maze of questions, most of them obvious, most of them meaningless, and all of them false. A bad historian picks the wrong ones and spends his time researching the useless. A mediocre historian tries to answer them all and spends his time doing background for conclusions that, when stated, will seem hopelessly obvious. A good historian looks at the issue and does . . . nothing. He sits and thinks and tries to find the few questions that are significant and central, hoping that one is so much a cornerstone that answering it will answer all the rest. And so I sat and waited, listening to them not breathing. I didn't know. I just didn't know. So I asked the unobvious, and hoped.

"Yeah," I said. I tried to sound casual. "All I want to know is, why does Randall want my permission to pay for Old Jack's funeral?" I heard a catch in Scott's breathing.

"What?" the Judge said. He looked a little annoyed, as if I were taking up his time with the trivial.

"I said, 'Why does Randall want my permission to pay for Old Jack's funeral?'"

"Well, I don't know," the Judge said, "but I presume that, even though you do not have control over the decision until you call for the property, Randall wanted to make sure you would not protest the expenditure as excessive at a later date. A prudent course . . ."

"You don't understand," I said. "Randall didn't want me to approve anything. He didn't want me to concur with anything. He wanted me to agree to let *him* pay. Personally."

"Ah, John," Scott said quickly, "I think you misunderstood me."

"Like hell," I said.

There was a long silence; the room was even quieter than it had been before, for no one was breathing, not even me. And then I suddenly realized that I had asked precisely the right question; it was so perfect that it answered itself. "Never mind," I said. "I know why. Because as trustee he would have to pay anyway, but if he had my permission it would never occur to me to go toddling down to the undertaker to find out who had picked up the tab, and then come toddling up here asking questions, and there won't be any kind of accounting, and nobody will ever figure out the nifty little shenanigans good old Randall has been up to with the trust funds. Tell me, Randall, how much did you steal?"

It was wrong. I knew that as I said it. I had extrapolated too far with no data.

"The financial portion of this estate is absolutely intact," the Judge snapped. "I told you that. And I'll thank you to refrain from making loose accusations."

"I'm sorry," I said. "I went too far. I skipped a step or two. Because the first thing that would happen if I came up here asking questions is that I'd find out about the Will, and then maybe I'd want to take the property out from under good old Randall's thumb—"

"What do you mean, find out about?" the Judge said. I hadn't been paying much attention to him; I had been caught up in the existential beauty of my own half-witted decipherings. But there was something in his voice that made me focus in on him now, made me realize that I had done it all wrong. Again.

"You thought I knew," I said.

"You didn't," he said.

We sat there for a long moment, looking at each other. "No," I said. "No, I didn't know anything. I don't know anything. I don't know what's going on here. . . ." I realized that my voice was climbing in both pitch and volume; I couldn't do anything about that. But at least I knew the next question. "Who," I said, "does the will say is responsible for informing the heirs of their inheritance?"

I didn't really need to ask. Because suddenly I knew why I had known nothing of this, and why the matches had been placed that way: they were waiting for my hand. Because Moses Washington had known that one day I would go climbing up into that attic, had believed I would follow the clues he had left there, and find my way to this place. He had been half right: I had tried. And failed. All I needed was confirmation.

"No one," he said. "It was not a part of the Will. Your father said he would make the charge personally."

I closed my eyes then, and folded my hands over my belly, trying to find some comfort in the darkness, and perhaps a little warmth. But then I heard the Judge saying: "To your mother."

I refused to look at any of them—especially at her.

"John," she said finally.

"Shut up," I said. "You don't want to talk when you're supposed to, you just shut up now, and let me think." Which was nonsense; I couldn't think. All I could do was shiver in the silence.

"I did what I thought best," she said. I looked at her, expecting her to drop her gaze. But she did not.

"I'm sure," I said.

"No," she said. "You aren't. You aren't sure at all. And that hurts you, doesn't it? See, I know you, John. You want to figure everything out. You go crazy when you can't. That's the way you were when you were a baby in your crib. I'd make you a toy and you'd take it and just sit there and look at it for a long time, you wouldn't even touch it, and then you'd pick it up and poke it and squeeze it and then you'd go to work and tear the stuffing out of it. And when you'd torn the thing to pieces you'd sit there and giggle. Your father used to love that. He'd give you things to tear apart, just to watch you go at

195

it. After a while he started giving you things that were harder and harder to tear apart. He'd bring them in and give them to you and wait and see how long it took you. And one day he finally got one that was too hard. I don't recall what it was made out of—canvas, I think. Maybe burlap. But he made it, and he gave it to you, and he sat there all day watching you while you tried to tear that thing apart. You'd beat it and you'd bang it until you were tired, and then you'd go to sleep, and then you'd wake up and you'd beat it and bang it some more. He sat there and watched you do it. And when it finally dawned on you that you weren't going to be able to tear the stuffing out of it, he sat there and laughed while you cried. . . . It almost made me wild, the sound the two of you made, him laughing and you crying. I couldn't stand it. I can't stand the thought of it now. And I couldn't stand the thought of it when he told me he wanted to give you another toy. Because you see, John, he left you a good one. I don't know what it was, but I know he spent all his time tearing it apart, just like you, and he never did. But I bet he went to Hell with a smile on his face knowing he was going to sit there by a warm fire and watch you beating yourself to death on it. But I didn't let it happen. I didn't tell you it was there." She stood up, smoothed her skirt. "Tell him," she said to the Judge. "Tell him it's all his now. Tell him he can have those damned books, tell him he can spend the rest of his life up there, going crazy just like his father." She folded her steno book with a snap, and headed for the door.

I watched her go, thinking how funny it would have seemed to anybody who knew: me slipping out of bed and going up there on tiptoe, and she walking around carrying a secret that wasn't a secret anymore. But then I realized that there had to be more to it, more than the books. The books explained her. But they didn't explain Scott.

"Mrs. Washington," the Judge said. His voice was soft, but it stopped her in her tracks. She stood there for a moment, perfectly still, then she turned and looked at him over her shoulder, a wary animal peeking from cover. "Come back and sit down, Mrs. Washington," the Judge said.

"Why?"

"Because I cannot continue unless all the principals are present. Those are the dictates of your husband's Will."

"My husband's Will be damned," she said. She turned her head back and walked towards the door.

But I got up then, got up and went and stood in front of her. "Sit," I said.

She didn't move for a minute, but then she turned and slowly went back to her chair.

"Thank you, Mrs. Washington," the Judge said mildly.

She nodded and opened the steno book again.

"John," the Judge said. "The next provision of the Will is, as your mother indicated, a bequest of books. The materials, described as 'books and records,' were to be kept in the premises described in the second trust, in the care and keeping of Yvette Stanton Washington until such time as you should call for them. Then you were to have the option of leaving them where they were or transporting them to another site. The only restriction is that you are not permitted to sell, bequeath, or otherwise divest yourself of their ownership until you have examined all volumes, including personal memoirs."

I wanted to laugh; I wanted to die laughing. "I understand," I said.

"Good," the Judge said. He paused, looked at Scott, turned back to me. "The final item is a parcel described only as 'miscellaneous documents of no financial value but great personal import.' These documents were to be held by the executor—myself—personally, until such time as you should choose to call for them." He stopped then, looked at Scott again. "I have to, Randall," he said. And then he opened a drawer of that old wooden desk and brought up the folio. He dropped it on the desk; he didn't lay it down, he dropped it, as if he were happy to get it out of his hands. It was then that my mother moved, jumping out of her chair and backing away and sagging into the one beside me. "Your legacy, John," he said. "Your legacy. If you acknowledge that you have come to call for it."

I heard my mother then; she was crying. The Judge reached into the inner pocket of his suit and brought out a handkerchief and, with a grunting effort, extended it across the desk. She did not see it. He looked at me expectantly. I did not move. The handkerchief, soft and white, hung there in the space between us. Our eyes met. The Judge held my gaze for only an instant, and then he looked away, put the

handkerchief down, and let it lie on the scarred wood, next to the folio. We both looked at it for a long while. Finally she fumbled in her
skirt pocket and pulled up one of her own. The Judge reached out
and touched his, toyed with it. Then he looked at me. "I was right to
fear you," he said.

I looked at him, and the surprise must have shown on my face.

"Oh, yes," he said. "That's the right word. Fear. I feared you
from the day he came in here with that damned gunnysack of his,
asking me to do him a . . . favor." He paused, smiled ruefully. "When
you see what's in that"—he nodded at the folio—"I expect you will
learn that I was one of your father's oldest and best customers. It was
a natural liaison: I have a taste for good whiskey; he made the best
there was. But there was more to it than that. Moses was . . . confi-
dential. When he supplied your private stock it stayed private; nobody even knew you had it. You could be a public teetotaler and a
private drunk; nobody knew but you and Moses and God Almighty.
That was part of what he charged for. 'The ability to maintain public
illusion and private delusion.' That's what he called it. That's what
he sold. And that's what I bought; what a lot of others bought too.
And found out that it was a mighty dear commodity. Because, you
see, Moses Washington thought like a white man, when it suited him.
That's the way he put it to me once. I remember the occasion. I had
tried to defend a colored man who had shot his wife and her lover. He
probably would have gotten away with it, but he shot them when they
weren't within three miles of each other. He got a gun and a horse
and went off and shot him, and then he came back and told her he'd
done it, and he waited until she had stopped crying and then he shot
her too. Then he rode to the sheriff and turned himself in. I tried to
help him, but I never understood why he didn't just divorce the woman, or abandon her, or wait until the two of them were together, anyway, and shoot them in the act. There wasn't a jury in the state would
have convicted him; they were all three colored. I asked Moses what
was wrong with that man, why he didn't think a little bit. And Moses
told me I didn't understand; that I couldn't understand, because I
was white, and thought like white people think. He said a white man
will scheme and plot and make plans, and expects his plans to work
out, and if they don't he'll say it was God's will. But a colored man, he
said, believes that this isn't the kind of world in which a colored
man's plans have any kind of chance of working, and so he just *does,*

and if it works out, then it's God's will, and if not, at least he's saved himself all that planning.

"But Moses had things both ways. He'd plan. We'd have a conversation, and halfway through, it would come to me that Moses had thought it all out ahead of time. We'd argue . . . there was no way to beat him in an argument. He'd start from a premise and it would be like an avalanche; once he was started there was no way to get out from under. But there was something else about it. Because the places he started from didn't make any sense at all. And so you'd sit there and listen to what he was saying and he'd make sense every step of the way and you'd have to believe it if you believed in logic, because it was logical, but the end was crazy, because it started out crazy. That's how he was with the things he'd plan. He was so logical and so cold about anything that anybody who knew how to think and who wasn't particularly troubled by having a conscience could follow along every step of the way, assuming you knew what he wanted to do. That was the problem. Because even though his plans made sense, the reasons for them didn't. You'd look back and see exactly what he did, no trouble with that, but you could never figure out why he did it in the first place. . . ." He shook his head.

"What he did with the whiskey was like that. He did what every white businessman would do with his business: he kept records. And yet there wasn't a white man who expected him to. Because it didn't make any sense to treat the bootleg whiskey business just like it was a dry goods business. But he did. And you should have heard them howl when they first found out about it. He had us all by then, back in the days when it was a dry county, and there wasn't a one of us could have stood up to the scandal. We had a sheriff then, an old fat fool they said was part of the Klan. Well, Moses paid him, just like he was supposed to, but that idiot decided to stage a raid and get some glory to go along with his money. I suspect he thought that nobody was going to take the word of a colored moonshiner against that of a duly elected sheriff, if Moses did talk about the bribe. Well, Moses got away, although he lost the whiskey he was hauling. But he let it be known in a day or two that one more little episode like that and there was going to be a whole lot of . . . discomfort. And so we all got together and let it be known that nobody was to interfere with him. And the funny thing was, he kept on paying bribes. I think what it was, he liked to own people personally, not secondhand. Or maybe he just liked to bribe. And I'll tell you another funny thing about him: he never blackmailed anybody. All he would do was to do what any good and respected citizen is supposed to be able to do in this fine democratic republic of ours: express his opinions. He would write letters to the people that made policy, or go see them in the dead of night. He knew who held the power around here as well as anybody, but he never came to anybody that wasn't duly elected. Oh, the word got back, and there was never much of a question that his . . . preferences would be strongly considered. But he never did a thing out of line. He used his power, but not like a whip. More like a leash. He kept people in check. He was fond of delaying things.

"He never came to me directly. I didn't have any legal authority. I was just a country lawyer with lots of friends. Until the day he came in asking for his favor. And God knows I was vulnerable then. I wanted to be judge. Judge of the Superior Court of the Commonwealth of Pennsylvania. Wanted that so bad I used to go in the washroom and lock the door and look in the mirror and say it over a few times. I liked the sound of it." He paused again, and shook his head. "So there I was, the weakest man in the world—a certifiable hypocrite with high-toned ambition—and Moses Washington came to the door. I told them to show him in. He came in, carrying that old gunnysack of his. I told him to sit, and he sat. 'Lucian,' he said, but I cut him off. I said to him, 'Moses,' I said, 'now, we've known each other for a long time. We both know you can ruin me. And we both know there's not a damned thing I can do to stop you. But the one thing that neither of us knows is just exactly how much I want to win that election. But I'll tell you this: I don't propose to be threatened, not by you or anybody. You tell me what you want, and I'll say yea or nay, and then you do what you will.' That's what I said. I thought at the time it was a pretty good little speech; I still think it was. But you know what he did? He laughed at me. Said he had been meaning to vote my way, but now he wasn't sure, seeing as I had such a guilty conscience that I was ready to start running before the hounds even got wind. And then he said all he wanted was for me to draw up his Will."

He stopped, looked at me. "I am rambling, John," he said. "I am not senile; I know what I'm doing. I am rambling. Do you mind an old man's rambling?"

"No," I said.

He took a deep breath, and leaned back in his chair. "We drank

200

together," he said. "Not often. Perhaps three dozen times over the years, he came and knocked at my door and we'd go into the study and pull the shades and drink together. He always came to the front door. He always came after dark, but that doesn't make any difference in this town—somebody always sees everything. I was nervous at first, knowing people were seeing him, but I often wonder if he didn't reason that out. I wonder how much of the success I had, especially in those early years, was due to the fact that people had seen him come and go and, since they didn't think I drank whiskey, wondered what kind of . . . secrets we might be sharing. But we shared no secrets. Moses never shared secrets. We just shared whiskey.

"And we talked. We talked history. We talked law. We talked land. Moses Washington knew more about the land in this County than any man alive. And he knew more about economics. I sometimes thought he could see into the future. He made no money that I know of, but he could have—I did, following what he said. We drank all night sometimes, back in the thirties.

"And we drank when he came for his 'favor.' But not until late at night. Moses' Will was a complicated thing. We worked at it all day. We got it all drafted by about sundown. He sat there while I typed it; he didn't want anybody else seeing the provisions, and I wasn't sure I did, either. We finished the last copy about midnight, and he signed them all, and I witnessed the signature. He gave me a whole stack of checks—cashier's checks, drawn on out-of-town banks, mostly Philadelphia banks, but one or two in Pittsburgh and one in New Orleans—to set up the endowments with, and he gave me the deeds to the land. Then he reached down into that gunnysack and brought up a jug, and we drank, and then I thought we were finished. But then he reached down again and brought up"—he nodded at the folio—"that.

"Of course, I knew what he kept in there. Everybody knew that. I expect they still tell the story about the time somebody tried to take it from him, down Clearville way. It was down in old man Minnich's store, and the gentleman who tried it was drunk on whiskey, probably Moses', and he reached over and opened up Moses' sack and took the folio out. Moses watched him do it. Then he said, 'Put that back,' That was all. The man stopped and thought about it, and then he put it back. Nobody said anything. Moses said, 'You know, you're lucky. The last man who touched something of mine died. I was going to kill him. First I was going to gut-shoot him, and then I was going to tie him up to a tree and dress him out like a deer, at least until the screaming got real bad. Then I was going to roast him over a slow fire.' And, as the story goes, that gentleman jumped up and ran out of Minnich's and headed down the road towards Chapmans Run, going about as fast as a man can on foot. Moses didn't move. He just sipped his whiskey. Then he said, 'Of course, I never got to do all that; he ran himself into collapse before I could catch him.' Well, they had a good laugh out of it. Until later that day when they brought that man in, draped over somebody's plow horse, dead from a heart attack." He stopped again. "I'm sorry, John," he said. "That was digression. Or perhaps not. Because I thought I was going to have a heart attack when Moses brought the folio out. Because I not only knew what it was, I realized that it was part of the Will: 'miscellaneous documents of no financial value but great personal import.' It was dirt, pure and simple. Otherwise known as power, enough of it to hold on to this County for another twenty years. It was slipping from me then, but I could have held it. All I needed was what was in that folio. And he wanted me to keep it, and he expected me not to use it."

He looked down at the folio, put his hand on it, stroked it. "And I didn't use it. Never." He raised his eyes and met mine. "You can see that the seal is unbroken, John. I didn't use it. I was tempted enough times. But mostly I wanted to destroy it. Because I feared you." He smiled at me, a little sadly.

"That's the word. Feared. If terrified isn't a better one. I don't imagine there's too much power in here anymore, in terms of politics. But there's a lot of pain in here. A lot of people could be hurt. Maybe they should be; there's truth in here, and there's a hell of a lot of hypocrites out there. And I rather imagined you would . . . enjoy exposing them. That's why I wondered why you didn't come. I thought surely he must have had your mother tell you that there was something powerful waiting for you, even if he didn't say precisely what, even to her. I watched carefully, expecting you to come. I know some of the things that went on when you were young. How you must have felt about them. When the cities burned, I thought to myself, thank God he doesn't have this; if he did, it would be just like that here—burning, looting. Oh, you couldn't have seen it, there wouldn't have been real fires—but it would have been the same. But you were too young—even if you had come, I would not have had to give it to you then. I was glad for that. But when you turned eighteen I expected you to come charging in here, ready to . . . to make us pay. I sat here until midnight the day before you turned eighteen, thinking about that. I almost burned it. I don't know why I didn't. And then I sat here until midnight the next day, waiting.

"But you never came. And I couldn't imagine why. It seemed to me I would have, if I had been you. But when you didn't come, I thought, well, maybe he isn't interested in all that old mess. Maybe he wants to put all that behind him. And when you won your scholarship and went away, I thought that was the end of it. But then your brother's name came up. I knew you would come then. But I didn't worry then, you see, because I knew that when you came you would want something tangible. There would be a basis for negotiation. I was afraid of righteous destruction, you see, but I knew we could survive a little blackmail. This County has been run by blackmail for years. But you didn't come then, and I started to worry again. When your brother ran away, I didn't know what to think. When he came back . . . I made sure he wouldn't go to jail. I knew if we did that to him you would surely come down upon us. But keeping him out of jail was the best I could do. I prayed that when you came I could make you understand that. And when you didn't come, I thought perhaps you did understand. . . . And then he . . . died. I *knew* you'd come then, full of . . . wrath. Fury. God, I feared that. But I sat here. The day of his funeral I sat and waited until the bus would have left, and then I called the Alliquippa to see if you had gone. They said you had. And then I felt safe. For the first time in ten years I felt safe. I knew you hated us, but I thought perhaps you hated us so much you were going to leave us alone to burn in our own hell. That you couldn't be bothered banking fires. I felt safe. I've felt safe for almost ten more years, thinking you didn't come because you didn't want to."

"I didn't come because I didn't know," I said.

"Yes," he said. He sighed. "You were to be told on your eighteenth birthday. Your mother was to tell you. I assumed it had been done. But I was the executor. I should have made sure."

"Why didn't you?" I said.

He shook his head. "There was no reason to suppose you had not been told. "This"—he nodded at the folio—"was not to be given to you until you walked in here and called for it, of your own free will. There was no way for me to . . ." His voice trailed off. He looked at me for a moment, then dropped his eyes. "No," he said. "No, that wasn't it at all. I hoped that she hadn't told you. Because I did not want you to have it." He raised his eyes and met mine. "Have you come to call for your legacy, John?" he said.

"Yes," I said.

"John . . ." Scott said.

"Be quiet, Randall," the Judge had said. "Go arrange a funeral."

Things look different in lamplight. That is a small fact, the kind of datum that escapes the notice of the average historian. He notes the sweeping changes in the American way of life that began when Thomas Alva Edison managed to make first bamboo, then tungsten, glow; probably describing the whole thing in terms of economics, or perhaps, if he is slightly above average, in terms of religion. But he misses the obvious—and therefore the significant—simply because he has never himself had to try and puzzle out the meaning of a text by the light of burning kerosene. And so he talks of longer man-hours or perhaps even an increased rate of information dissemination through reading, or perhaps even the effect of electric light on a religious matrix that had always revered fire and the sun. But he would forget the simple fact that things look different under lamplight. Edges are softer. The beginnings and ending of things seem to merge. Lines of print or handwriting on a sheet of paper are not stark black on white, but brown on gold. And the light flickers, so that anything seen is seen not only dimly, but elusively; inconstantly. And it is possible—for almost anything is possible, and the difference between logical cause and effect and magic is only a matter of which premises are chosen—that thoughts are different, too, in the soft light of a lamp. Not better, or nobler; just different. And one wonders—if one is a wonderer—if somewhere along the line things would not have been different if the electric light had come along earlier, or not come along at all. Could Franklin have written his "Essay on Populations" if he had had the unerring glow of incandescence showing up his bigotry? Could Lincoln have proclaimed Emancipation with the same glow highlighting his hypocrisy? Was the only difference between *Plessy* v. *Ferguson* and *Brown* v. *the Board of Education of Topeka, Kansas* the fact that the former was written by lamplight and the latter under—probably—a fluorescent tube? Could the Kennedys have changed from Commie-hunters to liberals in the age of whale oil? Could King have penned that hopelessly naive letter from the Albany jail with a flickering candle forcing him to stop and think while the words steadied before his eyes? Could I puzzle out truth better with a trouble light above my head, or perhaps even a flashlight? I wondered about this, and I answered myself as I had always answered myself when I wondered about it: things belong to their own time, their own place. Moses Washington had chosen not to wire his attic simply because there was no place for electricity. He had sealed his folio with candle wax; he had most likely written whatever was inside by the light of a lamp, or a lantern, or perhaps a glowing campfire. And I would open it by a similar glow.

The attic was warmer now—warm enough to allow me to move my hands, pausing only occasionally to hold them above the lamp chimney. And so I put my hands on the folio, feeling the leather cool and smooth and worn beneath my hands. I slid my fingers along the flap, watching as the wax seal crumbled, bit by bit by bit.

197903071030

(Wednesday)

IN THE YEAR OF OUR LORD 1441, a Portuguese sailing captain named
Antam Gonçalvez permitted a certain light-skinned Moorish gentleman, who was then enjoying the captain's hospitality, to ransom himself and two young male companions at the expense of ten dark-
skinned gentlemen and gentlewomen from the sub-Sahara. This
incident marks the beginning of the phenomenon known as the African Slave Trade.

In recent years the study of the Trade has become something of a
cause célèbre, for a perusal of its grim details offers white historians a
gold-plated opportunity to prove their liberality and objectivity, and
at the same time offers black historians—the few who can get jobs—a
chance to escape the paternalistic scrutiny of senior faculty members
who do not quite believe that the darkies can say anything useful
about anything that does not concern darkies. And so we know a
great deal—perhaps too much—about the ins and outs of the Slave
Trade; any historian worth his research assistant can shock the jovi-
ality right out of a cocktail party by saying, yes, between ten and
twelve million Africans were brought to the New World between 1510
and 1865 (a small matter of a fifth of the Christian calendar), and
that while losses sustained during the Middle Passage were much

lower than is commonly believed (a mere 13 percent to 19 percent), those incurred during the capture, the march to the coast, and the sojourn in the "barracoons" (hence the term "coon") awaiting transport were substantial enough to raise overall mortality to between 30.4 percent and 39.25 percent, indicating that between 14,367,000 and 19,753,000 Africans were actually kidnapped (in round figures, of course). If such dry business does not interest the ladies (who may be preoccupied with the concerns of the Women's Movement), he can always point out that as early as 1538 the Spanish Crown directed that at least a third of the Africans taken be female—tokenism, to be sure, but at least it had an effect; by 1773 the brigantine *Ann*, a slaver out of New England, was selling women for sixty-two pounds and men for only two pounds more, surely a victory for sexual equality. Then, having grabbed their attention, he can trot out a few specific incidents. He can tell them about the *Zong* incident of 1781, in which English traders were accused of having dumped one hundred and twenty-three blacks overboard into shark-infested waters in order to claim the insurance (the charge, of course, was conspiracy to defraud). Or he can discuss the 1659 voyage of the Dutch slaver *St. Jan,* whose captain was so untalented as to have lost one hundred and ten slaves (fifty-nine men, forty-seven women, four children) to various causes (including suicide) during the Middle Passage and then, having reached the Indies, to pile his ship onto a reef and have to abandon her with the rest of his cargo (eighty-seven blacks) shackled belowdecks. By that time everybody should need another drink (except the historian, of course; historians are used to such atrocities). The party may have become a bit morose, but never fear; the historian can simply tell the amusing tale of how captains in the employ of the famed patron of exploration Prince Henry the Navigator got so busy slaving they did very little exploring, and the Prince was forced to order them to refrain from actually kidnapping slaves, suggesting that they get them from native middlemen instead. Thus, in 1455, Prince Henry, always a visionary, became the first government official to issue regulations setting aside work for the sole profit of minority small business. That should get a laugh.

But what is really amusing is that even so knowledgeable a historian probably does not understand the African Slave Trade—certainly he does not understand it if he is white. Probably he thinks it has something to do with economics, or with greed, or with lust; most likely he thinks the effects of the Trade can be seen in the shifts of the worldwide balance of power, or the development of the British Industrial Revolution, or—if he is very honest and perceptive—the growth of the European Cultural Tradition. To an extent, he will be correct. But he will also believe that the African Slave Trade is over, that whatever its effects were, they are existing now in and of themselves, waves spreading across a pond, the stone that caused them having long ago come to rest. He will think this because to understand otherwise involves dealing with something so basic, so elemental, so fundamental that it can be faced only if one is forced to face it: death. For that is what the Slave Trade was all about. Not death from poxes and musketry and whippings and malnutrition and melancholy and suicide; death itself. For before the white men came to Guinea to strip-mine field hands for the greater glory of God, King, and the Royal Africa Company, black people did not die.

There was, of course, dying in Africa. It occurred in the proportion (one man, one dying) deemed by many appropriate for the apportionment of voting rights. But the decedent did not die—he simply took up residence in an afterworld that was in many ways indistinguishable from his former estate. Evidence for this is found in more recently observed African practices. Following an expiration, it is common for the living to report seeing the deceased, and carrying on conversations with him. It is also common practice to build him a house and to leave food about for his nourishment. Liquids, including alcoholic beverages, are poured out on the ground for the deceased to enjoy. Tools, such as hunting and fishing implements, are buried with him. The Kalabi fishermen of Nigeria rely on the deceased to enforce tribal kinship norms. In Dahomey, the folk tales report the existence of a "market of the dead," which suffers from a chronic meat shortage, much to the delight of living purveyors, who take the opportunity to "make a killing," as the European would say. The Nuer of the Sudan have an institution called "ghost marriage," whereby a deceased man is the father of all children borne by his widow, no matter how long the delay and even if she should remarry.

One might protest that these are current beliefs, having little to do with those that held sway five centuries ago. It is difficult to counter this protest, since the Europeans were far too busy "trading" to make even the most cursory study of African belief; it was widely believed by them that heathenism was not the proper concern of a white man. There exist, therefore, few records. However, one can counter the protest by pointing out that the first major schism in Christianity did not occur until that religion had existed for over seven hundred years, and the second did not come about for another eight hundred; to postulate a similar stability for African belief over a mere five centuries seems therefore reasonable. One might also protest that these are the primitive beliefs of primitive people. This is beside the point. The simple fact is this: if, following his "death," a man, never mind if he is accustomed to wearing breechclout or B.V.Ds, hangs about on the corner, talking to his friends, if he has an apartment, eats hoagies or hero sandwiches, drinks Pabst or Budweiser, goes on hunting or fishing trips as a means of relaxing from his job as a policeman or a judge, is vulnerable to price gouging, and can be slapped with a paternity suit, he cannot really be said to be, in the Christian sense of the term, dead.

But when the Europeans came, it was their avowed purpose to Christianize the natives. That avowal was not hypocrisy, or at any rate not purely so. Gonçalvez' rationale for accepting the suggested exchange was that ten souls are more than three, even if the ten were black, and one of the reasons that few blacks were taken directly from Guinea to the Indies until the late sixteenth century was that transshipping them in Lisbon offered an opportunity to baptize them; when the matter of direct shipment was argued, it was argued by religious sects.

Of course, one must point out that the traders were probably not unaware of the pacifying effect Christianity had had on the slaves of the Roman Empire. And surely the effect in the case of European-style slavery was much the same; thus, in 1845, a group of South Carolina slaveholders published a pamphlet on "the practical working and wholesome effects of religious instruction, when properly and judiciously imparted to our Negro peasantry." These wholesome effects, of course, would only be achieved so long as the more humane lessons of the Christian religion were not applied with too much zeal. (Such was the case; a manual, *On the Religious Instruction of the Negroes in the Southern States,* written for the enlightenment of missionary workers and published, in 1847, by the Presbyterian Board of Publications, advises that "civil conditions" be at all times ignored.) And so the Southern ministers and Northern missionaries, like the priests and vicars and whatnot who dealt with newly captured slaves, probably contented themselves with reading to the slaves the passages from the First Epistle of Paul (alias Saul the Enforcer) to Timothy, in which the Saint exhorts "as many servants as are under the yoke" to "count their own masters worthy of all honour, that the name of God and His doctrine be not blasphemed," a prescription he repeated in letters to Titus ("Exhort servants to be obedient unto their own masters, and to please them well in all things") and to the Church at Ephesus ("Servants, be obedient to them that are your masters according to the flesh, with fear and trembling, in singleness of your heart, as unto Christ"). Probably, too, the masters made sure the slaves heard the exhortation of Peter, in which the Rock upon which Jesus, for want of better foundation, was forced to build His Church extended the doctrine of obedience to unkind masters ("Servants, be subject to your masters with all fear; not only to the good and gentle, but also to the froward").

But even if there were ulterior motives, the fact remains: Africans were introduced to Christianity. And they embraced it. As to what the attraction of it could have been, one can only speculate. Perhaps it was that the notion of bodily dissolution was quite welcome to someone whose physical being was a mass of scars, sores, broken bones, empty guts, rheumy eyes, and the like. Or perhaps it was the belief that the European God must be greater than the African Great Sky God and his lesser companions, since otherwise how was it that only Africans were slaves? Or perhaps it was the idea that after all the suffering was over one went off to heavenly rest (probably being admitted through a side door), while those who caused the suffering were exquisitely tormented by a God so wise as to reserve the ultimate pleasure of vengeance for Himself. At any rate, they embraced Christianity and, consequently, became if not docile then more or less resigned. That they did so can be clearly seen in the negative example of the western end of the island of Hispaniola (what is now called Haiti), where the unenthusiastic efforts of a corrupt clergy allowed *vaudou* (or voodoo), an essentially African religion, to flourish, with the result that after a bloody revolution which cost the lives of most of the whites and a third to half of the blacks, France lost her most profitable colony and the world acquired its first black nation.

But while the Africans accepted Christianity, they did so only gradually, and never completely. Certain central Christian notions, while apparently adopted, retained a distinctly African character.

While it was accepted, for example, that the deceased no longer were in contact with the living, they were still believed to be living—they had simply "gone home to Guinea." (This, of course, explains the often reported "slave suicide" phenomenon, in which transportees would seemingly add to their misery by refusing such food or medicine as was offered, thereby ensuring their demise, or would actively pursue such demise by jumping overboard if the opportunity to do so presented itself. Nor was this kind of thing a matter of individual despair; the suicide attempts were often mass acts. One captain recorded an attempt that involved nearly a hundred men. The attempt did not follow a fit of despondency, but rather what the captain referred to as "a great deal of Discontent.") In some cases (Haiti being the most celebrated, but Trinidad being equally clear), the African beliefs proved so powerful that the structure of entire Christian sects (Catholic in the case of Haiti, Catholic and Baptist in the case of Trinidad) was bent to an essentially African form. In fact, it is possible that, had slavery been restricted to the islands of the Caribbean, on which the social structure was based upon European notions of class (masters were masters because they were members of a master class, not because they were members of the European race), the advent of abolition would have found all ex-slaves equipped with a religion that provided a model for sane rationalization of the realities of Africa with the realities of an essentially European New World. But slavery was not so restricted. It existed in a nation which held as its basic tenet the notion that class distinctions are not only false but morally wrong. Thus masters were masters because they were racially European, and it followed that any smart African who was dissatisfied with wearing a collar could aspire to change his lot by becoming like them. This was not as difficult as it may seem, since the Europeans had shown a certain willingness to mingle their blood with that of Africans, and had established the practice of assigning slaves having greater percentages of European blood to favored positions in the house (and, some centuries later, in the Senate), while the legal system actually stipulated that a person could have a certain percentage of African blood and still be considered a member of the master race—as much as one eighth, in the case of Virginia. So there was hope for upward mobility through miscegenation, the visible evidence being a light skin. But no matter how light a man's skin, nobody—not white people and not black people, either—was going to believe he

211

was a European so long as he went around shouting like an African in church, drawing funny pictures on the floor, and declining to believe in heaven, hell, the vengeance of the Lord, et cetera and so forth. The result was logical: smart Africans stopped being Africans in any way they could. They suppressed and repressed, on their own account, things African. They branded those who clung to Africanisms as stupid—and in some senses they were right: if one's freedom lies in being a European, one is stupid to read the future in chicken bones.

When Abolition came (as a by-product of a totally unrelated economic and political conflict), *de jure* slavery was replaced by *de facto* oppression (which later became a matter of law as well), but the basis of it was still race, and the smart Africans made use of their new-found freedom to pursue the physical and cultural appearance of the Europeans at every opportunity. The brightest (*double entendre* intended) of them revered "good hair" (and straightened theirs if they had to), respected education (to the point where any fool who could wear a suit and preach a sermon was called "doctor"—later, this applied to basketball players—and every piano player was a "professor"), pursued "society" (with elaborate cotillions in which the daughters of morticians, ministers, dentists, postal workers—essentially of middle-class families—impersonated French aristocracy and became debutantes for a day before taking jobs as typists), and, in their religion, emphasized pomp and circumstance to the point where a high-toned black congregation looked like an Anglican minstrel show. It was all useless, of course: the Europeans (now Americans) did not care if a black man was called colored, or negro (pronounced *knee*-grow), Negro (in 1931 *The New York Times* decided that the term should be capitalized), or Afro-American; they still regarded him as a spook, spade, smoke, jiggaboo, spearchucker, darky, or dinge—polite people never said nigger, except in anger.

Now, niggers aren't stupid. When it became apparent that there was no chance for them to be Europeans, they looked around for the little pieces of Africa they had lost along the way. They brought their hog maws and pigs' feet and watermelon out of the closet, and agitated for courses and whole academic departments to help them acquire a knowledge of their heritage. This, too, is useless; a heritage is something you believe in. One cannot become a believer by knowing facts or even by changing one's name, wearing a dashiki, and making a pilgrimage to the Guinea Coast.

Which is not to say that Africa is lost to us—it is not. It cannot be. The Africanisms—the anthropologists aptly call them "survivals"—exist in all of us, independent of our knowledge or our volition. Those of us who have learned about them can recognize them in our own behavior; those of us who were raised under conditions that reinforced the behavior can see it in everything we do. Those of us who know less about Africa than did the European slavers nevertheless tell tales that echo African tales, and sing songs that call on African patterns; nobody may know that the form is called "call and response," but that's the way you sing a song. And no matter how light-skinned and Episcopalian a black person is, he or she will never tell you that a person has died. "Passed away," perhaps. Or "gone home." But never died.

Now, many a liberal white has called all this a fortunate thing. Lucky niggers, heirs to two different cultural traditions. One such gentleman went so far as to suggest that a knowledge of the African past would make all the darkies happy and free and sure about their future. This is simplistic, romantic, half-witted drivel (the gentleman was not, of course, a historian). Because what it all means is that those of us who count black people among our ancestors (they are never *all* our ancestors) must live forever with both our knowledge and our belief. It is not that we must choose between traditions—that has been tried, and the attempt ended in failure. It is not even that we are caught in some dialectical battle between African thesis and European antithesis—then at least we could hope for the eventual synthesis. No, the quandary is that there is no comfort for us either way. For if European knowledge is true, then death is cold and final, and one set of our ancestors had their very existence whipped and chained and raped and starved away, while the other set—a larger proportion than any of us would like to admit—forever burns in hell for having done it to them. And if the African belief is true, then somewhere here with us, in the very air we breathe, all that whipping and chaining and raping and starving and branding and maiming and castrating and lynching and murdering—*all* of it—is still going on.

Or perhaps not. For we have lost some of our belief, and so we cannot *see* our ancestors, and it is therefore possible that things have changed in the Afterlife; that the slaves have rebelled and killed the masters (hardly a comforting possibility) or perhaps something has been worked out, and all the horror is, for the spirits, a matter of lit-

213

tle moment. That is possible. But I cannot imagine how it could happen. And I do not believe it has. Because when the wind is right, I think that I can smell the awful odor of eternal misery. And I know for certain that if I allow myself to listen, I can hear the sound of it. Oh, yes. Surely, I can hear.

The funeral was ending. It had been a pretty good funeral so far; not High Church, but stately and dignified. My mother, acting for Scott, of course, had arranged everything. The casket was top-of-the-line, lead-lined, hermetically sealed, guaranteed for five thousand years or until the Day of Judgment, whichever came first. The flowers were plentiful and beautiful. The only disagreement we had had was about how to dress him; she had wanted to put him in a suit, but I had insisted that he be outfitted properly, and so when I purchased my own supplies I had got the things myself: a new union suit of comfortable cotton, a warm flannel shirt by Woolrich, new overalls, Big Murphs, which look a little baggy but wear like iron, wool-cotton blend socks and a woolen watch cap, cotton painter's gloves, all he would need with the weather turning warmer. (I had bought him a new pair of shoes too, good sturdy hiking shoes by Georgia Giant, but shoes are a tricky thing, and I had thought it best to put his old pair in with him, just in case the new ones hurt his feet.) She had balked a little at all that, but I had simply ignored her, and I suspect that Scott managed to quiet her down, because when I came in with the Mail Pouch chewing tobacco and the mason jar of Georgia Moon corn whiskey, she had said nothing. But I had not been fooled—nobody beats Yvette Stanton Washington that easily—and I had got to the undertaker at the proper psychological moment and told him that she had made a mistake in the instructions, and the casket was supposed to be open at the funeral. (The proper psychological moment had been when I had brought in the things from the cabin, including his shotgun, along with a couple of boxes of factory loads.)

It was a pretty crowded coffin by the time I got finished. And when the final viewing took place, there were a few shaken heads. Quite a few. As a matter of fact, there had been a good deal of whispering; they all thought I was crazy. But Yvette Stanton Washington had stared them all into silence, her haughty glance giving the impression that everything was exactly as she had planned it, and if they didn't understand the deep religious significance of it all, it was simply because they were ignorant.

The preacher had done almost as well. The eulogy was a masterpiece, a web of half-truths and, if you knew anything about Old Jack, you would have had to add, of heresies, for he had possessed all the virtues the preacher called Christian without once embracing the faith.

The undertaker was good too, smooth without being slippery, and he had orchestrated the ticklish business of getting the casket out of the church and into the hearse with great style. The pallbearers, except for me, were old men not far from the grave themselves. But the dolly on which the coffin had sat rolled smoothly, and the undertaker had collapsed it at precisely the right time, and all we had to do was ease the box down the cement steps and onto the tailboard. And he had skillfully maneuvered the heavy hearse across the Hill, making it seem as though he were driving on solid pavement instead of a rutted, muddy track that only the charitable or the deluded could call a road. It was harder for the rest of us—we had to contend with the mud firsthand. But somehow we had formed ourselves into an oddly shaped stream of humanity, and we had flowed into the burial ground and pooled around the open grave: the minister, small and solemn, and the undertaker, professional and detached, both of them as comfortable in the presence of the dead as they were in the presence of the living; my mother and a few of what had once been the army of the WH&FMS ladies, seeming shrunken now, their once fleshy bosoms fallen almost to their waists; a few of the old men, Uncle Bunk Clay among them; surprisingly, Miss Linda Jamison, her face looking ravaged, but her body slim and her coat understated and expensive; and then, ranged out in a line down the slope a little ways where the earth had not been torn open by the gravedigging and they could stand on the grass that covered somebody else's grave so as to keep the mud off their shoes, Randall Scott and his buddies, the sons of those whom Moses Washington had suborned with whiskey and money.

Then the preacher began to pray, reading from the Book of Common Prayer instead of the Methodist Discipline, no doubt at my mother's request. But the words were probably the same, anyway: "Unto Almighty God we commend the soul of our brother departed, and we commit his body to the ground, earth to earth, ashes to ashes, dust to dust. . . ." I did not listen to him; I stood on that hillside and listened to the air. But there was no wind. It would come, though; I believed that it would come. ". . . Lord Jesus Christ; at whose coming in glorious majesty to judge the world the earth and the sea shall give up their dead; and the corruptible bodies of those who sleep in Him shall be changed, and made like unto His own glorious body; according to the mighty working whereby He is able to subdue all things unto Himself." The white men stirred a bit, thinking that the final amen was near, knowing that, in their church, it would have been. But it was not their church. And nothing was finished; it had just begun.

The minister looked at Uncle Bunk and nodded. Uncle Bunk stepped forward, stood in front of the casket and looked at those arrayed before it. "I knew this man," Uncle Bunk said. "Knew him well. He wasn't much for preachin' and he wasn't much for prayin', but he knew how to help as good as any Christian ever did. I mind a time, back before the War, end of the Depression, when didn't none of us have nothin' to eat. He come to my house and the eight of us, me an' my wife an' six kids, was eatin' boiled beans, and not much of that. He said to me, 'Bunk, how long you gonna eat them beans?' I said I didn't know, but there wasn't no work, an' I suspected we was gonna eat beans until they was gone, an' then start in on the walls. He just shook his head an' went out, but he come back later with four chickens. Now, we knew he stole them chickens. And some folks would say stealin' 'em made him a sinner. But the good Lord knows a sinner from a brother, and I thank God I do too. A sinner's a man who steals a chicken an' eats it. A brother's a man who steals a chicken an' shares it."

"Amen," the people said. The white men stirred again, shuffling their feet, thinking that was it. But it was only a small amen, not the final one. Because then Uncle Bunk began to sing, his voice off key and wavering and old: "My brother's gone to glory, I want to go there too. . . ."

And they caught it up then, fumbling a little as they found their way into a key that would accommodate them all, finding it and settling and strengthening:

"In bright mansions above,
In bright mansions above,
Lord, I want to live up yonder
In bright mansions above."

When the song died there was a silence, and Uncle Bunk moved through it, limping back to his place among them. The white men were looking confused, not sure what would happen next, lost without a printed order of service. But the rest of them waited patiently. For the spirit.

It came from among the women this time, through Aunt Emma Hawley, no words, just the thread of a song rising, in the old call:

"I looked over Jordan and what did I see . . ."

And they slipped in with the response:

"Comin' for to carry me home?"

The voices strong and steady, taking even the call away from her, doing it in unison:

"But a band of angels comin' after me,
Comin' for to carry me home."

And then the chorus, which even the white men knew, having probably sung it half-drunk at a lodge meeting:

"Swing low, sweet chariot,
Comin' for to carry me home . . ."

When the song died, we stood in silence. Waiting. And then she came forward, surprising me, not because she came—she hadn't planned this part, but she knew how it went—but because there were tears on her cheeks.

"I had a husband," she said, "and I have a son. This man was a brother to my husband. Walked with him, and talked with him. Saved his life, more than once. Saved him for me. I owe this man for that."

"Amen," they said.

"And this man was a father to my boy. Taught him things I couldn't teach him. Showed him things I couldn't show him." She turned her head far to the right, looking straight at me. "I didn't like that. It made me fear. It still makes me fear, sometimes." She looked back at the rest of them. "But he loved my son. And he taught him the things he taught him because that was what he believed a man should know. He taught him because he loved him." She paused then, for a moment, but we knew she was not finished. " 'And Jesus said unto him, Feed my lambs.' "

"Amen," they said.

And then she began her song:

> "Oh, sooner in the morning when I rise,
> The young lambs must find the way
> With crosses and trials on every side
> The young lambs must find the way."

It was not a song I knew, and not one that most of them were familiar with; and the singing of the response and the full chorus was a little tentative and thin. But they found the words inside them somewhere:

> "Oh, the old sheep done know the road,
> The old sheep done know the road,
> The old sheep done know the road,
> The young lambs must find the way."

And when they were done she gave me one look and went back to her place.

It should have been me then, but I couldn't move, couldn't think of anything to say. But they waited, calmly, patiently, not hurrying, as if they had all the time in the world. Then there was a little stirring, not much, among the ranks of the white men. For a moment I feared it would be Scott, seizing the time to make one of his speeches. But it wasn't; it was the Judge. His voice, clearly an alien one, rose. I resented it; I knew too much about him, or suspected it, anyway, not to. But there was nothing I could do but listen. At least he surprised me. From him I would have expected the Bible. But it was Tennyson:

> "Death closes all; but something ere the end,
> Some work of noble note, may yet be done,
> Not unbecoming men that strove with gods.
> The lights begin to twinkle from the rocks;
> The long day wanes, the slow moon climbs; the deep
> Moans round with many voices. Come, my friends,
> 'Tis not too late to seek a newer world.
> Push off, and sitting well in order smite

The sounding furrows; for my purpose holds
To sail beyond the sunset, and the baths
Of all the western stars, until I die."

He turned his head and looked at me, and he, too, began, giving the age-old call:

"Gonna lay down my burden . . ."

and getting the response, strong, quick:

"Down by the riverside, down by the riverside,
Down by the riverside."

And then they did something odd—they dropped away and let him carry the call solo, as if he were one of them:

"Gonna lay down my burden . . ."

And came in again, just as strongly, behind him:

"Down by the riverside,
I ain't gonna study war no more."

I did not sing with them. I was trying to think. Because I had to say something; had to: there was no more time. But I was too cold. I had drunk four strong toddies before the service, but still I was shivering, from the cold and the doubt; I had to speak, but I could not imagine what to say.

But when the song died someone else stepped forward: Linda Jamison. She came all the way to the grave, her steps light and easy despite the muddy ground, all the way to the grave. She turned to face them. "This man saved my children," she said. "They was sick, burnt up with fever in the middle of the summer. I had a doctor come—he give 'em pills and said for me to make 'em drink cold water and bathe them with cool cloths, to keep the fever down. That was easy for him to say; he had himself a Frigidaire. All I had was a spring. And I met this man here, the one you all used to call a heathen, while I was tryin' to haul water across from that spring fast enough to keep it cool. He never said a word to me, never even called my name, but he carried those buckets home for me, and then he went away. When he come back he was carryin' a hundred pounds of ice. He carried it all the way from town. He still never said a word. But he came back that evening with another hundred pounds of ice. I set up all night, bathin' my babies. Some folks come around, thought I should leave that an' take care a some other business. And maybe I would have. Maybe I woulda left my babies alone for just a little while—I never was no saint, nor much of a mother, either. But I was that night. Because that man who wouldn't even call my name cared enough about my babies to bring that ice to me, and I couldn't do no less. In the morning he come with more ice, and in the evening too. And that night he come and sat beside me, and he bathed my babies with cool water—he used those hands you all always said was so damn dirty. Maybe they was dirty. But he used 'em, and he stayed awake when I dozed off, and in the morning my babies' fevers broke. I told him thank you. He didn't say a word; he just went away. But every time one of my girls was sick he found out some way, and he come and brought whatever he thought they needed; and he give me money. He never said what for, but I knew; he give me money so I wouldn't have to leave my children just because somebody come wantin' a little pleasure. I'll never forget that. And when he was sick, I went to see if I could help him. But he didn't want help from me, or anybody on this Hill, either. He didn't want help at all. All he wanted was to see one boy that grew up over here and went away like anybody else with sense. He didn't think that boy would come back. But he did come back." She turned her head and looked at me. "God bless him," she said. She looked down at the grave a moment, and then she raised her eyes and looked at them standing there on the slope. "God bless 'em both," she said, "and to hell with all of you."

I heard them gasp a little, and heard the silence as she walked back to her place, but it was all right then. I stopped trying to think; I went on impulse and said the words that came. I saw the preacher's head rise, his face take on a puzzled expression, because what I was saying sounded biblical; it *was* biblical, but not their Bible.

"O death, how bitter it is to remember you for a man at peace among his goods, to a man without worries, who prospers in everything,
    and still has the strength to feed himself. O death, your sentence is welcome
        to a man in want, whose strength is failing, to a man worn out with age, worried about everything, disaffected and beyond endurance. Do not dread death's sentence; remember those who came before you and those who will come after. . . ."

And then, just when the words moved into the wrong stream, saying things I did not want to say, there were others:

"In their descendants there remains a rich inheritance born of them. Their descendants stand by the covenants and, thanks to them, so do their children's children. Their offspring will last forever,
    their glory will not fade...."

There was more to that too, but it wasn't right, but the words I wanted were there, in my mind; and this time I knew why I wanted them:

"I am black, but comely, O ye daughters of Jerusalem, as the tents of Kedar, as the curtains of Solomon. Look not upon me, because I am black, because the sun hath looked upon me. My mother's sons have turned against me, and bade me tend their vineyards; but my own vineyard have I not kept...."

I was finished then, and I stood for a moment, searching for a song. But before I could sing it, the song came from somewhere, the old slave call to clandestine worship or desperate escape:

"Steal away, steal away, steal away to Jesus;
    Steal away, steal away home,
    I ain't got long to stay here."

And humming it gently, without signal or ceremony they softly stole away.

The cabin stank of dying.

One of the world's most powerful smells, and one of the most ineffable. And intolerable. So after I got the fire going and the four galvanized buckets filled with water and set on the stove, I took down the wooden shutters that blocked the openings that served for windows, and I hauled the bedding out into the clearing, made sure it was downwind, doused it with kerosene, and set it alight. Then I went back in and began to take things off the shelves. By the time I finished that, the water was boiling. I poured strong industrial-strength detergent into a bucket and, with a long-handled brush made to spread tar, proceeded to scrub down the walls.

I did it three times, leaving the last bucket of water to wash the

221

implements, the tin dishes and cups, the pots and skillet, the trappings that a man builds up over years of living. The things I couldn't wash I wiped with damp rags. I oiled what needed to be oiled. And then I put everything back on the shelves, just as he had had it, his fishing gear and hunting gear and tools, his cooking utensils and the jars of food that were left. I got more water and set it to heat. Then I began to bring things over the ridge.

The job was difficult but not particularly time-consuming; by early afternoon I had the supplies on the shelves and the clothes hung on pegs, my old deer rifle racked and the new army cot made up with new blankets and set up against the far wall. The only things I could not neatly stow were the few books I had brought with me for reference, and my pads and cards and pens, and the two cases of bourbon, and the folio. The books I set on the floor. The rest of my equipment I set on the table. The bourbon I left on the floor near the stove. I did not know what to do with the folio. In the end I put it on the table too.

I put the shutters back in place and lit the lamp. The water was warm and I filled the old tin and sat in it, sipping a toddy and thinking of things I had forgotten. Lime. I would have to lime the outhouse. And maybe get some flagstones for the clearing, to make it a little less swampy. And I would need to rope the path; the storm would not stay stalled forever. And I would have to write to Judith.

When I finished my bath I dried with one of the new towels and put on a pair of sweat pants and a sweat shirt. (They weren't new; they were Bill's.) Then I made myself a strong toddy and settled down at the table.

For a long time I did nothing except sit and look at the folio and think, trying to decide something very simple: did I want to use the white cards or the colored ones? Simple, but important: for more than fifteen years the white cards had been reserved for recording the doings of Moses Washington. Finally I decided to use them to record the information contained in the documents Moses Washington had constructed his final fiction to protect, because he thought them valuable. He had been right; they were valuable. Any historian would say so. For they were the raw stuff of history: handwritten autobiography, drafts of published pamphlets, day-by-day journals. But Moses Washington had not really been a historian; at any rate, he had not cared about history. To him the papers were valuable because they told the story of a fugitive slave who had risen to social prominence, who had been both author and outlaw, gentleman and murderer, husband and whoremaster, and whose blood, he believed, flowed in his veins.

I opened the folio and took them out. I went through them. I took my time, not reading, but looking at each item carefully. I stopped when I got to the map. I looked at it a long time, memorizing it. It was an old map—it showed the County in perhaps 1830, when there were few enough farms for each name to have been printed on the map itself. And written in were lines and symbols designating, I believed, escape routes and redoubts and caches of food and perhaps weapons. Those were in black ink. There were other marks, in blue ink, marks that, I believed, showed the places where grain mash had been fermented, and whiskey distilled and casked and hidden. And then there was another mark, in faded red. I was certain I knew what it was for, what place it set apart: a man had died there. I thought I knew how he had died; I wondered if I was ever going to figure out why. I wondered if I—not the historian, but I, whoever I was—really wanted to know.

I stopped then and rose and stretched and made myself another toddy, hot and strong. I sipped it slowly and made another. Then I went to work with my fountain pen and my india ink and my cards, going through the documents and leeching out single events, tearing them away from the other events that surrounded them, recording them in bare, simple, declarative form on the white lined cards, in a hand as precise and unemotional as I could make it. I dated each one carefully, as precisely as I could, with a string of digits—year, month, date—in the upper-left-hand corner. Then each one was an incident. A single event placed precisely in history, but apparently free of any cause. For this is what one must do if one would understand: one must forget apparent causes, ignore apparent motivations. For things are rarely as simple or as complicated as they appear, and the only truth—and that only a degree of truth—lies in the simple statement of the incident: In the year of our Lord 1948 a child was born to Yvette Stanton Washington, wife of Moses Washington. One would say it that way because one can be convinced, but never absolutely certain, that a woman's husband is the father of her child.

But that is only an example. The incidents I recorded that afternoon were nothing so recent. They were the details of the lives of people long dead. Later, I would read those cards, looking carefully at the what and the when, and try to figure out the why. And then, if luck was with me, if I had grown at all, if somehow, somewhere—perhaps there and then—I could learn to imagine just a little bit, I could understand. But I had no faith that I would do it; I had never done it before.

I worked away through the afternoon, taking refuge in my incidents, letting my mind bounce around as I wrote down each date, trying to ignore the incident before me and concentrate instead on other things. Never mind that in the year of our Lord 1823 a young man's mother died of yellow fever, that he must have felt hollow and utterly alone; that was the year Nicholas Biddle was appointed president of the Bank of the United States. And never mind that in the year of our Lord 1832 that young man exercised the franchise, and must have felt elation, since a decade before he had been a slave; that was the year Andrew Jackson vetoed the recharter of the national bank, sending Nicholas Biddle into private business.

It was an amusing way to spend the afternoon, but the evening came on me inevitably, and I was out of time. So I put my cards away and took one last document from the folio. A simple message, dated in the spring of 1958, addressed to me. A message to pass on to Lucian Maccabeus Scott from the man who had been Yvette Stanton Washington's husband. I read it over. Then I took pen and paper of my own and wrote a message of my own. I made it simple—almost an incident—since an explanation that makes no sense is as useless as none at all. Then I signed it and sealed it and stamped it and put it in the pocket of Bill's field jacket. I filled my flask and changed into overalls and a flannel shirt. I checked to be sure the fire was dying, and that the flue wasn't overheating, and then I blew out the lamp and went out into the dusk.

I climbed to the ridge and went quickly down the Hill, across the river and into the Town, stopping from time to time to pull on the flask, trying not to think about anything. The lights of the Town seemed brighter than they ever had, bright and confusing; somehow I found myself sitting in the Square, near the hardy old men who sat there never minding the cold except in the very dead of winter. They chewed and spat and discussed the weather endlessly, and I sat there with them, not listening. Finally one of them leaned over and looked at me, his face close to mine, his breath hot on my face. He sniffed me, like a dog.

"You that Washington boy, ain'tcha?" he said.

"That's right."

"Thought so."

After a minute he took his face away, and looked at one of his companions. "Told you he was that Washington boy."

"Thought he was kilt," one of the others said.

"That was the other one. There was two."

"That's right. There was two."

"They laid that Jack away today."

"That right?"

"They say all the big shots went up there to the nigger graveyard to see 'em do it."

The first one leaned over to me again. "You don't mind him, he's ignorant. That Jack was a good boy. Best colored boy I ever knowed."

"Yeah," I said.

"Weather's gonna break," another one said.

"There's snow left yet," the first one assured him. After that they had not spoken to me. As night had fallen, one by one they had got up and moved away. If it had been summer they would have stayed, some of them, or gone and come back, but it was cold now, so they went away, nodding to me as they went, leaving me alone in the growing cold.

Eventually the flashing sign on the First National Bank told me that it was thirty-four degrees and seven twenty-two. I got up and stretched and went to see the Judge.

On the Heights it was darker; the streetlights were the old incandescents, and they bathed the street in a golden haze. The third house from the end belonged to the Judge. I mounted the wooden stairs to the porch, and knocked quickly on the big white door. I stood there waiting, the condensation exploding before my face in quick, violent puffs. A car cruised by in the street, went to the end, backed, filled, and came floating back down. It slowed from even its snail's pace when it came opposite the porch, I caught sight of a white face and peaked cap in the glow from the instruments, and then the light from one of the streetlamps flashed off the fluorescent paint and the bubble dome. The car drifted on down the hill a ways, then came

225

to a stop. I waited, but nothing happened; it just sat there.

I turned back to the door, raising my hand to knock again, but just then it swung open, revealing a round wrinkled face framed by a halo of white hair. Sharp blue eyes. "Good evening, Dr. Washington. He's been expecting you all day. Won't you come in?"

I stepped inside.

She stopped me in the wood-paneled vestibule. "Can I take your coat?"

I shrugged out of it, gave it to her. "Thank you," I said.

She turned away, carrying it carefully, as if it were mink instead of an old field jacket. I followed her, wondering who she was. She paused at a hall closet to hang the coat up, and looked over her shoulder. "He's in the study."

"Thank you," I said again.

"Oh," she said, "I'm sorry. I forgot you'd never been here. Not very many people come here at all anymore, and those who come are usually old ..." She hesitated.

"Cronies?" I said.

She smiled. "'Fogies' is more like it. They come in here, sitting up till midnight, talking about the old days and smoking cigars, and for a week the whole house smells. I don't know why he puts up with that; the doctor's told him it's bad for his lungs...." She stopped suddenly, peered at me with those bright blue eyes, turned suspicious now. "You don't smoke, do you?"

"No, ma'am," I said.

"And if he did, he's got better sense than to admit it to you." We both turned to see the Judge standing in a double doorway. Behind him was a crackling fire. "Edna, how many times do I have to tell you? Usher in my guests and make them welcome and spare them your damned lectures."

"It's bad for your health...."

"Don't worry, Edna, you're provided for in my Will."

She scowled at him. "You won't die. You're too sour to die."

"I died fifteen years ago," he said, "but the Devil and the Deity both claimed my soul, and they're still arguing the case."

"Humph," she said, and turned to me. "I'll bring tea in a moment. If you would like something more, feel free to ask." She went on down the hallway.

The Judge chuckled and waved me into a large comfortable room

226

furnished in old leather and dark wood. The light came from the fire and two wall fixtures. The ceiling was high, rimmed by a cornice from which hung a few ancient oils. It was impossible to tell what they depicted—there was not enough light, and they were badly in need of cleaning. There were shelves along the walls, loaded with books, and one freestanding case for the overflow. He closed the door and motioned me towards one of three chairs that sat in a semicircle facing the fire. He settled in the next one, separated from me by a low wooden table, and leaned forward, holding his hands out to the flames. The fire was blazing, but he was fully dressed, in a white shirt and a tie and a suit; for the vest he had substituted a handmade cardigan of soft wool. He worked his fingers and sighed. "I'm sorry about the heat, John," he said. "You get to be my age, though, the sun doesn't shine like it used to. They tell me I ought to spend the winters in Florida—everybody else does, including our mayor. But I don't play golf and I never could see the sense of going out in a boat and working all day to catch a fish that all you could do was take a picture of since he wasn't any good to eat. So I stay here, and sit close to the fire. I guess I ought to get used to that: when they do settle that lawsuit up there, I expect the Devil will win; he has prior claim."

The door opened and the woman came in, carrying an old but highly polished silver tray on which were placed a silver teapot covered, incongruously, by a hand-knitted cozy, and two thin china cups and saucers. There were silver spoons too, and a silver creamer and sugar bowl, and a butter plate on which were placed wedges of lemon. She brought it over and set it gently on the table. She was wearing an apron now, and she fished in the pocket and brought out a tea ball. "I'm sure you'd prefer to put this in yourself," she said to the Judge. She looked at me. "He says I can't brew it to please him."

"There's not a lot you can do to please me," the Judge said.

"There's not a lot you can do to please anybody," she snapped. "It's been nice meeting you, Dr. Washington. I can tell you're a gentleman, and I'm sure this must be a business call; you could surely pick better company. Good night."

"Good night," I said to her back.

"Good night, Edna," the Judge said mildly.

The door slammed, leaving us in the dimness.

The Judge shook his head, smiling. "That woman. Orneriest bitch in the County. I had a stroke a few years back, and they had private nurses for me; I have it in my mind Randall wanted somebody sitting by the bedside to make sure he didn't let his greediness get the best of him. She was one of those nurses. When the time came for me to get out of the hospital, Randall started this nonsense about how I was going to go to live with him. I told him I lived with him when he was messing in his pants and had pimples on his face, and I was not about to live with him ever again. So they said I had to have a nurse. So I hired her. Had her move in. Pay her nurse's wages. It sounds expensive, but anything else would cause talk. And she wouldn't do it, anyway. I asked her to marry me a year or two back, and she accused me of trying to get out of paying her salary. I told her she could keep her salary. She said that would make her a whore; she wouldn't have anything to do with it." He looked at me from under his eyebrows. "Am I shocking you, John?"

"No," I said.

"The hell I'm not. Anyway, what I was getting at is she's a funny woman that way. Now, I can't say we've done too much sinning, but she surely did cooperate when we did. But women have funny ideas about such things. Take this tea set." He waved his hand at it and snorted. "She knows I'm not going to drink any tea, but she won't just bring me the water and the sugar, she has to set up the tea. If I put bourbon in the water instead of orange pekoe, that's my account; she doesn't know anything about it. It's in that case over there, if you wouldn't mind."

I got up and went to the freestanding bookcase. I pulled out a book on each shelf, but they were real enough. I stood there thinking a minute. The Judge didn't say anything. I reached out then and grasped the shelf that was about chest height and pulled it towards me. One end came free, and I stepped out of the way and swung it open. There was a false back behind the books, and behind it racks of bottles; gin, vodka, Scotch, Irish, and rye, two or three brands of each, the best. But no bourbon. I swung that shelf closed and pulled the next one down. Behind the books was the bourbon, two of the best brands, and two of the best sour mashes, two or three bottles of each. I took out a bottle of Wild Turkey, brought it back, and set it down next to the teapot. "Excellent taste," he said. "I wish the old biddy would knit a cozy for this." He uncapped the bottle and poured stiff jolts into the thin china cups, added some sugar each, and then poured in the water. The steam rose, warm and sweet. He set the pot down, stirred, and handed me a cup without the saucer. "I never bother with those silly things. No man in his right mind lets good whiskey drip." He settled back in his chair and sipped contentedly. "Well, John, I guess you know it all now. If that folio wasn't enough, you know where I keep my whiskey, and you know about Edna. Anything else you want to know, I might as well tell you, because you already know the worst."

"Yes," I said. "I believe I do. And it doesn't have a damn thing to do with women, or whiskey either."

"Oh, I don't know," he said. "When you get to be my age, you find out there's precious little that isn't tied up with whiskey or women, and usually both. . . ."

"Don't joke with me, you hypocritical old bastard," I said.

He looked at me, shrugged his thin shoulders. "Is that what you came up here for? To call old men names?"

"Is that what you think?" I said.

"Oh, no," he said. "I know why you're here. You're here to tell me what you plan to do with what you know. I figured you were the kind of man who would give fair warning. By the way, I understand you spoke to Randall after the funeral. And I hear the County Commissioners are getting together with the Town Council. Something about paving streets and plowing snow."

"That's not why I came," I said.

"No?"

"No."

We sat there for a while, watching the logs turning to ash. We sipped our toddies. I finished mine quickly, not feeling the effects of it, or the ones I had had before. The Judge drank more slowly, and so I pretended to drink long after the whiskey was gone, waiting for him to ask something, to give me an opening, for the time to be right. The silence preyed on me, but I waited. And then a log burned through and, spitting sparks, fell off the andirons.

The Judge stirred, leaned forward, set his cup on the table. "I've finished mine," he said. "Finished it a while ago." He looked at me, with a cold smile. "I won't say how long ago. You finished yours a while ago too, I expect. And I don't expect you'll say, either. Now, either you were being polite, waiting for an old man, or you're doing what I think they call playing a power game. Well, if it was the last, I better tell you, I've been horse-trading over whiskey twice as long as you've been alive, and I don't need these funny new words to tell me what it is, or how it is. And I'll just tell you: I don't get all excited about who gets the whiskey, or who makes the drinks, or who finishes first or last. I don't mind silence, not a bit. So you might as well forget your games, because I don't play."

"I don't play, either," I said.

"That why they're paving the Hill?"

"You know why they're paving the Hill," I said. "They're doing it because it's the right and proper thing to do."

He looked at me sharply.

"That's right," I said. "That's why they're doing it. Because there isn't any power. There's only fear. The only people you can overpower are sniveling little people who are afraid you can do something they won't like. It's like a garter snake. A copperhead comes along and bites a man, and he dies. And for the rest of the summer garter snakes have power, because other people do all kinds of damage running away from something that can't hurt them. Now, if you raised a son that runs from garter snakes, that's your problem. And if he has a lot of friends that run from garter snakes, that's his problem, and theirs. Me, I'm just crawling along."

"Maybe," he said. "But you're no garter snake. You're a rattlesnake. You rattle, and make people run because they're afraid you'll strike. But I was wrong about the power; it's not power, it's terrorism."

"No," I said. "It's just exactly what I said it was. Grown men running from something that can't hurt them."

He looked at me sharply. "Are you telling me you won't use that—"

"I'm telling you," I said, "that there is nothing there to use."

He peered at me, his brow furrowed.

"There was nothing in that folio that would implicate anybody. No list of names and dates and amounts."

He stared at me then. "I don't believe you."

"You might as well. Because that's what I'm here for, to tell you that there's nothing more to fear."

He didn't say anything.

"I wish I didn't have to," I said. "But that was part of the package. One more of his little instructions: 'Tell Lucian what's past is ashes.' He burned it. And I'm a garter snake."

He started to shake, gently, almost imperceptibly, and then he began to make a strange, squeaking sound, and I thought that he was having some kind of seizure, but before I could get up he turned his head and I could see the shape of his mouth and the tears streaming down his cheeks; he was laughing.

So I settled back and waited for him to stop. He did, eventually. "That's good," he said. "That's very good."

"I'm glad you find it funny."

"Oh, God, yes," he said. "Don't you?"

"No," I said.

"No," he said, "of course not. You were all ready to come tearing through this town like an avenging angel, but you won't get to do that, will you? I guess you're a little disappointed."

"No," I said.

He looked at me thoughtfully for a moment. "Ah," he said. "He left you something else."

I didn't say anything.

"It wasn't exactly a gift, was it? It's just something you can't say no to. Something he knew you couldn't walk away from. It's not surprising; that was how Moses got his way, by putting things in front of people they couldn't walk away from, and then being there handy to collect. If it had been him who tempted Jesus in the wilderness—"

"Spare me," I said.

He looked at me and smiled a wintry smile, then he leaned forward and took my cup. He set it beside his, uncorked the bottle, and began to mix fresh toddies. "That damned woman," he muttered. "I don't mind her pretending this is afternoon tea, but I wish she'd set out decent-sized cups."

"You're not angry," I said.

"Me? Why should I be angry? It's nothing to do with me."

"Of course it is," I said. "Because he knew what you couldn't walk away from. Power. You used the folio."

He stopped his mixing and looked at me. "I told you—"

"You lied. Oh, not right out. You're a lawyer; you probably never told a real lie in your life. You're too good for that. You tell the truth and let the poor fools make up their own lies. You said two things. You said the financial portion of the estate was intact. You were being specific because you couldn't really say the nonfinancial portion was intact."

"That's a little feeble," he said.

"And you 'demonstrated' the folio hadn't been used because the seal was intact. But you didn't need to open it to use it; I used it this morning and I knew there wasn't anything to speak of inside it. Because everybody in the County knew about that folio, knew what he kept in there. And everybody was wondering where it was. So all you had to do was let somebody see it. Accidentally. Somebody comes into the office and you look upset and hide it just a second too late. That's all it would take. And they wouldn't know your name was in there. So you had all the power. Rattlesnake power. It wouldn't have occurred to anybody that you didn't have any venom in your fangs."

He looked away, and finished the mixing, pouring the hot water carefully over the whiskey and sugar. He set the pot down. "You couldn't prove any of that, of course."

"Why bother? There's no law involved that I know of. But it doesn't matter. I'm not a lawyer, I'm a historian. I don't have to prove anything, I just have to know."

"And that's what you came for? To have me confirm that?"

"Among other things."

He nodded slowly, then he leaned forward and handed me my toddy, looked at me for a long minute. "All right," he said at last. "I used it. I used it just that way." He shook his head. "I suppose nowadays that seems unremarkable, but I have lived with the guilt. . . . The worst part of it was before, though. I wish now I had kept a record of all the times I looked at that thing. For a while I was afraid to touch it. I put things on top of it and tried to forget it was there. But then I got so I'd take it out and stare at it. What I'd think then was that maybe I could take out some of the evidence, the part that had to do with me and a few others. We weren't the real crooks, you know; we just bought the stuff. I know, you think we're all the same. But there were things that went on in this County that went beyond questions of who held power and who made money. I know for a fact that at one point there was a power struggle going on between the Party and the Klan, and it looked for a while like the Klan was going to win. So some bright boys down at the Courthouse hatched out a scheme to arrange to have some colored boy lynched, and they had it all set up to blame it on the Klan. It never happened—somebody got wind of it and called it off. But that was what there was to choose between— men who were ready to lynch somebody for no good reason and men

232

who were ready to lynch somebody for politics. That's what we were fighting against. And I suppose that's why I never opened that folio, even after I realized that I could pick and choose who got hurt; I figured if I was going to violate that kind of trust on the grounds that I was just a hypocrite and not a real criminal, I was going to be just as bad as the real ones. Well, that lasted for a while. Then I stopped caring about using it, I just wanted to destroy it. And then..." He paused and sipped at the toddy. "I used it only twice. In the spring of 1959. June fourth. And in the winter of 1960. January twenty-seventh. Before then I hadn't really needed it, but by that time I was a little too far out of things to protect people I hadn't planned on protecting. The only thing I could have done then was to compromise myself as a judge; I compromised myself as a lawyer instead." He seemed to shrink a little, hunching his shoulders, staring at the fire.

"You were supposed to use it," I said. "He expected you to use it. He expected you to use it just as you did. He knew you would keep your word. He knew you wouldn't open it. And you didn't."

"It was a compromise," he said. "I wanted to keep my integrity and have my way too. You can't often do that. I think sometimes it would have been better to have done one thing or the other. Less cowardly." He smiled and shook his head. "And now you know."

"I knew," I said.

He looked at me. "So you came all the way over here because a dead man left you note? I doubt that."

"There are other things I want to know," I said.

"Such as?"

"Such as why, if you were so damned worried about your reputation, you went to his funeral."

"He was my friend," he said.

"He didn't have any friends."

"I didn't say I was his friend. I don't know, but I suspect you're right, he didn't have any." He stopped, stared into the fire. "To say that about most men would be a terrible thing. But not for Moses. If he didn't have any friends it would be because he didn't want any. But he wanted to know me. That was why he'd come to see me, usually; because he wanted to know me. It wasn't anything he needed, not anything he wanted like a man might want a woman, or a drink of whiskey, or anything; he had a reason there in his head, something that said Moses Washington ought to get to know a white man. I just happened to be the white man that he picked. That's the way it seemed. And I never knew why he picked me. I know that in some ways I didn't suit him; he kept . . . guiding me. I recall one time when I wanted to . . . use power. I was in a good place; I had some backing, and a little money, and some men were going to come to me, ready to give me anything I wanted. Well, I thought I knew what I wanted, some big, flashy things that would have done, I thought, a lot of people a lot of good. So I sat and waited for them to come—I didn't know exactly when it would be. But Moses did. He showed up one evening just about dusk and he told me they'd come the next day. I thought maybe he was going to ask me what I was going to do, but he didn't. He told me. He didn't give me any orders, or even make suggestions, or say he was giving advice. He just . . . told me. As if it were something somebody now had written down about what happened then: how Lucian Maccabeus Scott had done this and that and the other, and people did this and that and the other, and what was funny about that was that what he said they were going to say and do wasn't anything that I would have wanted to have happen. And everything he said sounded true. I think that was because he wasn't making predictions. He didn't know anything, and he wasn't pretending to; he was just looking at the situation and imagining how it was going to work out, people being people. He believed he was right, and he didn't give a damn whether I did or not. And I didn't. Because I knew I wasn't going to do anything he said I was. Well, when he was done he finished his toddy and he went away. He made me mad, not asking if I agreed with him, even. And I said to myself, that bastard's going to be surprised when he finds out what I did. But he wasn't. Because when those men came I found myself doing exactly what he said. I don't really know why—I wasn't afraid of him. Well, when the news got out, people acted just the way he said. But I didn't care, because Moses had said it would be that way, and . . . I don't know. It was comforting. He'd never said things were going to work out all right, and I didn't necessarily believe they were going to. But I got through the bad part because Moses had told me what was going to happen. Later on, it was the same; I'd tell him what I planned, and he'd imagine the future for me. I don't think I ever changed my course again because of what he said—that wasn't even what I did the first time. But when the bad times came, after I'd done something, I could stand back and just watch it happen, because Moses had made it seem inevitable. That's what he did for me. It was precious. And that's why I went to his funeral. I owed him that."

"Touching," I said. "Should I cry now, or wait for intermission?"

He didn't say anything.

"No," I said. "I don't believe you. And no, I don't know exactly why. Because I can't imagine things like you say he could, but I know people, and there's only a few things that could bring you up there like that, make you take a chance like that, and friendship isn't one of them."

He didn't say anything.

"Loyalty is one," I said. "But you're a politician."

He didn't say anything.

"Greed is one," I said. "But you already had everything you were going to get from him."

He still didn't say anything.

"The only thing left is guilt."

He looked up at me. "You forgot love, didn't you?"

"I never forget anything," I said. "There's a lot of things I can't do, and forgetting is one of them. And walking away is another. I can't forget you know something. And you're going to tell me what it is, because I'll sit here until you do."

"Funny you can't figure it out," he said.

"Maybe I can. Maybe I just want to be sure."

"Maybe you can't. You said you couldn't imagine."

I didn't say anything. I just looked at the fire.

"And if I lie?" he said.

"I'll know."

He sipped his toddy silently. "All right," he said. "I'll tell you. I'm too old to lie anymore. But you like puzzles; I'll give you a puzzle. A man like Moses Washington comes in one day to make his will. Not the kind of man you would expect to make that kind of move, and not the kind of man to do it out of the blue. But he comes. And he dies a month later."

"I imagine that happens often," I said carefully. "Old people have a premonition—"

"Moses was sixty-seven, but he wasn't an old man by any other standard. And if he had thought Death was trailing him he wouldn't make a will; he'd take his shotgun and go up in the hills and try to sneak up on Death before it could sneak up on him."

235

"Maybe that's what he was doing," I said.

"I know what he was doing."

I didn't say anything.

"When they found him they knew it was trouble, so they sent a man—I guess there were phones down there then, but they were party lines, and God knows saying something over a party line is just about like putting it in the paper. And God knows they didn't want to have everybody in the County knowing that some farmer named Ames had seen something up on a hillside and gone up and found Moses Washington shot deader than a doornail. They didn't want anybody to know that. Not in an election year. Not when they found the body in Southampton." He looked at me. "It had to be Southampton, of course." He paused, sighed, sipped his toddy. "I lied to you before; they didn't just talk about lynching a man, they actually tried it. I don't know why they didn't do it—I'm not even sure they didn't. I just know it never came out. And I know that they picked Southampton Township to do it in, and I know they picked well. Because it's a little piece of the South down there. It started out being Virginia. It was Virginians who settled down there; I forget the name of the man who led them, but I used to know. I recall that it was a dozen or so men who came. Somebody gave me a book once. I don't know why whoever it was gave it to me, but I suppose it was because the man who wrote it lived around here and was a judge. There was something in there about Southampton, about how it was the most primitive part of the County, and how they didn't have a single piano or an organ, or a buggy or a carriage, in the whole township, and how nobody down there took any paper but the *Gazette,* and only six of them did that. I don't know when he was writing about—"

"Eighteen forty-nine," I said.

He looked at me.

"The book was called *Reminiscences and Sketches.* It was published in Harrisburg, in 1890. The author was Judge William Maclay Hall." He was staring at me now. I didn't look at him, but I could feel his eyes. "And the name of the man who found the body was Iiames, or that name with a variation in spelling, because Richard Iiames was one of the original settlers. And there were thirteen of them, not a dozen, and they were led by a man named Joseph Powell, who was the grandson of Thomas Powell, who was the first white man to set foot in Southampton." I looked at him. "Or in the rest of the County," I said. "Bear that in mind; he discovered the whole damned place."

He didn't say anything.

"Oh," I said. "And you know who gave you that book. Or lent it to you, rather. It was Moses Washington."

He sighed.

"No," I said. "I can't imagine what the truth is, but I'll know if you lie. So stop it."

He didn't say anything.

"Or maybe you've forgotten."

"No," he said. "I haven't forgotten. I'll never forget any of it. Not that day. Not that ride. We went slow out of town, so as not to attract any attention, and we went down through Cumberland Valley and up over the mountain, so if anybody did see us going they'd never connect us with Southampton. We had to go through Rainsburg, and I ducked down low in the seat; nobody saw me. We went up over the next mountain and we came down into Chaneysville. I didn't even bother to duck down; nobody in Chaneysville sees anything, and if they do, they don't talk about it. It was a stupid place for Moses to get himself killed. Anyway—"

"What?" I said. "What did you say?"

"I said it was a stupid place for your father to get himself killed. But I suppose you're right—any place is a stupid place to get your head blown off in. Anyway, we went on through Chaneysville, we went up a hill and came down close to the creek. I recall it was cool in there, cool and green and quiet. It made me angry. . . . No. It offended me, being quiet and peaceful as Eden, when the day before somebody had gone up on a hillside and blown a man's brains out. But then, I suppose that's what Eden was all about, wasn't it? Murder in the middle of peace and beauty."

He looked at me, and I raised my cup to hide my confusion. Because I knew he wasn't lying. He was telling the truth, as he saw it. I thought for a minute, going over everything, wondering if maybe I could be wrong. Again. But I was as sure as I had ever been about anything. So I kept the feeling out of my voice, and I said, "Yes. That, and the knowledge of Good and Evil."

He nodded, sipped at his cup. "Well," he said. "I was angry. But then I stopped being angry. Because we passed this cement bridge, County Bridge number twenty-four. Eight hundred and ninety-nine feet above sea level. I didn't have to get out and look, because that bridge was part of a deal I had made with somebody about something—I can't recall who or what, and I couldn't recall then. But I saw that bridge and all the anger went out of me. Because I realized I was a part of whatever had happened down there, one way or another. I don't imagine you understand that. Or believe it."

I didn't say anything.

"A mile farther on we parked the car. We had to go on back in the woods on some old—I don't know if it had been a road at one time. Maybe. It ran along the stream. Then we went up over a hill. And we came on the place. It was somebody's burial ground, maybe that farmer's. I don't know. But there were a lot of gravestones, and a wall, and just beyond the southeast corner of the wall, there was Moses. They hadn't touched him. I figured that he had thought to take cover behind the wall and someone had taken him from behind. I know, it's hard to believe anybody could take Moses Washington in the woods, but he hadn't been in the woods that way for a long time, and he wasn't a young man anymore, either. And whoever had done it wasn't a fool; he had tried to make it look like suicide. Smart, as far as it went. The coroner believed it. But nobody who really knew Moses Washington would have believed it, not for a minute. So we put it down as an accident, and your mother collected on the insurance, and—"

"And that's why you came to his funeral. Because he was your friend but he had the bad sense to get himself killed in an election year, and so you covered it up and let some slack-jawed hillbilly murderer run free. So much for justice."

He glared at me. "Maybe Moses getting killed, that was justice. Poetic justice, if nothing else. He killed his share."

"And you were worried about somebody else lynching somebody."

He didn't say anything.

"And your precious integrity too, worried about opening a folio, breaching a sacred trust . . ."

"All right," he said. "That's why I came. Out of guilt, like you said."

"Guilt, hell," I said. "You just wanted to be sure they got him in the ground so you wouldn't have to smell the stink. But I've got news for you—they never bury anybody that deep."

He didn't say anything.

I raised the fragile little teacup to my lips and drained it. I set it down. "I think I'll be going now," I said. "Don't bother to see me out." I got up and went to the door. I stopped and stood there, just at the edge of the hallway, looking back at him. He wasn't looking at me, he was hunched close to the fire, and I knew he would be shivering, just as I was. I almost told him then, almost told him the truth. But he had made his own lies. And I had told him about the folio; I had been kind enough for one night.

"What's going to become of us?" she had said. We were lying in the bedroom, windows closed, heat turned high, lights out.

"There are a couple of incidents that can be used to argue to the contrary," I said, "but it's safe to assume we're going to die. What happens after that is a matter of theology, not history—"

"I'm not talking about history," she said. "I'm talking about us."

"Are you implying our romance is less than historical? You don't think we're as important as Antony and Cleopatra, or at least the King of England and Wallace Simpson?"

"John," she said. "I want to talk about this."

"I don't."

"Oh, I can see that."

"So don't push it."

"I'm not."

"*Somebody* is."

"Mother Nature," she said.

I didn't say anything for a minute; I was busy thinking. Counting. "You're not pregnant," I said.

"Of course not," she said.

"Then what are you talking about?"

She didn't say anything for a while, and I lay there listening to her breathing. "I was born in 1948," she said finally. "I am thirty-one years old and I have been with a man—with you—for five years. We have been living together for three. We get along. We have a lot of problems, but we get along. And I would happily go on forever, but there's a part of me that wonders if that's all there's going to be. Because when a woman is with a man like I am with you . . . No. I take that back. I suppose it isn't true for some women. But it's true for me: I think I would like to have your child."

239

I didn't say anything.

"What's frustrating," she said, "is that you won't even talk about it. And time is running out."

"There plenty of time," I said.

"No," she said. "No, there isn't plenty of time. There's barely enough."

"There are tests. . . ."

"Jesus, John" she said. "I'm a doctor. I know about tests. But it doesn't matter. I'll wait. I'll wait until I'm thirty-five, or thirty-six. Or forty. All you have to do is say that it will happen then. But you have to say it now."

"Why?" I said. "Why now?"

"Because I have to decide if what I want is your child, if what I want is *a* child. And if what's important to me is the child, then I have to have time to get away from you and find somebody else, and build a relationship. . . ."

"I don't know how you can say that," I said.

"I don't know how I can't. What do you want, for me to start forgetting to put the jelly on my diaphragm or something? Then I can come in one day and I will be pregnant. Well, I won't. Because I don't intend to raise a child of ours by myself."

"Right," I said. "And you couldn't, could you? Because there wouldn't be any help from the old folks at home if their daughter turned up with a half-breed baby and a bastard to boot. . . ."

"John," she said quietly. "Do you hear what you just said?"

"What?"

"You as much as admitted that if I were pregnant, you'd leave me."

I didn't say anything.

"Oh, I don't blame you, in a way," she said. "I'd leave me too, if I were you and I thought I was trying to do something that devious. But the thing is, it might not be devious. It might be an accident."

I didn't say anything.

"You don't trust me at all."

"You don't understand," I said.

"You think I don't," she said. "You don't give me enough credit. You think I've just decided I love John, and John loves me, so hey, let's have a baby. You think I'm one of those stupid white bitches who sticks her fingers in between some black man's fingers and says, What pretty babies we could make. Well, I'm not. I've thought a whole lot about just what kind of garbage a child of mine would have to face if his father was a black man. And I don't like the idea at all. If it turns out I want to have a child and it can't be with you, I wouldn't dream of having it be a black man. And I think if you were almost any other black man, I wouldn't dream of having your child; if I decided I wanted one, I'd just . . . leave. But I want it to be your child, because I love you, and I think that maybe your child would have a better chance than any man's child, black or white. . . ."

"Why on earth," I said, "would you think that?"

"Because you could tell him things. You could explain things to him. He'd have a father who wasn't afraid of anybody. . . ."

"That's not true," I said.

"I said 'anybody,' not 'anything,' " she said. "You're not giving me enough credit again."

"And you still don't understand. What am I going to do, tell him the glorious story of the black people in America? Well, let me tell you, a lot of it isn't all that glorious. . . ."

"I *know* that," she said. "You think I've been listening to your little lectures for five years without knowing that? 'History itself is atrocious.' I hear it in my sleep. But I also hear you saying that the problem is not the horror, it's the lies, the ones they tell and the ones they don't mention. And our child will know the truth. . . ."

"Lucky him. We'll give the little spearchucker an African name and a set of *rada* drums for Christmas. There's only one thing you're forgetting."

"No," she said, "I'm not forgetting it." Her voice was suddenly soft, forlorn. "I think about it every time I think about saying all this to you. Because I grew up on stories about *my* ancestors. And yes, those stories made me proud and strong. But there was one story about . . . well, I'm not even sure he was one of my ancestors. My father always said he was, but he'd claim anybody who was named Powell who had anything to do with Virginia and who did anything halfway illustrious. He claimed a man who was a pianist once, and we almost got sued, because he was no relation at all. And this story was so old, and there are so many Powells in Virginia. . . . Well, anyway he claimed this man. His name was John Powell. He was a sea captain. His ship was called the *Seafoam*. When I was a little girl I thought that was just the prettiest name. But my father was more interested in the fact that John Powell came into the James River in 1620, the same year as the *Mayflower* reached New England. He'd make a big point out of that; he'd sit there by my bed and he'd say, 'The same year as the *Mayflower*, Judith, and it could be, a month before.' He never tried to find out for sure, because he might have found out it was a month after, or maybe even that great-great-however-many-great-grandfather was no relation at all. He didn't care about the truth; he was too busy being proud. And I was proud too, even though I didn't know what it meant. But you know, now I think, what if how-ever-many-great-whatever John wasn't just a sea captain; what if he was a slaver? What if the *Seafoam* was a slave ship? They all had pretty names, didn't they?"

"Not all," I said. "Some. Like *Desire*. And *Jesus*."

"And that's the trouble," she said. "You know those things. And I suppose if you found out the *Seafoam* was a slaver, you'd tell our child that his mother's ancestors kidnapped his father's ancestors and chained them and tormented them and sold them into slavery."

"Well," I said. "I wouldn't worry about it. 1620's a little too early for an Englishman to be a slaver. There isn't any evidence of English slaving on a large scale until 1660 or so. Oh, it's possible—the English were in Africa then, and they'd carried some slaves before—but it's not likely. So probably you folks weren't slavers, you were just a bunch of salt-of-the-earth tobacco farmers. Probably you didn't steal us and sell us. Probably you just owned us."

She hadn't said anything then, for a long while. But I had been able to hear her breathing harshly in the darkness. "You don't show anybody any mercy at all, do you?" she had said finally.

The metal of the mailbox was cold and a little damp with the moist air; it stuck to my skin. I pulled the door open and stood there for a long time. Then I took the envelope out of my pocket and dropped it into the chute. I heard it fall. It made a solid strike against bare metal; they had already made the pickup for the day. I wondered if they would pick up again in the morning, or if it would be another day before the letter went out. It didn't matter; she was going to say the same thing whenever she got it: that I showed no mercy.

I let the door swing shut, wincing as the metal shrieked against the night. I turned away and headed back towards the Hill, thinking as I went that she would be wrong, that I did show mercy, to her if to nobody else. Because all the while she was imagining things about her however-many-great-whatever John, the captain, I could have been telling her the truth about her maybe however-many-great-whatever Thomas, the explorer. Or worse, about his for-certain grandson Joe.

197903110600

(Sunday)

THE STORM HAD ENTERED ITS MIDDLE PHASE. The change had come almost gently; the mass of moisture-laden air had come drifting up from the south, and the snow had begun to fall almost as if by afterthought. But the gentleness was deception. Soon the snow would come driving down. Soon the south wind would blow. But not just now. Just now everything was silent. Just now everything was still. No strong wind came whistling down from the high ridges to stir the branches and rattle the briers. No squirrel chattered. No bird called. The only sound came from the snowflakes drifting down, invisible in the mist, tinkling as they fell like ten thousand tiny bells. It was just about sunup; just before or just after. There was not much light, but enough to see that more light would not have done any good; the air was full of fog and falling snow, and it was all too thick for any real vision. I could easily have been lost, for all the landmarks were shifted and changed by the grayness. But I was not lost; a hunter is never lost so long as there is a track to follow. And, amid all the grayness and all the quiet, the tracks were there, sharp and bright and clear and plain and crisp as cracking ice.

I sat on my heels and studied them. They were fresh, of course—the snow was falling fast enough to obliterate a trail in minutes; I would have to follow swiftly, or lose the spoor. But I did not hurry. Because it is patience, not impulse, that follows tracks; it is knowledge, not haste, that saves time.

In three minutes I knew what the tracks had to tell me. I knew he was a male, because of the way he dragged his feet; a female would have pranced more, stepped more precisely. I knew he was not large, perhaps ninety pounds, and I knew he was alone, which made him young; not a yearling, but no more than two or three. And I knew, too, that I had a chance to catch him, depending on what he did and on how well I remembered old lessons. Not a good chance, but a chance.

I stood up and invested a few minutes in stretching. It had been a long night—I had covered forty miles since sundown—and now my muscles were cramping and my mind was as gray as the forest around me. I could not afford either. Cramped muscles make for jerky, unnatural motion which in turn makes for abrupt, unnatural sounds; the kinds of sounds that alert any game. And a tired mind makes for mistakes that, with a gun in hand, can be fatal. So I stood up carefully and massaged my shoulders and arms and especially my legs, and washed my face with snow. In a few seconds I felt wide awake, although my hands were cold—almost numb. The alertness was temporary; the numbness was not. But for the time being I would be all right. I shrugged into my pack, retrieved my rifle from where it rested against a tree, and checked the safety and then the bore, to be sure I had not somehow clogged it. Then I loaded. And then I started off after him.

He was headed south, moving nose-to-wind as they almost always do, along an old game trail etched into the mountainside a hundred yards below the ridge. I moved along behind him, sticking to the trail, not only because the going was easier there, but also because that trail had been a whitetail highway for as long as I could remember; if he heard my movements coming from that direction, he would think I was another deer. I was dressed properly, in cotton and in wool, so that the sounds my clothes made against the brush were soft and natural; I was not overly worried about noise. I was worried about the wind. There wasn't any to speak of—just a light northward drift—and that meant I was at the mercy of chance. Wind, even a strong wind, is not a constant in the hills; the pattern of the land, the presence of water or bare rock, any one of half a hundred things, can set up minor eddies of the air which, unopposed by strong currents caused by weather or sun, could go almost anywhere. One of these could carry a ravel of my scent to him. And then he would be gone.

But if the relative stillness of the air worked against me, the storm, at least, was with me. It deadened hearing and obscured vision, but he was the one that most needed to hear and see. And the snowfall provided a constant gauge of my progress; after twenty minutes of trailing I knew that I would catch him: the tracks were getting fresher.

By then I knew even more about him. I knew he was a little larger than I had thought, because when he went through higher drifts his chest caught on the snow, turning his trail into a trough. That meant he was older; definitely a three-year-old. He was smart too; he had read the weather, had felt the air moving in from the south, and had known—as I had—that here at last was the big storm that had been threatening. And now he sensed—as I sensed—that this storm would not sweep through, but would stall and hang over us, dumping its entire load of moisture before its air became light enough for it to float away over the mountains. Then there would be hell to pay. Then the temperature would fall and the winds would come driving out of the west, whipping the snow into monster drifts. He sensed that, as I did, and so, even though he had left off his feeding in order to go in search of shelter, he was stopping now and then to browse, storing up against what could be a long fast. That helped me make up ground, of course. But it wasn't certain that that would do me any good, because I also knew from his tracks that he was, like most of his kind (at least those who reach advanced age), a paranoid. There were times when he would stop, not to browse, but to wait in heavy cover, looking over his backtrail. The odds were he would hear me or scent me long before I could detect him. I would come up on him, but I would probably not get a shot.

But I followed along anyway, trying to be quiet, trying to listen for the little tattletales that can give things away—the chirp of a bird, the chatter of a squirrel. But mostly I concentrated on my breathing, on keeping it even and slow and deep and quiet, because the panting of a man is a sound unlike any other, and it can be heard a long, long way. And it was hard not to pant. Not because I was moving so swiftly; because I was excited.

For I was coming up on him, bit by bit. Every step brought me closer—that excited me. But what excited me even more was that with every step I was getting better. The old knowledge was coming back, the old tracking sense, the feel for which way a branch would spring, for where, below the snow, lay rock or clear ground. I began to feel the heat running in my veins. Not blood lust; trail lust. I was getting good, and I was getting close. And then, suddenly, he left the game trail and moved up towards the crest of the ridge. I stopped dead.

I didn't know why he had done that. It could have been something done out of habit—deer are creatures of habit—but it could have been something else. There was not a lot of time to consider; I moved on up the trail, crouching low, acting on the assumption that he had gone up there towards the ridge so that he would have a good vantage from which to examine his backtrail. It was not a familiar tactic, but it could be effective; perhaps he had learned it at the hoof of some venerable stag, just as I had learned at the foot of Old Jack. The fact that he had used it did not have to mean anything—he could simply be being cautious before heading into some protected bedding ground. But I thought not. I thought I knew what was happening: he was aware of me.

A hundred yards up the trail I stopped and waited a few minutes, and then I slid off, climbing up the slope parallel to the track he had taken. I stopped short of the ridge, stopped and waited and listened. And I heard him, moving away to my left; over the ridge. I had just missed him. But he had missed me too. I still had my chance. I would have to be doubly careful now, though, because he was alerted, not to me, maybe, but to something. I moved off, going easily, going patiently, with no expectation, as Old Jack had taught me.

He came down off the ridge on the other side, and angled off to the south again. The breeze was stronger here, on the eastern face of the hill; the hill curved away to the west a bit, so his line would bring the scents from the valley to him. I wondered if he had known that, if he had consciously run the risk of the move up to the ridge in order to gain, eventually, a greater security. There wasn't much point in thinking it: if he was that smart, I'd be lucky if he didn't end up chasing me. But whether he knew what he was doing or not, I was in a bad position.

I slipped quickly off the track, moving upslope, removing the danger that he would scent me. It was a smart move. But it was a mistake; it took me away from the tracks. I could see them, but not well enough to read them. And so I did not know precisely when he sensed me.

He had stopped to check his backtrail, and it might have happened then, but I didn't notice it until I had to move down again to avoid a shelf of scree. When I came down to the tracks I saw that they had changed.

I knew what had happened; he had become aware of me. Not just something; me. He hadn't spotted me, or scented me, and he wasn't aware of what I was, but there was no doubt in his mind that there was something back there behind him where nothing ought to be, and so he was moving more sharply, bellied down in the snow. But I still had my chance. Because he wasn't running.

I was not surprised; I knew him well now. He was old enough to be wise, but young enough to be foolish. He was old enough to be cautious, but he was young enough to be curious. And he had pride. Too much pride for his own good. He would not go bounding off in healthy alarm. Not until he knew what it was on his backtrail.

And I knew just what he would do. He would move along quickly, opening up some distance, and then he would turn and circle upslope, accepting the risk of having the wind at his back just long enough to come around, then he would backtrack downwind of his trail until he crossed my trail line and scented me. It was a good set of moves for him, but it could be his undoing. Because if I was good enough, if I had managed to somehow get my trail sense back enough, I could counter him, and his good moves would bring him to me, bring him right across my sights.

I took my time. I didn't have much of it, but I took what I had and I used it, thinking hard and furiously, then mentally backing away from it, letting the thing roll out, checking to see how it looked. When he turned I would have to turn too, turn and climb far enough to get above his return line, and then move forward just far enough to be well in advance of where he would first begin to sense my trail. Then I would have to still-hunt, not moving at all, hardly breathing, so that when he came prancing back, full of curiosity, I would get my shot from above. It would not be an easy shot, but it would be a shot. It would be my only chance.

I followed him, going quickly, letting my intuition work on the first problem: guessing when he would make his turn. I had to turn then too, as soon as he did, because if I waited too long his strategy would work or catch me out of position, and if I turned too soon he might never cast back far enough to reach me. The situation was logical, but the solution was beyond logic; I just moved, waiting to *know* when he turned. But it was a long time, and despite everything I could do, I started thinking that surely I had come too far, surely he had turned by now, surely . . .

I made my move without thinking. I climbed easily and quickly, keeping quiet, breathing as heavily as I dared from the very beginning, not letting the carbon dioxide build up in my lungs and force me to pant. I was working on a new question now, trying to sense how high up to go to come out above him, but close enough to see him. And then I knew that too, and I turned and headed south again, working on the next problem, using a little logic too now, choosing the spot that felt right but also estimating how quickly he would move, how far along the slope the wind might take my scent. I found the right spot. I stopped. I waited. And I listened.

I listened, it seemed, forever. My ears grew tired from listening. And I did not hear him. I should have, but I didn't. And I felt my stomach knot, for I knew that I had guessed wrong; he had never turned at all, or he had turned a long time back and had crossed my line and moved away without my knowing, or . . . And then I knew he was there. I couldn't see him; I could feel him. He was up there. But he wasn't circling. He was listening, just as I was. He had his strategy—I had been right about that—but he was too wise to commit himself until he was certain that he was not being stalked. And what he would do was teeter for a while, and hearing nothing, come to believe that there was nothing behind him, or come to know that what there was behind him was deadly, because it had taken such pains to hide. Either way he would be gone. And so I reached out and broke a twig.

The sound was not loud. The twig was damp and the slight crack it made in breaking was muffled by the snow and the heavy air. But it reached him; I knew it reached him. And almost immediately he started to circle. I couldn't see him and I couldn't hear him, but I knew. And, with the excitement boiling within me, I swung the gun up and braced myself to hold it there as long as I needed to. And then I waited for him to come within my range.

I do not know how long I waited there; it was not a question of time. There *was* no time. There was only the slow shifting of sensations: the sting of the snowflakes falling on my face; the slow ache of my arm muscles as they grew tired from the weight of the gun; the growing numbness in my hands. At first none of it mattered, but slowly I became aware of the little things that usually go unnoticed: the beginnings of a blister on my right foot; the harsh tickle in the back of my throat which could only be cleared by a cough; the slight, almost pleasant ache in the small of my back; the droop of eyelids. I waited. Awareness became discomfort. I waited. Discomfort turned to pain. I waited. The pain became boredom. Then it was dangerous. Because then my mind began to drift, began to doubt, began to think it was all a bunch of silliness, mushing through the pinewoods like some half-witted Daniel Boone, trying to kill something wild that I would have to dress out and butcher and pack out, taking the risk of running afoul of the game warden, when I could just buy my meat at the A&P like normal people. . . . And then I heard him move. He was closer than I had thought he would be—the storm had deadened sound so that he was on top of me before I heard him. And he was not below me, sniffing on his backtrail: he was coming straight at me.

I heard briers rattle as they would have had there been wind. But there was no wind. I swung the gun slowly, cursing stiff muscles and dead fingers. I peered into the gloom, waiting for him to emerge.

He stopped. I heard the briers give a final rattle and then there was silence. But I knew where he was; the silence was almost visible, a little dead spot in the creakings of the forest. About a hundred yards. I knew he was there, even though I couldn't see him.

I wondered if he could see me.

I waited some more, getting impatient, working on the impatience as a way of avoiding boredom. My muscles ached. My fingers were lifeless. When he moved again I would have to be careful; when the moment came to fire, my numb trigger finger might make me jerk. But he didn't move. My toes went numb. I could not last long.

I considered shooting into that dead spot. It's something you always think about at times like that, when you're cold and tired and you know there's nobody else out there with you. You think, oh, it won't matter this time, and then it's either shoot or put the gun up and go home, and if you're any good you put the gun up. Because there *might* be somebody there. You might believe you're alone, but the truth is, you don't know.

He moved. Before I realized it, he had closed to maybe sixty yards, the sound of his passage little more than a whisper now, an intermittent rattling in the briers. He stopped again, matching his patience against mine, and I had the eerie sensation that it was he who was the hunter, and I the stalked. I waited, wondering if deer think as we do, wondering if he was standing up there, not just waiting and listening and watching, but actually *wondering* if this would be the time when his curiosity would kill him. And then I heard him move again. One step. Then another. And I realized I could not fire. The cold had numbed my hands and cramped my arms, and I could not hold the gun steady. There was only one chance. I waited until I heard the first whisper of his next step and then I moved as swiftly as I dared, lowering myself to the ground, settling in prone. I waited for the next step, and when I judged it was coming, I got the gun set and lined it on the sound of him. And then there was only one problem: the safety. It would make a small sound coming off, small but totally unnatural. It would be all he would need. So I needed sound from him to cover it. I waited two more steps, reestablishing the rhythm of his movement in my mind. I waited and listened, and then, when I *knew* he would be taking a step, I slipped the safety off.

He had not been taking a step.

He heard the sound, stopped dead. I waited, knowing it was useless, but knowing too that to rise now was to lose all chance. And then the wind sprang up suddenly and swirled the mist and snow into a new pattern, and for just a moment the air between us was clear, and I saw him. He was standing thirty yards away, beneath a barren sugar maple. I couldn't see much of him, because his coat was thickly covered with the wet snow; just the outline of an antlerless head, a sloping chest. There was nothing I could shoot at. Nothing I could be that sure about. But I saw him. For a moment or two I watched him and he watched me, neither of us moving. And then the freakish wind that had cleared the space between us died, and the sight of him was lost to me. But through the gloom I heard him move again, quickly now, and confidently, in no great hurry but not wasting time, not alarmed, just moving on. Because he was finished there; he knew what lay behind him, and now it was time to be about more pressing business.

I lay there for a few more minutes, the snow falling gently on me, making me cold. There was no point in following him—I would never find him. I was not that good. So I clicked the safety back on and got to my feet and headed back the way I had come.

A mile and a half from the cabin, at the short end of a ridge that provided them with shelter from the steadily worsening storm, I found a small herd. I circled above them, looked them over and then, with a long and fairly difficult but unhurried shot, dropped a small buck. I dressed him out and butchered him, cleaned my hatchet and knives, and left, taking with me both haunches and a shoulder, the meat wrapped in the flour sacking I had carried in my pack.

It was early afternoon when I reached the bottom of the slope. I climbed up slowly, in part because the snow was deep now, making the footing uncertain, especially to my numbed feet, in part because I was feeling the fatigue now, in my legs and in my back. Just below the spring I stopped and put down the pack and the gun and the meat and tried to work some feeling back into my hands. I did not get any—they were too numb—but I got enough flexibility into them to get the pack fastenings undone and get out the rope and hang most of the meat. Then I moved on up the slope. I should have gone carefully—there were such things as game wardens, although they weren't given to prowling the Hill's far side—but I was too tired, and so I went wearily and without caution. But something made me stop when I reached the edge of the clearing. Something made me stay there, just at the edge of cover, stop and look at the cabin.

There was little wind in the hollow; the smoke from the chimney rose straight up for fifty feet before even starting to drift. There was nothing odd about the smoke; I had taken the risk of not dousing the coals entirely before I left, and a little smoke was to be expected. There was nothing else odd, either; the woodpile was as it had been, the logs I had cut and stacked as they had been, except that all was now covered by a white layer of snow. But something was wrong. There was somebody in the cabin.

I stood there wishing that I had a better angle so that I could see if there were tracks leading into the cabin. I considered circling around, hesitating because it had been a long night and I was tired. I tried to tell myself that I was simply tired and a little uneasy about having taken a deer out of season, but that made no sense, really; I had done it before. I tried to think if there really was any likelihood of danger, if maybe, after all these years, some fool had decided to come gunning after Moses Washington's folio. But there was no way to decide. And so I started to fade back into the woods, getting ready to begin the circle. And then I began to think again, to reason, and I stopped and looked up at the path where it came down from the ridge.

There were tracks on the path.

It looked that way, anyway. There were indentations in the snow, at fairly regular intervals, the way it would look if somebody had come down that path after the snow began, but not recently—say more than an hour ago. But the indentations did not have to be tracks. They could have been caused by many things—they could have been shadows.

And so I reluctantly stripped off my gloves and fumbled rounds into the rifle. Because that's the way it always is: you assemble your facts with all the diligence in the world and come to the best conclusions in the world, you check the conclusions against the facts with all the care in the world and, if you want to be professional, you check them again. But in the end preparation is procrastination; you have to go in and see.

I did not crawl. A purist would have insisted on it, but I had hands that had lost all feeling, and I wanted to be inside *now*, wanted the fire and a toddy. So I went more quickly than I should have. I reached the side of the door and put my back against the cabin wall and waited, listening for movement inside, hearing nothing. I checked the rifle, made sure the safety was off, and then leveled it. I was about to hit the door when a chance gust of air brought the scent to me: coffee. And strongly made. Judith.

I took my time. I slipped the safety on and unloaded the rifle. I stood outside the door, trying to get my breathing under control, trying to figure out what to say and how to say it. And then I realized what I was doing, figuring all that out: I was wasting time. Because I was afraid to go inside. Afraid of finding out that it wasn't her, or that it was; afraid of the truth. But the feeling was gone from my hands, and the rest of me was as cold as it had ever been, so finally I just opened the door and went in.

She was sitting in the chair that had always been mine, her back to the door, reading a thick file by the light of the lamp. When the door opened she turned and looked up at me over the square lenses of her reading glasses. She had a slightly sour expression on her face. She took the glasses off and looked me up and down, taking in my snow-and-blood-covered boots, my bloody hunting coat, the rifle held in the crook of my arm.

"Who the hell are you supposed to be?" she said. "Davy Crockett?"

I pulled the door closed behind me, stood there for a moment, feeling the warmth. "No," I said finally. "Old Davy, he was into bears. That's too much for me." I went and racked the rifle. Then I let the pack slip to the floor and shrugged out of the coat. I hung it up behind the door, where it could dry without the heat making the blood sour. I leaned against the door and struggled with the laces of my boots, trying to get them off using only my thumbs and forefingers; I couldn't control the other fingers anymore. I got the laces undone finally, and got the boots off, feeling the pain in my toes. I slipped off the heavy wool trousers; they were wet, but the jeans I wore underneath were still dry. I hung the pants up next to the coat. "You're serious, aren't you?" she said. "Those aren't somebody's old clothes; you actually went out there and shot at something."

I turned to look at her. She was staring at me. The lamplight made golden highlights in her eyes.

"I didn't shoot *at* something," I said. "I shot it."

"A deer," she said.

"That's right," I said. "A whitetail buck. *Odocoileus virginianus,* if you care about such things."

"You killed it?"

"Of course I killed it. You don't think I'd leave it out there wounded, do you?"

She shook her head. "Oh, no," she said. "No, that would be against the Code of the West or something, wouldn't it?"

"It would be against the code of common sense. A wounded animal is unpredictable. It's liable to charge. You get hit by a hundred-pound deer going maybe seventeen miles an hour, you're the one who has to be put out of misery."

She shook her head, closed the folder, laid it carefully on the table. "Are you just going to stand there?" she said.

"No," I said. "I'm going to have some coffee as soon as my hands get warm enough to pour it." I really wanted a toddy, but I didn't want to tell her so.

Her gaze moved from my eyes down to my hands. I didn't have to look to know they were pale and wrinkled with the cold. She sucked her breath in, got up quickly, and came to me. She took my hands. The heat in the cabin had begun to warm the skin, and the thumbs

253

had already begun to tingle, but the fingers were still numb; I saw her touch me, but I couldn't feel it, not even when she squeezed. "They'll be okay in a minute," I said. She stepped closer to me and thrust my hands into her armpits and held them there with her own. Slowly I felt the sensation come back, felt the warmth and the pressure from her, the swell of her breasts against my wrists. I tried to catch her eyes, but she would not look at me. Her eyes stared straight ahead, at the five days' worth of stubble that was growing on my chin. Her jaw was set. I looked down at her, along the inch of air that separated our bodies, seeing her cheek and belly and the faint hint of thigh beneath the material of her slacks, and I remembered how it felt to have the cheek against my chest, the belly and thighs solid and warm against mine. I tried to draw her to me, but she resisted, swaying with the first slight pressure but refusing any contact beyond that of my useless hands. I eased off the pressure, doing it gently and slowly so that she did not lose balance, so that she would not stumble or even sway, so that we would not acknowledge any of it. After that we just stood there, waiting for my hands to warm, waiting for the numbness to go away. When I had feeling back in the fingers I ended it. "I'll have that coffee now," I said.

She let my hands drop immediately, as if she were glad to be rid of them. She went and got the cup she had been using, while I poured coffee into mine and added sugar. I poured hers for her. And then I went and sat down in Old Jack's chair. It felt strange—I had never sat in it before. But the cup was warm in my hands, and the coffee was hot and soothing in my throat. Suddenly all the tension left me; it was almost as if I had just come back and made the coffee and settled down, with no one to explain anything to. I closed my eyes and let my head loll back. I held the cup in my left hand and wriggled the fingers of my right around. They ached slightly: a little frostbite, not too much.

"Don't you have gloves?" she said. She was still standing by the stove, and her voice came to me out of a haze of heat. I realized that she must have worked hard at getting the fire up, and not without a few false starts; the faint odor of smoke still clung to the air.

"Sure," I said. "But you can't wear them all the time. You can't handle a rifle very well with gloves on. And you can't gut—"

"All right," she said.

I heard her leave the stove and go sit down; heard her sipping at her coffee. I waited for her to speak, but she didn't. The waiting was hard on me, and after a while my concentration started to go; for a while then I was back there, tracking him, my feet driving through the underbrush, making the dry leaves rustle despite everything I could do, the moonlight filtering down through the clotting clouds and the first flakes of snow falling as I struggled up the slope, searching in the shadows for the greater darkness of a cave entrance, because the map said that he had hidden the whiskey there, or at least that's what I thought it said, and I needed the whiskey, because I was cold, terribly cold, and it was the thing I believed would warm me. I moved as quickly as I dared, searching, not finding, shivering, doubting, despairing, and then I found it, a log fallen across the opening, detritus clogging it, but a cave, and I dug the opening clear and crawled inside, into the darkness, searching with my hands and finding, not nothing, but a bit of broken crockery that might have been the remains of a jug—and might not have been; that might not have been crockery at all. . . .

"Don't you need a license or something?" she said.

"Huh?"

"To hunt. Don't you need a license?"

I opened my eyes and looked at her. She had a strange look in her eyes, and her lips were a thin line of whiteness against her pale face. "You don't *need* anything besides a decent rifle and a lot of patience."

"But you're supposed to have a license. Aren't you?"

I closed my eyes again.

"Aren't you?"

"Yes," I said.

"Do you have one?"

"No," I said. "But it doesn't much matter; the season's been over for months."

"What's that make you, a poacher?" There was a bite in her voice. I didn't like it.

"Yes," I said.

"Well, congratulations. Now you're a minor criminal. It was pretty ingenious, coming up with poaching. It's a lot quicker to buy a rifle than to try and set up a still. But then I guess your father was a poacher too."

I opened my eyes again. "Please," I said. "This is a small cabin. There isn't any room in here for a couch."

"That's too bad," she said. "I think you need one."

I looked at her closely then, because she never talked that way. Never. We had had our fights, but her style of combat had always been the blunt frontal attack, so honest it was sometimes physical; she had never resorted to sniping from ambush. Never before.

"I guess you don't agree with me," she said. "You probably prefer something else. What is it now? Bonfires? Hot-water bottles? Or is it your old friend Jack? Jack Daniel's, I mean."

There was something wrong with her eyes. They were narrowed, as if from anger, and reddened, as if from exhaustion, but there was more wrong about the look of them than could be ascribed to fury and fatigue; lurking behind the narrowness and the redness was a haunted look: I could not understand what caused that.

"There's nothing wrong with me," I said. "I'm just—"

"Cold," she said.

I didn't say anything.

"No," she said, "there's nothing wrong with you. No. It's just perfectly normal for you to walk away from everything to come set up housekeeping in a one-room shack with a dirt floor. Why, you've got an outhouse and you've got a spring, you've got a gun and a stove and a kerosene lamp; everything for gracious living—if you happen to like the seventeenth century."

The odd look was still in her eyes, but now I knew what caused it. Hurt caused it.

"I'll bet you've got it all figured out," she said. "You'll can your vegetables and dry some fruit and salt some pork and jerk some beef—that is what you do with beef, isn't it? Jerk it?"

"Judith," I said.

"You can get a vat and make lye soap," she said. "You'll be good at using lye."

"Judith," I said.

"No, no," she said, "there's nothing wrong with you. It's all my fault. I'm a hysterical woman, I guess—when you say you'll come back to me at a certain time, why, I'm stupid enough to believe you. And to worry if you don't. Especially when you don't call. I know, I don't understand; that's what you always say. Well, you were right. When you didn't come back I didn't understand. I guess you could say I was a little frantic. But then your letter came, and I calmed right down. It wasn't that you were overdue—you weren't coming back at all. Oh, I know you didn't say that; but I could read it between the lines. All four of them."

"Judith," I said, "I'm sorry."

She closed her mouth and stared at me for a minute.

"I'm sorry," I said.

"Oh," she said. Her voice was sharper now, cutting like a whip. "Oh. Well. Well, then. Why didn't you say so before? That changes everything. I feel much better now."

I didn't say anything; I just closed my eyes.

"Don't you do that," she said. Her voice was almost a shout; I had never heard her shout before. "Don't you *do* that, you bastard. You open your eyes and you *look* at me."

"I said I was sorry," I said.

I heard her move, and I opened my eyes just in time to see her coming for me, charging around the table. I got my hands up to protect my face, but she wasn't planning on hitting me. She just stood over me, fists clenched, staring down. I lowered my hands and looked up at her.

"I don't need you, you know," she said. "I could get along without you just fine."

I kept very still, not even blinking. After a minute her shoulders drooped, and her hands seemed to unclench. But the look was still there. I looked up at her for a while, and then I lowered my head. But I could still feel her eyes on me, hot and angry. And suddenly I was angry too, and I raised my head and looked into her eyes. We held each other's gaze for long minutes; then she blinked. I looked at her a few seconds longer, and then I got up, moving slowly and cautiously, but moving, and she had to step back. I stepped around her and went to the stove and poured myself another cup of coffee. I stirred in sugar. I took a sip. Then I turned my head and looked back at her. She had moved; she was still standing in front of Old Jack's chair, facing it as if I were still sitting in it, but she had stepped back even farther than she had had to; her body was pressed against the table, the edge of it cutting into her flesh. I turned my head away.

In a minute I heard her moving, sliding away from me, around the other side of the table. I heard the creak of the chair as she settled into it. I gave her a minute, and then I turned and went back and sat down in Old Jack's chair.

"I've had a hard time," she said.

"I know," I said.

"Do you?"

"Yes, I do."

"Then why are you doing this?"

"What's this?" I said.

She stared at me for a minute, then shook her head. " 'What's this?' *This*"—she waved her hand around at the cabin—"is this. You want a name for it? I'll give you a name for it. Going native. Turning into a Goddamn homesteader with forty acres and a mule. Where *is* the jackass, by the way? Or are you playing all the parts?"

I felt the anger come again then, a cold rush in my veins. But then I realized that there had been a change in her voice; the angry words were there, but the whiplash sting was gone. "You're a little mixed up," I said then. "A mule is the sterile offspring of an ass and a horse—they aren't the same thing, a mule and an ass."

She just looked at me.

"And homesteaders got a hundred and sixty acres—the forty acres were what the Southern freedman expected, as compensation for servitude. And never got."

She didn't say anything.

"I don't want you to talk like that anymore," I said. "I know you're angry, but I've had enough. I don't want to argue. And I don't want you to talk to me that way again. Not now, and not ever."

She stared at me, but I did not look away. She lowered her eyes. We sat there for a minute, with the silence hanging there like a mist. She didn't move, but eventually I heard her breath come out in a long, slow sigh, and she seemed to shrink a little in the chair.

"Judith?" I said.

"What?"

"What I'm doing here isn't because I hate you or because I love you. It has nothing to do with you at all."

"You son of a bitch," she said. Her voice was wrong—flat, dead. It made the words sound like a weather report. "You Goddamned son of a bitch. After five years and God knows how much . . . Oh, God, I don't even know what to call it. But after all that, you have the nerve to sit there and tell me something you're doing has nothing to do with me."

"That's right," I said.

She looked at me for a minute, then she shook her head. "I understand," she said. "I wish I didn't, but I do. It's taken an awfully long time, but I understand. You know where I figured it out?"

She stopped, waited, wanting a response.

"No," I said.

"On the bus," she said. She shook her head again, gave me a small, watery smile. "It's a long ride."

"It is that," I said.

"I drank a pot of coffee before I left the apartment."

"You shouldn't have done that," I said.

"I know. Now. I found out the hard way. That's the point. We were only half an hour out when I had to go the the rest room, but I wasn't the first one; the man who had been in there before me hadn't bothered to put the seat up, so I couldn't sit. I had to squat. Or try to. But before I did I looked down in that hole. . . . Anyway, I was squatting there with that . . . *mess* sloshing around underneath me trying not to breathe and praying we weren't going to hit a bump and cursing you with every word I could think of. Because you never told me about it. . . ."

"Of course I told you," I said.

"No," she said. "You didn't *tell* me anything. You gave me one of your little lectures. I remember it. It was just after we had moved in together, after I practically made you move in with me, and I was supposed to pick up toilet paper on the way home, and I was tired, and I forgot, and when you found out you got dressed and went out— it must have been eleven o'clock—and went wandering around all over West Philadelphia looking for someplace to buy toilet paper. And I sat there, waiting for you to come back, drinking coffee and crying, because I thought you'd take it as a chance to move out, or something—maybe it was stupid, but that's what I was afraid of. And when you got back you just took the toilet paper into the bathroom and came back and made yourself a toddy and sat down and didn't say a word. And I tried to apologize. But you wouldn't listen, you said it wasn't important, but I knew it had to be, because nobody goes running around in the middle of the night over something that isn't important, but you wouldn't talk about it. And I kept pressing you—I shouldn't have, but I did. And finally you started talking, and you gave me this amusing little lecture, all about trains and planes and buses, and I thought it was the funniest thing I had ever heard, because I thought that you couldn't really be angry, not really, if all the while you had been running around on Baltimore Avenue or wherever you went, you were thinking up something that funny. And I was so happy, I didn't know what to do. Because I didn't know you then.

259

Didn't know how you are when you're angry, and when you're frightened—didn't know how you hide things by putting them in a lecture and bringing it out all neat and logical and precise, and I didn't realize then that you only do that when something has you so mad you could kill. So I was happy. I didn't know that what you were doing was taking vengeance. Because that's what you were doing that night. So you never told me about what it was like back there in that stinking little room. And do you know what I realized when I thought about all that?"

"No," I said. I was wondering what, if Judith had been upset by the relatively benign aroma of a bus rest room, was going to happen when she had to visit the pungent precincts of Old Jack's privy.

"I realized that you hide things. Not just some things; everything. You don't even think; you just hide them. You've got a big lead vault in your head and you put things in it. If there's anything you haven't figured down to the last quarter inch, anything you're not absolutely sure about, anything you haven't torn to pieces a hundred times, you keep it in there. And if there's something you never understand in there, it will stay; nobody else will ever see it."

She looked at me, waiting, but I didn't say anything.

"You never shared anything with me," she said. "You told me how you acted when your brother died, and I thought it was intimacy. But it was just a little piece of something you had figured out and finished with. It was a bone and you threw it to me, and I chewed on it for a good long while. But it didn't have anything to do with much of anything, did it?"

"No," I said, "it didn't."

"Well, that's what I figured on that bus. Because I realized you've never told me anything about this place. Nothing at all. You told me lies. You made this place, this . . . *shack,* sound like some quaint little cabin with a nice warm stove and a kindly old man who told tall tales to little boys and kept them out late and made their mothers worry. You told me about hunting, but it was always some nice story about sitting around drinking watered whiskey with the old men and then following dogs and treeing something just for the sport of it and letting it go. You never told me anything about . . ." She waved a hand at my coat, hanging on the door, dripping pink onto the dirt floor.

"You lied to me, John. You lied to me from the beginning. And then you write me a letter and think I'm supposed to accept what you're doing. I'm supposed to understand. But how *can* I understand? You've never told me anything. You didn't even warn me not to drink so much coffee."

She stopped then, and rubbed her hands over her face. I waited for her to go on, to say what she had to say. I knew what it was, but I waited for her to say it.

"I know why you do it," she said. "You do it because you don't trust me. I don't know why, but I know that. And I know I can't take any more of it. I need you to share with me. Now. I need that." She stopped then, waited, leaving the rest of it unstated. But I knew it was there, hanging.

I waited too, trying to think of a way around it all. But there wasn't any way around it. I took a deep breath. "There's nothing I can do about that right now," I said. I looked at her and saw the hurt come back into her eyes.

"You mean you don't care about what I need," she said.

"I care."

"But you won't do anything about it."

"Not now."

"You're too busy," she said.

I gave myself time, looking for a way to soften it, finding none that would be true enough to satisfy her. "Yes," I said.

She didn't say anything. She just closed her eyes.

"I'm sorry," I said.

She took a deep breath. "I kept thinking—on the bus—I kept thinking about how little you'd ever shared with me. And I kept trusting you less and less and less. When the sun came up we were in the mountains. They were nice, friendly, low mountains, not like those monsters they have out West. There was snow on them, but you could see the shape of the rocks, and the green of the pines, and the fields were white and pure. And the clouds rolling along, tumbling all over themselves, black in some parts and gray in others, and sometimes there was this little wave of mist across the ground. . . . Oh, I can't explain it. It was just lovely. And I started to think that you really loved it here, that you never brought me here because you didn't want to share even that. But I know the first part of it isn't true. You hate it here. There's something here that terrifies you. But you won't share it either way. . . ."

261

"There's nothing to share," I said. "Nothing that's any good."

"Then share the bad. You're hurting, John; you need help."

"I need no help," I said.

"Oh, yes, you do. You need it. And you want it. That's part of what you're afraid of, needing me to help. You'd rather get your help out of a bottle."

I just looked at her.

She didn't say anything.

I took my cup and got up and went to the door and opened it. The snow was falling gently but steadily; the woodpile was hidden now, and the limbs of the trees looked like the shadows of the weight of snow they bore. They creaked with the weight of it. I threw the rest of the coffee out into the whiteness and watched it stain the snow. It steamed for a moment, and then it froze. I turned back inside and shut the door.

"Go home," I said. "You don't belong here. Go home."

She didn't say anything, just watched me as I went to the stove and pulled the kettle over the heat. I could feel her eyes on me, but I did not turn around; I just stood and waited until the water boiled, and then I took down the sugar and the bottle and made myself a toddy. When it was made I went and sat down again and sipped it. I did not look at her.

"When's the next bus?" she said.

History is a dinosaur. To precisely what genus and species it belongs is difficult to say—possibly it is a triceratops, but most likely it is a brontosaurus, a large, gray-green thing, so large and cumbersome that to the uninitiated, its head appears to be in only vague and intermittent contact with its tail. It is cold-blooded, taking whatever warmth and passion it might possess from its surroundings. It is so far-flung of extremity and so limited in terms of central nervous capacity that, while it may have some dim sense of purpose, its movements are effectively aimless. It is, in general, slow-moving, but its speed may vary; at times it seems to leap forward with a velocity that fools the eye, at times it seems not to be moving at all. But it does move. Always. And always forward. And as it goes it knocks over everything in its path, not out of malice, or even out of indifference, but simply be-

262

cause it is too ponderous and stupid to notice. It is a minor miracle that history is not, like the other Great Lizards, extinct. But there are strong indications that this will soon be the case.

Reasonably enough, given the antediluvian nature of the beast, the study of history is based on the assumptions of antiquity. In fact, the basic tenets of "modern" historical study have their roots in the writings of the Greeks (Herodotus, recognizing history's saurian nature, wrote lucidly of the crocodile), and there have been no recent branchings of any great significance since the good old days of the seventeenth century.

Those were the salad days of history. William Shakespeare dusted off the *Chronicles* of Raphael Holinshed and proceeded to turn history into popular fare. Ben Jonson followed suit. That started a ratings war. Marston, Dekker, Middleton, Heywood, Webster, Beaumont, Fletcher, Massinger, and Ford all took up the pen, and soon it was history, history, history, Greek history, Roman history, Scottish history, English history, everybody's history, in prime time and on every network, not just PBS. Of course, these playwrights paid about as much attention to research as the average TV producer does; but then came Isaac Newton.

Newton was, as many experts will tell you, the founder of the science we call physics. And it is true that, during a rather idle youth and while on an undesired sabbatical from Cambridge (the university was closed for a few years on account of political difficulties), Newton did amuse himself with "discovering" the law of gravitation, the laws of motion, the fundamental principles of optics, which led to the idea that light was composed of discrete particles or corpuscles, and for a bit of comic relief, the fundamentals of the calculus of variations, all of which we have come to associate with the physical sciences. However, these discoveries were of far greater importance to history than to science, a fact that, while probably not obvious to either the layman or the scientist, or perhaps even the historian, was certainly appreciated by Newton himself, who, in his later years, referred to mathematics and physics as "recreations" and turned his mature attention to questions of history; in particular, to the fundamental problem of chronology.

This did not indicate, as many have supposed, a change in the direction of Newton's intellectual thrust. For the basis of both seventeenth-century science and seventeenth-century history was the same. There was a single, fundamental assumption: that every event has a preceding cause and a proceeding effect. To that assumption there were two major corollaries. First, that each event was discrete: separate and, given sufficient accuracy of measuring instruments, separately visible from both cause and effect. (In historical terms, this means that it occurs at a specific point in time, that it can be dated—that it is, in other words, an incident.) Second, that while cause and effect might appear to be broad, vague, and diffuse entities, they were, in fact, vectors: the sum total (in terms of both magnitude and direction) of a very large number (possibly an infinite number) of events—or incidents.

Things, of course, changed rapidly for the physicists. In two hundred years they had abandoned the corpuscular theory of light for the more complicated wave theory and then, eventually, wedded the two in quantum mechanics. Still later, Heisenberg came mouthing the heresy that one could not look at an event without changing it, which offended nearly everybody, including Einstein. But he didn't offend the historians; they ignored him.

We still do. We still believe that, by whatever haphazard means, the past is created, fixed; that its understanding depends on finding out exactly when whoever did whatever to whomever. Some of us get a little crazy about it, but most of us have learned to accept the idea that we will never know everything, so long as we labor here below. But we also believe in Historians' Heaven: a firmly fixed chamber far removed from the subjective uncertainties of this mortal coil, where there is a gallery of pictures of the dinosaur taken constantly from every angle, and motion pictures, and cross sections. And we believe that if we have been good little historians, just before they do whatever it is they finally do with us, they'll take us in there and show us what was *really* going on. It's not that we want so much to know we were right. We *know* we're not right (although it would be nice to see exactly how close we came). It's just that we want to, really, truly, utterly, absolutely, completely, finally, *know*.

Except one wonders. One wonders if Newton really turned away from physics and took refuge in the immutable past because, as some suggest, no one could agree whether he or Leibniz was first to discover the calculus, or if it was something deeper; if it did not have something to do with the fact that there was a problem that he could not solve with classical mechanics, something ordinary and observable, something that he should have been able to figure out: the motion of a fluid in an excited state—the motion of water around the prow of a punt, the movement of air around a candle flame—turbulence. Maybe he ran against that one and turned away. Maybe he suspected, looking at his candle or his lamp, using the light to work out his equations, that there was something in it that made everything he was doing suspect. It had to bother him. Because it bothers historians now.

There were two of them. They were rectangular, three inches by five, and white (although the second one was a bit yellowed), with ten thin light blue lines and one red one at the top. The numbers were neatly placed in the upper left corner, and the letters were ranged below, centered as much as possible. I had used india ink, and the dates and words seemed to leap off the white surface, even in the uncertain lamplight, tearing events loose from their surroundings, an incident isolated and pure. In the year of our Lord 1890, in the ninth month, on the twentieth day (exact time unknown), a son was born to Cora Alice (née O'Reilly) and Lamen Washington. In the year of our Lord 1958, in the eighth month, on the seventh day (exact time unknown, although it was certainly not before three in the afternoon, probably not before six, and perhaps as late as sundown), that son departed this life. In the intervening years, he carried out the normal activities of men: he had at least one woman, whom he married, but one suspects he had others, whom he did not; he had two known children, both acknowledged, both legitimate; he made money, ate food, drank water and whiskey; of that there is evidence aplenty; one assumes he urinated and defecated. His life had the same amount of meaning that the lives of other men have; it was of vital interest to some, of great irrelevance to most. The significance was on the second card: his death, unlike that of most men, had significance. Or at least he had intended it to be so, had imbued it with meaning and wanted someone—me—to puzzle that meaning out. And I had come with my methods and my training and written it down, in india ink on a white file card. It floated there before me, in black and white. And it meant nothing.

I heard a sound behind me; the cot creaking. For a minute I was confused, and thought that it was Old Jack come back from the dead to give me some guidance. But it was not; it was only Judith.

"What are you doing?" she said. Her voice was clear and the sentence was fully formed; she had been awake, lying, waiting, watching me, for a long time.

"I'm failing," I said. I took up another card. In the year of our Lord 1907 in the third month, Moses Washington appeared in a small town located in the Allegheny Mountains, on the Raystown Branch of the Juniata River, a tributary of the Susquehanna. He had advertised his arrival by taking up station on a stone bench in the town square and dispensing, to all and sundry, farmer and laborer and idler and judge, cupfuls of home brew whiskey that went down as smooth as an oyster and packed a kick like a mule. I reached out and turned the second card face up and looked at it. It still meant nothing.

"You know," she said, "I've never seen you work before."

"Of course you have," I said.

"No," she said. "No, I haven't. I've seen you writing and going through books and making notes, and I've heard you lecture. But I've never seen you struggle with anything before."

"Struggling," I said, "is like defecation. It's natural and necessary, but it's vulgar, and ought to be done in private. Polite people don't even mention it." I wished she would be quiet and let me *think*.

"You know who you remind me of?" she said. "My mother. She has some very precise ideas about what constitutes proper behavior. When I was little she just gave orders, but when it was time for me to go to boarding school she sat me down and laid out the rules for proper behavior for young upper-class ladies. You know what the first one was?"

"No," I said. It wasn't like her. Usually she knew when I did not want to talk.

"Never do anything that might work up a sweat."

"I see," I said.

"It's not the same as struggling," she said, "but it's close."

"Yeah," I said. I picked up the next card. In the year of our Lord 1910 (exact date unknown), the man calling himself Moses Washington invaded the back room of the general store then run by Walter Jackson Hawley, the venue of a perpetual and only occasionally crooked poker game, there making the acquaintance of John "Old

266

Jack" Crawley, shoeblack, free-lance political adviser, and Joshua "Snakebelly" White, itinerant laborer and albino. I looked back to the second card; it still made no sense.

"You know," she said, "I always thought the two of you would get along."

"Yeah," I said.

"I wish you'd meet her. I think she'd like to meet you. I don't think she's terribly happy about us, but I think she might be ready—"

"What did you do," I said, "tell her I only drink the best bourbon?"

She didn't say anything to that, but you couldn't have called the result silence; it was too thick for that. I turned over another card, not sticking with the order anymore; I wasn't getting anywhere that way. In the year of our Lord 1942, in the seventh month, Moses Washington was assigned to the 92nd Infantry Division, an all-black unit officered by white Southerners (because they *understood* negroes), which served in Italy, losing three thousand men and collecting 1,300 Purple Hearts, one of them his, 162 Bronze Stars, two of them his, and 65 Silver Stars, one of them his. And the second card still made no sense.

I heard her get up and come up behind me. Her hands reached out and touched me, kneading my shoulders. "What are the numbers?" she said. "Dates?"

"Yes," I said. I turned the cards face down. She took her hands away.

"Excuse me," she said. "I didn't mean to pry."

"No," I said. "I just couldn't stand to look at them anymore."

"Sure," she said.

"I'll explain it if you want," I said.

She hesitated.

"It's not terribly complicated, anyway," I said. "Each card lists an incident. The number in the corner is the date as precisely as I can figure it. Twelve digits: four for the year, two for the month, two for the date, four for the hour and minute. You don't often get it down that close, but sometimes you can, or at least to morning or afternoon. The cards are color coded, according to scope of event. The gold ones are international, the red national; those are pretty standard. The orange ones are more restricted in this case: those are events that took place in Pennsylvania. The blue ones are local."

She was kneading my shoulders again.

"The cards don't really do anything," I said. "They just help to order events. No suppositions or connections. No cause and effect."

"Why?" she said.

"Why what?"

"Why not causes?"

"Because that's what history is all about," I said. "Finding out what happened and then figuring out why. The first part's harder than it sounds. The second part is even harder than that. Because there are a whole lot of things that look like direct causes that aren't, and a whole lot of things that are causes that you'd never think of. So you set up the cards, and you read through them and read through them until you've gotten them pretty much memorized, but while you're doing that things occur to you. Part of it's just deduction. Maybe you see that the legislature instituted a severe sentence for a particular type of crime, and that tells you that you ought to check on the possibility that there were a lot of such crimes going on at the time. But there's more to it than reasoning. . . ."

"Imagination?"

"No," I said. "No. Not at all. There's no imagination in it. You can't create facts. But you can discover the connections. If you're good, there's a point where all the facts just come together and the ideas come out. It's like a fire, smoldering, and then it catches, and the flame catches other things, and then it's like a forest fire. . . ." I stopped.

"But that isn't happening," she said.

"No," I said. "That isn't happening."

She didn't say anything for a while, she just stood there behind me, working the knots out of my shoulders. I closed my eyes and let my head loll back, feeling the warmth of her hands, wondering if I was going to have to do without that, wondering if I could remember how. Then her hands stopped moving.

"Suppose," she said, "that there was something that you were leaving out. On purpose. Subconsciously."

"This is history," I said, "not psychoanalysis."

She straightened up, but kept her hands lightly on my shoulders, as if she were holding me down. I looked at the table.

"What are the white cards for, John?" she said.

I felt my shoulders tense, and I fought it, but I knew her fingers had felt the muscles move beneath the skin. "Those are the facts you're trying to explain," I said carefully. I let my head sink forward until my chin was on my chest, and I waited. After a minute, her hands began to move, digging into the muscles on my shoulders, easing the tension. I brought my head up.

She stopped massaging my back and moved away. "I won't push you," she said, "but I won't let you lie to me, either."

I turned my head to look at her. She did not look good. Her hair had escaped from the fastenings that had held it in a loose bun, and wisps of it stuck out at odd angles. Her eyes were still red, and her clothes were rumpled from sleeping in them, and the light fawn wool slacks she had worn were soiled; there was a smudge on the right hip, black and oily, from where she had brushed against some soot-laden surface. She hadn't noticed it, probably. When she did, it would bother her. She returned my gaze for a minute, and then padded towards the stove on naked feet. I had kept the fire going, and by now the floor would be warm and not a shock to her feet, but it was still dirt; I wondered what her mother would have said about that. I watched her as she dipped warm water from the reservoir on the stove into the dishpan and began to wash the coffeepot.

"I know what's on the cards, John," she said. "It's something about you. Something personal. I know because it's the kind of thing you wouldn't tell me about. And that's what I want to know."

"You do know," I said. "You know all about me. All the lurid details—"

"I don't want lurid details." She set the pot down hard. "I don't want local color. I don't want good stories. I want to understand what you're doing and why you're doing it. Maybe you don't think it's important that I understand, but it is. It is to me. Because I love you. And I'm not going to leave you alone. Unless you make me. Force me. Oh, I'll go away from here if that's what you want, but I'll be waiting for you somewhere. Unless you tell me you don't want me anymore." She stopped and turned back to the dishpan. Then she turned again, as if something had occurred to her. "Or was that what you were telling me?" she said.

"You know better than that," I said.

"No, I don't," she said. "I don't know anything for sure right now."

"No," I said. "That wasn't what I was telling you."

She nodded, turned back and finished washing the pot and rinsed it with cold water from the pail. Then she dried her hands on her pants. "All right," she said. "I'll leave you here. But I want you to know, I think it's wrong. I think it's dangerous. And I'm going to worry. I'm going to damn near die with worry. So I have to know the whole thing makes sense. So tell me, all right? Don't lecture me, just tell me."

She looked at me for a minute, then turned back to the stove and started to make the coffee, lifting the canister down, measuring grounds with only her hand. She moved deftly, her hands fluttering in the lamplight like golden birds. She finished preparing the pot and slid it onto the back of. the stove, where the heat would not be too high. I realized that she had done something to surprise me—and her mother. She had learned how to make good coffee in an old iron pot on a wood stove—no mean feat. She wiped some sweat from her forehead. She looked at me. "Stove's hot," she said. Her voice was noncommittal.

I looked down at the cards.

She moved then, crossing the cabin with quick steps. I heard the rasp of material as she caught up her coat, the grunts of effort as she jammed her feet into her boots without bothering to unzip them, the complaining of the door as she tore it open and went out. Suddenly the cabin was freezing. I looked up, but she had closed the door behind her. I got up and went to the stove and put in more wood. Then I went back to the table. I wasn't through the cards yet, but I tried a little correlation. Moses Washington had arrived in the County in the same year that Upton Sinclair wrote about the disgusting conditions in the packing plants. There was a little bit of a connection there— the public sentiment that Sinclair stirred up spurred Congress into passing the Pure Food and Drug Act, which was the first step towards Prohibition, because it required that the exact proportions of alcohol or narcotics included in food be reported on the label—but it was pretty weak. . . .

The door opened and she came back in, closing the door quickly, but not before the cold had swept in. Her coat was open and her cheeks were flushed; she almost seemed to glow. "It's beautiful out there," she said.

"It's cold out there," I said.

"Cold and beautiful." She took off her coat and hung it on a peg. She stepped out of the boots. The coffeepot was starting to make simmering noises. She went across and pulled it farther towards the back of the stove. "John," she said, "why doesn't anybody live here?"

"You mean on this side of the Hill?"

"Yes. The other side, it's so . . ."

"Ugly?"

"Well, not exactly ugly. Just . . . used up. People have been living there so long, I guess, but it looked . . . I don't know. Gray. Like an old mill town. Or maybe it was just the snow."

"No," I said. "It's not just the snow."

But she went on as if she hadn't heard me, her eyes bright with something—discovery, maybe. "But over here, it's so different. Like . . . like . . . Walt Disney. Those nature films, where the fox had a name and struggled for survival, and the seasons changed. . . ." She stopped, looked at me.

"I know what you mean," I said.

"I was just standing out there looking at it," she said. "Thinking about it. It doesn't make any sense; all this beauty over here and all that . . ."

"Fatigue," I said.

". . . whatever over there. You'd think somebody would have moved."

"They don't move," I said, "because they're afraid of the ghosts."

The excitement in her eyes died and was resurrected as anger. "Right," she said. "Ghosts."

I looked at her for a minute, then I reached out and took up the blue cards, and flipped through them as I spoke. "I'm serious. They didn't move because they were afraid of ghosts." I found the card I wanted. "There used to be people living over here, beginning in about 1849. But there was a smallpox epidemic in"—I flipped through the cards—"1872. It killed practically everybody. But there were enough people left to make a comeback; there was a sizable settlement here in"—I flipped more cards—"1904. Then the second epidemic hit. Typhus, this time. I'm not sure exactly what time of year."

"Fall," she said. "Or late summer. Peaking in the winter and early spring. That's the way it usually goes."

I nodded. "It's transmitted by body lice, right?"

"The epidemic form is," she said.

271

"Makes sense. It's under control in the summer and early fall, when the air is warm and people bathe more frequently, but come winter, when nobody wants to haul water and heat it and nobody's about to go skinny dipping . . . It makes sense." I took up my pen and made a note on the card.

"How can you *do* that?" she said.

"Do what?"

"Makes notes about something like that. You're talking about a death rate of—"

"Close to a hundred percent, in this case," I said. "I make a note because it's a fact I didn't know; the epidemic probably started in the late summer or fall. And it doesn't bother me because I heard the horror story a long time ago. Old Jack told me. He and Uncle Josh White were the only ones who survived."

"Out of how many?"

"Who knows?" I said. "When the ground's clear you can count the old foundations. There were twenty, maybe twenty-five cabins over here. You figure four or five to a cabin. . . . Anyway, Old Jack and Uncle Josh were lucky. They got the disease first, when there were plenty of healthy grownups around to take care of them. They got well. But more and more people got sick, and there were fewer and fewer to take care of them. Old Jack and Uncle Josh did what they could, but they were children. And at the end they were all that was left. They had figured out that people caught the sickness from each other, but they didn't know they were immune, so they stayed in cabins as far apart as they could get, and they sat there looking at each other across the hollow, each one with a shotgun ready to blow the other one to kingdom come if he got too close."

"How old . . ."

I flipped the cards. "Old Jack was twelve. Uncle Josh was thirteen."

"Dear God." She closed her eyes. I put the cards back in place.

"What about the rest of the people?" she said. "The people on the other side of the Hill?"

"They brought food," I said. "They left it up on the ridge."

"That's all?"

"They mounted a guard to make damn sure Uncle Josh and Old Jack didn't come across the ridge." I looked at her. "Nobody understood typhus, you see. They thought it was contagious. It *is* contagious, if lice are a part of your life. So they isolated potential disease carriers and they kept the whole thing quiet as the grave."

"Kept it *quiet?* But why?"

"Because they worked in town, most of them, the women doing days work and nursing children and the men working in the hotels, cooking, waiting, hopping bells, and if the word had gotten out that there was sickness over here, and that—" I stopped; something occurred to me. "Yes," I said. "And if it was winter, like you said, the hotel season would have been ended, and if there was any money coming, it was going to have to come from the women—the men would have been out of jobs until spring anyway. And if the word had gotten out that there were colored people dying like flies, nobody was going to be having a colored woman taking care of a child. So they kept it quiet. I guess maybe Old Jack always figured it was the women's fault. But anyway, that just about did it for this side of the Hill. Old Jack and Uncle Josh lived over here—I never knew when they decided it was safe to get close to each other—but nobody else wanted to come near. They were still afraid. And they told the children that there were ghosts over here, and that Uncle John and Old Jack were boogeymen, to make sure the children didn't come exploring—"

"Oh, no!"

"Oh, yes," I said. "And a good thing, too, because those lice live a long time. But I guess the stories outlived them; the stories were still around when I came along, but I never caught anything. Or maybe I was just lucky."

She turned back to the stove and went about the business of pouring herself some coffee.

"I'll take some of that," I said.

She whirled around. "I don't understand you at all," she said.

I shrugged.

"I mean it," she said. "You just sit there on top of all this . . . I don't even know what to call it. Death. Horrible things. And you make notes on little cards and then you ask for another cup of coffee."

"Sometimes I'd rather have a toddy," I said. "But if I did, people would say I was too weak to face reality."

She looked at me but did not reply; she just poured me a cup of coffee and brought it to me. I took it from her, holding it in both hands.

"I don't understand how you can be so calm about all the things you know about and still be so afraid of this town."

"I'm not afraid of it," I said. "I just hate it."

"All right," she said. "Tell me why you hate it."

"Isn't typhus enough reason?" I said.

"You said it yourself; they didn't know anything about typhus in 1900."

"No," I said. "But they knew that they didn't want to live in dirt-floored shacks with a hundred people taking water out of the same spring. The Town built a waterworks in 1817. Maybe they didn't know what caused typhus or typhoid—there was typhoid over here too—but they did know they didn't want to live that way. And they let people go on living that way. And they made sure nobody ever made enough money to move. They made that epidemic as surely—"

"All right," she said. "But that's not enough. Maybe it's enough reason for Old Jack to hate, but you weren't even born yet. And you didn't lose anybody. To you it's just—"

"History," I said. "And I'm a historian."

"Oh," she said. "Is that what being a historian means—hating for things that don't mean anything anymore?"

"No," I said. "No, it means hating for things that still mean something. And trying to understand what it is they mean, so you can hate the right things for the right reasons."

She turned away from me and went back to the stove. She picked up her cup and sipped at it, still not facing me.

"You're thinking," I said, "that I'm talking about black people and white people."

"No," she said. She turned and looked at me. "I'm thinking you're talking about you and me."

I didn't say anything.

"You're the man with the logic," she said. "Here's some for you. You hate white people. I am a white person. Therefore you hate me. Only you say you don't; you say you love me. Which seems like a contradiction. So I guess you must be lying about something. Either you can't hate so much or you can't love—"

"And you're the psychiatrist," I said. "You know it's not that simple."

"I know," she said. "I know. You can hate me and love me at the same time. But you see, that's not what I want. I don't want you to hate me at all. I don't want to live like that. If I have to, in order to be with you, then I will, for as long as I can. But if I'm going to do that, I have to know more about the hate, about where it comes from. Because you're talking about hating me."

"No—"

"Yes," she said. "Yes, you are. If you think that what somebody did or didn't do to a bunch of people who died fifty years before you were born is something you ought to take personally, then when you say you hate white people I have to take it personally."

I didn't say anything.

"I *am* white, John. You know that? I am. I don't think you ever have realized that. Because if you did, then you'd have to hate me—"

"It's not that way," I said.

"Then how is it?"

I sat there for a minute, thinking, getting the words in order. "It looks that way," I said. "I suppose that's the basis of it all; hate, black people, white people, those simple things. But it's so much more complicated than that. It has to do with . . . atmosphere. I don't know exactly what it is. Corruption, maybe. But every place has corruption. Bigotry. Self-righteousness. All those things. So what it comes down to is atmosphere. This place stinks. It makes me choke. It's not the people; it's not the mountains; it's not anything in particular. It's just a stench, like somebody buried somthing, only they didn't bury it quite deep enough, and it's somewhere stinking up the world."

She looked at me and shook her head. "All right," she said. "It's the smell you hate."

"I don't hate the smell, I hate . . ." I stopped.

"What?" she said.

"I don't know," I said. "I guess I'm trying to say that it's a funny kind of smell. One of those things that gets in the air and makes the lemmings run to the sea. Whatever it is that's in the air, it makes people be just as bad to each other as they can be. It makes them treat each other like dirt."

"That happens everywhere," she said.

"Yes," I said, "I suppose it does."

She shook her head. "John, what you're saying doesn't make any sense."

"No," I said. "No, I guess maybe it doesn't make any sense. But you want me to tell you things before I understand them." I looked at the cards, reached out and pushed them away, set my coffee down where they had been. It was rich and dark, and the aroma was sweet in my nostrils, but I knew it would taste bitter; I longed for cream. "You came in on the local, didn't you?" I said.

"You mean the bus?" she said.

"Yes. You came in on the local and you went into the Alliquippa and got the desk clerk to phone you a taxi."

"John," she said' "what the hell . . ."

"It's what you'd do," I said. "And they'd know right away you were from the city, because of the way you dressed, and because they'd never seen you before, and because you'd call it a 'cab.'" I looked at her. "Around here, it's called a taxi, you see."

She was staring at me now, as if she thought I was crazy.

"You probably didn't bother asking directions. You just told the cabdriver that you were looking for me. And he told you where to come. Not just to the house; he knew I'd be over here. Didn't he?"

"Yes," she said.

"That's what this town is like," I said. "You sneeze and seven people say God bless you. And I'll tell you what else it's like: when you got to the foot of the Hill, the driver stopped and let you walk up the Hill. Didn't he?"

"Yes," she said.

"You know why he let you off there? You know why he didn't bring you on up the Hill? I'll tell you why. You see, the only time Jobie—that's the driver—the only time he drives people up here is when they're white ladies coming to talk to Aunt Dorrie about getting some sewing done. There's not too much of that anymore; they drive themselves now, those that come. But before everybody had a car, he used to drive the white ladies right up the Hill. But he'd let the colored people walk. See, there's no pavement on the Hill, so every time Jobie'd come up, at least in winter or spring or after a decent rain, he'd get that old Checker stuck hub-deep in mud, and he'd have to find a colored man and pay him a quarter to help push it out. It didn't matter to the white ladies—he'd just charge them an extra fifty cents fare. But the colored folks couldn't afford an extra fifty cents, so they'd walk up the Hill and save Jobie all the trouble and themselves two hours' wages. Now you. If you had just got in the cab and told him to take you to the Hill, or even to Washington's, he'd have brought you right up and charged you the fifty cents extra. But you asked for me, and I guess he figured there was something between us. So he let you off at the bottom of the Hill." I looked at her, but she didn't see it; there was nothing on her face but puzzlement. "It's interesting," I said. "Around here they have never become sophisticated enough to develop the concept of 'nigger-lover.' They just sort of figure it rubs off. So you walked up the Hill. Now, I don't know what you saw, because I don't know which way your head was turned. But I know what you smelled. You smelled the old rotting timbers in those falling-down houses, and you smelled a little sweet-sour smell from something that had died in the weeds, and you smelled pinewood smoke, and you smelled gassy smoke from coal, and you smelled fresh earth from the graveyard. And you smelled the stink from the outhouses. They still use them, you know. There's a sewer line now; they ran it in ten or fifteen years ago, because the state government gave them a grant to pay for it. But nobody was giving any grants to pay for people hooking on, and anybody who could afford it was using the money to get off the Hill. So you smelled the outhouses. Not just the ones now; you smelled maybe a century and a half's worth of outhouses. You smelled a hundred and fifty years' worth of . . . shit."

She didn't say anything.

"I was lucky," I said. "I didn't have to worry about a sewer line, because Moses Washington had dug himself a cesspool, and I didn't have to worry about a spring because he had dug himself a well—two wells, as a matter of fact. So I had a toilet in the house, and it was warm for me in the mornings, because I had a furnace too. And I was clean, because I had a shower on top of all that. I was better off than anybody. But I still had to breathe the air."

She was looking at me, and I could see she was confused.

"The smell used to be a lot stronger," I said. "There were more people over there then. And there were a lot of dogs; just about everybody had a dog. And pigs. Floyd used to keep his pigs up behind the graveyard, and when the wind was blowing the wrong way it got pretty bad. That part of it got to the Town, and they started enforcing a state regulation that made him cook the garbage before he fed it to them. It's really the garbage that smells, you see, not the pigs. So that got rid of some of the smell. Got rid of the pigs too, eventually, because it cost too much for Floyd to cook the garbage, he had to build an oven or something, and he couldn't get the money from the bank, or it was too much trouble.... I don't know. Anyway, he stopped keeping the pigs, and the smell got better. But it was still there. Because the Hill smelled. And the people smelled too."

I stopped and looked at her, but she didn't say anything. "I'm serious," I said. "The people smelled. I remember back when I was in high school, they used to laugh at some of the kids from the Hill because they didn't smell just like Barbie and Ken were supposed to. I remember one of the home ec teachers caused all kinds of trouble when she took some of the girls aside and gave them a little talk on the subject of personal hygiene and antiperspirants and soap and water. I tell you, they had a whole delegation from the church after that poor woman's head for saying those girls smelled. It wasn't her fault; she was trying to be nice. But nobody on the Hill understood her, and she didn't understand the Hill. I guess maybe she could have figured out how hard it is to keep clean when you don't just step into a shower stall and dial hot or cold, when you have to get up before sunrise and carry water two buckets at a time for a quarter of a mile, and then heat it over a stove after you chop the wood for kindling and get the fire up, and then take your bath in a tin tub and then get all sweated up hauling the water away. She was teaching home economics, but the girls she was talking to had to come home and do the laundry with a washboard. I guess somebody could have explained that to her. I guess somebody could have explained that when your life is made up of a thousand little sweaty tasks you just don't get in the habit of confining your perspiration to one set of clothes and calling it a sweat suit. And I suspect she would have understood and felt sorry. But she still would have thought those girls smelled bad. Thing was, there wasn't anything wrong with the way they smelled. If everybody lived the same way, nobody would have thought they smelled. Nobody would have noticed any odor at all. Or they might have liked it.

"I guess all that's pretty normal. People live in a different way, they tend to not understand each other. But I was in the middle of it, you see. Because I had a toilet and a shower and a furnace and a wringer-washer. I was lucky. Only I didn't understand, either. Because I'd smelled that air all my life, and I didn't think the people or the Hill smelled any different than it should have; the Town didn't smell the same way, but it was different, not right or wrong."

I took a swallow from my cup and looked at her. She wasn't looking at me; her eyes were lowered.

"Come to think of it," I said, "I do know which way your face was turned when you came up the Hill: away."

She looked up at me.

"There's nothing wrong with that," I said. "It takes some getting used to, I guess. I don't know. I never had to get used to it. I always saw it that way. I grew up over there, smelling the smells and looking at those houses falling apart, breathing that air. And I grew up over here. When I was at home I used a toilet, and over here I used an outhouse. So you see, what you see as being strange for me isn't strange at all: I can't go native; I *am* native."

She lowered her head again. I took another sip from my cup.

"No," she said softly. She brought her head up again and looked at me. "No. It's not good enough. You're getting closer to it, but you aren't making sense yet. Oh, it's a reason for what you feel, but it's not the reason you feel it. It's something you can use to explain it and justify it without telling me why you feel what you feel. It's just a symbol."

"It sounds corny to say this," I said, "but these are my people."

"You're right," she said. "It sounds corny. It is corny. It might be true. But I know you better; you're no font of brotherhood. You don't like anybody that much."

I set the coffee down. "All right," I said. "All right, I'll tell you. I'll tell you how they killed my brother."

"No," she said. "You've used that one. I fell for that one already."

"No," I said. "I never told you this. I never told you how they murdered him." I waited a minute, but she didn't say anything. "It goes back a long way. Most murders do. And it was slow. So slow you wouldn't have thought they were killing him at all. It looked like they were doing fine by him; he was a high school hero, and they gave him block letters for his sweater, and they actually made him the King of the Pigskin Hop and the Winter Sports Dance. They wrote him up in the newspaper. You really would have thought they liked him. They probably *did* like him then. Because it didn't matter; he was already dead by that time, living on borrowed time. And this is how they killed him. When he was fourteen years old he was supposed to take algebra. He wasn't stupid, but he wasn't much interested in studying, either. He flunked the first quiz. He flunked the second. He flunked the first test. He flunked the second. He was going to get an F on his report card. But it was football season, and he was the starting halfback on the junior high school team. An F would have made him ineligible. So the coach talked to the teacher. Bill promised to get help. They gave him a C. I tried to help him; it wasn't any use. Oh, he did a little better, passed a quiz or two, but he flunked the exams. Only when the second marking period rolled around, it was still football season. So they gave him another C. Then it was too late. I kept on trying, but even if he had wanted to catch up, he couldn't; by then he didn't even know what they were talking about. He couldn't have passed a test for love or money. And he didn't think he needed to. He figured so long as he could play, they'd pass him. And he was right. Because by the time the third marking period rolled around it was wrestling season. Wrestling is a very big thing in western Pennsylvania, and they let ninth-graders try for the Varsity. He tried. He made it. So it didn't make a bit of difference that he didn't know an exponent from a subscript; he got his C. And they gave him his C the last marking period because that was what determined eligibility to play in the fall. The next year they gave him Algebra Two. And they gave him C's. The next year it was geometry. And chemistry. That was his junior year. He set the state rushing record that year. He went to the State Wrestling Tournament that year. He won it. They thought he could do it the next year. They gave him C's. The trouble showed up when he took the College Boards. Oh, he did okay on the aptitude tests, but he did so badly on the achievement tests in math and science, he would have been better off just flipping a coin; he knew just enough to pick out the wrong answers. Well, that didn't matter; he could take the tests again, and stay away from the math and science. All he had to do was be good enough at football. So they gave him C's in trig. They even let him take physics. And they passed him. Right through football season. And they had the first undefeated year in about twenty. They passed him through wrestling season, and he won the States for them again. He was twelve weeks away from graduation. He was ignorant as sin, but his grades weren't bad. Syracuse and Michigan and Ohio State wanted him. They would have gotten around the Boards; they do that all the time. But Bill had already delivered everything he could for the local people. So they flunked him. And there wasn't any way the scouts or whoever could get around the fact that he hadn't graduated from high school. And so he went to work on a loading dock to try and build himself up to try out with the pros. He lifted weights and ran the hills and threw boxes around. He talked about how Big Daddy Lipscomb never went to college, either. He worked for a year, almost. He might have made it. But he was born in the wrong month; he turned nineteen before the tryouts. Instead of getting drafted by the NFL he got drafted by Uncle Sam. You know the rest of it. But what it all comes down to is they killed him so they could have a better chance of winning a couple of junior high school football games."

She looked at me for a long time. Then she moved, leaving the stove and coming over and putting her hands on me. But she didn't rub my shoulders this time. She leaned over and wrapped her arms across my chest and held me tightly. She held me for long minutes. Then she spoke. "I'm sorry, John," she said. "It's still not good enough."

I came up out of the chair, tearing her arms from around me, whirling around. "What the hell do you mean, it's not good enough? Who the hell are you to tell me what's good enough? That was my *brother!*" I knew I was shouting; I had to be—the lamp flame flickered with the sound.

"Oh," she said. "Aren't we noble. *My* people. *My* brother. Next thing you'll be telling me how you have a dream. And of course you're going to shoulder the burden for all those poor dead darkies that got exploited to death, and for the ones that moved away and got good jobs too, the ones that don't even know how beat on they were. That's mighty big of you, Johnny boy. But I'm not sure you're big enough."

"What do you *want* from me?"

"The truth," she said. "I want the truth."

Suddenly I needed to be out of there. I went to the door and pushed it open and went outside and pushed the door shut behind me.

She had been right: it was beautiful out there. The sky was darkening, but the sun was strong enough to make sharp highlights in the clouds. The snow was stopping, gradually, and it seemed that I could make out the individual flakes. But I had been right too: it was cold out there. And as I stood looking at the tracks she had made going down to the outhouse, the south wind suddenly gusted fiercely, sweeping a cloud of snow over the ridge and dumping it down into the hollow. I turned and went back inside, shivering.

She was waiting for me, sitting in my chair, her back to the door. I went and stood by the stove, warming my hands. Then I turned to warm my back and looked at her.

"When I was six years old," I said, "I went to school. Up until then I don't think I had ever really talked to anybody white. Not really. And I know I had never played with any white kids. And it's funny, nobody had ever said anything about white people that I can remember. I know there was a lot of bad feeling from time to time, and I know that sometimes older kids would get into trouble with white kids, but I just never paid much attention. Anyway, I went to school. I didn't know what to do in school. For one thing, I had never been anywhere without Bill before. For another thing, I knew how to read already, so there wasn't much to do for a long while, except color. I loved to color. I remember how every morning they'd give us something made with that purple ditto ink, and we'd color it. I was always the neatest in the class, except for this one girl, I think her name was Lisa. . . . I don't know. But the other thing was the playground. It was stupid; they put guards at the crossings so we wouldn't get hit by a car crossing the street, and they had blunt scissors so we wouldn't cut ourselves, but they'd turn us loose on the playground and let us try and kill each other."

"Did you get into fights?" she said.

"Fights? Me? No. No, I didn't know how to fight. Not for a long time. For a long time it never even occurred to me that I ought to fight. I remember the first time a little boy punched me; I didn't even know what he'd done. All I knew was it hurt."

"Why did he punch you?"

"Because I was black."

"Oh," she said.

"Oh, that's nothing," I said. "There was that kind of stuff, and name calling. I guess that's supposed to be real traumatic. Maybe it was; I don't remember it that way. They called you a nigger and chased you home; they called the little kids runt and chased them home. The teacher wouldn't believe I could read all the way through the Dick and Jane book after two weeks and made me stand in the corner; she said I'd gotten somebody to read it to me and memorized it—that was worse than being called nigger. Or maybe it was the same thing. But what I remember from the playground was this joke. Stupid joke. You go up to somebody and say, 'Shake hands with Abe Lincoln.' After the other kid shakes, you say, 'Congratulations. Now you're a free nigger.'"

"I remember that one," she said. "We all laughed. We didn't know what it meant. And there weren't any blacks in the school. . . ." She stopped.

"Yeah," I said. "You have to have a nigger handy to make the joke funny. I don't think the kids who were doing it knew what it meant, either; they knew about calling people nigger but they didn't know who Abe Lincoln was. I knew who he was, but I didn't understand the joke any better than they did, so I laughed too. And I went home and tried it on my mother. She just about went crazy. She wanted to know exactly who had told me that joke, and where they lived, and she told me not to worry about it, she was going to call their mother, and I still didn't know what was going on. But right in the middle of all of it, Moses Washington came in. He'd been up in his attic and he came down I don't know why. Maybe he heard all the noise she was making. And he wanted to know what was happening. And she told me to tell him the joke. So I did. Or I tried. I got as far as 'Now you're a free . . .' and he laid one up against the side of my head. . . . Well, I guess it wasn't that hard, really, because he didn't knock me down, but my ears sure did ring, and I could barely hear him, which was funny since he was shouting. He shouted a good while; I don't know what he said. And then he picked me up and carried me out into the back yard and he set me down, and he said to me, 'Don't you ever say anything like that again.' I tried to tell him that I was just repeating what a white boy said, and I wasn't calling him a nigger, but he didn't want to hear it. He said, 'I don't care about words, or white boys; but I want you to know this: your great-grandfather had his freedom before Abraham Lincoln was out of short pants. He didn't beg for it and nobody gave it to him. He didn't even buy it. He took it. And if some white man ever looks at you and says, "Congratulations, boy, now you're free," you look right back at him and say, "Jackass, I *been* free."' And then he started to go away and leave me there, but he turned around and came back and picked me up and carried me back inside, and he set me down on the floor and he kissed me and he said, 'I'm sorry I hit you. I didn't mean to do it.' And I said, 'That's all right.' And he said, 'No it isn't. A man shouldn't hit another man unless he means to do it.' And then he went back to the attic.

"I went to school the next day and that same boy came up to me and tried that joke on me, and I let him deliver the punch line, and then I said, 'Jackass, I *been* free.' And that's when I learned how to fight. I didn't like it. I got beat. And I knew I'd have to do it all over again. I was right. The next day, first thing in the morning, he came up to me. There were a whole lot of other kids around. He went through the joke. Did the punch line. Only nobody laughed; they were waiting to see what I'd do. What I did was wait until the silence got real heavy, and then I said, 'My great-grandfather was free before Abraham Lincoln was out of short pants. And he didn't beg for it, and nobody gave it to him, and he didn't buy it. He took it.' And nobody said anything. Because they didn't know what to say. And that boy didn't know whether to hit me or not. So he had to let me walk away. That's when I learned about knowing. That's when I learned that knowing nothing can get you humiliated and knowing a little bit can get you killed, but knowing all of it will bring you power. A few years later I read some of Lincoln's speeches and I found out he was about as much an emancipator as George Wallace, and it was a good thing too, because as soon as I got to high school they started in with that Emancipation Proclamation nonsense, and I was ready for them. I just about gave the American history teacher heart failure. I loved it. I just gobbled history right up, and after a while it didn't have anything to do with protection or getting even. It just had to do with history. And just about that time I found somebody just like me. His name was Robert. He was a little runty white kid with thick glasses and pop eyes and hair about the shade of dishwater, but he was just like me: he loved history. The Civil War was what got him going. He knew everything about the Civil War, right down to the times of the charges and the three-hour delay at Gettysburg. It was funny; otherwise he wasn't very smart at all. He was in Special Education. Couldn't read anything but history, and he couldn't read that very well, but he studied and he worked, and he never forgot a thing. And he had history books all over the place. I don't think anybody in the school even knew it. I forget now how I found out. But I did, and we'd spend hours talking. We'd sit down by the creek and he'd set up the whole battlefield and move the rocks around: this was somebody's cavalry, that was somebody's infantry. He lent me books. And I lent him a few; I didn't have many, but he took a long time with them so it didn't much matter. And I could get books out of the library; they wouldn't let him in. Well, everything was fine. I think I was even happy. And then school ended for the summer. But I had a whole bunch of his books, and I knew he had a whole lot more, so one day I went over to his house. He lived over in the Scott Edition—well, it wouldn't mean anything to you. A pretty good section of town. Not the best, but pretty good. They complained when the truckdrivers started making enough money to move in. Anyway, I went over there with the books. He wasn't home, but I left the books. Later that night, it must have been about nine o'clock because it was dark, there was a knock on the door, and I opened it, and he was standing there with the books of mine he'd had. He hadn't had them long; I knew he couldn't have finished them. So I said to him, 'Just because I brought yours back, it doesn't mean you have to bring mine back.' And he said, 'I'm done with them.' But I knew he was lying; he couldn't read that fast. But he handed me the books and he turned away. I remember it was so dark he disappeared right away. But I could hear him going down the Hill. I was just about ready to go back inside when I heard him stop. And he said, 'Johnny?' and I said, 'Yeah?' and he said, 'My mother said for you not to come to the house no more.' And then he went on down the Hill. I listened to him going all the way to the bottom, and then I heard a door slam and a car start up, and then I heard it drive away."

I had to step away from the stove then; I could smell my clothes starting to scorch. But I didn't feel the heat.

"I don't understand," she said. "Why . . . Oh."

I didn't say anything.

"You don't have to hate, John," she said. "I'll do it for you."

"For us," I said. I turned to the stove and mixed myself a toddy. When I had mixed it I stood there, feeling the warmth of the stove but not being warmed by it. "There was a girl." I listened, waiting for her to say something, but she didn't; there was nothing for me to do but go on. "Her name," I said, "was Mara. She was the younger daughter of Miss Linda Jamison. Miss Linda was . . . well, you couldn't call her the town whore, since there were other women—

white women—who did that kind of work. Miss Linda was more of a courtesan. She didn't have customers, or even clients; she had friends. Powerful friends. She had a house on the Hill, but Miss Linda never had anything to do with colored men. Strictly white trade. I don't think she had anything against colored men; it was just that she didn't think white men wanted their women having anything to do with black men, even if the women were black themselves. I suspect she was right.

"Anyway, she had two daughters, both by white men—nobody knew exactly who, and Miss Linda wasn't about to tell them, if she knew, because she was collecting money from five or six different men who were all afraid she might be able to prove one of those girls belonged to one of them. She didn't try to hide it, either—they knew about each other, and they liked it that way, because then they each had something on the others. And if one of them got a little behind, they'd cover for him for a month or so, but if he decided he wasn't going to pay at all, they'd jump on him real fast, because they were afraid Miss Linda would expose them all. It was beautiful; she never even had to threaten. And she kept it quiet. Nobody on the Hill even knew about it. They thought Miss Linda made all her money on current fees; they didn't know she was collecting royalties."

I stopped then, and sipped at the toddy. It didn't seem hot enough, somehow, and I poured in more hot water, sipped again. I heard her move, and again I waited for her to say something, but she didn't. "Mara was a year younger than I was," I said. "I knew her; there weren't many children on the Hill, and we all played together. My mother didn't like it, Bill and I playing with Miss Linda's daughters. She and Moses Washington had a fight about it; she wanted him to make us stop, and he said he would, if she would explain to us exactly what it was that Miss Linda did that made it bad for us to play with her children. That ended the whole thing real fast. I don't know what she was worried about. And I think if she had known me better, she wouldn't have worried at all. Because about that time, Mara started school. I was in the second grade; Bill didn't go to school yet. So it should have been natural for Mara and me to go to school together. But we didn't. I took her down the first day with me, but after that she walked down by herself, and so did I. And even though we'd play together in the afternoon, she'd walk home by herself and so would I. Sometimes I'd see her a block ahead, walking, and I knew she knew I was there behind her sometimes, but I never hurried up to catch her, and she never stopped to wait. I never knew if she wanted to, but she didn't. And during the day, we didn't talk at all, on the playground, or anywhere."

I stopped, sipped at the toddy. She still didn't say anything. I wished she would, but she didn't. "After Moses Washington died, my mother told us not to play with the Jamison girls anymore. It didn't matter much to me—I was busy with other things. So I didn't see Mara at all, really—she didn't come to Sunday school or church. It was sort of funny. In a lot of ways Mara Jamison was the girl next door. God knows she was pretty enough for anybody. Even for the Town. They made her a cheerleader. It wasn't all that simple; there were some folks who didn't think a black girl ought to be a cheerleader. But Miss Linda talked to some of her 'friends,' and that was enough to get Mara on the junior high cheerleading squad. That was about the only thing I knew about her. Until one day—I was sixteen, so she would have been fifteen—she came to the house. My mother wasn't home from work and Bill was at football practice or something. So I answered the door. She stood on the porch and said she wanted to talk to me. I told her to come in, but she didn't want to talk there. She told me to meet her in the woods. She told me where, and when. So that night after supper I went out and met her. It was fall, September maybe; it was just dusk when we met. It was up along the ridge, above the graveyard. She was there waiting for me, sitting on a log. I sat down beside her. I didn't know how to ask her what she wanted, so we just sat there until it got dark, not saying anything. Just sitting. Finally she told me what it was. Her mother wanted her to sleep with a white man. He was a lawyer. Big in the town. He was married, and he had a wife and a daughter a year younger than Mara. She didn't say who he was, but I knew. And her mother wanted her to go with him, and get pregnant, and have his child, and be set for life. I said I didn't know what to tell her to do. She said she knew what to do if I'd help her. I said I would. So she explained Miss Linda's theory about white men, how they wouldn't want a woman after she'd been with a black man, and she asked me if I'd be with her.

"So we did it. Right there, in the woods up above the graveyard, up above where Floyd used to keep his pigs. That's just about as romantic as it was, too. The ground was hard and the sky was clouded over. There was a cold wind blowing up the slope. I was afraid and nervous, and at first I couldn't do anything. Miss Linda must have told her things to do in case that happened; anyway, she tried everything. Nothing worked. Finally she gave up and we just lay there, shivering in that wind. She was crying. I told her to stop, that we'd try again tomorrow, but she said that was too late, because he was coming that night. I don't know what happened . . . No, that's a lie. I know what happened; I started thinking about how excited he had to be, thinking about what he was going to do. And then I could.

"When we were finished we just left. We straightened our clothes out and went away from each other; we didn't kiss or hug or anything. It hadn't been anything particularly soft or warm or gentle. But it was good; she was safe. Because she could go down there and tell Miss Linda—tell him too, maybe—that she'd been with a colored boy. And I could go home and sit up there in Moses Washington's attic and know that I had done something like the things he did; I had cheated one of those white bastards out of something. I was probably wrong about that—Moses Washington would have seen eye to eye with Miss Linda—but I didn't think so then. I thought he would have been proud of me, taking something right out from under the lion's nose."

I drank the rest of the toddy in one quick swallow; it was cold, and made a cold place in my belly. I mixed another one quickly, not bothering with the sugar, using only enough whiskey to give it taste. I wanted the heat. Judith still didn't say anything. I wondered what she was thinking.

"It didn't work," I said. "It was never going to work. All you had to do was to look at the facts to know that. Her mother made her living catering to white men that way. So did her sister. What was she going to do? Get a job as a secretary? Nobody was going to hire her for that. Work in one of the factories? There weren't that many jobs, and if business got bad she'd get laid off first. Waitress? She'd spend all day or half the night dodging passes from truckdrivers and guys on the night shift, anyway. And so one day it came to her that there wasn't any reason for her to fight so hard. Not a reason in the world. And so she went into the family business. But she made them do it differently. Oh, yes indeed. Because Mara was as smart as she was beautiful, and she'd gotten a little bit too close to somebody who spent all his time, or almost all of it, fooling around with books. She knew how to do things right. And before long she and her mother and her sister had moved off the Hill and down into a place in Town.

They bought one of those old houses the Town Fathers keep wanting to put plaques on, and Mara insisted that the place be redone, and she had the plumbing contractor send away for three bidets, one for every bathroom. It was funnier than hell; Bill kept writing back from Vietnam, talking about how he'd trade in all the bar girls in Saigon for five minutes on Mara Jamison's bidet, and how the first thing he'd do when he got home would be to march down there and tell her she was drafted into the service of the United States Marine Corps. He had always had a kind of crush on Mara, you see; she was his girl-next-door too. He didn't know about Mara being with me. Nobody did. Mara never told Miss Linda who it was she was with, and I never told anybody. Not after the first time, and not later on, when we . . . when I went over and asked her to be with me again. I went in the dead of night and tapped on her window, and we went up along the ridge and I built a shelter and made a fire, and we stayed there together all night; we sneaked back in just before dawn. We kept that up for years, until I went away." I stopped then, hoping she was going to let me leave it there. But I knew better; Judith, in her own way, is more merciless than I.

"And you think it's your fault that she . . ."

"Yes," I said.

"Because you went away?"

"I was always going away."

"Because you didn't take her with you?"

"She was always staying," I said.

She didn't say anything.

"I loved her after a while," I said. "I started out wanting to keep her from them, and after a while I just wanted to keep her; I guess that's love. But I never admitted it."

"You never told her you loved her?"

"Oh, I told *her,*" I said. "I just never told anybody else. I told her that people would talk if they knew, and I didn't want anybody saying things about her, like they did about her mother and her sister. So I insisted that we meet in secret. We did. We'd go up in the hills and spend the night, and sneak back before dawn. But when we were back on the Hill, or in Town, we acted like we barely knew each other. That was how I wanted it. Because I knew that sooner or later she was going to do what her mother wanted her to do. And when it happened, I didn't want anybody thinking that those white men had got-

289

ten something that I wanted. And I knew they would. I hoped they wouldn't but I knew better; I'd actually sat down with a piece of paper and a pencil and figured out all the pressures that were going to be on her when I was gone, and I figured out just about when she was going to give up. She fooled me, in a way; as close as I was ever able to figure, she lasted six months longer than I thought she would. She actually tried all those jobs; she fought like hell. She'd write me letters and tell me about it. Then the letters stopped coming, and I knew what had happened. And nobody ever knew about us. I'd never written her a letter or anything; there was nothing to connect us. But I used to think sometimes that maybe if I hadn't known so much, maybe if I'd believed in her a little bit . . ."

"Yeah," she said. "Maybe you would have won."

I didn't say anything.

"You know, I've always wondered what the hell you wanted with me. Why *you* would have anything at all to do with a white woman. I thought maybe you wanted to make me suffer, brutalize me in some way. But you never did. So I started to think that it was just a kind of accident, that you had fallen in love with me the same say I had fallen in love with you, and you were as confused by the whole thing as I was, and that what was stupid about it was that there should have to be a reason for us, any more than there would have to be a reason for two other people—two black people, or two white ones. That's when I decided it was all right; there were going to be problems, but they weren't the kind of problems . . . Oh, hell, you know."

"I know," I said.

"But I was wrong, wasn't I?"

I didn't say anything.

"You wanted me because I was a white man's woman. I was a white man's daughter and when you met me I was a white man's lover, and if you hadn't come along I would have become a white man's wife and probably a white man's mother, and if I wanted you then you could cheat them all. That was it, wasn't it? That's *still* it. I'm just like Mara, only this time you're not just keeping something from them; you're taking it."

I didn't say anything.

"John," she said, "you've got to answer me."

"I didn't want you at all," I said. "I wanted to stay as far away from you as I could. Because when I thought about being with a woman, you were exactly the kind of woman I thought about being with, except for one little thing. But you wouldn't let me stay away, and it all happened just like I knew it was going to happen, and I ended up loving you. But I didn't know why. Oh, I believed it was for every reason that's right and good, and for none of the reasons that are anything else. I still believe it. But I don't know it." I stood there by the stove, so close to it that I could smell my pants starting to smolder.

"You're never going to be sure, are you?" she said after a while.

I stepped a little away from the stove then, but not too far; I could sense the pain from the burning, but I could not feel the warmth at all. "I can't imagine how," I said.

I had tried all the combinations; I had merged the white cards with the blue, I had mixed in the red, I had tried red and white alone. I had put in the orange. I had cut out the white cards and mixed in the gold. I had made notes. None of them made any sense. Now I went through the laborious process of separating out the cards, isolating each color once again into its own stack. When I had them isolated I started in again, going through the red ones first, one by one, looking at each, memorizing it almost, getting the context set in my mind. Then I went to the white ones. I went through slowly, making associations. I pulled a legal pad to me and started making notes. Once or twice I thought I had something going, but it was nothing but smoke. I went back to the beginning and tried again, working only with the new white ones at first. In the year of our Lord 1787, on a plantation in western Georgia, a child, later named "Zack," was born to a slave woman; her name is unknown, as is that of the father, but she claimed that he was a full-blooded Cherokee brave. In the year of our Lord 1790, on a plantation in northern Louisiana, a child was born to a quadroon house slave named "Marie." In the year of our Lord 1805, on the same plantation in Louisiana, a child, later named "Brobding-nag," was born to an octoroon house slave named "Hermia"; the child's father, apparently, was Zack. In the year of our Lord 1856, in the mountains of southwestern Pennsylvania, a child, later named Lamen, was born to "Bijou," a former slave-prostitute of unknown age and ancestry; the father was almost certainly a man calling himself C.K. And in the year of our Lord 1890, in the city of Philadelphia, a son, later named Moses, was born to Cora Alice and Lamen Washington. That was all comforting. That was all clear. Then I took up the old white cards, the ones that were yellowed with age, and looked at the last one. In the year of our Lord 1958, in the eighth month, on a hillside approximately four and one-half miles south of the town of Chaneysville, Pennsylvania, Moses Washington departed this life. It still made no sense. I took up my pen and added a notation: departed this life probably by the action of his own hand. And it still made no damned sense. I picked up the pad and tore off the sheets with the notes on them and balled them up. I went and dropped the papers into the fire, watched them crisp brown and blacken and burst into flame. For a minute I thought about doing that with everything: the cards, the notes, the notebooks, everything. For a minute I wanted to burn it all.

"Nothing?" she said.

I put the lid back on the stove. The flames left an afterimage dancing in my eyes. I turned around. My eyes adjusted slowly, but I waited until she was more than a shadow, until I could make out the details of her face in the lamplight.

"No," I said. I turned back to the stove and pulled the kettle to the front. I could have used water from the reservoir, but I wanted the toddy hot; as hot as I could get it. Hotter. So hot it would burn.

"Can't I help?" she said.

I took down the whiskey and the sugar. I mixed in the old way, measuring sugar with my thumb. I didn't use much whiskey; the heat was more important than the alcohol. The water boiled and I filled the mug to the brim, glad that it was a thick earthenware mug, not one of the Judge's bloody demitasse cups. I pushed the kettle to the back of the stove and went and sat down.

She sat across the table, her jaw set, and watched me take the first sip. She had been reading something in a folder; she looked down at it, reached out and took up her pen and made a note, then closed the folder, put the pen down, and rubbed her eyes. "I don't know how you see anything in this light," she said. Her voice was neutral, but when she brought her hands away from her face I could see her jaw was still set and her eyes were still on the mug.

"It seems," I said, "that I don't."

The clench went out of her jaw and her eyes softened. "Maybe . . ." Her voice trailed off.

"Maybe what?"

"Maybe if you talked to me about it."

I shrugged and took another sip. The toddy was not as hot as I wanted it; I would have to drink it fast before it cooled even more. "There's nothing to tell you," I said. "That's the problem. I've got lots of facts and none of them connect."

"I don't even know what you're trying to find out," she said.

I sipped the toddy.

"And of course you won't tell me until you know all the answers."

"Look," I said, "that's the way I am."

"All right," she said. "I'm sorry. I just feel like there's something I ought to be able to do to help you, and I can't do anything because you won't tell me anything."

I finished the toddy, sat looking at the empty cup. The warmth hadn't made a dent on the cold in me. I looked at the cards.

"John," she said.

I looked up. "What?"

"Is it all right if I talk to you?"

"Sure," I said. "Isn't it always?"

"No," she said. "It wasn't before. I made you talk. I don't want to do that anymore. I don't want to stop you from doing . . . whatever it is you're doing."

"I'm not doing anything," I said.

"Oh," she said.

"What do you want to talk about?" I said.

She opened her mouth, closed it. Then she smiled. "I don't know," she said. "I just . . . All the way up here I was waiting to talk to you. I was mad and I was worried and I was scared, but what I wanted was to talk to you. So I get here and all I can do is yell at you and badger you and act like . . . I don't know, like a Southern belle who can't have everything nice and neat and clean the way she wants it, and so I haven't gotten to talk to you at all really, when that was what I wanted all along."

"It's good to see you," I said.

She smiled again and got up and went to the stove and poured herself some coffee. She came back and we sat there, drinking together, not saying anything, for a long time.

"John," she said finally, "how did you get here?"

I looked up. "What?"

293

"How did you get here? It sounds so horrible. It sounds like nobody wanted you here and you didn't want to be here. . . ."

"Oh," I said. "You mean black people. That's a good story. Three stories. Well, four, but the last one isn't very interesting. You see, the Hill has two sides, actually: there's the Hill and there's here, what they used to call Far Side, only nobody much calls it anything anymore. Anyway, the thing that separates them isn't geography, it's history. Because the people who lived over here all came from one place, the plantation of one Thomas O. B. Carter, in Fauquier County, Virginia. They arrived in a body in"—I stopped, set the mug down, and reached for the cards—"1849 or '50. Anyway, they came because of—" I stopped again. Something had occurred to me. I took up the red cards, flipped quickly. I knew the date I wanted; I was checking details.

"What is it?" she said.

"I don't know," I said. "Probably nothing. But . . . yeah. John Marshall was born in Fauquier County."

She looked at me blankly.

"And you're from Virginia too," I said. "You ought to be ashamed."

"If I tried to remember the name of every Confederate colonel in Virginia . . ."

"He wasn't a Confederate," I said. "Far from it. He was a Federalist, and he was a real bigwig around the turn of the eighteenth century. He was a relative of the Randolphs and the Lees and the Jeffersons, as in Thomas. But they didn't get on, because, like I said, he was a Federalist and supported Adams against Jefferson in the 1796 election. He was Secretary of State for a while. But mostly he was the fourth Chief Justice of the Supreme Court. He sat on the most important cases in history, the ones where they were still trying to figure out what the Constitution was all about. Marshall wrote the opinion of *Marbury* v. *Madison,* which established the power of the Supreme Court to declare a legally passed law void because it violated the Constitution. Up until then nobody was sure whether or not the Constitution was the supreme law or just the first one. And he wrote the opinion in *McCulloch* v. *Maryland,* which said the U.S. Constitution superseded state laws. He was pretty much a liberal; he wouldn't let Jackson forcibly relocate the Cherokees. Jackson did it anyway."

"And he came from the same place these people did? Did he have something to do with their being here?"

"No," I said. "Probably not. Still, you never know. There are connections and there are connections. No, actually, John Wesley had more to do with their being here than John Marshall."

"John Wesley," she said. She was looking at me as if I were crazy.

"Yep," I said. "John Wesley started the Methodist Church. And Methodism got exported to America just about the time the Colonies were going through a really crazy period of religious fervor. John Wesley was right up there with William Wilberforce when it came to not liking slavery. He published a pamphlet on the subject in"—I stopped and flipped quickly through the gold cards—"1774. *Thoughts on Slavery.* He may have thought a lot about it, but he sure didn't think much of it; he said that slave buyers were 'on a level with man-stealers' and that the people in England who owned plantations, or stock in the companies, were 'principally guilty of all these frauds, robberies, and murders.' Well, that little broadside didn't have too much of an effect for a while, since Americans were too busy getting their own freedom to worry about anybody else, but it was a part of the Methodist Doctrine: no slavery. There was a conference in Baltimore in"—I flipped quickly, knowing it would be in a leap year—"1784, right around Christmas, and it was voted that every member of the church should emancipate his slaves, and do it legally and formally, and if they didn't want to do it they could get out; they were still members, I suppose, but they were to be excluded from communion; after 1784, no slaveholder was supposed to be allowed to take communion in the Methodist Church. That didn't last, of course; by 1796 they were waffling all over the place, saying now that slavery was an evil, and that no slaveholder should be admitted to the church until the minister had spoken to him, and that it was all right to buy slaves, so long as they were only kept in bondage for a stated period of time and if the children were freed at twenty-five if they were men, twenty-one if they were women; the only thing they were adamant about was that nobody should sell any slaves. And things got less and less stringent after that; by 1820 the Methodists weren't even discussing slavery anymore. But for a good long while there, any man who was a slaveholder and a Methodist and who lived in the Upper South had to make a choice between going to heaven later or going into bankruptcy now."

"Wait a minute," she said. "You lost me."

I put the cards down and rubbed my eyes. "Yeah, well, it's complicated. Because a lot of things were going on at the same time. The First Fugitive Slave Law was being passed in 1793. The slave trade was closing down, then reopening for a while, then closing down again, theoretically, although it never really did...." I stopped. "Okay," I said. "There was a compromise in the Constitution, and it was agreed that Congress should not be allowed to illegalize the slave trade before 1808. I'm not sure that anybody was really all that hot to shut off the slave trade, but the important thing is that the Southerners accepted 1808 as a cutoff date. Which means they estimated that within twenty years or so from the ratification of the Constitution, they would have a sufficient slave population in this country to make the system self-sustaining. In fact, they beat the limit by quite a few years, and by the time the Christmas Convention was saying no more slavery for Methodists, there was a complex but highly effective breeding system in operation. It was essentially an internal slave trade; the states in the Upper South bred an excess of slaves and sold them to the states of the Lower South, where there was a demand for large masses of labor. By"—I stopped, flipped through, looking for the exact date—"1830, Virginia was exporting so many slaves that her own black population was just about stable; for the next thirty years she sold slaves at the rate of ten thousand a year, which was just about forty percent of annual interstate exports. In the same period Maryland exported twenty-five hundred a year. Slave breeding was big business, and it naturally affected the composition of the slave-holdings. Because if you were going to work the land you wanted men, but if you were in the breeding business, you wanted women, and you wanted to end up with a lot of children. There was one guy in Virginia who owned one man and eight women."

"What's that got to do with the Methodists?" she said.

"Oh," I said. "Yeah. The Methodists. Well, all those figures come from pretty late, but the Southerners could estimate capacity way back in 1787, and know there would be plenty of breeding going on in twenty years to meet demand. And the Methodists in the Upper South were some of the people who were going to do it. But then along comes the Christmas Convention and tells them to free their slaves, and even when things loosened up, by 1796, they were allowed to free their slaves, but they couldn't sell them; the church was adamant about that, if nothing else. So there they were. They were denied their main source of revenue. They could always work the slaves, but that wasn't enough to keep them afloat; they needed profit. But they couldn't sell their slaves for profit, and they couldn't get rid of unproductive slaves by selling them, they couldn't get rid of women, who were maybe two thirds as productive as males, and who were always getting pregnant and producing children who couldn't do enough work to support themselves for maybe six years and who couldn't be sold, either. They couldn't make money and they couldn't cut their losses or reduce their overhead or even keep their costs from rising due to increasing unproductive population. The only way they could feed their slaves was to plant more acreage in food crops, but they couldn't buy more land so they had to divert acreage from cash crops, which meant that they had less and less work for the slaves to do. It was incredible; the Methodist Church took what had been a profitable, productive, sensible capitalist system and turned it into a welfare state complete with built-in inflation and a decreasing productivity spiral. So the slaveholders did about all they could think of to do—"

"Gave up slavery?"

"To do what? Slaves were the only labor supply available."

"They could have used them as free workers—"

"Living where? Fed by whom? With what? And besides, most states had laws against either manumission or residence by freedmen. No, a lot of them quit Methodism. One of the reasons the Methodist Church changed its position was because some smart bishop looked at the membership rolls and discovered that they were attracting a whole lot of poor, enslaved blacks and losing quite a lot of rich, free whites; at one time the Methodist membership in America was about forty percent black. It couldn't last; power follows money, and three rich slaveholders who made their slaves be Methodists were worth a lot more than three angry slaveholders leaving the church, and the church saw that. In the meantime, a lot of the slaveholders solved their problems by sending their slaves north. Not the productive ones. The excess. Women and children and older men. They'd give the overseer some money and send him north with a coffle with instructions to take up land for the slaves. Some of them made it, and some of—"

"Wait a minute. What happened to the ones who didn't make it?"

I looked at her. "The average Southerner was not a slaveholder.

About three fourths of the Southern population didn't own a slave and wasn't even related to anybody who did. But everybody knew that the key to wealth and power was the ownership of slaves, and the cheapest way to acquire a lot of slaves was to acquire a few female slaves. So now you figure: you're an overseer for Marse Tom, a big Virginia slaveholder with a hundred and fifty slaves, a man rich enough to afford religion. Marse Tom decides he'd rather take communion than make money, but he doesn't want to go broke, either, so he puts together a coffle of breeding women and young children who can't work too well, say about twenty-five, and he gives you some money to take them north. But you aren't rich and you don't care about communion, and as soon as you get out of sight of Tara it suddenly comes into your head that you've got a little bit of money and a nice bunch of slaves, and you can either go on a long hard trip all for the benefit of a bunch of junglebunnies who don't know what's going on anyway, or you can take a little jaunt over the mountains and set up housekeeping in Kentucky or someplace, and become the wealthiest man in the region overnight, and—"

"I get the picture," she said.

"Or maybe you're tired of farming. You don't want to be a planter; city living is more your style. You think you can make it big on the cotton market. So you take the money and herd the slaves south to the slave market in Alabama or somewhere. A prime field hand was worth maybe $1,500 on average. Of course, you probably didn't have too many of those; Massa kept them home. But women were going for $1,200, depending on proven fertility, and if you couldn't have them all pregnant by the time you got to—"

"All right," she said.

"And the kids weren't worth much; maybe only $875. And of course, if there was a light-skinned little girl in there you let her alone; she'd fetch a fine price in New Orleans—"

"I said all right."

"And some of the overseers actually brought the people north."

"I'm glad to hear it," she said.

"Yeah," I said. "Of course, most of those boys weren't above making a quick buck. Massa said buy land, he didn't say how much or where or what kind. Or maybe he did, but all he was going to know was what you told him; there weren't any slaves who were going to write and tell him different. So they brought the people just across the Mason-Dixon Line and bought them the cheapest land available. And what could be cheaper than the northern slope of a hill full of rocks and hollows twenty-five miles from the Mason-Dixon Line? And that's what happened. Mr. Thomas O. B. Carter got religion. Or maybe not; maybe Mr. Carter was like a lot of his fellows and figured out how dangerous it was to have too many slaves and not enough work for them; maybe there was no market. . . . I don't know. I do know that the slaves sent included children; one of them was a two-year-old girl named Mary. She was one of Old Jack's grandmothers."

"So that was this side," she said.

"Yes," I said. "The other side, the Hill, was pretty much populated by the indigenous slave population—"

"You mean ex-slave."

"I mean slave. Chattels personal, as the phrase went. Not indentured servants. Not apprentices. Slaves."

She looked at me blankly.

"Good God," I said, "don't tell me you're one of those people who thinks they only had slavery way down South im de land ob cotton? You probably believe in Santa Claus and the Easter Bunny too."

"I'm not stupid," she said. "And you don't have to be sarcastic."

"So why the look?"

She dropped her eyes. "I don't know. . . . I guess I just don't like to think about that sort of thing. And it just seems . . . John, this is such a pretty town."

"Yeah," I said. "Ain't it? But what difference does that make? There were slaves here when there were slaves everywhere. The first record of slavery in the County that I can find was"—I pulled out the blue cards, flipped through quickly—"1763. Owned by an innkeeper named Pendergrass. That's not too certain; it comes from a novel. But Hervey Allen was pretty reliable, for a novelist. The state started recording slaves in"—I flipped again—"1780. There were three slaves registered then. All males. One was fifty-four, one was thirty, and one was seventeen. So it sounds like there were a few women somewhere too. Anyway, after"—I flipped the cards again—"after 1780 slavery was abolished in Pennsylvania; at least, that's the way it looked. But the Act for the Gradual Abolition of Slavery was really a masterpiece of putting off to tomorrow the things you don't want to do today. First of all, it applied only to blacks born after March 1, 1780, so anybody who was alive before then was a slave for life. Secondly, the blacks born after that weren't free; they owed their masters a twenty-eight-year indenture. The life expectancy of blacks was about twenty-one, but that takes into account the high infant mortality rate—"

"All *right*," she said. "So the people who were brought here were free, and after the indenture the ones who were born here were free. Why did they stay?"

"Why not? The transportees didn't have it so good, true, but doing days work or any kind of free labor, or even trying to scratch out a crop on a rock pile, probably beat chopping cotton for Massa."

"Well, how about the others? The ones who became free. If it was so bad, why didn't they leave?"

"Oh, I don't know. Maybe they figured there wasn't anywhere to go. Or maybe they were sentimental fools and didn't want to leave their children."

She looked at me again, but this time the look wasn't blank.

"'He that hath a wife and children hath given hostages to fortune,'" I said. "Sir Francis Bacon. He said it in 1625, but he could have been a member of the Pennsylvania Assembly." I got up and went to the stove and pulled the kettle over the heat. "There were quite a few who didn't stay," I said, without turning around.

"They moved on? Where?"

"Not on," I said. "Back. They were runaway slaves. They came north, those that knew which way north was, looking for freedom. There was an organization to help—"

"The Underground Railroad," she said.

"That's right. Most of the publicity went to Philadelphia and Cincinnati, because those were the most successful routes. There was another in eastern Pennsylvania. And there was one through here."

"Here? Why here?"

"Geography. The mountains run north and south, pretty much, but they curve away to the northeast. So if you wanted to go due north you had to cross them. So the people stuck to the valleys, the bottomlands where there were streams to lose the dogs in and—" I stopped, looked at her.

"What's wrong?" she said.

"Nothing."

"Why are you looking at me that way?"

I didn't say anything, I just got up and went to the shelf and took down the folio. I brought it back to the table, opened it, drew out the map, spread it slowly. "This is the County," I said. "The way it was in about 1849. This part here, the lower twenty miles or so, is the South County; before the Mason-Dixon survey cleared up the boundary dispute, it was legally part of Maryland—it had always been settled by Southerners anyway. So the sentiments were not precisely abolitionist sentiments; there was surely some slaveholding, but the records are a little sketchy, because it was better to register slaves in Maryland, where they would be slaves for life, than to do it in Pennsylvania, where they would be free after a while. Anyway, that's the territory that runaway slaves had to come across. The first route they used was this one: up through Cumberland Valley, on the west side of Evitts Mountain, here, through these little towns, Evitts and Cruse and Centerville and Patience, and up here into town. But just about nobody made it that far, because the slave-catchers knew that route, and they'd just sit there, waiting. So after a while there was an alternate route, that split off somewhere south of the Line and came into the County east of Evitts Mountain. That route was safer, but not by a whole lot, because here, it came up along the western side of this . . . well, it's not a mountain, exactly, more a hill, called Iron Ore Ridge, to this little town, Hewitt. There was another route, that came in from central Maryland, and it came along the eastern side of Iron Ore Ridge. So at Hewitt—or outside Hewitt someplace; nobody was stupid enough to go into a town—the two routes came together. That's when it got dangerous. Because for the next six miles or so there was no place to go except north, or north by a little east, through this little valley—around here they're called coves. About halfway between Hewitt and this town, Chaneysville, it's extremely narrow—a half mile across, maybe less. It was easy to get caught there. But I don't know how many did; not that many, it looks like. I don't think the slave-catchers knew the land well enough to use that bottleneck. And they didn't need to, because once the slaves got to Chaneysville, they either went this way, north by northeast, up Black Valley and into a town called . . . well, then it was called Bloody Run, and over here and into the North County, or they went this way, up over this ridge and along this valley through Rainsburg and Charlesville and on into town. There were people here who helped if they got that far. Old Jack's grandfather was one of them, and there was a country man named John Graham who used to carry people in the bed of his wagon, hidden under hay, and there was a preacher named Fiddler and another man, named Rouse; I don't know what he did. They hid people in a lot of different places; one was a butchershop. That was the Underground Railroad. And there were some white people involved in the Underground Railroad; a lot of them were Quakers, up here in Fishertown. But for everybody who helped, there were a few who didn't. Which is why the slave-catchers didn't bother going down into Southampton Township—that's where Chaneysville is—and sitting around with dogs and horses and camping out. It was just as effective, and a lot more comfortable, for them to come in and take a room at one of the hotels and put out a few handbills and wait to see if some of the local boys didn't want to do their work for them. There were quite a few local men who made a habit of latching on to strange black folks and turning them over for a reward. In one incident, two men, Crissmun and Mock, told two runaways they'd protect them, and then locked them up in a schoolhouse and sent for their master. Typical." I looked at her. "Another funny thing about Fauquier County. About twenty-five years before Mr. Carter sent his overseer north, somebody—maybe even Mr. Carter—sent his slave-catcher up here. And he hauled back two runaways. Hunted them down in the mountains. One of them was named 'George.' The other one was named 'Henry.'"

She shook her head. "But once they got across . . ."

"The Mason-Dixon Line? Once they made it north they were in free territory, and all they had to do was turn around and thumb nose at Massa? Nope. Didn't work that way for anybody except thieves and murderers like Bonnie and Clyde. They passed the Hot Pursuit Laws to stop them, but there was a hot pursuit law for niggers all along, since 1793. First Fugitive Slave Act . . ." Something clicked in my mind. I went back to the table and picked up the cards, flipping through the red, then the orange. "Yeah," I said. "There's your connection. The First Fugitive Slave Act was passed in Congress in 1793. It provided for the seizure of a fugitive slave in free territory. There was a lot of trouble about it, but the first challenge came in *Prigg* v. *Pennsylvania,* in 1842. Seems that the planters had gotten a little fast and loose with the Fugitive Slave Act, and they would come across the border and claim a free black and find a tame magistrate and get a certificate of remand and haul the poor bugger back South. There was a murder case involved. A freeman named John Read killed two white men who came into his house to take him. They found handcuffs, rope, and whips at the scene. There was a mess about it, and Read was acquitted of killing Griffith, who was supposed to be his master, but found guilty of manslaughtering Shipley, who had come along to help Griffith. The state had pushed for the death penalty, but the jury of Read's peers only gave him nine years. The legislature passed the Personal Liberty Laws, which made it harder for a free black to be taken, since he had to be given due process under the laws, where he didn't under the Fugitive Slave Act. Then along came Prigg, a Maryland man, who sued in federal court, and the Supreme Court held that the Pennsylvania laws were unconstitutional because they were in conflict with a federal statute, which they wouldn't have been able to do without John Marhall's opinion of federal legal supremacy in *McCulloch* v. *Maryland*. There's your connection."

"And they didn't have to prove that the black was a runaway?"

"Only to a magistrate. And . . ." I flipped through the cards again. "Here we go. In 1816 the justice of the peace in Town owned two slaves, one a woman named Milla, the other a child named Bonaparte. Sorry. Bonaparte was legally an indentured servant; Milla too, probably. But imagine exactly how fair a hearing a scraggly runaway was going to get. And that's if he got this far. Down in the South County, in Southampton Township, a man named Jacob Adams was justice of the peace. I don't know what his politics were, but he hailed from Loudon County, Virginia. He was the justice of the peace"—I flipped through the cards again, more slowly this time; my eyes weren't as quick as they had been—"for thirty-five years. Then his son took over."

"And they were crooked?"

I looked at her. "What do you mean, crooked?"

"Well . . ."

"There's no evidence that anybody did anyting illegal. There is every reason to suspect that they scrupulously upheld the law. Which said that a runaway black was exactly the same as a runaway horse, and that interfering with an owner or his agent attempting to regain his property was exactly like interfering with a man trying to catch his horse; the same as being a horse thief."

"They were people—"

"No," I said. "No, they were not people. That was the one thing everybody agreed on, including Abolitionists. Legally, a slave was not a person. And good old Judge Marshall comes in here again; he made the Constitution supreme, and the Constitution recognized slavery. It regulated it, and it gave Congress the power to tax imports at the rate of ten bucks a head. In fact, towards 1860, certain people started advancing the proposition that there was nothing illegal about enslaving white people—"

"I don't understand you," she said.

"What don't you understand?"

"It sounds like you're defending it."

"Defending what?"

"Slavery."

"It was a fact. I'm a historian."

"What about your family?" she said. "Were they runaways?"

"No. God, no. The Professor would have died. No indeed, that's the boring story. The crazy niggers who came here out of choice. The Stantons were good Tidewater house slaves. Got freed about 1800; I don't know the exact date; the Professor had the papers, but he gave them to a library. But it had to have been before 1806, because that's when the Virginia legislature made every freedman get permission to stay in the state, and I remember the Professor had a certificate dated 1806. That's in the library too. The family stayed in Dinwiddie, Virginia. There was some kind of connection with somebody, because they were all educated after the Civil War; the Professor wasn't the first one to go to college. A couple of doctors, a lawyer or two, and three or four preachers. The Professor got his Ph.D. and taught in Washington. Didn't come here until 1942."

"What about the Washingtons?"

"What about them?"

"When did they come here?"

"That's a long story," I said.

"Which you aren't going to tell me."

"It's not interesting," I said.

"I'm interested."

"I'm not."

She didn't say anything. I closed my eyes and leaned back and let the toddy warm me. Tried to. I heard her get up and move towards the door. Her steps were short, quick; angry. She stopped suddenly, spoke abruptly.

"That's it, isn't it? That's what you're trying to figure out. What your father was doing here."

"Lord, no," I said. "I know all that. That's why it isn't interesting. I'm trying to figure out why he died."

"What do you mean? I thought his death was an accident."

"Yeah," I said. "Me too. But it wasn't. They covered up to make it look like an accident. They thought it was murder made to look like suicide but they knew nobody would believe that, so they made it out to be an accident. But it wasn't murder." I shook my head and got up and went to the stove.

"You've just discovered your father committed suicide," she said.

"Not just," I said.

"How long have you known?"

"Since Wednesday," I said. "Since I wrote you the letter. I wasn't sure then; I waited until I was sure before I mailed it."

"And you're trying to find out why he killed himself."

The kettle boiled. I poured the water in and stirred the toddy with my finger, burning myself. I carried the mug back to the table and sat down heavily, spilling a little of the toddy on the note pad. She was watching me, so I had to struggle to hold the mug steady while I sipped at it. I tasted the toddy and realized I had forgotten the sugar. It didn't matter. She watched me drink. I set the cup down carefully and took up the cards, starting to merge them all into one stack. It looked like a rainbow. I was confused; the lamplight flickered, not steady now, and I could hardly read the dates. She watched me for a while—fumbling with the cards and sipping at the toddy, spilling it—then she got up and came around the table and took the mug out of my hands. She put her hands on my shoulders and pulled me up, turned me. I could barely see her; the lamplight was betraying me. All I could see was the blue of her eyes. Her fingers moved over me, unbuttoning my shirt, undoing my belt. She undressed me quickly, efficiently, as if she were undressing a child. I did not resist her. She led me to the cot and pushed me down on it, then went back to the table and blew out the lamp.

In the darkness I heard her undressing, the clink of buckles, the rasp of a zipper. In a few minutes I could see her a little, the pale outline of her body glowing in the ruddy light that escaped from the

305

chinks in the stove. In a moment she came and slid onto the cot beside me and I felt her against me, her skin hot where it had been closest to the stove. She pulled me to her, her arms strong and her fingers spread against my back. She did not move after that, just lay there holding me immobile, her muscles tensed, her body hard, unyielding. I knew she was waiting for me to do something, but she held my arms prisoner; I could not touch her. I tried to; I struggled, but she tightened her grip and held me still. "Shh," she said, in a tight harsh whisper. "Shhh . . ." I stopped moving then, stopped doing anything, breathed as shallowly as I could, waiting and waiting, until the keening of the logs in the grate became a lullaby and I thought that I would fall asleep, fall away from her. And then, just when perhaps I would have, she gave one deep sigh and her breathing quickened, and I felt her thighs move, slipping around me below and above, and I felt her belly against me, and then the softness and heat and moistness that lurked below.

I stood on the ridge, exposed to the full force of the wind that came driving out of the south. The snow had stopped but the wind kicked that which had already fallen into great white clouds, full of icy spicules that stung my face. On the slope below me the drifts were building; they would be even worse on the eastern slopes; because of the mountains' northeastern swing, the drifts would build there too, but the wind would not be slowed by the contour of the land. And what it meant was that if I was going to go, I would have to go now, before the eastern slopes were fully drifted, before the inevitable swing of the wind into the west drifted the western slopes and choked the valleys too.

I did not want to go. I did not want to go at all. I would rather have sat in the cabin, sipping toddies, listening to Judith's snoring, even looking at those damned cards. But there was nothing in the cards for me; I knew that now. And I had gone to every other place on the map, visited the caves and the hollows and the hideouts, all of it. There was only one place left. Only once chance left for me to understand. If there was a chance at all.

I shifted the pack to make it ride more easily, and fumbled in the pocket of Bill's field jacket for the flask. I took a sip, keeping it small; the whiskey in the flask and in the bottle in the pack was going to have to last...I figured quickly. A forty-five-mile round trip, at maybe three miles an hour, allow for rest and delay due to the snow-fall...Call it twenty hours, perhaps twenty-two. I realized that I should have brought another bottle. But I would not go back; I might wake Judith. And I was wasting time thinking about it; I shifted the pack again and started down.

I stopped when I got as far as Moses Washington's house. I don't know why I stopped. But while I stood there I wondered, for the first time, if she knew the truth about what he had done. Probably not. Probably it was the kind of thing that she would work at not know-ing, or at least, at not believing. Just as I had. But then I realized that it made no difference what she knew, because for a dozen years she had lived with a man who was so crazy that one day he was going to walk twenty-two miles just to find a nice spot in which to blow his brains out, and so preoccupied as not only to do it, but not to care enough about the effect of it on his wife—and his children—to try and make it look like an accident; a man who showed her no mercy. And then I thought of Judith, waking in the morning to find me gone.

And so I climbed up onto Moses Washington's porch and opened the door of Moses Washington's house, and stepped inside, shivering a little, trying to be silent.

But the house was not silent. The darkness echoed with electron-ic static scratchings and the raspy sound of an announcer's voice; she was listening to the radio, some all-night call-in show from Boston or Detroit. The sound of it grew louder as I climbed the stairs, made my way through dark familiar rooms: "My grandfather got off a boat from the old country, Dan, and he was discriminated, but he worked hard and he made his way, and I think anybody can do the same thing...." I went and stood at the doorway of her bedroom, looking at the mound her body made beneath the handmade quilts. "...hard work is the American way, even if you are discriminated..."

"John?" she said.

"...don't like it, just go back where they came from. My grand-father had to fight to get here, and they didn't have to do a thing..."

"Yes," I said.

"Well, I don't know if that's quite the way to look at it."

"What do you want to know?"

"Well, Dan, that's the way I look at it. I think if they took the welfare money and bought boats..."

"How can you listen to that garbage?" I said.

She reached out and turned the radio off. "I don't really listen to it," she said. "It just keeps me company."

I didn't say anything.

"What do you want to know?" she said again.

"Nothing," I said. "I don't want to know anything."

"You always want to know something," she said.

I didn't say anything. The radio scratched in the darkness. She reached out again and turned it off.

"Why did you marry him, anyway?" I said.

"I wanted to have children," she said. Her voice was flat, matter-of-fact, as if she had expected the question.

"There were lots of men."

"No," she said. "There weren't any. Not here."

I didn't say anything.

"We were allies," she said. "We didn't want the same things, but what we each wanted was close enough.... I wanted children, he wanted sons. He wanted two sons. He said that at the very beginning. I said I hoped he knew you couldn't always control that kind of thing. He said he could. He had read and studied a lot of books and the Laws of the Old Testament, and he said that if we lived the way the children of Israel lived, then we would have sons. So we did. Part of the month he would sleep in the other room. And we had sons. And after your brother was born, that was the end of... that part of things. Because he had what he wanted, and I had what I wanted...."

"Didn't you ever want anything else?"

"You mean love?" she said.

I didn't say anything.

"Yes," she said. "I wanted it. I suppose you could say I didn't get it. Moses didn't love the way most people would think a man should love.... I don't know. I had what he gave me. Maybe it was love, maybe it wasn't."

"Was it worth it?" I said.

She didn't say anything. But suddenly I could hear her breathing, there in the darkness.

"Was it?" I said. "Was it worth it?"

308

I heard her move then, heard the bedsprings creak as she reached out and turned the radio back on. I heard it hum as the tubes warmed.

I turned away from her then, and went into the powder room, wondering if what I was doing was the right thing, or even a kind thing; if Moses Washington's way had not been better; if she had not, when they came to tell her that her life with him was a finished incident, breathed, somewhere inside her, a tiny sigh of relief. I stood there in the smell of hair pomade and stale perfume and wondered. But then the radio began to crackle again, and some insane insomniac began to chatter about the salvation of God, and I took the keys down and slipped them into my pocket and quietly went away.

197903120400

(Monday)

WE CAME SLAMMING DOWN OFF THE HILL, the tires half rolling, half sliding over the snow, giving me a minimum of control. I wasn't steering, I was aiming, but that didn't worry me—I had learned to take a car off the Hill long before my mother had found the money to buy snow tires—but Judith, sitting rigid in the right-hand seat and watching Railroad Street come flying up towards us, was frightened. "Shouldn't you slow down?" she said.

I didn't answer her; I was running out of Hill. I had time to flick the headlights and hit the horn, just in case there was somebody on Railroad Street, and then we went diving down into the hollow at the base of the Hill, the speedometer reading thirty-five. The rise beyond the dip killed some of the speed, but the wall of the warehouse on the other side of the road came roaring up at twenty-five, and I heard Judith say something, but I was too busy to listen, too busy hitting the clutch and holding it down and jamming the transmission into second, and then stabbing at the brakes once, hard, and cranking the wheel around to the left. The rear end kicked out, and I flicked the wheel just a little. The rear end came around then, and straightened out, perfectly square, and I had traction and control, and drove on, steadily, sedately.

"Jesus," Judith said.

"It's the only way," I said.

We came rolling up towards Richard Street. I made the turn at twenty, let the speed climb a little more, and then we were going up the grade into the center of town and I kept the engine speed constant while the wheel speed fell off. We coasted to a stop at the traffic light, and there I had to make my first decision. There were two ways to go: east, out towards the Narrows and then turning south on state highway 326, through Charlesville and Beegleton and Rainsburg; or due south into Cumberland Valley, through Burning Bush to Patience and then east from there to Rainsburg. The first route was likely to be unplowed; the second would be clear as far as Patience, but then I would have to climb Evitts Mountain on a road that might be plowed and might not. I thought about it for a minute, sitting at the traffic light wishing I were on foot. The mountains angled away to the northeast. The wind had not yet kicked around to come out of the west. The western slopes should be fairly free of drifts, and warmer, so less icy. It wasn't much of a theory, but otherwise the decision was a toss-up, so when the light changed I took us south, up the long incline on Richard Street and down into the valley beside Shobers Run. The road was twisting for a mile or more, but the turns were gentle, the rises and falls small.

"It's lovely," she said.

It was. There was no wind in that valley; it was protected by a curious configuration of the mountains: they pinched down into a narrow pass, creating almost a box, really. And so the air was still and clear. The headlights reached out and tapped the snow and sent back golden sparkles that added to the silver thrown up by the moonlight. But far above us the clouds were fleeing north across the sky, propelled by a wind so strong it tore them apart as much as it pushed them, and I knew that half a mile farther on, where we would come out of the lee of the mountain, the wind would be driving up the cove.

"Yeah," I said. I looked over at her.

She had turned her head back and was staring out the windshield. Her face was calm, composed, and contented, her profile sharp and distinct against the background of the moonlit snow.

Her face changed then, but not into a smile: her eyes widened in fear, and I realized that I should have been watching the road. I spun back. We had been coming down an incline towards a turn, and I had let the speed get away from me, and ahead of us loomed the outline of a square solid building, its near corner only a few feet from the edge of the road. It wasn't as dangerous as it looked; I just shifted back to second and steered the car around it.

"That's a dumb place to put a building," she said.

"Actually, it's a dumb place to put a road; the building was there first. On the other hand, there wasn't any other place to put the road; all that over there was water."

"What . . . ?"

"It's an old mill," I said. "Built by"—I let the cards flip in my mind—"Dr. John Anderson, around the turn of the century. All that out there was the mill pond."

She shook her head. "I know you said this place was backward, but they were using water power in 1900?"

"Sure," I said. "But I meant the turn of the nineteenth century."

"It's still standing?"

"They built to last. There were mills all over the place, and a lot of them still stand. Or parts of them do."

"Still . . ." she said. But I couldn't listen to her; another turn was coming up, the first of the bad ones, close above the creek and cambered wrong, which is what happens when you try to build a highway over a route best suited to horses. I got the speed down with some careful braking, and came around it with enough speed to straighten out. I heard Judith gasp, but it wouldn't be the road this time.

"The Springs Hotel," I said. I turned and looked. It was a sight. A long, creamy edifice, with a columned, two-storied central section and long, pavilioned wings reaching out on either side. The snow on the lawn was smooth and unblemished, and the moonlight danced on the facade.

"It's beautiful," she said.

"And old," I said. "A hundred and seventy years or so. Built by Dr. Anderson"—I stopped to think, letting the cards flip—"in 1806. Just a few years after Vincenz Priessnitz invented the sponge bath, the wet sheet pack, and the douche, and started cleaning up in Austria with mineral water spas. The fashion came across the Atlantic. Along about 1804, a mechanic . . . nobody knows his name, so maybe it's just a story, but anyway, he was fishing right over here and started drinking the water, and before long his rheumatism was cured and the sores on his legs were gone. So Anderson built his hotel, and a couple of years later he bought more land, with three more springs on it, and the word got around. For a while this was the most prestigious resort in America, the vacation spot of millionaires and Presidents. Local people made plenty, and they stopped complaining about hard water."

A right angle was coming then, and I got the speed up and started to bring us around the turn.

"I don't—" she said, but the wind hit us then, and pushed us into a little skid. I started to correct, but then I saw what was going to happen, and I let the rear end come around until the wind caught the left side of the car and slammed it back into line. I relaxed then; from there on until the climb over the pass into Cumberland Valley it was going to be easy. Judith twisted around in her seat, looking back to get a last glimpse of the Springs. "Quite a sight," she said. "When did it close down?"

"It didn't," I said. "It's just shut for the winter. Opens the end of April."

I felt her tense. "I see," she said. "Just one of those little things about this place you didn't tell me, right?"

"It's just an old hotel," I said. "How am I supposed to know you'd be interested in an old hotel?"

"One that looks like that? I . . . Oh, never mind. Tell me now. What's it like inside?"

"I don't know," I said. "I've never been inside."

I heard her twisting around again, and I knew she was staring at me.

"I've never been inside," I said again. "I wouldn't set foot in the damned place."

We were up the incline now, and I made the turn that put the Springs out of sight. The road ran straight then, at a slight upgrade, across the face of the mountain. The trees were tall on either side, their branches arching over us, blocking out the moon. I shifted back up into third gear and let the speed climb.

"John," she said. There was an edge on her voice.

"It's a long story," I said.

"Good," she said. "It'll keep my mind off your driving."

I thought about it, not wanting to, hoping the facts would elude me, but they didn't, they came springing into my mind, names and dates as clear and sharp as india ink on red card stock. "Buchanan," I said. "James. Born 1791. Graduated Dickinson College, Carlisle, Pennsylvania, 1809. Elected to Congress 1821. Appointed minister to Russia 1832. Elected senator—this was back in the days when the senators were elected by the state legislature—1834. Stayed in the Senate for eleven years, and then went to work as secretary of state under Polk. Buchanan messed up foreign relations for a few years, hewing to the expansionist line. He presided over the acquisition of Oregon and the annexation of Texas, which got us into the Mexican War, much to the delight of the Southerners, who had visions of turning the entire Southwest into slave territory. They won the war but lost the political battle, because Zachary Taylor became a hero in the Mexican War and ran for the Presidency as a Whig, and won, which put Buchanan out on his ear. But Taylor died of typhoid fever. Millard Fillmore couldn't hold the Whigs together, and lost out in 1852, but the Democrats managed to compromise on Franklin Pierce, who was a war hero and soft on slavery, and he was elected. He made Jefferson Davis secretary of war, and he made Buchanan minister to Great Britain. At the same time, the minister to France was a man named John Young Mason, a Virginian, and the minister to Spain was a French-born immigrant who had gotten to be a big-time Louisiana Democrat, a man named Pierre Soulé. Now, the way it worked out, the Southerners were hamstrung by laws that controlled the expansion of slavery into the North and West, but nobody had ever said much of anything about the South. They thought they were going to make out well after the Mexican War, but all they got was Texas. So they set their sights on Cuba. The first thing they did was to try and steal it, and they sent seven hundred and fifty Mexican War veterans under a man named Narciso López on a little expedition. That was in"—I had to think for a while—"1848. That didn't work. It didn't work when they tried it again in 1850. When they tried it again in 1851, they came close; they actually got a foothold on the island. But López was captured and killed. So they got Pierce to make noises about annexing Cuba in his inaugural address, trying to stir up favorable public opinion, and tried to promote a war over a customs hassle involving a cargo ship called the *Black Warrior,* which had violated some regulation and was being held in Havana harbor. But the North refused to go to war over a six-thousand-dollar fine. So then they got Pierce to get Soulé to try and buy Cuba. But Soulé had really screwed up pushing the *Black Warrior* thing, had actually issued an ultima-

314

tum on behalf of the U.S. government that nobody in the State Department had authorized, and the Spanish wouldn't listen; they didn't want to sell Cuba, anyway. So Pierce told Soulé to get together with Mason and Buchanan, and they held a conference in Ostend, Belgium, and came up with a document called the Ostend Manifesto, which was a pretty obvious suggestion that if Spain wouldn't sell Cuba, the U.S. government ought to go and take it. That got nowhere; the secretary of state was no great liberal but at least he wasn't a fool, and he repudiated the document as soon as the news leaked out. But it didn't hurt Buchanan any; it kept him in good with his Southern buddies, and with their help, and the help of some of his Northern buddies who were just as bad—in between 'My Old Kentucky Home' and 'Dixie,' Stephen Foster wrote Buchanan's campaign song—he got the Democratic nomination for President, and because the liberals couldn't decide between Frémont and Fillmore, and because of some shenanigans about the Dred Scott Decision, which his Southern buddies on the Supreme Court held up announcing until after the election because they were afraid if they did it beforehand half the country would vote Republican, he managed to get elected President. First Pennsylvanian ever elected President. And the last one, too; people do learn from their mistakes, if the mistakes are bad enough. And Buchanan was bad enough. If you went looking for a worse President you could find one, I suppose, but you'd look awful hard to do it. Maybe Nixon. But then, Nixon never really came close to destroying the country, and he had six years; Buchanan just about did destroy it, and he managed in four. He started out by appointing a crony to every job he could find. He made a man named Bowman, who had been the editor of one of the local papers, the *Gazette,* for a long time—"

"Local . . . you mean here?"

"That's right. He was a Democrat, and his idea of journalism was to print darky jokes and run accounts of slaves slaughtering white people and then eating them, so Buchanan made him the public printer in Washington, and after four years Bowman ended up with a hundred thousand dollars, which wasn't bad for those days. Of course, others did even better. Buchanan had another buddy, a Virginian named John Buchanan Floyd—I never could find out if they were related—who started out as a cotton planter in Arkansas and went broke, but he helped Buchanan get nominated, so Buchanan

315

made him secretary of war and he managed to 'lose' $870,000. Those guys did okay, but everybody else was going broke; there was an economic panic so bad that the farmers in Illinois decided it was cheaper to burn their corn than to send it to market. Buchanan didn't do much about that; he was too busy trying to make his Southern buddies happy by getting Kansas admitted to the Union with a constitution that would have made it more of a slave state than Alabama, a thing called the Lecompton Constitution. The Kansans were against it about four or five to one, but Buchanan arranged it that when they went to vote, the only choices they had about slavery were limited slavery or unlimited slavery, so the people who were against slavery didn't vote. Buchanan brought it up before Congress, but the deal stank so bad that even guys like Stephen Douglas, who wasn't exactly what you could call an enemy of the South, couldn't stomach it. And that set the stage for the Civil War, because the Southerners were mad at Douglas, so when he was nominated in 1860 they bolted the Democratic party and nominated Breckinridge and split the vote, and Lincoln sneaked in between. So Buchanan ended up destroying his own party; the Democrats didn't elect a President again for twenty-four years. But that wasn't enough for Buchanan. By 1860 everybody knew there was going to be war—William H. Seward had been talking about the 'irrepressible conflict' for two whole years—so Buchanan let his Southern buddy Secretary Floyd send a hundred and fifteen stands of arms to Southern arsenals for safekeeping, and order Anderson not to defend Fort Sumter. . . ."

"John," she said, "will you please tell me what this has to do with that lovely old hotel?"

"That was the bastard's headquarters. After he was elected he made it the Summer White House, but he'd been coming here for years, long enough to have kids named after him and make twenty-buck contributions to the local Episcopal church. He would hang out down there, being the big man with his local lackeys, like Bowman and a man from the West County, a guy named Jeremiah S. Black, who was smart enough to get to the State Supreme Court but not smart enough not to become Buchanan's attorney general and end up getting blamed for mismanaging the South Carolina secession. But I guess it was a thrill for a lowly state judge to hang out with Buchanan's other buddies, that compromising idiot Henry Clay and that damned sellout Daniel Webster and Associate Justice Robert Grier, who was a Polk appointee, even though he was from Pennsylvania. Of course, he wasn't the only Supreme Court Justice down there. They were all down there. They spent the summers down there. That's where they hatched out the dirty deal over the Dred Scott Decision. Buchanan didn't make a single campaign trip, but he came here to talk with his buddies, Mr. Chief Justice Roger Brooke Taney, from Maryland, and Mr. Associate Justice James Wayne Moore from Georgia, and Mr. Associate Justice Peter Vivian Daniel from Virginia . . ."

"John . . ."

". . . sitting down there with their own personal slaves waiting on them hand and foot, just like back home, bringing magnesia water to cure old Massa's rheumatism, and then they'd send the niggers out to the quarters, just like they did back home in Dixie, and they'd switch over to iron water and go to work deciding exactly when they were going to tell the poor dumb darkies that they weren't citizens, and weren't ever going to be citizens, even if they managed to get free, and that they didn't have any right to property, or to appeal in a court of law, and that the 'status of slavery is perpetual and self-perpetuating,' so they couldn't be free and their kids couldn't be free . . ."

I realized that my voice was too loud, that my fingers were aching from gripping the steering wheel, that my foot had somehow come to press the accelerator nearly to the floor, that we were flying over the highway at nearly sixty miles an hour. I felt a flush of adrenaline in my belly, and eased off on the accelerator gently, feeling sweat running down my spine. I let the car roll to a stop and sat there in my sweat. I took my hands off the wheel but I couldn't hold them up; they were shaking. I put them in my lap, and felt them trembling on my legs. When my hands had stopped shaking enough I reached into my coat pocket and got out the flask. I took only a small sip, but I took it slowly, and I knew Judith was watching me. When I was finished I took the flask away from my mouth and put the top back on and got the car going.

From there it was easy. The road went downhill fairly steeply, but my guess had been right: the western slope of the mountain was free of drifts. Down in Cumberland Valley the wind was throwing up minor tornadoes of snow, but the plows had been through recently, to clear the drifts from the road. I knew the road well—I hated the valley, but I knew it—and I put the speed up to forty-five and we made good time, rolling south through Burning Bush and on into Patience. The climb to the top of Evitts Mountain was quick and easy; they had plowed the back roads too, for some reason.

At the top of the mountain I let the car roll to a stop and looked over at Judith. She had said nothing at all during the long, easy run, and I thought maybe she was asleep, but she wasn't; I could see her eyes glinting in the light from the instrument panel. I started to call her name but changed my mind. I just took a sip from the flask and sat for a minute, looking down into the valley. I reached out to adjust the heater, but it was on full. "Must be windy up here," I said.

She didn't say anything. I shrugged and got us moving again, down into the valley towards Rainsburg. The road was clear; it was going to be easy. I risked taking my hands off the wheel, one at a time, and blowing on them. Judith looked at me. "Are you cold?" she said.

"Just my hands," I said.

"It feels warm to me," she said. "It's the whiskey that's making you feel cold."

"The whiskey's the only thing making me feel warm," I said.

We came to the bottom of the mountain then, and I dropped down into second gear to negotiate a long curve. Then we were on the valley floor, rolling easily into Rainsburg. The road was still clear; we were still in the lee of a mountain, and the wind wasn't pushing the snow across the road at all. But there was wind; I could feel it.

Rainsburg was asleep, the few houses and the store dark, but the road as bright as daylight in the unearthly glow of the vapor lamps. I turned right and moved slowly south, towards the bulk of the mountain. At the lower end of town, where the road turned east and began to climb, I let the car come to a stop and killed the engine. I felt for my gloves and hat, found them, and then found the flask. I took a good pull this time, and capped it, and then started to pull on the gloves.

"Are we there?" she said.

"Not yet," I said. "Stay here." I took the keys and got out, closing the door reluctantly, huddling for a minute beside the car. Then I straightened up, expecting to take the wind full on my face. But there was no wind. The air was calm and still. But cold.

I went around and opened the trunk. I unearthed the jack, and the chains. I worked quickly, jacking the car and slipping the chains on without trouble. I put the jack in the trunk and got back in the car. My hands were shaking, and I had trouble getting the key into the ignition. When I had the engine running I took out the flask again. I needed a toddy, but cold whiskey was better than nothing.

"I want to know where we're going," she said.

"Maybe no place," I said. "It depends on what the wind has done to the road up here. It won't be plowed, but we ought to do all right with the chains, providing the snow hasn't drifted. And once we get to the top we should be able to get down into the cove on the other side."

"What's there?"

"Chaneysville," I said.

"John, what's in Chaneysville?"

"I don't know," I said.

I put the car in gear and took us out of Rainsburg, working the speed up as high as I dared, looking for the place where the surface changed from macadam to gravel. It was about there that they would probably have stopped the plow, there that the hard going would begin. But I never saw the surface change, because they had stopped plowing before then, and the road had vanished into just a swath of white. Then I felt the increase in traction as the chains started to bite through snow into loose stone, digging deep, and I shifted down into second and settled back for the climb.

The first mile or so was easy; the mountain had killed the force of the wind. But then we came around the shoulder of the hill and the drifts were there. Light at first, and at an angle to the road—I had enough speed to slide through them—but they would get worse. I started to speak to Judith; then I realized that the slow speed had lulled her—she was asleep. It was just as well. The mountain was looming on our right side, and to the left the land fell away in a sheer drop of about fifty feet into a creekbed lined with rocks and fallen trees, and hitting one good drift at the wrong angle would have us over there, and if we went it would be better if she was relaxed. That wasn't likely—the chains were biting well—and I began to think we were going to make it without any problem. But then there was a turn and I had to let the speed drop off, and then there was a hill and I went into the climb with too little speed. I didn't dare give it gas; that would break the rear wheels loose. All I could do was keep one eye on the steadily falling speedometer and watch the road, hoping that the grade would lessen. It didn't. It got steeper. The speed fell off. A quarter mile into it, with no end in sight, I knew I wasn't going to make it anyway, and the speed was so low it hardly mattered, and I risked giving it gas, slowly, just a little. The speedometer leaped to the left as the wheels spun, and I was about to ease off, but the chains dug through to gravel and got an instant's traction, and then we were skidding, the rear end going off to the left, swinging towards the drop. It happened quickly, but it went almost in slow motion, and I eased the wheel around and killed the skid in what seemed to me to be no time. But when I looked in the side mirror I saw the tail end hanging over nothing. It took all the will power I had not to spin the wheel to the right, but I held it and got lined up and fed in the gas, and the car straightened out, still moving at maybe ten miles an hour. But little by little the speed dropped off, and there wasn't enough traction to get it up again, and then the road disappeared. I could see where it had to be, because there was mountain on one side and drop on the other and the trees formed an avenue, but I couldn't see road, or hint of road. There was nothing but snow. I stopped the car, killed the engine and the headlights, and sat there, looking out at the snow and listening to the wind howling and the faint ticking of the engine as it cooled. Judith stirred beside me, twisting into a more comfortable position. I got out the flask and sipped at it while I looked out at the snow and thought about what to do. The situation didn't really merit much consideration, but I made the thinking last as long as possible, and then, when I had reasoned everything through far more than was reasonable, I put my hat and gloves on and got out to go and make camp.

I had slept. I had slept and while I had slept the wind had died and the moon had gone down, leaving the woods black and still.

The fire was glowing happily now, the wood hissing gently, the coals throwing out good heat, enough, almost, to warm me. I checked the kettle; the snow had melted, making enough water for maybe two toddies, and it was hot. The coffeepot had more water in it; I had kept adding snow as what was there had melted. I rummaged around in the pack and found the coffee and dumped some in the pot and set it back over the fire.

It had been a long time since I had made a winter camp; fifteen years, at least. It felt good to do it again. I thought about plans. My watch read 4 A.M.; daylight in three hours. No new snow had fallen; we should be able to get across the rest of the mountain on foot in an hour, and then another hour in the valley. We would be there by nine o'clock.

For the moment I was content to lie there, wrapped in blankets, by the fire, with Judith beside me; for a while I was relaxed and happy. But my mind does not turn off; it never has. Bit by bit the thoughts came slipping in, the facts and the calculations, the dates and the suspicions. There was no pattern to them, nothing I could grab on to; it was just random cerebration; a mind chuckling to itself. But it brought me out of my stupor, made me feel uneasy, made me remember where I was and where I was going. The wind kicked up then, chilling me. I straightened up and reached for the bottle. Judith stirred.

"John?"

"Here."

"Whereat?"

"Right here."

"No, wherewe?"

"The same place we were when you went to sleep: halfway up the side of a mountain."

"Coffee?"

The pot was humming gently and the smell of the coffee was on the air, but she liked it strong. "Be ready in a minute," I said.

She hauled herself ungracefully into a sitting position and rubbed her eyes. A gust of wind came whipping over the top of the windbreak and chilled us to the bone. "Jesus," she said.

"He had enough sense to get born in a warm climate," I said.

She stretched her arms out wide, then leaned over and wrapped them around me and hugged me. "This is fun," she said.

"Some fun," I said.

"You're right," she said. "Fun isn't the right word. I was so tired last night I thought I was going to die, and then I thought I wasn't going to have the chance because from what I could see we're so stuck we'll probably die up here, but what matters to me is that you brought me. I don't know if that means anything, but it means something to me, and I don't care if we do die of starvation—"

"Exposure, maybe," I said, "but not starvation. Remember the Donner Party?"

She didn't say anything.

"The coffee should be ready now," I said.

"You can ruin anything, you know that?" she said.

"You haven't even tasted it yet. Maybe it's not as good as your coffee. . . ."

She pulled her head away from me and looked at me, then she put her head back on my chest and hugged me again. I maneuvered my cup past her head and took a sip.

"Don't you want your coffee?"

"Yes."

I poured a cup for her. She took it, sipped. I settled back and she leaned back beside me, her right hand holding the cup, while her left sneaked out and searched for mine. I shifted my cup and took her hand. I felt the calm come back over me, her hand in mine, the warm whiskey sliding down my throat. I gazed into the red heart of the fire. I squeezed her hand.

"John?" she said.

"What?"

"Will you tell me now?"

"Tell you what?"

"Where we're going. Not why; just where."

"I told you where."

"You told me the names of places; they don't mean anything to me. You know they don't."

I shrugged my shoulders, settling deeper in the blankets to avoid a tendril of wind that had somehow crept over the windbreak. I took a sip of the toddy. "We're going to see the place where Moses Washington blew his brains out."

"Do you think that will help?" she said.

"I've done everything else," I said. I felt suddenly colder, and I pulled the blanket closer around me. I sipped at the toddy and stared at the fire, at the flames dancing around in the wood.

"It's another long story," I said. "If you want to know, I'll tell you."

"I want to know," she said. "You know I want to know."

I took a deep breath. "All right," I said. "Give me a minute."

It took longer than a minute. I sat there, staring at the flames dancing, and tried to make my mind work, trying to forget everything, all the clashing facts on the red cards and the gold cards and the orange cards, trying to separate out the ones on the white, and trying to forget I didn't know the why of any of it. It took more than a minute, but after a while the dates were in order, at least as far as they went.

"It starts in 1787," I said, "on a plantation somewhere in northwest Georgia, when a slave woman, whose name I don't know, gave birth to a son. Actually, the story must have started at least nine and a half months before, when she managed somehow to come in contact with a full-blooded Cherokee brave, whose name I also don't know, who according to her was the baby's father. The master, whose name I also don't know, must not have been a man of much imagination; he named the child Zack. Or maybe I do him an injustice; maybe it was a large plantation, with lots of births, and he had used up all the fancy names. Or maybe he had gotten tired of having niggers named Hannibal and Caesar running around. Anyway, after a while Massa must have gotten tired of having Zack underfoot: in 1801 he sold him. Zack had been trained as a blacksmith, and he was worth a lot of money—probably a thousand dollars or more—to a man named Hammond Washington, who owned a large plantation near a place called Independence, in Louisiana. And now the story gets a little complicated, because there's another point where it starts—on Hammond Washington's plantation, in 1790, when a baby girl was born into bondage, the daughter of a house slave named Marie, who was probably an ex–French chattel; anyway, she was a quadroon. The child's father, being an educated man, named her Hermia." I looked at her, but she didn't say anything. "Evidently, Hermia led a rather privileged existence, possibly due to her mother's high status as a house slave and concubine, and partly due, of course, to her own relationship to Hammond Washington. She was from the beginning groomed for a position in the house. But somehow she managed to come into sufficient contact with the new blacksmith for a courtship to take place. On September 27, 1803, she was permitted to marry Zack. Although the ceremony had no legal standing, the union was legitimized to a higher degree than most slave marriages, because Hammond Washington, who was evidently a scrupulous and careful man, drew up a license for them. He also drew up a second document, which he gave Zack as a wedding gift, which enjoined the Washington family from disposing of them separately, or of disposing of them at all while Marie should remain alive. In addition to this, Zack was to be permitted, from the day of the marriage forward, to hire his own time and collect his own wages. The stipulations were: that Zack would be responsible for the upkeep of himself and his wife, even though she was to continue working as a servant in the Washington household; that he should pay to Hammond Washington a flat weekly rate of three dollars, and a third of anything he earned beyond what he required for that payment and the upkeep of himself and his wife; and that, should Hermia become pregnant, during the time that was spent in lying in and in nursing the child Zack should compensate Washington at the additional rate of two dollars per week, to be taken out of his profit. Whatever was left in profit could be applied by Zack against a price of two thousand dollars, which was Hammond Washington's estimate of his value. When that sum was paid, Washington agreed to manumit Zack, at which time the three-dollar flat fee would no longer be payable, although the percentage rate would continue so long as Zack or any of his family would continue to be the property of Washington or his family. After Zack was free he could begin paying towards the value of Hermia, which Washington fixed at eight hundred and seventy-five dollars. There were additional clauses in the document concerning children, which gave Zack the right to pay towards their price, which was to be established by their worth on the open market, and the stipulation was that the children had to be purchased before Hermia could be. Zack obviously understood the implications of the document, even though he was forbidden by law to even try to read it; he knew time was against him. So he went to work, and in the next two years he paid his fee and percentage to Hammond Washington, and made regular payments of about twelve dollars a week towards his freedom, which Hammond Washington scrupulously credited to him in amendments to the document. In twenty months or so he had paid half the price. But time and nature caught up to him, and in the early part of June 1805, the payments dropped off by about three dollars a week, and on August 12, 1805, Hammond Washington amended the agreement to allow Zack to pay, after his own freedom was purchased, on the freedom of a male child who was five-sixteenths black, and a quarter Cherokee, and whom Hammond Washington, evidently an admirer of Jonathan Swift, named Brobdingnag.

"The effect of the child on Zack's economic circumstances was pretty damaging. It's possible that Hermia had a difficult time, and wasn't able to return to Hammond Washington's house for some time. At any rate, in early September Hammond Washington began to debit the amount he had credited towards Zack's freedom at the rate of three dollars a week. It was only a temporary setback, however, and the debits stopped in mid-October. But Zack paid no more towards his freedom until January of 1806, and from then on the sums only averaged about ten dollars. Still, he made good progress, and by March of 1807 he had managed to get the balance due to Hammond Washington down to only about four hundred dollars. He probably would have been able to purchase his freedom within twelve months, but sometime that year the Louisiana legislature passed a law limiting manumission to slaves over thirty, thus making the agreement between Zack and Hammond Washington not only technically illegal, which it had been from the beginning, but impossible to execute, even informally. I don't know exactly when the act was passed, but on December 14, 1807, Hammond Washington amended the document, deferring the manumission of Zack, Hermia, and any children until such time as manumission should be legal under the laws of the state of Louisiana, but stipulating that as soon as the originally agreed upon amount of two thousand dollars should be paid, the flat fee would end, and any sums paid would be applied to the price of the freedom of Brobdingnag."

"So nothing much changed," she said.

"Everything changed," I said. "For one thing, while Zack might have been freed by 1817, and Hermia by 1820, Brobdingnag wasn't going to be free until 1835, assuming he survived that long, and even if he did, the odds that Zack was going to live to see it were pretty slim. For another, there was no guarantee that Hermia would have no more children; if she did, Zack was going to end up buying his children out of slavery until he died, and probably working himself to death trying. But the crucial factor was Hammond Washington, who from all appearances was as fair as a slaveholder could be. Since he fathered children in 1790, he was probably born around 1775 or perhaps a year or two earlier; it wasn't likely that he was going to live until 1835 to manumit Brobdingnag, even less until 1838 to manumit a second child even if Hermia had conceived right away. So it would be a question of whether his heirs would honor the agreement; the document, no matter how long it had been in force, had no legal standing at all. So what was basically a gentleman's agreement, likely to be kept because the person charged with the keeping was the author of the agreement, became a highly unlikely promissory note drawn on somebody else. I don't know any details about Hammond Washington's family; it's possible that he had children and Zack could see that they were unlikely to keep the bargain. Or it's possible that he had none, and Zack didn't know who might inherit. It's impossible to tell what Zack thought, or exactly what he did, but I do know what he stopped doing: paying on his freedom. The amounts credited to him dropped off drastically. By mid-1808 he was making only occasional payments on his freedom, and on November 7, Hammond Washington began to debit the sum already paid at three dollars a week . . ."

"Hermia was having another child," she said.

"No," I said. "No, it just seems that Zack wasn't able to pay the flat rate. It could have been that he wasn't working very hard, but on April 27, 1809, Hammond Washington debited a large sum, five hundred and twenty-four dollars, and noted that it was for payment of debts in Zack's behalf. Exactly what the debts were is hard to say, but since slaves couldn't own anything or buy anything, Zack must have been involved with something shady, and since the amount was large and the indebtedness honored by Hammond Washington, it's pretty clear that Zack had been gambling with white men. Anyway, the debits continued, and then, in late May, there is another large debit, two hundred and seven dollars, for payment of debts on Zack's behalf. On June 4, 1809, Hammond Washington amended the document once again, this time suspending Zack's right to hire his own time until such time as he should be able to do so 'to the profit of himself and his master,' taking over the responsibility of paying the upkeep for Zack, Hermia, and Brobdingnag, and placing what remained from Zack's freedom payments, the sum of seven hundred and seventy-nine dollars, in trust at a rate of two percent simple interest.

"What happened for the next year I don't know. But it appears that Zack managed to get back the faith Hammond Washington had placed in him, and on June 12, 1810, Hammond Washington amended the document again, restoring Zack's right to hire his own time and his responsibility for his own family, using the same percentage rate but eliminating the three-dollar flat rate. Zack could have paid off much more quickly, but it appears that he had given up any dream of his own freedom; the new amendment stated that, at Zack's own request, the money would be paid against the price of Brobdingnag's freedom only, which was to be figured at the free market rate in 1835, when Brobdingnag would become eligible for manumission under the Louisiana law. It also appears that Brobdingnag was to be trained as a blacksmith, because the amendment awarded to him the right to hire his own time after the year 1826, on terms similar to those originally granted to Zack, providing Brobdingnag showed himself worthy of trust. Zack began to make regular payments almost immediately, averaging around five dollars a week, which would have meant that, considering the interest, he would have put aside enough to pay over three thousand dollars for Brobdingnag by 1835, regardless of what the boy might earn on his own behalf. Hammond Washington evidently gauged the progress, and on June 12, 1811, exactly a year after the previous amendment, he added a new amendment, making sum in excess of the free market price payable to Brobdingnag on the day of his manumission. He seems also to have been pleased with Zack's return to respectability; the amendment formally permitted Zack to seek labor in New Orleans for six months out of the year, providing he should not be absent from the plantation more than one month at a time.

"But Zack evidently worked hard and kept his nose clean; no more debits, no more gambling—or at least, if he gambled, he won— and a steady record of payments right into 1812 . . ." I stopped then, letting the facts reorder themselves in my mind.

"You're not stopping now," she said.

"No," I said. "No, I told you it was a long story. And it's complicated too. Because I haven't said anything about the Napoleonic Wars, or the economy of Virginia, or—"

"Never mind that," she said. "Just tell the story."

"It *is* the story," I said. "Or part of it. But now it gets complicated. Because what happened was that England and France went to war in 1803, and the British navy was short of sailors, so they kept taking American vessels and impressing sailors, and also, incidentally, lifting the cargoes. Just about the time the Louisiana legislature was passing the law against manumission, a British man-o'-war called the *Leopard* opened fire on the U.S. *Chesapeake,* and Thomas Jef-

327

ferson, who had enough sense to know that the United States couldn't win a war with England, but who had to do something since the country was in an uproar, asked for an economic embargo. In December 1807, Congress passed the Embargo Act, which prohibited the export of American goods. The idea was a silly one in some ways, but it worked from Jefferson's point of view; all the patriots who had wanted to go to war over the *Chesapeake* affair dropped their flags and grabbed their wallets, and Jefferson managed to get out of office and get his candidate, James Madison, elected with no real problems. But it caused a general economic depression of no little magnitude, especially in states like Virginia, which produced a lot of goods, tobacco especially, for the European market. And one of the planters who fell on hard times had to make money by selling his house in Richmond and the slaves that staffed it. At least one of them was sold south, to a Mr. Waters Clarke, of New Orleans. The slave's name was Lewis Bolah.

"Bolah was not that old a man, probably in his late twenties. He got around pretty well, it seems, and was fairly well known by the black community in New Orleans, well enough so that in 1812, or perhaps early in 1813, some of them came to him and, so he later claimed, offered him a captaincy in a rebellion that they were planning. Exactly what part Bolah played in later events is not clear, but at the very least, he informed the authorities of the existence of the rebellion, and they apprehended the leaders of the rebellion and placed them on trial, found them guilty, and executed them. The usual form of execution in these cases was to behead the slaves and place the heads on stakes along the Mississippi as warnings to other insurrection-minded slaves. Bolah's part in it all brought him a lot of credit, and on February 13, 1813, the Louisiana legislature passed a resolution emancipating him and instructing the state treasurer to pay Mr. Waters Clarke the sum of eight hundred dollars . . ."

"What's all that got to do with . . ."

"Zack?" I said. "Zack was one of the ones they executed."

I brought the mug up to my face and drank down the last of my toddy. It wasn't much of a toddy anymore; it was as cold as ice.

"So they killed him," she said.

"They killed him," I said. "Not that they had much choice. It was a major revolt, five hundred slaves involved, and they were scared about that kind of thing, anyway. I don't know what the slave

328

population of Louisiana was then, but it was probably about a third to maybe two-fifths of the total population. There was no way the whites were going to keep all those people in line just with force; they had to use propaganda, and they had to use terror, and putting sixty-six black heads on stakes was a pretty good way to terrorize people."

"I guess so," she said. "But I didn't mean that. I meant they killed him when they passed the law against manumission."

"Oh," I said, "that. Maybe. But then, there's nothing to prove that he was really conspiring. Maybe he was. But maybe not. Maybe he had made what you psychiatrists call a good adjustment and was contented with his lot and the hope that his son was going to be a free man, even if he himself wasn't going to be. Maybe he just got caught in the wrong place at the wrong time. I don't know; there aren't any real facts one way or the other. Unless of course you want to believe in Louisiana justice." I leaned forward and picked up the bottle. I mixed myself another toddy and settled back, sipping it.

"I don't know what happened to Hermia and Brobdingnag. Not right away. I know that Hammond Washington took care of them, and I know Brobdingnag spent a good bit of time in the house, even though he was officially a field hand—"

"Wait a minute. He was eight years old."

"That's right. He had probably been working since he was six. Anyway, I know he was favored enough to spend some time in the house, because when he was twelve he was discovered in Hammond Washington's study with a copy of *Gulliver's Travels*. Hammond Washington had pointed it out to him one day, to show him where his name had come from, and he went back in alone to look at it. He couldn't read, of course, but it didn't matter; he was discovered, and he was punished, although Hammond Washington was minded to go easy on him; he was only given three stripes. I don't know what effect the flogging had on him, but it certainly wasn't the desired one. Three years later, when Brobdingnag was fifteen, he was found drawing in the dust, and even though he tried to scuff out what he was doing, part of it was left to be seen; the letters *C* and *K*. Hammond Washington was not minded to be merciful this time: he had the boy heavily flogged and, as a reminder, branded with the letters.

"From then on, it seems, Hammond Washington had no more trouble with him. But not because Brobdingnag stopped his rebellious ways. His mother had made the error of giving him the docu-

329

ment that Hammond Washington had drawn up, and by the time he was sixteen he had memorized every word of it, letter by letter, punctuation mark by punctuation mark. He had no idea what the words meant—he didn't really understand that they were words—but he knew the order of the letters and could reproduce the whole thing, date by date and amendment by amendment, with a stick in the dust. But that seemed to satisfy him. He worked well in the fields, and Hammond Washington spoke to Hermia about the possibility of having him trained as a blacksmith as his father had been. But that never happened, because in 1822 Hammond Washington caught cholera and died.

"That changed everything for Brobdingnag. Evidently Hammond Washington had a wife, and his wife was not terribly happy about the special place Hermia had held in the household. As soon as Hammond Washington was dead, she put Hermia to work as a field hand, at age thirty-two. Hermia died a year later. By this time Brobdingnag seems to have managed to learn the rudiments of writing and reading; he forged a pass for himself and ran away. It wasn't a terribly complicated thing to do, since most whites couldn't read or write either, and no slave could; the assumption was that if a slave had written authorization, it came, at the very least, from a white man. At any rate, he doesn't seem to have had much difficulty. And it's possible that he never would have had any had it not been for the fact that he somehow also wrote a check and withdrew seventeen hundred dollars from the local bank. That was just about what the money Zack had paid against his freedom would have amounted to, with interest. Probably, Hammond Washington's wife would have been happy enough to get rid of him if it hadn't been for the money. In any case, she sent slave catchers out after him, and they managed to track him, since he didn't know the first thing about woodcraft, and he had to kill two of them, and three dogs, in order to make his escape.

"I don't know what happened to him precisely for the next few years. It's fairly certain that he didn't stay in that area, and it's likely that he didn't go to New Orleans, either, since although it was a big city it was fairly well organized, and a black with a brand on his shoulder would have been easy to spot, especially one with money. But he managed to stay free and he rejected the name his grandfather had given him and began to think of himself as C.K. And he managed to learn more about reading and writing; enough so that by

1825 he could look up the trial proceedings and the acts of the legislature relating to Lewis Bolah. And then I know exactly what he did. He began to hunt for Bolah.

"Bolah was a free black, and the one thing the South kept very close tabs on was the movement of free blacks. They were all scared to death that too many free blacks would upset the balance between the poor white yeomen and the aristocracy. Which made sense, since racial superiority was the bone the planters kept throwing to the poor whites. They had tried various schemes to get rid of free blacks. The North didn't want them; as late as 1860 the good citizens of western Pennsylvania were petitioning the state legislature for more laws restricting blacks, and just about everywhere else a free black had to put up a good behavior bond, or something; anyway, the North didn't want the excess. So the South got the federal government to set up the American Colonization Society, and to buy land in Africa, and send the free niggers back. But there were still enough left in the South to scare the white folks. So they kept real good track of them. There was hardly a state they could settle in without the permission of the legislature. So all he had to do was to go to the capital of each state and look up the records of petitions by freedmen to remain in the state. So he went North on a riverboat—"

"Wait a minute," she said. "He was passing as a white man?"

"Not exactly," I said. "He was, after all, nearly half white to begin with, and just a little more than a quarter black. But he didn't try to hide the black blood, although he did profess to be ashamed of it. What he did was to mix up the way he was descended, claiming that it was his mother who was half Cherokee, her mother, a white woman, he claimed, having been raped by an Indian. His father, he said, was a half-breed, the son of a planter and one of his slaves. Which made C.K. a quarter black, but which also made him free, since slavery was based on the legal principle of *partus sequitur ventrem,* which means, basically, that if your mother was a slave you were a slave, but if your mother was free, even if you were black as the ace of spades, you were free too. It didn't work out that way in practice, but the principle was there—and it helps explain why white Southerners were so worried about the possibility of black males copulating with white females. So C.K. carried forged papers attesting to the fact that his mother was a free woman of mixed white and Cherokee parentage, and that his father had been a mulatto, and nobody wanted much to do with him, but he got to Cincinnati and then made his way east, and eventually got to Washington, D.C., where he began to search for Bolah in the records of the American Colonization Society. But he hadn't really expected Bolah to go to Liberia—he was certainly hoping he had not. What he wanted was the experience of looking up records at a place where he could pose as a newly freed black looking for a relative and not have to worry about trying to pose as a white while he polished his reading and learned how to use records. By the time he had exhausted the possibility that Bolah had been relocated in Liberia, he was ready to tackle the most likely source of information. He went to Richmond, where Bolah had come from, and searched the records of petitions from blacks desiring to remain in the state. He didn't have to look far. On December 6, 1824, Lewis Bolah had begged permission to reside in the state of Virginia, citing his service to the state of Louisiana and his service in the War of 1812 under Commodore John Shaw, and saying that he was afraid to go to Liberia or Haiti because he was afraid of what might happen to him in any country governed by 'persons of colour.' The petition had been granted.

"So in the spring of 1826, C.K. found Lewis Bolah. He tracked him down to a small town called Dinwiddie. Bolah was living in a cabin in a little area just east of the Post Road—Route One, it would be now. C.K. waited until the middle of the night, then set fire to the house. When Bolah came running out he jumped him, tied him, cut his head off with an ax, and planted it on a stake."

I stopped then, to sip at the toddy before it got cold. She didn't say anything. "You know Dinwiddie?" I said.

"My family used to own land near there," she said.

"Well," I said, "this happened a long time ago."

"We owned the land a long time ago," she said. She drained her mug. "What did he do then?"

"I don't know," I said. "I don't have any information on what he did for nearly a year and a half."

"He must have done something."

"He must have. But I don't know what."

"Well, God, John, that's the interesting part. Here he is, he's managed to escape from slavery, and it sounds like ever since he was young he'd been focused on this man Bolah, and he escapes and he tracks him down and he gets his revenge, and then he must have just felt . . . empty. I mean, can't you imagine—"

"No," I said. "I can't imagine." I sipped my toddy, sucking at the warmth of it.

"All right," she said. "Tell me what you know."

"I know that in the spring of 1827, C.K. Washington, which was what he had taken to calling himself, arrived in northwest Georgia and presented himself to the tribal elders of the Cherokee Nation, claiming citizenship in that Nation by right of his grandfather's membership in the tribe. I don't know what the procedure for such things was, but evidently the situation was confused by the fact that the Cherokees were changing their form of government, and just that year they had adopted a constitution that called for an elected chief, a senate, and a house of representatives, but the elections had not yet been held. So while they got their government running, C.K. lived with them, learning how to be an Indian, how to hunt and how to fish, how to find shelter, all the elements of woodcraft that no slave knew or was permitted to know, simply because it would have made running away so much easier. The things he learned were to him as important as reading and writing. But he studied too, because the Cherokees had a written language, and he found that the best way to learn it was to study it in written form. At that time, in fact, he read and wrote the Cherokee language better than he read and wrote English. The rest of his time he spent searching up and down the Cherokee country, looking for someone who might remember his grandfather and be willing and able to testify. But he found nobody. What he did find was gold. I don't know exactly where, but it was river gold, washed down from a mother lode somewhere. He found it one day while he was fishing in a creek, and he panned for it whenever he could, and he hid it. Because he wasn't sure about what the Cherokee elders were going to say about his membership in the tribe, since nobody had ever heard of a Cherokee brave and a slave woman who had had a child together; the Cherokees were proud people, and there were quite a few who weren't happy about his mixed parentage. I suspect he believed that, in the final analysis, he might use the knowledge of the gold to prove his loyalty to the tribe when the case was finally decided. In 1828 the Cherokees elected a principal chief, a man named Kooweskoowe. He was of mixed blood. C.K. believed that the mixed heritage would make him more sympathetic. But C.K. forgot that the half of Kooweskoowe that wasn't Indian was white and Southern and named John Ross, and that John Ross had served with Andrew Jackson in his wars against the Creeks, or maybe he didn't know; but when the case was decided, in December of 1828, the tribal government determined that the man calling himself C.K. Washington was not a Cherokee because his mother was not a Cherokee, and his father's mother was not a Cherokee."

"So they kicked him out?"

"C.K. was strong and able-bodied; he'd been free for several years, taking good care of himself, eating well, so forth. By any standard he was a top-grade field hand, and top-grade field hands were worth a lot of money. So no, they didn't kick him out; they made a slave of him."

"You mean they *sold* him?"

"The Cherokees were a civilized people," I said. "They had had a representative government since 1820, and they were busy as beavers building roads and raising grain and making cloth, and in order to make cloth they were growing cotton, and in order to raise all that cotton the Cherokees used exactly the same method the whites used. Chattel slavery. And there were quite a few slaves on the Cherokee plantations that were half Cherokee the same way there were a lot of slaves on white plantations that were half white. C.K. made one more.

"He slaved in the Cherokee cotton fields for nearly two years. He knew enough about survival in the woods by then to escape, and while he probably couldn't have eluded a bunch of Cherokee trackers forever, he had a chance of making it, and it was probably worth a try. But he didn't try. He concentrated on being a good little field hand, and on sneaking away whenever he could and panning for gold and hiding it, and on listening to what the Cherokees were talking about. And what they were talking about was their white neighbors, the Georgians, who had passed a law as soon as the Cherokees had set up their Nation, declaring that the Cherokee Nation should come under Georgian law. The Cherokees weren't stupid; they knew the purpose of the law was to get their land. Some of the hotheads were ready to go to war, but John Ross counseled calm, because the Georgia law wasn't supposed to take effect until June 1, 1830, and Ross's old army buddy, Andrew Jackson, had been inaugurated President in

March of 1829. In September of 1829, C.K. allowed some of the gold to fall into the hands of a white man. The word of the Cherokee gold spread like wildfire, and in December of 1829 Andrew Jackson made a speech to Congress and said that he didn't think the Cherokees had a right to independent government so long as they stayed inside the state boundaries of Georgia, and suggested that if they wanted to be independent, the Cherokees ought to move West. What he proposed was that they move to lands set aside as Indian territory, which was Oklahoma, where there sure as hell wasn't any gold, or any cotton plantations either, and that they should do it voluntarily. But if they didn't, they would only be able to keep the land they needed to live on—not farm on—and they would be under Georgia law. And Congress passed a bill to that effect in May of 1830.

"On June 3 the Georgia authorities initiated actions to parcel out the Cherokee lands to the adjacent counties, and the Cherokees went to the federal courts, and the mess lasted nearly a decade, not that the delay did the Cherokees any good; they ended up marching west on what they came to call the Trail of Tears, and thousands of them died, and they were so angry they ended up fighting for the Confederacy in the Civil War, but none of that made a lot of difference to C.K. because at the end of June 1830 he escaped from the Cherokee plantations, eluded pursuit, recovered his hidden gold, and made his way to Philadelphia."

"So," she said. "He was free."

"Yes," I said. "He was free. Unless somebody kidnapped him, remember."

"Don't tell me . . ."

"No," I said. "No, nobody kidnapped him. In that sense, he was free. And Pennsylvania was a pretty liberal place when it came to slavery. The first known protest against slavery had come from the German Mennonites way back in 1688. But Pennsylvania had always been sudden death for free blacks. Early on, in the eighteenth century, they were punished as severely as slaves: execution for raping a white woman—there wasn't any penalty if the rape victim was black—for homosexuality, murder, burglary, and the second offense of interracial fornication—providing, of course, the male was the black; castration for attempted rape of a white woman; flogging for carrying arms or gathering in groups of more than four. In 1725 they got around to passing a special law, 'An Act for the Better Regulation of Negroes,' and they made it pretty clear what they thought about free blacks. The preamble said 'free negroes are an idle, slothful people, and often burdensome to the neighborhood . . .' and so they said a master couldn't free a slave unless he put up a bond insuring the slave's good behavior, and giving any magistrate the power to bind into service any black who was able to work and didn't, and they ordered that all children under twenty-one, and male children under twenty-four, be bound out—"

"Wait a minute," she said. "You mean the children of slaves . . ."

"I meant what I said. Women under twenty-one, men under twenty-four. Blacks. All."

"But you said that if the mother was free . . ."

"That was in Louisiana."

She didn't say anything.

"Oh," I said. "I forgot. Under that law I could be bound into service for seven years for living with you. You'd have to pay a fine, though. Of course, if we were to get married I'd be sold into slavery immediately. Only it would never get that far; they would have killed me after the second time we made love."

She didn't say anything.

"But then, I never would have met you; if somebody had caught me more than ten miles away from home, I would have been whipped. Or outside at all after nine at night. Of course—"

"All right," she said. "This isn't 1725."

"No," I said. "But it's still Pennsylvania."

"So why did he come here?"

"I don't know," I said. "I guess because he didn't know where else to go. And even though the law was the way it was and public sentiment was the way it was, there were some hopeful signs in Pennsylvania. By 1780 the manumission act was passed, and for some strange reason the legislature had never gotten around to saying blacks couldn't vote—maybe because the property restrictions on suffrage made it unlikely that a black man could vote. But when C.K. arrived in Philadelphia there was a large body—the largest in the United States—of free blacks. They had formed a society of free blacks in 1787. In 1797 four blacks who had been freed in North Carolina even though it was illegal, and who had come to Philadelphia, sent the first petition from blacks to Congress, and another petition from Philadelphia blacks in 1800 had Congress in an uproar for a while. The first fully independent black church was begun there in 1816, and the next year they sent another petition to Congress, protesting the American Colonization Society. By the time C.K. got there, there were at least forty-three black societies, sixteen male, twenty-seven female, paying out relief moneys, and Philadelphia had hosted the First National Negro Convention. I don't know if he knew all that before he went; possibly he had picked up word of it when he was going through the North the first time. But he went to Philadelphia, and he bought land, and set about becoming involved in the community. In 1832 he had satisfied all the requirements, and he voted in the elections, and in the beginning of 1833 he was hard at work in the Philadelphia Negro Library, which had just opened.

"I don't know too much about his day-to-day life. I know that he held a job as a laborer, but I don't know if that was because he hadn't brought enough gold to live on, or because he was afraid of attracting attention to his money and having it confiscated, and himself sold back into slavery. Probably the last; it was against the law for a free black to be idle in Pennsylvania, whereas an ounce of gold bought about as much goods then as it does now. But in any case he spent most of his time in the Negro Library, working to improve his reading and writing. On the advice of a man named James Forten, who was a Revolutionary War veteran and about the most prominent black in town, he began writing his personal history as a way of improving his writing—"

"Is that how you know all this?" she said. "You've got his diaries?"

"They weren't exactly diaries. His personal history was an account of his life up until 1831, when he arrived in Philadelphia. It was pretty sketchy; in the beginning he couldn't write all that well and just getting the facts down and the grammar right was an effort. So he left out a lot. Then, by the time he was getting to the end of the story, he was busy with other things, and his writing had gotten better, which was all he wanted out of the account, so he skipped even more. The style itself is a problem. At the beginning he couldn't manage more than a straight declarative sentence, so the relationships he expressed seemed simple, even though they obviously weren't, and it's hard to tell how he felt about them. And when his style developed it got worse, in terms of information, because he cluttered up the facts with hyperbolic metaphors and literary allusions. It's obvious that he loved writing, and he loved his own style, which is understandable; when you've been flogged for trying to read your own name and branded for trying to write your father's name, it's probably quite a thrill to not only read books but quote from them in your own hand, even if nobody else is going to read it. The journals are pretty much in the same pattern. . . ."

"Wait a minute," she said. "How did you get all these things?"

"I'm getting to that," I said.

"Slowly," she said.

"Okay. Mid-1830s. The Philadelphia blacks were the largest and most prosperous group of black people in the country, probably in the hemisphere, possibly, in some senses, in the world. They were civically minded, had access to the sciences and literature of the Enlightenment, and were proud of it all. They liked to think they were responsible, and they were. They were moderates; they would have approved of, mostly did approve of, nonviolent protest. But they were politically naive. In 1832, when the state legislature was considering laws that would have practically prohibited the immigration of free blacks into the Commonwealth, they had written a petition against it, going on and on about what good citizens they were, how the welfare rolls were only four percent black when the city population was eight and a half percent, and how black people paid over a hundred thousand dollars a year in rent, and how there was church and other institutional property owned by black organizations that was worth more than a hundred thousand dollars, and how black beneficent societies paid out over seven thousand dollars a year, and how there were four or five hundred blacks in trades, and some blacks were wealthy enough to send their children to private schools. They thought that would make the legislature recognize their worth; they didn't see that their worth was the reason the immigration restrictions were being considered in the first place. Because if there's one thing a white man hates more than a free nigger, it's a free nigger who isn't on welfare and who pays his rent on time and goes to a big church and has a good job and sends his kids to a decent school. . . ."

"You mean 'hated,'" she said quietly.

"I mean what I said. 'Hates.' It's true now and it was true then, only then it was easier to see—the white folks tended to start riots. They started one in 1834. And C.K. Washington, on his way home from a meeting of some society or other, ended up in the middle of it.

338

He got himself out of it, and while he was doing it he rescued a young woman named Priscilla Langley. I don't know exactly how, he didn't say. But anyway, he rescued her, and they fell in love, and a year later they married." I stopped and took a sip of my toddy.

"They were married, on September 23, 1835, in Bethel Church, which was the mother church of the African Methodist Episcopal denomination; I don't know if C.K. was a member, but they held the wedding there, and I know it was a risk, because C.K. could have been recognized by somebody. But he wasn't. I don't know much more than that for quite a while, but it seems he had an arrangement with a white Abolitionist whose name I don't know, whereby the white man said C.K. was working for him, and was therefore not an idle black. But what C.K. was really doing was becoming more and more involved with the local black community. He was becoming an activist, a pretty prominent one, although he still tried to stay as anonymous as possible. He kept up his reading, and evidently his writing was approved of by the local people, because in March of 1838 they called on him to help draft a petition.

"What had happened was that way back in 1790, Pennsylvania had drafted a new state constitution, and the framers had specifically stricken out the word white as a qualification for franchise. But the public sentiment was against blacks in general and free blacks in particular, and the Pennsylvania Supreme Court—the chief justice was a man named Gibson, who was part of the Springs crowd—had decided a case called *Fogg* v. *Hobbs,* which held that that was mistake, basically ignoring both the constitution itself and the minutes of the convention, which made the intent clear. There was no appeal from that, of course. So the black people concentrated on writing petitions to the convention that was supposed to produce a new constitution, asking them to restore the vote to blacks. They didn't. So the Philadelphia blacks organized a mass meeting that was aimed at defeating the ratification of that part of the new constitution. And of course the way they protested was to publish a pamphlet. They entitled it *Appeal of Forty Thousand Citizens, threatened with disenfranchisement, to the people of Pennsylvania.* It wasn't a badly written document in terms of style, but it was the same naive garbage about how in Philadelphia alone there were over eighteen thousand free blacks holding one and a half million dollars' worth of property and such, and paying a hundred and fifty thousand dollars a year in rent, which would have made them good citizens if it hadn't been precisely the reason they were being disenfranchised. But anyway, C.K. helped write it. How much of it he did, I don't know, but there are a few ringing hyperbolic phrases in there that sound a lot like him. He stayed anonymous, of course; although I don't know if the real reason for that was modesty or a fear of being discovered and returned to slavery. I don't know if it would have made much difference; the *Appeal* appealed mostly to the already converted, and the constitution was ratified with no problem, and the black people went right on paying rent and taxes, so it was a pretty good deal from the point of view of the white power structure. But what had happened was that C.K. had gotten all involved in the Philadelphia moderate way of thinking about things, and he decided that the best thing to do was to publicize the prosperity and the responsibility of the black community. So after the *Appeal* was finished, he started writing a book.

"He did it anonymously, of course, but he didn't use a pseudonym. In fact, through his whole life, when he could have lived far more publicly simply by changing his name, he didn't; I can't imagine why. The book was published as *Sketches of the Higher Classes of Colored Society in Philadelphia, by a Southerner;* it was only in the text that he identified himself as a black man. And you couldn't really tell from the writing; it sounded whiter than white. It really wasn't much of a book. It was heavy on the names and on giving credit where it was due and probably where it wasn't, and there was a definite elitist tone to the whole thing, and it hewed close to the Philadelphia moderate line—good citizenship, measured protest. It got lousy reviews from the blacks in New York, who were getting on with the business of calling for armed insurrections and such by 1841, when it was published. And it surely did no good in Pennsylvania. It made things worse, as a matter of fact. Because the same old anti-free-black sentiment was running strong, even stronger because times were bad and if white people don't like rich blacks when times are good, they like them even less in the middle of a depression. So in 1841, the blacks of Pennsylvania called a convention in Pittsburgh, and C.K. went as a delegate. It wasn't an easy trip, three hundred miles across—"

"I know," she said.

"Yeah," I said, "and there's another hundred miles west of here. And C.K. didn't have a Greyhound and a Turnpike. There was a stagecoach, but Jim Crow was no stranger to Pennsylvania—as a matter of fact, the term originated in the Fifth Street Theater in Pittsburgh. So C.K. went on horseback. But he followed the stage route, west through Lancaster and York and Gettysburg, and then to Chambersburg, and then over the mountains through McConnellsburg. He passed through here on the fourteenth of August. He tried to get a room at the local inns. One, which was called the Rising Sun, wouldn't take him. Another, the Washington Hotel, would, but there were so many slave-catchers hanging around that he felt uncomfortable, and he moved on early in the evening and made a camp for himself a few miles west, on the east bank of the river, not far from the town of Wolfsburg. He caught a few fish and built a fire within sight of an old gristmill that at the time belonged to a man named Morrison. He didn't know that, of course, but he did describe the mill: three stories high, made of fieldstone, with four stone mill runs. He wrote a lot about that place; maybe it was the fact that he was used to writing and didn't have much of it to do since the book was finished; I don't know. But he wrote well into the night, describing the town and the prevalence of the bounty hunters, and the beauty of the country. He was still fairly elitist; he wrote about the black people he had seen in a not terribly complimentary way, said they were beaten out and defeated-looking, and that the only one with any substance was a bootblack named Nelson Gates. But he was impressed with the country, and he wrote on and on about that, and wondered if it might not be a good thing to bring his wife here—"

"So," she said, "that's how your family came here?"

"No," I said. "This was 1841. Things weren't that simple in 1841, not for a black man. He had to worry about being taken back into slavery, remember, and the slave-catchers he had seen couldn't have reassured him. And he could read a map; he knew he was only about thirty miles from slave territory. But he did speculate. I guess you could call it a daydream, if you made allowances for his awful style. He sounded like a real Romantic, going on about 'peaceful sylvan springs' and things like that. Interesting, because he had never really written like that before, but terrible.

"Anyway, he finished his writing and doused his fire and went to sleep. But sometime in the middle of the night he heard sounds, and he heard his horse whinny, and he came awake. He was carrying a pistol, even though it was illegal for a black to be armed, and he got it

341

out and crept off into the brush, and he waited. In a few minutes he saw movements near the mill, and he thought maybe it was a bounty hunter that had come to kidnap him, so he went sneaking up there and found three slaves, runaways, who were hiding in the water under one of the wheels. As soon as they saw him they came out and spoke to him, asking if he was the man who was to come for them. He told them he wasn't, but he offered them what was left of the fish he had caught and some bread and they came with him and ate it. They told him they had come north from a farm near a place called Independence, and at first he thought they were talking about Louisiana, and the truth was they didn't know what state it was in, but they said they had run to Charleston, Virginia—"

"You mean West Virginia."

"It was Virginia then. Anyway, that and the time they had spent helped him figure out that it was Independence, Virginia, they were talking about. He spent a long time asking them questions and writing down their answers, trying to make sense out of where they had come from and how they had come, but they really didn't know. They had heard of 'North,' and that a man could be free there, and that if you spoke to a particular man in a particular way, he would show you how to get there, and so they had run away to Charleston and found the man and he had passed them on. They had come up the valley under cover of darkness, twenty-five miles in one dark night, and a preacher in town had hidden them through the day and then told them to come west until they saw a three-storied mill and wait there.

"So they waited, eating C.K.'s food and making jokes about slavery, and how good it was to be free, and asking C.K. questions about what life was like in the North, and how long it took a black man to talk as well as he did, and wear a suit, and ride a horse. C.K. kept trying to quiet them, trying to explain that they were a long way from being free, but they wouldn't listen. It was lucky there wasn't anybody around.

"Just before dawn two men came, black men with a hay wagon. They wouldn't give their names, but took the slaves and hid them under the hay, and drove on. And an hour later, just after dawn, a party of slave-catchers came by, searching the woods on either side of the road with bloodhounds. But by that time C.K. was bathed and shaved and mounted, and was watching from the other side of the river."

"They would have taken him, wouldn't they?" she said.

"I don't know," I said. "Maybe. You can't tell. And he couldn't, either. So he made sure of his safety in the only way he could: he rode hard and slept light and didn't go near a town until he got to Pittsburgh. And it worked; he made it without being bothered.

"But not without being changed. The experience had done something to him. It shows in his writing style. While he was writing about this area he was really emotional, enthusiastic, and even though the style was flowery there was some enthusiasm for the content as well as the style, and it isn't half as bad as the other stuff about so-and-so, the great colored citizen. But what he wrote after he got to Pittsburgh—and he didn't write anything else until he did get there—was just like the earlier stuff, only worse. It seems like he lost the enthusiasm for the style too. The style didn't change—he was still throwing around quotes and tossing off metaphors—but it wasn't really a style anymore; more like an empty form. He wrote about the convention as though it were . . . I don't know. There were a hundred and forty-seven delegates, and Pittsburgh wasn't even a major black population center, so it must have been an important gathering, but C.K. makes it sound like a tea party. I don't know what actually caused the change, but I suspect it was being so close to slavery again, and being afraid of being taken, because when he got back to Philadelphia, he started writing about the things he was doing to protect his wife against kidnap, even though Priscilla Langley had evidently been born free. The fear he had wasn't unreal—a lot of free blacks were being kidnapped, especially attractive females, of which she was evidently one—but he made more out of it than he had before. He had papers of manumission forged for himself, and he had affidavits drawn up testifying to Priscilla's freedom, and he hired people to watch the house when he was away. So he must have been preoccupied with the whole thing, but you couldn't tell it; the style stayed florid and empty for a solid year, right up until the riot in 1842. And then he dropped the flowery style and started putting down the facts, nothing else: names, dates—"

"Wait a minute," she said. "You lost me at the riot."

"Sorry," I said. "The anti-free-black sentiment erupted again in 1842. Actually, it had been going on all along. There was a major riot in 1834, when C.K. met Priscilla, and one a year later, and in 1838 they had burned down Pennsylvania Hall, which had been built by the Abolition movement, and they had done it while the Anti-Slavery Convention of American Women was meeting there, so they were getting pretty unchivalrous in their anger. Part of it was due to the Panic of 1837, which made for a lot of idle whites and resentment, but some of it was just ... I don't know ... background hatred. It wasn't just Philadelphia, either; the black section of Pittsburgh had been burned down in 1839. Anyway, in 1833 the British Parliament had passed a law ending slavery in the Empire as of August 1, 1834, and in 1842 the Philadelphia blacks got together to celebrate the anniversary, and evidently a gang of whites didn't like the idea of blacks taking a day off and celebrating freedom, so they went tearing into the Negro section, beating up on people and killing a few, and burning property left and right. It was a regular Long Hot Summer act, and the militia had to be called out to quell the riot. And C.K. was right in the middle of it. He dropped the florid style like a shot and he just set down fact after fact. He got everything. Names, dates, places, ages, everything."

"And he didn't feel a thing."

"Of course he did," I said. "As a matter of fact, after the riot a white Abolitionist named Henry C. Wright wrote to him asking for information, and C.K. wrote back and said ..." I stopped for a minute, to remember the exact words. " 'To attempt a reply to your letter, now, is impractical.' He couldn't give the man facts, you see; he was still sorting through things—"

"Sorting through things," she said.

"Yes," I said. "Rubble. And emotions were part of the rubble. In the same letter he wrote: 'I feel that my life, weighed down and crushed by a despotism whose sway makes a hell of earth ...' But those weren't facts. The white folks didn't mind; they published the letter in *The Liberator,* anonymously, of course. But C.K. was—"

"Busy sorting through things," she said. "I know. Just like a good little historian. You like him, don't you?"

"I admire the hell out of him," I said.

"And you want to be just like him. You think there's something good about getting the feelings out of things. Don't you?" She was looking at me hard, and I could see the fire's glow reflected in her eyes.

"Yes," I said. "Not ordinary feelings; a historian has to have ordinary feelings—a little sympathy, a little anger. That's what makes him human. But if the feelings are so strong they get in the way of the facts—"

"And you think that's what he had?"

"Yes," I said.

"I don't."

"I don't give a damn what you think," I said. "Because you don't have the facts. But I'll tell you, it takes one hell of a historian to sit at a desk with a quill and ink and write down, without even making a blot, that among those killed was Priscilla Langley Washington, aged twenty-seven, and in her seventh month of pregnancy."

She didn't say anything. I didn't look at her, just sat there, looking at the fire. It was dying a little now, the glowing center eating into the fourth log. I could already feel myself chilling. I pulled my clothing close about me and stirred.

"Where are you going?" she said. There was a little alarm in her voice.

"More wood," I said. I pulled my hat and gloves back on and stood up. The wind hit my head and chest, hard and frigid, and I felt the chill drive into the pit of my stomach. I climbed quickly over the windbreak, shaking as the wind sliced at my knees, and plowed to the wood I had piled. I had to spend a moment estimating, but it was all right; there was enough there to last. I picked out two logs and carried them back and laid them carefully on the fire, trying not to break the structure of it, trying to keep it going while adding to it. When I had it done as well as I could, I sat down again. My cup was half full, but the toddy was cold. I added hot water to it and sipped, feeling the warmth run through me, feeling the cold go away; not far, but away.

"I'm sorry," she said.

"What for?"

"For . . . being impatient."

I shrugged. "I get impatient too," I said. "I want to hurry. I want to know everything *now*. But history doesn't work that way; the truth is usually in the footnotes, not in the headlines. One of the local historians said history was 'the sayings and doings and surroundings of individuals; their rivalries, and quarrels, and amusements, and witticisms, and sarcasms; their mechanical and professional pursuits; their erection of houses and fulling mills and grist- and sawmills . . . their births and marriages and deaths; their removal to other localities, and how they prospered, and what descendents they left. . . .'"

"C.K.?" she said.

"What?" I said. "Oh, no. No, a man named William Maclay Hall."

"Does he come into it?"

"Yes," I said. "He comes into it." I didn't say anything for a while then, and she left me to my silence, snuggling down next to me and laying her hand against my belly. But I could not feel her hand through my clothes, and though the fire blazed brightly, I felt the chill growing in me. When I began to shiver I leaned forward to mix another toddy. She took her hand away, but said nothing. I sipped the whiskey and, for a time, felt the chills recede.

"I don't know exactly what he did then," I said. "I know he buried her and I know that he stopped attending meetings and things like that as soon as he did, because he kept the journal, and there's nothing in there about any of that. But there isn't anything in there about grieving, either, nothing about anger. All I know is that he went about the business of selling everything that he had, converting everything into cash, and that on Christmas Day, 1842, he donated the entire sum to the Abolition movement. Or most of it; he must have kept something back, or perhaps he went to work to live. He doesn't say. For the next six months the journal is nothing more than a list of books he's finished reading. Up until this time, he'd make casual reference to a book, or quote from it; for those six months he simply listed titles and quotations. He was reading fast—three, four books a day. And he was reading different things than he had been: literature. He finally read Jonathan Swift, and he read Sir Walter Scott, and Charles Dickens—evidently he had met Dickens when he was in this country in 1842—and a lot of the Romantic poets, especially Wordsworth and Shelley. He read contemporary criticism too, and he spent an awful lot of time reading Southern writing, not that much of it was worth reading. But he followed Poe's career carefully, and managed to meet the man during that year—Poe was living in Philadelphia at the time. He doesn't mention any of his old associations, but I suspect they were after him to become active again, because in July of 1843 he wrote that he had been selected to attend the National Negro Convention in Buffalo, and that he had decided to go.

"I don't know what all the reading had done for him; it may have changed his outlook, but it didn't show. He wrote about the Buffalo convention in a very flat style, recording votes, positions, and not doing much else. He made it sound like a sewing circle, when actually it was one of the most important events of the decade. The New York blacks had always been more militant than the Philadelphia people, and the ones in Buffalo were downright rebellious, and during the course of the convention, a man named Henry Highland Garnet got up and called Denmark Vesey and Nat Turner patriots and called for revolt among the slaves. Tough words: 'You cannot be more oppressed than you have been—you cannot suffer greater cruelties than you have already. Rather die free men than live to be slaves.' It caused quite a stir, and a motion was made to adopt it as the sentiment of the convention. They called the roll in alphabetical order; C.K. was the last delegate to vote. He voted no. The motion failed by one."

"After all that, he voted no?"

"That's right," I said.

"*Why?*"

"I don't know," I said. "I don't know any more about it than that. There's nothing more in his journal about that, or about anything to do with the Abolitionist movement. Maybe he got disgusted with it. There were all kinds of factions now; the whole movement was dividing over militancy, and over whether or not blacks should be more or less prominent, and whether it was proper to buy slaves in order to free them, and whether or not women should be allowed to vote in meetings—all *kinds* of things. Maybe he just walked away from it all. But the next things he writes about are trails and points of vantage and concealment, and the wholesale price of corn."

"What . . . Oh. Moonshine."

"That's right. Moonshine. Sometime in the fall of 1843 he left Philadelphia and came across the mountains, and spent a good bit of time exploring the mountains hereabouts. I'd say he must have arrived in mid-September. Not that anybody saw him; it just seems that he would have needed that much time to scout the area as thoroughly as he did. He drew maps, routes of access, charted caves, everything. He spent some time improving shelters, expanding natural caves and such. And he bought corn. He bought it through an agent, a man named Mickle, down in the South County, and he had Mickle believing he was a white man who was buying food for a plantation owner in Virginia. It didn't make a lot of sense, but he waved enough money in Mickle's face to keep him quiet and honest. And he bought

347

the corn, and picked it up at a South County mill, and nobody figured out what it was going for. Or where it was going. Which was up in the mountains, a little here and a little there. By the end of November he had everything set up—I guess he brought the hardware with him, or maybe he made it; I don't know. He let his mash ferment, and in late February he started to cook.

"He didn't cook much that year, just a few hundred gallons. But he cooked carefully and did different batches in different ways. In late April he came down from the mountains and looked up his buddy Mickle and told him that he had come up with some whiskey. Mickle was greedy enough to handle the selling for a large profit. But I don't thing C.K. was much interested in profit; he wanted to know which one of his formulae had worked the best. He found out by how much of each Mickle sold, and how fast. That fall, he had Mickle buying more corn, but without the pretense about the plantation. Of course, Mickle still thought C.K. was a white man. C.K. cooked again that winter, using the most popular recipe, adding a few variations. And that spring the whiskey that sold the best was exactly the formula he thought it would be. And then he was ready to go into business.

"He has it all laid out in the journal, exactly what he did and exactly how he did it: transactions made, actions taken. There isn't a single place where he puts down a question, or a doubt; it's all facts and logic, step by step. First he went out by himself, at night, looking over cornfields by moonlight, rousting farmers out of bed and buying their corn before it was halfway ready. He bought the best corn, and arranged contracts for delivery. When the time came, Mickle delivered wagonloads to points C.K. set up. By late November he had gotten the mash stored and the accounts paid. Then he killed Mickle and—"

"What?"

"He killed Mickle," I said. "What did you expect him to do?"

"I don't know. Not that."

"Why not? It's perfectly logical. He couldn't have somebody like Mickle knowing what he was doing and how, and probably even where. He had to kill him."

"But you said he voted against—"

"A call for slave insurrection. It was a stupid idea, and Henry Highland Garnet didn't know what he was talking about. He had been born in slavery but had gotten out of it when he was a child; he spent the rest of his life being a pampered darling in Troy, New York, and screwing liberal white ladies. C.K. was probably laughing all the time. And whatever he thought, that vote doesn't make him nonviolent."

"But—"

"The man had been a slave twice and could have been taken back at any time. He'd lost a wife, maybe seen her killed. You think he was going to lose sleep over some piece of poor white trash? The man couldn't be trusted; he had to go."

"Well, why didn't he find somebody he *could* trust?"

I just looked at her.

"You're going to say there was nobody he could trust, aren't you?"

"No," I said. "No, I'm not going to tell you that. Because I've already told you enough times, and you don't understand. But it's true anyway, whether you understand it or not."

"All right," she said. "Never mind the reason. He killed the man."

"Yes," I said. "He killed the man. And then he made his mash and cooked his whiskey, and in the spring of 1845 he loaded it into a freight wagon and hauled it over the mountains to Philadelphia. He sold it there. I don't know exactly how he went about it, because he evidently didn't take the journal with him, and all he wrote down when he got back was the money he had made and the places where he had deposited it. All solid banks. And it was a good bit of money for the time, evidently. I'm not too sure about the conversion. But none of that is really all that important at this stage. What is important is that he had some whiskey left, not enough to make it profitable to haul it east, but too much for private consumption. As a matter of a fact, C.K. didn't even drink whiskey, or anything else besides water. I don't know why; I guess he had just never gotten into the habit. At any rate, he didn't know enough about the stuff to judge on his own what was good.

"Anyway, he decided to sell the stuff locally. He drove his wagon into town with just one barrel loaded on the back, and he stopped on the shady side of the town square, right in front of the old jail, and he tapped the keg and took a tin cup and handed out free samples to all the old bench-sitters and railbirds and farmers that were hanging around, and then, when the barrel was empty, he just drove away

349

without a word to anybody. Then he waited about a week, until the word had time to get around, and then he came back, but he came at night, with the whiskey in jugs instead of kegs, and he went to the houses of all the top men in town, the doctors and the lawyers and the men on the civil list, and he sold it to them, six jugs a man, no more, no less. They had heard about it by this time—everybody had heard about that whiskey; it was the best whiskey anybody around had ever tasted, and this was whiskey-making country. So they bought, and they paid his price, and for weeks after they talked about it; not so much about the whiskey—they all knew about the whiskey by now, from the railbirds and the bench-sitters—but about who hadn't been offered any. It was a good way to assure a market, and I have a suspicion C.K. liked the idea of a bunch of white men giving each other airs over a colored man's whiskey, not even knowing that he was colored or that what they had gotten was the bottom of the barrel. But that isn't really important, either. What is important is that selling that whiskey made him a part of the Town. It brought him into contact with the most powerful men and the best-known men, and it made him well known. That was about the best way to be sure of his safety; because if somebody saw him and said, 'Isn't that a runaway nigger?' thinking to haul him south and sell him, they'd take him before a local magistrate, and that local magistrate would think he was white; and what's more, he wouldn't want to see the source of the best whiskey he'd ever had going south. So after that, C.K. became a lot more open. Not that he let anybody know where he came from, or what he did, or where he hid out in the mountains, but he did come into town now and again. And that meant he got to know people. He became good friends with Nelson Gates, the bootblack, and with two other men, John Crawley and John Graham; he got to know them because he recognized them as the two who had been on the wagon that came for the runaways. They introduced him to the preacher, John Fiddler, but C.K. never had much use for him, even though he did write that his first impressions about the local blacks had to be wrong if even the ministers were risking working for the Underground. And he met William Maclay Hall.

"C.K. met Hall after the second time he sold whiskey locally, in 1846. Hall had just come to town to read law for the bar examination. He had been here before—his father was the local Presbyterian minister—but he had been away in college. How he and C.K. met, exactly, I don't know, but I do know their acquaintanceship, at the beginning, was based on whiskey. Up until that time, C.K. didn't drink at all, but he had written about something that Gates and Crawley drank—he didn't say anything about Graham drinking it—which he called 'grog.' It wasn't, really, since true grog doesn't have any sweetening; Gates and Crawley drank theirs with molasses. C.K., it seems, was afraid to try it, but then he came into contact with Hall, who evidently didn't have a whole lot of experience with whiskey, and C.K. started experimenting on him, feeding the stuff to Hall to see how much of it he could take. C.K. found Hall's limit and noted that 'the brew is seductive. Seven such mixtures, taken over the course of an evening, is sufficient. More violates the limits of sanity.' Then C.K. figured he knew enough to start drinking himself. So Hall probably changed C.K.'s personal habits. And he also changed his mind. I don't know when they talked, or how often, but they must have done so at great length whenever they did, and seriously; the journal is peppered with notes on the conversations, thoughts C.K. could not understand, or wanted to think about and refute—"

"So he did end up trusting somebody," she said.

I thought about it; it hadn't occurred to me that way before. "No," I said, finally. "I don't think you could say he trusted Hall. There's no evidence that he told Hall anything of his history, or anything like that, or even where he made whiskey, or even that what he sold locally wasn't the only whiskey he made, or even who he sold it to around here. But I suppose you could say he trusted Hall's ideas, at least enough to give them a trial. Because in 1848 Hall convinced him that the solution to the slavery question—they had some arguments about that too; C.K. had taken Hall up strongly by saying that any man who thought slavery was a question ought to be shot—was through the political process. It was a pretty sophomoric idea, but Hall was a young man, and he convinced C.K. that it was worth a try. So in 1848, C.K. gave Hall money to publish broadsides on behalf of the candidacy of Martin Van Buren, laying out all the arguments for Van Buren, and the anti-expansion slavery position, which Van Buren supposedly held. Well, it turned out that Van Buren wasn't any better than anybody else as far as slavery was concerned, and as for C.K.'s little experiment with the electoral process, in this County Martin Van Buren got exactly one vote—Hall's.

"After that, C.K. gave up on politics. But the business with Hall had gotten him involved again in what was going on in the world. The notes he made in the journal started to move beyond just comments on the conversations, and notations about what corn to buy, and at what price. He started to speculate about what kind of action *would* be effective against slavery. It's pretty clear that he had come out of whatever isolationist shell he had been in, and was ready to do something again.

"In early 1850 he came into contact with the slaves who had been brought here and freed on the old Methodist plan and he began to speculate that he could plow some of the profits he was making from the whiskey into purchasing slaves and freeing them in Canada, or in Liberia. But he rejected the idea, mostly because he saw it wouldn't do any good. For one thing, prime field hands were going for about two thousand dollars a head by this time, and he couldn't have purchased that many, even though his profits were good. And to C.K.'s way of thinking, it wouldn't help anybody. Oh, a few individuals would be freed, and that would be nice for them, but C.K. wasn't overly concerned about individuals; he wanted to attack the system. And buying individual slaves was never going to do anything about that. Even if he could somehow manage to buy enough to affect the market, the only effect it would have would be to stimulate it. So he discarded that idea, and the others that occurred to him—contributing to Abolitionist newspapers, that kind of thing. Because one thing Hall had done for him was to make him think in terms of larger processes: politics, general movements; in particular, economics.

"C.K. had never thought much about economics—few people at this time had—but when he did, he realized that there was simply no way to attack slavery. It was entrenched. It was the basis of the Southern system, and the South produced cotton for the North, so it was the basis of the whole national economy. Even the Abolitionists never really approached the question from that angle; they talked of morals and they talked of politics, but they didn't talk about the fact that if they had abolished slavery, the economy of the entire nation would have been destroyed.

"But C.K. realized it and recognized what it meant: that all the newspapers and all the pamphlets in the world weren't going to do any good. Because slavery was not a moral evil, it was an economic system that worked very well, and the only way to get anybody to change it was either to come up with something better or to make it work less well. He thought about that, and he realized that the only sane way to attack slavery was in more or less the same way that Fiddler and Crawley and Graham were attacking it: by stealing slaves out of the South. Not that they thought of it that way; C.K. wrote that they were too busy helping people to do anything useful. But what he figured out was that the whole slavery 'question' revolved around a single issue: whether a slave was a person or a thing. That's what the constitutional argument had been about. That's what the Dred Scott arguments were about. But the weakness of the arguments and the system was that a slave was both. Yes, he was a self-perpetuating, self-repairing, self-sustaining, highly intelligent work animal, but he was also a person, with a will, and a brain. And, most important, feet."

"You lost me," she said.

"Feet. To walk with. Look. The slaves in the South were worth, at this time, about six billion dollars. And that wasn't a theoretical figure; slaves were money. Actual coin of the realm. The states in the Upper South bred slaves and sold them to the cotton-producing states in the Lower South. So a slave in the Upper South represented a tremendous investment, but his value was only potential. Steal him, and the potential was never realized. The planters of the Lower South not only worked their slaves, they borrowed money against them. The only other collateral they had was the land itself, and the land was worse than worthless without slave labor to cultivate it. Steal the slaves, and the planter had no way to repay his loans, and the bankers had nothing to foreclose on, either. Six billion dollars, and every dollar's worth had a pair of feet. And to bring the whole system crashing down, all you had to do was to encourage a sizable percentage of those people to use their feet at the same time.

"Now, C.K. was no fool; he knew that it was next to impossible to get that many slaves to run north, especially since most of them didn't know which way north was. But the beauty of his thinking wasn't that it was necessary for the slaves to actually escape; all they had to do was to be unavailable for work or sale for a long enough period of time to cause a collapse, or if you wanted to make it even easier, but slower, all you needed to do was get a few to keep running all the time, to drop the profit margin, raise the interest rates because of the added risks, that kind of thing. Never mind that most of the slaves that tried it wouldn't make it; all you had to do was get them

353

out of the fields, running anywhere. What you needed to do was to promote the idea of escape.

"But that was a problem. Slaves couldn't read and there wasn't much travel, and the planters had already set up a strong anti-escape mentality by circulating stories about how Northerners ate Negroes for breakfast and such things—not that that was far from the truth. But C.K. figured out a way around that: the planters talked to each other, and what one planter said to another in the study eventually ended up in the slave quarters, and the thing that planters were most likely to talk about was lost money. So if somehow you could manage to get a lot of women and children to escape—"

"What—?"

"Women and children. A woman was a breeder; an escaped female might represent a loss in breeding potential worth five or six thousand dollars. A child of six represented six years of investment and a return that existed only in potential: a sale value of maybe eight hundred dollars, or twenty years of labor. And these were the slaves the least likely to run. Unless somebody made them. And they were the least likely to escape—unless somebody helped them. And the planters would know that. So if a lot of women and children started disappearing, they'd talk, and the word would get around that Massa was mighty worried about disappearin' poontang and picka-ninnies, and people would get ideas. And any strong man would think, if a woman and a six-year-old can make it, I surely can. And they'd run.

"And so, in the spring of 1850, when C.K. took his whiskey to Philadelphia to market, he asked a few questions and found out who was pretty much running the Underground Railroad in that part of the country. It turned out to be a man named William Still. Still's operation was fairly passive; the idea was to assist people who managed to make their escape, settling them in places where they were unlikely to be recaptured, or if the pursuit was hot, to try and get them into Canada. That took a lot of money. C.K. made a sizable donation, and used the fact that he was a bankroller of the operation to try and influence Still's thinking, to encourage him to become more active in promoting escape. Whether that worked I don't know, because C.K. didn't write much about it; he probably continued to work on Still, and he gave more money, but he wasn't involved in the operation. And something else: he was in love.

354

"Her name was Harriette Brewer, and she was technically a runaway, but only technically; her mother had been three months pregnant when she had left a plantation near Savannah because the child she was carrying belonged to her master, and the mistress of the plantation seemed to have some designs on both her and her child. So she ran away and got to Savannah and stowed away on a ship in the harbor. It was fortunate for her that the captain was something of an Abolitionist, or she could have been sold, but he was, and when he discovered her he took her into his cabin and protected her and delivered her to Philadelphia and set her up as his mistress. So Harriette had been born free, but she could have been taken back at any time; legally she was a slave, the property of her father.

"When C.K. met her she was thirty years old, as beautiful as her mother must have been. But that wasn't what impressed him. What impressed him was that she was educated and intelligent—her mother had evidently parlayed her attraction for the captain into opportunities for her daughter—and she had what C.K. called the strongest moral sense he had ever encountered in man or woman. She was working with Still, keeping records for him. She had worked out a code, and she kept the records in it, and eventually Still was going to be able to decode and publish the accounts. But she was more than just a talented chronicler. Because of her ancestry and her education, she could pass for white, and she undertook some of the most dangerous jobs, helping to take escapees who had made it as far as Philadelphia on north. She knew the safe routes, and safe houses, and she was tough enough to have killed a couple of slave catchers. And C.K. fell in love with her.

"I don't know the details of the affair. I know he asked her to leave with him and come back to the hills. But she wanted to put C.K.'s plans into effect. Evidently they argued about it, C.K. insisting that it was too dangerous, and that they were the brains and money of the operation, and didn't need to get down in the trenches, she insisting that you couldn't ask anybody to do what you were afraid to do yourself. The argument ended in a compromise: she stayed and worked with Still and tried to put C.K.'s plan into some kind of operational form, and he came back to the hills to make more whiskey, and the agreement was that when he came back in the spring he would look at what she had set up and maybe she would do it and maybe they would do it together.

"That's the way they left it. C.K. came back and sold his remainders to the locals. He went back to Philadelphia for a while after that, to be near Harriette and work on the plans. He came back to buy corn, went back, came back in September to set up to take delivery of the corn.

"But his mind wasn't on business, and it wasn't on the economics of slavery, either; it was on Harriette Brewer. For about two months the journal has nothing in it about plans, and only the barest sketch notes about corn and whiskey-making, but it's full of really bad sophomoric poetry, imitations of Wordsworth, I think, but I'm not sure. After two months the poetry stops, and there's nothing much but notes about the whiskey-making, but he didn't stop writing poetry; he just stopped practicing. Sometime in late December he took the risk of leaving everything to make a quick trip east, to see her and to deliver a whole sheaf of soupy love poems to a publisher in Philadelphia, and when he went back in April, he took delivery of five hundred leather-bound volumes of a book of poems called *Untrodden Ways,* and before he even sold the whiskey he took the whole load to her—"

"Don't make fun of it," she said. "I think it's lovely. And I'll bet she thought it was, too."

"No," I said. "I don't think she ever knew about it. Because sometime in February she had decided that the best way to make plans was to try them out, and she had gone South, and she hadn't come back.

"C.K. waited. He didn't know where she had gone; she had written out all her plans, but they were in code, and not the one she kept the other records in; Still couldn't read them. So there was nothing for C.K. to do but wait, hoping she had just gotten delayed. He sold his whiskey and tried to break the code, but he gave that up eventually. So he started reading every Southern newspaper he could get his hands on. But that didn't do any good, and it probably wouldn't; she could have been taken in a hundred ways, for a hundred different things, and it probably wouldn't have made the headlines anywhere, or perhaps only in some small town that nobody had ever heard of. It was hopeless. After two months C.K. came back and sold his remainders. And he made his plans. And in May he made his first trip south."

"Looking for her," she said.

"No," I said. "Oh, there may have been some hope in it, maybe more than a little. But C.K. was no fool; he knew the South was a big, dark place, and that his chances of finding her were practically non-existent. He may have hoped that somehow, some sense would guide him, but I think he just wanted to carry on with what they had planned. He may have been angry; it doesn't show in the way he wrote, and he makes no mention of it, but he may have been. It doesn't really matter. He went south in May, and by late June he had brought out seven women and six children. He bought his corn in July and went back—"

"Wait a minute," she said. "How did he bring them out?"

"I don't know. He kept records in code, just like Harriette Brewer; all he kept in plain language was the records of how many people he brought, and their sexes and ages. I don't know where he brought them from—that's in code, although it seems, judging from the length of time his trips took, that he was going into the Deep South, Mississippi and Louisiana and Alabama. I don't know where he sent them when they left here, although I imagine he spirited them north to New York State, maybe through Williamsport; that would have been the easiest and probably the safest route, valley the whole way. I don't know where he relocated them, if he let them stop in this country or took them on to Canada. But I do know that an important part of what he did had to do with letters. Before he left them he would take down their words, messages to relatives, anybody, and he would help them sign their names. And he'd mail the letters. Of course, the slaves couldn't take delivery, or read the letters. But the masters could, and did. And in those letters there was always mention of C.K., how he had taken them out past all kinds of dangers. I doubt that the adventures were true ones—they probably would have identified too much. And if they were true, I don't know why C.K. kept copies. I have the idea that he used a series of form letters, and the adventures were designed to be good stories, and to get repeated enough so that even slaves heard about C.K. Washington."

"He used his own name?" she said. "Why? I would think it was dangerous."

"It was. Maybe he was hoping that Harriette Brewer would hear the name and get word to him somehow. Or maybe he was hoping that the word would get back to his old mistress; maybe he was looking for a little subtle revenge. Or maybe he was building his ego. In

357

any case, he built a reputation. By 1852 rewards were posted for him in Louisiana, Alabama, and Mississippi. Five hundred dollars for capture. By 1853 newspapers in the Deep South were printing reports of his activities, warnings about him, descriptions of him. By 1855 the rewards were five thousand dollars for his head—there was no mention made of the rest of his body. I don't know what his precise activities were, but in those four years he made three trips a year, the first a short one into the Upper South, the other two into the Deep South. They were always well planned; I can tell from the amount of material in code, even if I don't know how to read it. He had brought out over two hundred slaves—ten men, the rest women and children. It doesn't sound like much, but that was over two hundred thousand dollars' worth of slaves, and a tremendous loss in potential, and the planters certainly must have felt it. And if they didn't mind the loss, they surely minded the propaganda. You could hide which way north was from a slave, but you couldn't hide the fact that four women and twelve children disappeared one night and they weren't sold and they weren't dragged back kicking and screaming."

"So his plan was working?"

"I don't know. I don't know how to tell. I know his idea never destroyed slavery; it took the Civil War to do that, although the North used a plan very much like C.K.'s to deny the South supplies. . . ."

"They did?"

"The Emancipation Proclamation," I said. "But I don't know if C.K. cared about that anymore. I think he did begin to see the whole thing as something of an ego boost, at least in the mid-fifties, when the rewards got very high. And I know he got arrogant and careless, because the third trip he made that year wasn't coded. And the plan itself was just plain crazy. He started it in the journal, wrote down that he was in need of the physical release that could only be provided by a female, and that in order to ease his discomfort and accomplish his higher aims at the same time, he was going to avail himself of the services of a nunnery."

She just looked at me.

"C.K. had read Shakespeare," I said. "He was going to liberate a whorehouse."

"A whorehouse," she said.

"Absolutely," I said. "Now, there wasn't really a whole lot of prostitution in the South; the fact that Massa could tip on down to

358

the slave quarters and practically any other white man could too, or just pick a woman out of the fields—"

"You mean rape one," she said.

"Not rape," I said. "You can't call it rape if the woman doesn't have a right to say yea or nay to begin with. Bestiality is more like it—they weren't people, remember. But that's beside the point. There wasn't that much prostitution, except in the cities. There there was a bit. But it wasn't highly organized and it was mostly white prostitution; hardly a part of slavery, or at least not the kind C.K. was interested in. But the one place where black prostitution was not only highly organized but also an integral part of the social structure was New Orleans. There it was common practice to have spring dances to show off the most beautiful black women of mixed blood, and the white men would come to these—they called them 'octoroon balls'—to purchase a concubine. Very often a father would pick out a young girl for his son as a birthday present. Sometimes the relationships were formalized by a kind of 'left-handed marriage.' But there was a lot of the more traditional whorehouse kind of prostitution, usually for women who were too dark to make it in octoroon society. And C.K. went to steal a whorehouse.

"He had a detailed plan. It was going to be an expensive one, and he didn't want to pump any money into the Southern economy, so there was another plan to provide a bankroll. After he had bought his corn futures in July, he headed west across the mountains to Cincinnati, and took passage on a riverboat heading south to New Orleans. He was posing as a Southerner who had gone north to claim an inheritance, a man with lots of money and no sense, and he spent the first part of the trip in the card room, losing every bit of the seed money he had brought with him, about three thousand dollars. By the time they were halfway down the river every man on board knew he was a sucker and practically broke, and they were lining up for chances to take what he had left. But just about then he had a run of luck and won back all of his stake, and about five thousand more. Then he lost that. By that time they were in New Orleans, and he had nothing more than his original three thousand, but he had a reputation for being a dumb cardplayer with streaky luck. And more important, he had a set of acquaintances to go with his fake name. And he had an entrée into the best poker games in New Orleans.

"I don't know where he had learned to play poker, maybe on his

359

first trip up the river, but he knew, and he knew how to catch cheats too. In a month he was well known as a gambler and a dueler, and he was just about even with the money; he hadn't beaten anybody badly enough to be thought ill of, but he was known. He let that reputation build for a while, and then he promoted a big game and won the fifty thousand dollars he needed. It was a lot of money, but he was careful to take it from a lot of different people, so nobody was bankrupt, and nobody was mad, and everybody thought he was a fine fellow, and thought it was just a great way to spend a lot of found money—"

"What was?"

"His vacation. Two weeks in a rented house in the country near Hammond, Louisiana, with the top fifteen women from the best house in town. He took all the men who had lost money to him, and he let them spend the first weekend enjoying good food and drink and women and probably some more poker. And then he packed them off with a strict injunction not to bother him until the last two days of his vacation, when they were all supposed to come back for another big party. So the top gentry of New Orleans went back to town, laughing and joking and full of liquor and good will, and ten days later they came back, ready for another party, and found an empty house and no women and a letter from C.K. Washington thanking them for showing him such a good time in New Orleans. They put out the alarm, of course, but C.K. and the women had a ten-day head start, and C.K. had disguised the women as a coffle of boys being sold west, with C.K. as the driver, and nobody could imagine fancy women dressed up and made up that way; they made it here by late September. I don't know what the other trips were like, but C.K. remarked on the lack of adventure in this one.

"The only problem was that it was too late in the year to move them on. C.K. had to take delivery of his corn and get about his whiskey-making. So he taught the women how to build cabins and they set up a little commune in the hills, and helped him cook that year, and I imagine he got his physical release. When spring came he had gotten more than that. Nine of the women moved north to Canada. Five chose to stay with the profession, and C.K. took them to Philadelphia and gave them enough money to buy a house and set themselves up in business. . . ."

She made a face.

"They were free women now," I said.

"All right," she said. "But your arithmetic is off."

"No it isn't. One of the women stayed with C.K.

"Her name was Bijou, and she was the darkest of the women; that's all he says about her. He never even mentions the fact that sometime during the winter she became his mistress. I doubt that she was the only one who did, but she was the only one who stayed, although that was probably more her decision than his. All he did was record the fact, and mention her from time to time, and chart the progress of her pregnancy; there's nothing to indicate that he cared about her, or even thought about her. He didn't change his activities in any way that I can see. The next year—1856, that would have been—he made the same three trips, and he didn't get back from the third one until long after she was due; when he did get back she had had the child and named him Lamen—God knows why.

"But he did change shortly after he came back from his first trip in 1857. I don't know where he went that time; the New Orleans trip seems to have restored some sense of discretion to him, and he started putting things in code again. But wherever he went, he came back wary and . . . I don't know. Apprehensive. He became absolutely fanatical about security. He moved Bijou and the child further into the hills, and he started expanding his escape routes, setting up a system of provision caches all the way to the eastern side of the mountains, and another one stretching north as far as Williamsport. And he stopped going to town as frequently as he had; he more or less disappeared—"

"He was afraid," she said. "He'd already lost one woman and he was obsessed with idea of losing another one."

"Maybe," I said. "But I don't think so. I think it was something else."

"What?" she said.

"All right. I have to go back to the beginning again. Another story, about a man named Pettis. F. H. Pettis. Pettis was a lawyer in New York. About 1840, he had seen the lucrative possibilities represented by fugitive slaves, and he had begun to advertise in Southern newspapers, offering to track down and return fugitive property for a flat fee of one hundred and twenty dollars, providing the owner would provide a description and pay twenty dollars in advance. I suspect it was just a scheme, and that Pettis had every intention of taking the twenty dollars and forgetting the whole thing, maybe writing back in a month or so that the slave had reached Canada, and was therefore beyond capture, but that, being a good con man, he decided it would be smart to actually capture a few, just to look reliable. Or maybe he was serious about the business all along. It doesn't really matter, because either way, he made the attempt to locate a few fugitives, and given the fact that there were relatively few blacks in the North and that the laws governing them were so restrictive, requiring all kinds of registration and bonds and so forth, he discovered that tracking down runaways for a hundred and twenty dollars paid better than not tracking them down for twenty. In a year or two, Pettis was legitimate, and his business was expanding to the point that he no longer relied on slave owners' contacting him, and had developed informants in the larger black communities who kept him abreast of new arrivals. That wasn't hard—Philadelphia had the largest black community, and there were less than twenty thousand people in it. If Pettis discovered a black who looked to be a runaway, he would scan the wanted posters and newspaper advertisements and eventually come up with a probable owner. Then he would contact that owner and offer to return the slave for a reasonable fee. A third of the slave's value was the usual amount at the time; Pettis probably got more, but even if he didn't, that would have been an average $250 a head. It might have ended there, but there is some evidence that he was irked by the amount of money he spent investigating blacks who turned out to be free, and so he began not only to investigate the identities of legitimate owners but to assess the interest of potential ones. That, he found, was formidable. For some years there had been a subtle imbalance in the slave market, with the breeders failing to keep up with increasing demand. The situation in 1840 was not as bad as it was going to be twenty years later, but it was serious enough for Pettis' inquiries to meet with enthusiastic responses from slaveholders. And so he had gone into the kidnapping business, carefully selecting blacks who were young and strong, but mostly limiting himself to skilled craftsmen or attractive young women—who could be considered craftsmen of a sort—and sending them south.

"By 1847 Pettis had come to be viewed by many a Southern planter as a genteel and civilized alternative to absorbing losses on runaways, and had begun to be called in on cases of missing and valuable slaves long before the black had a chance to get out of the state, let alone out of the South. Pettis had capitalized on this confidence, and had developed a larger and more efficient organization in other Northern urban centers, and in Southern cities as well. And he had cadres of slave catchers, men and dogs trained in the arts of trailing men and capturing them and bringing them back to their owners more or less undamaged. By 1850 he was installed in the minds of the planters as the man to call on to solve any problem involving slave security, from the capture of runaways to the gathering of intelligence regarding planned insurrections, to the activities of the Abolitionists and the Underground Railroad.

"By this time Pettis had reorganized his business, entrusting everyday operations to lieutenants, while restricting his own activities to policy-making and active involvement in only those cases that were particularly unusual, or highly lucrative, or offered the best opportunities for gaining recognition and political advantage. He was hired by slaveholding interests to operate against Haiti, and he was so successful that they asked him to work on the problem of Cuba, and he orchestrated Narciso López's third expedition, the one that came closest to success. Then, it seems he got tired of foreign adventures, and turned his attention to uncovering slave insurrections. It was a profitable business, and some of the insurrections he exposed probably even existed; one in Texas, for example, in 1856.

"But the things that really interested him were those cases of escape that involved large bodies of slaves. In 1847 he had personally investigated the escape of nearly fifty slaves in Kentucky, and although he met with only partial success, he had developed contacts which made it possible for him to detect and foil a plot of nearly seventy-five slaves to escape the next year. Pettis' work resulted in the recapture of all seventy-five, the execution of three of them, and the incarceration, for a sentence of twenty years, of the white man who had planned and led the escape. Five years later he was back in Kentucky, investigating the escape of twenty-five slaves from a plantation near the town of Boone City. In 1855 he purchased a plantation in Kentucky, and more or less retired to drink mint juleps and enjoy the revenue from his various enterprises. It would have been that way, probably, but he had two embarrassments in 1856. The first involved the investigation of an alleged slave insurrection in Tennessee; Pettis took personal charge. The black who had been implicated refused to betray his fellow conspirators, or at least, failed to do so before Pettis had whipped him to death, an outcome which Pettis found both embarrassing and frustrating. The second involved the escape of thirty-one slaves—four young men, fifteen women, and twelve children—from a plantation only a few miles from Pettis' own. The escape was engineered by C.K. Washington.

"Evidently Pettis had known of C.K. Washington for some years, and had no hatred for him. But C.K.'s incursion into his territory turned Pettis' attitude into one of flaming hatred, and he vowed, publicly, that he would not rest, or allow anyone in his employ to rest, until C.K. Washington had been taken. Not just taken, but taken legally, caught in the act of transporting slaves or aiding and abetting an escape, or some other legitimate violation. And when that happened, Pettis vowed, he would have C.K. hanged. Not lynched, but brought to a legal trial and given a legal sentence of hanging. The vow made headlines all across the South.

"C.K. probably learned about Pettis' interest in him—he probably knew about Pettis already—on that first trip in 1857. And at the same time he learned how good Pettis' organization was. Because the handbills that were out, offering a reward for information about him, didn't just call him C.K. Washington; they described a Negro slave named Brobdingnag, calling himself 'C.K.,' escaped from the plantation of one Hammond Washington in 1823, now aged fifty-two years, having light skin and a brand on his shoulder in the shape of the letters *C* and *K*. Pettis had tracked down C.K.'s past. And most important, he had come up with a legal reason to hold C.K. if he was captured. So C.K. probably was more than slightly worried when, in the summer of 1857, the local paper listed F. H. Pettis among the prominent men vacationing at the Springs. . . ."

"He'd found C.K.," she said.

"No," I said. "Probably not. Most likely Pettis' presence was largely a matter of fortune, call it good or bad. While Pettis was dedicated to tracking down C.K., he was also an aging man, plagued by aches and pains. He was also one of the *nouveau riche,* and probably had the usual love of hobnobbing with the rich and the famous. He probably came to the Springs Hotel to take the medicinal waters and swap cigars and brandy with the most powerful men in America—the Supreme Court and President Buchanan and the rest of them. And C.K. probably saw that. But he couldn't be sure. And maybe he was right not to be. Because if Pettis' people could nose around the black community and pick up rumors about runaway slaves, they probably

had managed to locate a few of the people C.K. had helped to freedom, had managed to figure out the routes they had taken, and had
come up with the fact that this area, or western Pennsylvania, anyway, was a common denominator in all that activity. So maybe Pettis
was combining business with pleasure. I don't know. I do know that it
had an effect on C.K. He canceled the second and third trips in 1857,
and spent his time mapping trails and building redoubts. And he took
Lamen and Bijou over the mountain and set them up in a house in
Philadelphia. In 1858 he didn't even plan any trips. He had cooked an
extra measure of whiskey the year before, and he laid that away, and
then he just hung around in the hills, watching what went on in the
South County. He recorded at least thirty-five different incidents in
which slaves were hunted down in the mountains and taken back to
the South, usually with the help of local bounty hunters and trackers
and dogs. The groups were usually fairly small, about four or five people, but there was one that numbered twenty. So any way you look at
it, C.K., personally, saw a hundred and fifty slaves dragged back to
bondage. He tried to stop it when he could, especially if the groups
included a large proportion of women or children, although child escapees were fairly rare. He doesn't list too many details, he just notes
the number of people whom he helped escape. He kept a running total, debits against credits, and at the end of the year he had watched
over a hundred more people taken back than he had helped. I think
that bothered him. I think he wished that he could go in and help
them all, even when it seemed that he would be taken, too, if he
failed. I know why he didn't, and I know he knew why. It's there in
the diary, the logic of it, but it's obvious, anyway; he had looked
around and seen what was happening and sensed that the time for
the kind of actions he was involved in was long past, sensed that the
forces moving in the land were too ponderous to be deflected or even
much affected by a single man, no matter how daring he was. But
while he couldn't do much against slavery, he could do a lot for it; all
he had to do was be captured. Because what he had done was turn
himself into a symbol of hope to any slave who heard about him, and
if the Southerners could capture him they would kill that hope. And
so he was careful when he intervened, for good reasons. But I have it
in my mind that he hated those good reasons. Or maybe not. Because
there was more to it.

"That summer, instead of going south, he had gone to Philadelphia. When he came back he was a different man. The diary was different. He was . . . frank. Almost as if he were writing things that he might want somebody to read someday. His prose was straightforward and clear, but it wasn't flat and factual. It was, for him, tremendously emotional. And so I think the decision he had reached was emotional, rather than political. . . ."

"*What* decision?" she said.

"He had decided to retire. Give up, maybe, if you want to be hard about it. I would say he was probably harder on himself about it than anybody else could be. It wasn't so much a decision as a realization; he realized he was tired. He had been politically active for a quarter of a century. He had moved from being wholly anonymous to being famous—or infamous, if you happened to hold slaves. He had, through direct action, deprived the Southern economy of two million dollars' worth of slaves—more, if you considered labor potential and the potential of offspring locked up in the loins of the females he had taken. His example had probably inspired the escape of several millions of dollars' worth more. He had probably cost the South two million dollars' worth of man-hours in trying to track him down. Call it all ten million dollars' worth of damage; he had been a success. But now he was getting old. Each morning was a little harder for him, each night spent in the open a little more of a trial. He wasn't showing any particular strain as yet, but he felt the strain. And he longed for some ease. He was absolutely honest about that; he wrote: 'My life is not easy, I long to make it so. I have learned that there is no weakness in softness, no evil in taking rest.' I don't know precisely what made him decide that, but I think it had to do with Bijou, and probably with the child. At any rate, he wrote that that winter would be his 'final sojourn in the cold,' and that in the spring he would go to Philadelphia and take the woman and the child and leave for either Liberia or Haiti or the British West Indies, where slavery was a thing of the past.

"I don't know why he wrote all that down. I have it in my mind that he was trying to convince himself. That he felt some kind of guilt about turning away, and that he wanted his thoughts out there in black and white so that he couldn't just pretend he had never thought them. But that's just guessing; I know him well enough to guess, not enough to be sure. But I am sure that he didn't act like a man who had decided to give up; he was even more active locally than he had

366

been the year before. He developed a new technique; he would slip down into Maryland and pick up handbills advertising for runaways, and then he would try to pick up their trails near the border and steer them to Underground Railroad stations where someone could help them on. He must have steered forty or fifty people away from the route up through Cumberland Valley, because it was long and dangerous and there were no stations on it. He didn't intervene directly, though; I think he realized that was too dangerous, and that he could be of even more help giving runaways directions and telling them where the danger spots were. And he actually helped more people that way, it seems. Because the forty or fifty all came in a space of two months, while he was involved with taking his corn and setting up to brew, so he was only working at it part time. There's no telling how much good he could have done when he was finished making whiskey."

I stopped, sipped my toddy.

"John," she said.

"That's it," I said. "The journal ends there: December 23, 1859."

"That's *all?*"

"That's all."

"What happened to him?"

"I don't know. Something. Nobody ever heard of him again."

She looked at me. "You bastard," she said. "After all that, you're just going to let it fall like that?"

"There's nothing else to do," I said. "That's all I know, all I can figure out. There's no more record, and there's nothing in code, just December 23, a routine notation about the whiskey, a brief comment about the weather: the first snowstorm of the year was brewing, and he decided to go into town for supplies before it broke, and, if he had time, hunt. That's the end of it; a period at the end of the sentence. That's the way history is sometimes. Sometimes you don't even get periods."

I leaned forward and began to mix a toddy. The logs had burned low, but the wind was letting up, it seemed. I decided to wait to build up the fire.

"All right," she said. "So you don't know what happened to him. So now you can tell me how you got the journal."

"That's another story," I said. "And it's not a very long one, either, because nobody kept any journals on it. Just brief notes, names, addresses. So all I've got is what I can figure out. It takes place in Philadelphia, and it starts on September 20, 1890, when a son was born to Lamen Washington, a fairly prominent black mortician, prominent enough to have the event written up in the local black newspaper, and his wife, Cora Alice Washington, née O'Reilly—"

"O'Reilly?"

"Her father was an Irishman, fresh off the boat, and he married her mother. Such things were happening in 1865 or so, when she was born. But anyway, the event of the birth was not as joyful as it might have been, because Mrs. Washington died in childbirth. Lamen Washington took care of his wife's body—"

"You mean he did it himself?" she said.

"Yes," I said. "The note on that is quite specific."

"Who made these notes? . . . I know, you'll get to it."

"Yes," I said. "Lamen Washington buried his wife and then got about the business of naming his son, and he did it by sticking his finger into the Bible. The kid was lucky; Lamen's finger could have landed in the 'begats,' and he would have ended up with a name like Abinadab, or Bezalel, or Segub, but it landed in the second chapter of Exodus, and the child was called Moses."

"Your father," she said.

It wasn't a question, so I didn't answer it. "I don't know much about Moses Washington's childhood. Lamen evidently did not remarry, so I expect that someone was hired to look after him. His upbringing probably was as normal as it could be under the circumstances, although there is some evidence that he was not particularly fond of his father, perhaps because his father did not seem to be particularly fond of him. He was probably well cared for, well fed, all that, because Lamen would have been an important man in the black community, and a fairly wealthy one. Moses was well educated; he went to the Friends School, and he probably did well there, because he had a passion for books. He read everything he could get his hands on and took copious notes on all of it.

"I really don't know much more about him until he was fifteen, and for some reason he became interested in the history of Negroes, particularly in Philadelphia, and he somehow got a copy of the *Sketches*. . . ."

"C.K.'s book."

"That's right. Although Moses didn't know that. To him it was just a book. Until at some point Lamen found him reading it, and took it away from him and burned it. I doubt that helped father-son relations any. What it did do was to arouse Moses' curiosity, and he got another copy of the book and spent weeks reading it and rereading it and taking notes and trying to figure out what it was that his father had objected to. He finally decided that it had to have something to do with the author, who was, of course, anonymous, but that didn't stop him. He set about cataloging all the anonymous writing that had been done by Philadelphia blacks about that time, and he eventually came up with the book of poetry and the letter that had been published in *The Liberator,* and a lot of other things that probably didn't belong to C.K., anyway. He was spending a lot of time and getting nowhere in particular because he really didn't know what he was looking for; the identity of the author of the *Sketches,* but maybe that was only a first stage. . . ."

"He was fifteen years old?"

"Sixteen, I figure, by this time. He didn't do all this overnight."

"How long did it take him to figure out who C.K. was?"

"He didn't. He had practically driven himself into a collapse and his grandmother managed to figure out what he was doing. . . ."

"Bijou," she said.

"Bijou."

"And she told him?"

"No," I said. "No, she didn't tell him. I don't think she knew. I don't know if it was the kind of thing C.K. would have talked to her about. I know she hadn't read the diaries—"

"How do you know that?"

"She was an ex-slave; I don't think she knew how to read."

"She could have learned," she said.

"I suppose so."

"She probably did learn; she had his books, and she loved him, and she'd want to read them—"

"I don't know that she loved him."

"She kept the books, didn't she? She kept the book of poems."

"So?"

"So she kept a book of poems that her man had written for another woman. I'd say she loved him."

"All right," I said. "Maybe so."

"And how did she get them? How did she get the books?"

"Maybe he left them with her."

"And the journal? It went right up until the time he disappeared. How did she get that?"

I didn't say anything.

"I'll tell you how," she said. "That woman came up here looking for him, and she went to all the places she knew he might be, and she didn't find him, but she found his books, and his writing, and she took it back with her, because that was the only thing she had of him besides his money and his son. That's what happened."

"Maybe," I said. "It makes sense." But I wasn't really thinking about that. What I was thinking was that if it was true, whatever had happened to C.K. wasn't a question of somebody finding him and killing him or taking him; they would not have left the diary undisturbed, probably. Whatever had happened to him had happened outside, in the woods. "Anyway," I said, "he kept notes on the books as he read them, and used the journal to figure out which of the anonymous pieces he had found belonged to C.K. That took him a few months. The last entry in his notebooks is dated December 1907. . . ."

"December twenty-third?"

"Thirty-first," I said. "This is history, not a fairy tale; everything doesn't work out that neatly. But you've got the right idea—"

"He came here and used C.K.'s notes and maps and set himself up in the whiskey business."

"Methods too; he followed C.K.'s techniques pretty closely, right up to the point of selling to the powerful. He didn't take his whiskey to Philadelphia—times had changed—but this area still had a fondness for untaxed whiskey, maybe just because it was untaxed, and he must have made out all right, and then came the Volstead Act and moonshine was the only shine, and he made a small fortune—"

"But that wasn't what he was doing, was it?"

"No, not really."

"He was trying to find out what had happened to C.K."

"Yes."

"Did he?"

I looked at the fire. The last log was starting to crumble, but the coals were red and alive. I looked up. The eastern sky was lightening; false dawn, but light—we would be able to move in an hour. There was no point in wasting wood. I settled back against the snow, feeling the chill of it against my back.

"No," I said. "No, I don't think so. No."

It wasn't easy going in the valley. The plows had been through, but that had been a long time ago—the afternoon before, maybe. The snow came to within a few inches of the top of my boots, and I knew it would be at the top of Judith's.

We had been moving for two hours, since the first redness of dawn. We had made good time considering the snow, and covered six miles, maybe seven. I started looking for the signs. I tried not to think about anything, and it was not hard; the night had exhausted me. My throat was raw from wood smoke and talking, and the toddies and lack of sleep had put a dull ache in my head. I moved now only because not to move was to be cold.

I looked back and saw that Judith had fallen behind by about thirty yards. I stopped and waited for her, watching her come up to me. The steam cloud was large in front of her face and there was sweat on her brow. I had been pushing too hard. She stopped when she got to me and leaned against me, panting. I put my arm around her, trying to feel the shape of her shoulders through the bulkiness of the coat.

"How far do we have to go?" she said.

"It can't be far now," I said. I was lying, it was probably another two miles, but it wouldn't do any good to tell her that. "Look for a concrete bridge on the left."

"And that will be it?"

"The next turn to the left." I didn't say it was maybe a mile.

"A concrete bridge, and then we turn left?"

"That's it."

"Sounds simple."

"It is simple," I said. "Everything's simple when you've got a nice road to follow."

"It's a damned sight simpler when you've got a nice car to follow it in," she said.

"Ah," I said, "your mother was so right about the gentle constitution of the Southern lady."

Twenty minutes later, she spotted the bridge. I went back to work counting the paces, figuring fifteen hundred to the mile. The count was off. Sixteen hundred and seven paces later, I detected a wider than normal gap in the trees to the left and turned off the road.

"Where the hell are you going?" she said.

"This is it," I said. "This road."

"What road? I don't see any road."

There was a road there. It was hard to believe for the first hundred yards, but then the trees on either side thickened and there was more underbrush and the path through it was more distinct. The trees had kept the snow from drifting deep, and we made good time. Thirty yards farther on I caught the sound of a stream on the right, gurgling to itself down beneath the snow. I stopped and let her catch up.

"You want a drink?" I said.

"Where?"

"Listen," I said.

We held still. There was no sound, none at all, except the whispering of a light breeze high in the trees and the dripping of water as some of the snow melted in the sunlight, and under it, the slow chuckling of the stream.

"I don't hear anything," she said.

"You don't?"

"No."

I shrugged, took her hand, and led her off the road and down towards the stream. Through the snow I felt the beginning of a sudden drop-off; I stopped and probed with my toe. The cover of snow cracked and crumbled, opening a hole two feet wide and showing clear water running swift and shallow over a sandy bottom. I pulled my gloves off and knelt carefully at the edge of it. "Hunker down," I said. I cupped my hands and dipped them into the water. It was icy cold; my hands were numb in an instant. I took them out and brought them up to her face. She brushed her hair back with one hand and put the other under mine and held the heels of my hands against her chin and drank. When the water was gone, she kissed my hands softly and took her face away.

"More?" I said.

She nodded. I dipped my hands again, and she drank again, but this time she did not let my hands go, she held them with hers, folded them together. "Now you," she said, and slipped her gloves off and dipped her hands.

The coldness of the water was a shock to her—I saw her flinch but she said nothing, and raised the water to me. I drank it quickly. "No more," I said.

She wiped her hands on her scarf and pulled her gloves back on. I wiped mine on my pants and picked my gloves up.

"Touch me," she said. "Touch my face."

"My hands are cold," I said.

"I know that. Do it."

I put my left hand up and touched her cheek. My fingertips tingled with the cold.

"The right one too," she said. "And hold my face."

I did.

"Your hands are bad, aren't they?"

"No," I said. "Not really." I put my gloves back on and stood up.

She stood too. "Where now, O great Gitche Gumee, who knows the ways of the forest?"

"Up," I said, "yours."

"At least it's warm there," she said, and started up the bank. I started to follow her, but as I turned my toe caught on something hard and rough beneath the snow. I looked down. More of the snow had crumbled away, dropping into the water, showing the edge of the stream was not a bank but a curb of stone laid in a haphazard but definite pattern.

By that time she had reached the road, turned, and seen I was not there. "John?"

"Yeah," I said. I knelt again and brushed away more snow, enough to see that the pattern of the stones was preserved with a rough, grainy mortar, applied carelessly and rudely, but long enough ago for the water to have worn the edges smooth.

"What is it?" She was above me now; she had come back from the road.

I stood up again and looked downstream, trying to find a pattern in the placement of the trees. "Nothing, really," I said. "Just some stones and mortar that must have been part of a millrace down there."

"Does that mean something?"

"No," I said. "There were mills all over the place, on every stream that had enough size to power one."

She turned her head, faced upstream. "I don't see anything."

"You have to look downstream," I said. "And you probably wouldn't see anything anyway; it might date back as far as 1730. They built to last in those days, but the thing could have stood for two hundred and fifty years and still be nothing more than a pile of rocks now."

"Couldn't we find that?"

"Probably. All we'd have to do is follow the millrace until we fell over some rocks and got our feet wet—assuming the rocks haven't been hauled away to build something else."

"Oh," she said. "It's important, though, isn't it? To find it?"

"No," I said. "It has nothing to do with where we're going."

"Then why are you still looking for it?"

"I don't know," I said. "I'm just curious." I stopped looking and made my way back up the bank. "It's not far now," I said.

We went on, forging through the snow. In a hundred yards the road stopped being a road at all; I could sense it through the snow, from the feel of the ground, but it made curious twists and there were fairly large trees growing in the center of it. I stopped and looked at one closely, wishing I had a saw.

"What . . .?"

"This is an old road," I said. "It was built before they had bull-dozers to knock down trees or dynamite to blast stumps; that's why it turns so much, to go between trees too big to blast out with black powder—"

"I see you twisting and turning," she said, "but I don't see any trees, except the ones you practically run into."

"That's because the trees it was going around aren't there any-more. Maybe somebody cut them down later and the stumps rotted, or they just died. But the others are new growth—"

"That's a new tree?" she said. "It's pretty big."

" 'New' meaning thirty or forty years. Which means this road stopped being used that long ago. Which means nobody much was using it when Moses Washington came up here and shot himself."

"Does that mean—"

"Stop asking me if it means anything. I don't know if it means anything. I don't know if anything does."

I turned away and went on, moving badly, faster than I had to, getting the snow higher on my legs than I had to. I heard her behind me, floundering to keep up, and I knew that it was wrong, that I should slow down for her, but something was pushing me, and I just kept on, and then I heard her calling me, and whatever it was that was making me move that way went away and I stopped and turned and went back to her. She was standing in the middle of the road, the breath exploding from her mouth, the steam rising from her forehead. It took me almost a minute to get back to her.

"I'm sorry," I said.

"*I'm* sorry," she said.

"No," I said. "You didn't do anything. . . ."

"I know that," she said. "I'm sorry that I got you mad enough to try to kill me." She smiled at me and put her head on my arm and rubbed it.

I took out my handkerchief and wiped her brow. "You can't get overheated. You'll catch pneumonia."

"I know that," she said. "You're the one that forgot."

"Yeah," I said, and put the handkerchief away.

"Never mind," she said. "I'll survive. Only for God's sake tell me how far we have to go."

I realized that I had lost track of distance, of elapsed time, even of direction, had lost track of everything but the meanderings of the road. I looked around. "Just . . ." I stopped.

"What is it?"

"Here," I said.

"Here?"

"Yes," I said. I pointed to the left. "Up there."

"That," she said, "is not here."

But I barely heard her. Because I had left the road by that time and had gone blundering through the underbrush, searching with my boots for a path. In a moment I found one, or at least a smoother way that could have been a path, and was following it up along the curve of the ridge. I came to the top of the rise and started down the other side. And then I realized that the slope was falling away to my right and that as I followed it, the sun was moving to my left; the hillside was twisting, coming around to face south. I moved faster then, surer of where I was going. The trees thinned rapidly, then stopped altogether; I came to a halt there, at the edge of the timber, where a ruined stone wall thrust up from beneath. Beyond that the hillside was smooth and clean and white, interrupted only by the rounded tops of the gravestones. The hillside fell away into a silent valley, the snow cover deep and cottony-looking, shining golden in the sun. A few giant shapes moved across the snow, the shadows of clouds.

In a few minutes I heard her coming up beside me, breathing deeply. She stopped and I heard her breath catch, and I knew what she would be thinking: that it was beautiful down there. I was ready to agree with her. But then the wind came driving up the valley, lifting the calm snow into a white whirlwind, not so much drifting it as driving it forward in a wall. Then the wind hit me, tearing through my coat and skin and into my bones, and I remembered what hillside that was, and I stood there, shivering with the cold and looking out over the place where Moses Washington had died.

"Here," she said, after a while.

"Yes," I said.

"It looks like . . ."

"A graveyard," I said. "Family graveyard. Belonging to a family named Iiames."

"He killed himself in a graveyard?"

"No," I said. "Not in it. Just beyond the edge of it. The southeast corner."

"You need to find the exact spot," she said.

"Yes," I said. "Just looking at it isn't helping anything."

"How are you going to do that?"

I sighed. "I'm going to go in there and tramp around over people's graves and figure out where the graves stop and the field begins." The wind kicked up then, and I shivered. I reached into the pocket of my coat and brought out the flask, raised it, drank. The liquor tasted raw and it didn't do any good. I wiped my mouth on my glove and put the flask away. She didn't say anything. "I guess I'd better get at it."

She stepped back then, back behind me, and put her arms around me, holding the base of my belly with both hands. I stood there for a minute, but she wasn't helping any more than the whiskey had, and so I reached down and pried her hands loose.

I climbed over the wall, moving stiffly, and went to the nearest gravestone. I checked the name, not because I wasn't sure, but because I wanted to be certain. The letters of the name were hard to make out, but I managed to trace out an *I* and an *A* chiseled into the gray stone. Enough. Enough for me to go flipping through the cards in my mind: in the year of our Lord 1758, in the first month, on the twenty-sixth day, Richard Iiames was buried on the farm which he owned. And in the year of our Lord 1958, in the eighth month, on the seventh day, Moses Washington, son of Lamen, son of C.K., son of Zack, son of some philandering Cherokee, had seen fit to blow his brains out in close proximity to Richard Iiames's remains. And it still made no damned sense.

"Something wrong?" she said.

"No," I said. I started walking along the ranks of stones. They were set about six feet apart. There were twelve stones in the full row; that made sense. An even dozen. Twelve pews on each side of a church. Twelve disciples, if you counted Judas. So when they had made the graveyard, they had decided on twelve across, and when they got to the twelfth they had started again, on the right probably. I went back to the beginning of the rank and paced off the distance between the first and second stones in the file; about eight feet. I looked along the second rank. Some of the stones appeared to be missing, but that wasn't so strange—they had probably been there for two hundred years; it made sense that some would fall down or break off. I paced off the distance to the third file. Eight feet. But when I looked at the rank it seemed that most of the stones were out of line; I got down and sighted along the rank to be sure. They *were* out of line. But the ones that were out of line were in line with each other; some were three feet too close to the second file, some were two feet too far away. And then I saw that two of the ones that were out of line were in the same file. I nodded to myself.

"Did you find something?" she said.

"Not really," I said. "They started out burying twelve across, probably leaving space for a wife next to her husband, or vice versa. But reality complicated that little pattern. That man there"—I pointed to a stone—"lost a wife, and remarried. And that woman there"—I pointed again—"lost two children. She may have died in childbirth—"

"How can you tell all that?"

"From the spacing. The children were buried at the mother's feet. There's a full grave, eight feet long, for the mother, then a shorter one, five feet, for the children. The other full graves, the ones beside the mothers, are probably the husbands—"

"But there aren't any children at the feet of the ones you say are the husbands—"

" 'It's a wise father that knows his own child,' " I said.

She didn't say anything.

"You wanted to know about this place?" I said. "You wanted to know all about this County? Well, it's all right here in this graveyard. Somewhere in here is the grave of a man named Richard Iiames. He was part of a group of thirteen that came here in 1728. Oldest continuous settlement in the County; west of the Susquehanna, for that matter."

"Where did they come from?" she said.

"Virginia," I said.

She didn't say anything, and in a way I was glad, because if she had I might have told her the rest of it. But in another way I was not; in another way I was hoping she would say something, would ask a question, give me something more I could explain. But she didn't. So I climbed back over the wall and walked to the southeast corner. And then I stood there.

I don't know what I was expecting. I don't know what I was hoping for. A flash of light, maybe. Maybe thunder rolling. Or just a burst of insight. Certainly I was expecting something. And certainly whatever it was I was expecting, or hoping for, didn't happen. I just stood there, shivering a little more than usual, maybe, but that was all. After a while I fumbled out the flask and drank from it, drank it all. I capped it, and put it away. And then I stood there some more, with the whiskey turning to ice in my belly.

"Anything?" she said.

"What?" I said. "What would there be? Twenty years ago somebody blew his brains out and bled into the dirt. They took the body away, so there'd be no bones, and the blood soaked into the soil, and that's covered up with snow. So what the hell would there be?"

"You're the one who wanted to come," she said softly.

"Yes," I said. "I'm the one who wanted to come."

I stood there some more, looking out over the valley, and waited.

"All right," I said finally. "That's it. Let's go." I turned quickly, too quickly, and felt my feet go slipping out from under me. I went down heavily, and my arms wouldn't move fast enough to break my fall; I landed on my back, and felt something hard and solid slam into my head.

"John?" She came running, bent over me. "John? You . . ."

"I'm fine," I said. My eyes wouldn't focus properly; I saw two of everything. "What the hell did I hit?"

"A rock," she said.

I shook my head. It cleared; I was seeing okay again. I looked at the rock. It was shaped strangely; a solid triangle. It was dark in color, almost black. I got to my feet. My head ached, and I was dizzy, but I stood practically on top of the stone and faced across the slope. I paced off six feet and found a second stone, and six feet farther on, a third. I paced on six more feet and kicked around in the snow, but that seemed to be the end of the rank. I went back to the third one and paced down eight feet. I found a stone. I paced below that and found nothing. I went back up and went across the slope, below the second stone. Eight feet below it was a stone, another five feet below that, another five feet below that, nothing below that. I went back up and kicked around eight feet below the first stone. I found nothing.

"John," she said.

I looked up and saw that she had paced off six feet from the first stone, but in the direction opposite the one I had taken. And she had found a stone. "Go—"

"I know," she said. She went on beyond, found nothing, came back and paced down the slope. Eight feet down the slope she found a stone. She paced on, found two more in the file, spaced five feet apart. That seemed to be the end of them.

"What *is* this?" she said.

"Another graveyard," I said. "Another graveyard right beside the other one."

"But why would they put some of the family over here?"

"Maybe it wasn't some of the family. Maybe it was something that belonged to the family."

She didn't say anything.

"Yeah," I said. "They came from Virginia to pioneer, but they brought a little help with them . . ." but then I realized that didn't make any sense. "No," I said. "Not help. They must have decided to go into the breeding business. It's hard to tell how they did. This woman here had three children that died; there's no way to tell how many got old enough to sell. This one, well, either all her children lived, or she was a lousy breeder. The other two, probably so-so. You wanted to know about the County; well, here it is. How do you like it? Think I've been cheating you out of anything worth mentioning?"

"Men," she said.

"What?"

"If they were breeding, what about studs?"

"Oh, that's no problem; they're probably over there on the other side of the wall. I mean, why pay good money for a nigger and give him a harem when you can do the work yourself. Anything else you want to know?"

And I was hoping there was. Because just for a minute I wanted to tell it all to her, tell her all about how Richard Iiames had come with Joseph Powell, grandson of Thomas, brother of John, captain of the *Seafoam;* for a minute I wanted to watch her face when I told her that. But she didn't say anything. She just went kicking across the slope, her feet throwing up frenzied clouds of snow. I didn't say anything, feeling the anger going out of me as she kicked, knowing what she was feeling, what it was like to go that way, searching, not knowing how, or for what. And I knew what it would be like for her when she failed to find anything at all.

But she didn't. She didn't fail. Somewhere down the slope, in line with the two stones in the last file, she found another one. I heard her suck her breath in when her foot hit it, but she did not cry out; she just sucked her breath in and stood, panting, looking down. And then she looked up at me. She glared at me, angrily. Then she came back up the slope, stood beside me.

"What about that marker down there?" she said.

"Probably a man," I said. I looked down over the valley, watched as the wind kicked up more snow, and braced myself for the blast that would come in a minute when the cold gust reached us. But as I shivered, the number of them came to me: one man, four women, seven children; twelve.

"I was wrong," I said. "They weren't breeding stock."

She looked at me. "What were they doing here, then?"

"Dying," I said. "Let's go."

We were halfway up the slope when she caught her foot and stumbled. As I helped her up I saw that she had stumbled on another

380

marker. It was like the others, the same size and shape, and it had nothing written on it, but it was not in the pattern at all, it was above it, closer to the southeast corner of the Iiames family plot, almost exactly where he would have been when he killed himself.

"Somebody marked his death," she said.

"Yeah," I said, and went on, not wanting to tell her it wasn't a death that somebody had marked, it was only a grave.

197903121800

(Monday)

THE STORM WAS IN ITS FINAL PHASE. The south wind had gone, had taken with it the moisture and the clouds. Now the sky was clear and black, the air crisp and dry and cold as steel. Now the west wind blew. I knew it was the west wind—I could hear it singing.

That was what I had called it when I was a child; that was what it had sounded like to me. And that was what I had believed it was, even though nobody else thought it sounded like singing, not even Old Jack. He had claimed it was the souls of the Indians who lived and died in the mountains, long before the white man came, panting as they ran in pursuit of deer and bear and catamount in their hunting grounds beyond the grave. But he had never argued with my interpretation. Because it was not the kind of thing you could argue about. He heard panting, I heard singing; we both heard something, and believed what we wanted to believe.

Eventually there had come a time when I had not needed legends to explain it. I had been in my last year of high school then, studying physics, and I read in my textbook how the passage of a gas over an irregular surface sets up vibrations, the frequency of which varies in direct proportion to something, and in inverse proportion to something else, and I had realized that the sound I called the singing of the

382

wind was not singing at all, or panting, either; that it was just a sound, like a car honking; that if you knew the shape of the land and the velocity and temperature and direction of the wind, you could sit there with your slide rule and come up with a pretty good idea of what the pitch would be. It was something that you didn't have to believe in; it was something you could know. And so I had copied down the equations in my notebook and I had waited anxiously for the first of the winter storms, and when the snow had fallen and the sky was clearing, I had gone to the far side to sit with Old Jack and drink toddies and listen to the sound the wind made and to glory in the power of *knowing* what it was. I had told him what I had learned and he had looked at me blankly, and shaken his head and said he didn't give a damn about what the book said; it was the souls of Indians. And I had realized for the first time that even though I loved him, he was an ignorant old man, no better than the savages who thought that thunder was the sound of some god's anger, and for the first time, I had argued with him about it. But then it had started, and I had left off arguing to listen. And what I had heard had filled me with cold fear. For I had not heard a sound like a car honking; I had not heard vibrations of a frequency that varied directly or inversely with anything at all; I had heard singing. I had sat there, clutching my toddy, trying to perceive that sound as I had known I should, trying not to hear voices in it, trying not to hear words. But I had heard them anyway.

In the days that followed I had spent every spare minute studying the physics of sound, studying harder than I had when I had needed to pass an exam. But it made no difference. For when the west wind blew, I heard it singing. And so I had done what I had to do; I had gone away from the mountains, down to the flat land, where there were no irregularities of surface. And I had promised myself I would never hear it again, that I would never go up into the mountains again. I had kept that promise, until now. Only now I knew where the lie had been: I had stopped hearing, but I had not stopped listening.

It was cold in the cabin; I could not recall its ever being as cold there—or anywhere—before. It was the wind that made it cold, not only stabbing through every crack in the walls but slicing over the top of the chimney, creating a fearsome draft, making the fire burn strongly but without heat, making it give off nothing but a hard, cold, fierce, unholy light.

I saw Judith leave the stove—not Judith, really, just the shadow of her, moving against the glow of the stove. She set a steaming cup on the table before me. I did not need to taste it, or even smell it, to know what it was: coffee. I did not want coffee. I wanted a toddy. I needed one. But I could not expect Judith to understand that. There was a lot that I needed that she would never understand. For she was a woman and she was white, and though I loved her there were points of reference that we did not share. And never would.

We had come back easily, more easily than I would have thought possible. We had to struggle down from the hillside and out to the main road, but when we got there we found that it had been plowed and cindered, and within half a mile of walking we were offered a ride in a battered red GMC pickup by an aging farmer with a ruddy, weather-beaten face. He said little to us, only asking if we wanted a ride and how far we were going, and sharing his opinion on the timing of the inevitable shift in the wind. He dropped us at the base of the mountain, and we had made our way up. The sun was high then, and shining on that slope, and the air was cold but still; we made the climb in half an hour, and brought the car down in just a little more, slowed only by an occasional deep drift and the fact that we were going in reverse.

I bought gas in Rainsburg, and we made good time from there. I stayed in the valley, coming north through Charlesville and Beegletown, swinging west at the Narrows, tooling slowly through the Town. I expected to have to climb the Hill on foot since it was rarely—if ever—plowed, but when we got there I saw the Town's road-grader coming down; Randall Scott was an honest politician—he stayed scared.

The cabin was cold, but not as cold as I had feared it would be; there were still coals glowing in the grate. I built a tinder fire on top of them to force a draft. In half an hour the heat was coming up well, and the frost no longer blossomed before our faces. By then I had made tea, and we drank it loaded with sugar, and I heated stew and fried venison steaks, and we wolfed them down. Then I loaded the stove with wood to burn while we slept. By the time I finished, Judith was already lying down, huddled under the blankets. But she wasn't sleeping—her breathing was too regular for that. I mixed myself a toddy and stood by the stove. When I had drunk it all I went to lie beside her; she moved quickly to make room. Then we lay there, listening to the fire roaring in the chimney.

"John?" she said after a while.

"What?"

"Are you going to tell me *anything?*"

"I'm not sure I can," I said.

She didn't say anything.

"Tell me what you want to know," I said.

"I want to know who the hell is buried down there," she said.

"Oh. That. Slaves are buried down there. Runaway slaves. A subject of a local legend; not much of one. No heroes doing great deeds. Nobody much has even bothered to write it down, except for one local historian, and we know about local historians. . . ."

"John."

"A group of slaves came north on the Underground Railroad. They got across the Line all right, into what they probably thought was free territory. Only there wasn't any such thing. And so they were about to be captured and taken back. But they decided they'd rather die. Some kind soul in the South County did it for them. Anyway, that's the legend."

"And you think those are the people buried down there?"

"Yes," I said.

"And you think it has something to do with your . . . with Moses Washington."

"Sure," I said. "You know, it's really amazing when you think about it. I mean, mathematically it's perfectly possible, but for a man to take a mathematical possibility and turn it into reality . . . it's amazing. I don't know whether you'd call it obsession or dedication, but it surely is amazing."

"John," she said. "Will you please slow down and talk to me? *What* is amazing?"

"Moses Washington's search. He started it when he was sixteen years old. He dedicated his life to it. That's easy to say, but you can't understand it until you sit down and figure out how he must have found those graves. He wouldn't have known they were there, or even what he was looking for. And so he would have had to look everywhere for something. And he would have known, before he was twenty years old, that he was going to have to do it that way and he would have had to accept, at twenty, the possibility that he was going to end up looking at every square yard of this County, on foot. And he would have had to accept the fact, at twenty, that he wasn't going to be finished until he was . . . I don't know. The odds would make it at least forty-five. And so he would have had to set up a plan, a pattern, that he was going to follow for a quarter of a century, longer than he'd been alive. It was perfectly possible; there's about a thousand square miles of County, and he could have eliminated some of it—plowed fields, rivers, towns, so forth—but even if there were a thousand square miles, he could have searched a square mile a week, which isn't much. But it would take twenty-five years. And it took longer. It took him thirty-five years, even though he naturally prowled the County most of the time. So by then he must have actually searched most of the County. Maybe all of it; maybe he missed them the first time, not knowing what he was looking for—"

"Missed the graves," she said.

"Yes."

"But how did he know that that was what he was looking for? When he found it, I mean. And how was it—"

"He knew because there were only twelve runaway slaves. That's what the legend says. Well, it says a dozen, which could be taken as an approximation, but could be dead accurate. And he knew the legend; it was one of his favorites."

"But there are thirteen graves," she said.

"That's how he knew he'd found him."

"Found who? You mean . . . C.K.?"

"Yes," I said. "C.K."

She didn't say anything.

"Thirty-five years," I said.

"Why thirty-five?" she said. "He died in 1958, right?"

"He found them in 1942," I said. "He would have found them in the fall or early winter, because the ground would have had to be clear. Or maybe he found them in the spring or summer and took the time deciding what to do."

"What did he do?"

"He joined the army," I said.

She didn't say anything.

"You know," I said, "it's funny. You spend years fiddling around with facts, trying to put them in the right places, trying to explain them with each other, and maybe you come pretty close, and everything fits except maybe one or two things, and that's usually because you've made a mistake right from the very beginning, overlooked something so obvious that when it finally dawns on you you just want to cry. I spent the better part of fifteen years wondering what happened to him in the army that made him change. I guess it seemed reasonable to assume that was where it had happened; everybody knows war changes men—that's why they keep having them. But the war didn't change Moses Washington. He would have had to change before he would go to war. Otherwise it doesn't make any sense. Moses Washington, fifty-two years old, volunteers, hell, *bribes* his way into a white man's army, a segregated army, to fight a white man's war; he would have had to change in order to do that, or have had a pretty strong reason."

"So you think he found the graves before that, and that's what changed him?"

"No," I said. "I don't think he changed at all. I think he went to war for the same reason he married my mother when he came out, for the same reason he did everything else: to get himself ready to find C.K. Washington."

"But he'd *found* him."

"No," I said. "He'd found his grave."

She didn't say anything.

"I know," I said. "It sounds like the same thing. That's what I thought too; that's the way historians think. I assumed that if Moses Washington went looking for his grandfather he'd really be looking for signs of his grandfather: records, old campsites, markers, graves, maybe even a skeleton. And he was. So I assumed that he was acting just like a historian, and when he found whatever it was, he'd set up a marker or something, and that would be it. But I forgot that Moses Washington wasn't a historian, any more than he was a moonshiner or a real estate speculator. If he was anything, he was a hunter. And he did what any good hunter does when he's going off to trail dangerous game: he left trail markers, so that if somebody wanted to they could follow him, and he more or less made sure somebody would want to. . . ."

"You're talking about you, aren't you?" she said.

"Yes," I said.

"All right," she said. "So he was a hunter, and he left a trail for you to follow. But what was the point of it if he'd already found the grave?"

"He wasn't looking for a grave," I said. "He was looking for a man. That's what he was looking for all along: a man. He knew when he came here that C.K. Washington was dead; if he wasn't he would have been a hundred years old. So he was looking for his grave or a skeleton or whatever the same way a hunter looks for a hoofprint, or bedding grounds, or signs of feeding or droppings—it was a spoor. And when he found it he did what any good woodsman would do: he put himself into the mind of the game and headed off after it."

"Wait a minute. You're saying that because C.K. Washington died there Moses Washington committed suicide there?"

"No," I said. "Not suicide. I was wrong about that. We were all wrong. Everybody thought it was an accident. The Judge thought it was murder. I thought I had discovered it was suicide. But what it really was was a . . . a hunting trip. That's where he said he was going. That's what he told his wife, and that's what he told Old Jack: he was going hunting. And that's what he did."

"That sounds . . . crazy," she said. "You're talking about a man chasing after ghosts."

"No," I said. "Ghost isn't the right word. Ghost is a word that was invented by people who didn't believe, like the names the Spaniards gave the Aztec gods. Ancestors is a better term, or—"

"I don't care what you call it. It's insane."

"Maybe," I said. "I guess maybe that's what insanity is, somebody believing in something that doesn't have any kind of reality for you. Napoleon's dead; anybody who thinks he's Napoleon is crazy. There are no ghosts; anybody who chases ghosts is crazy. The thing is, if you accept his premises, everything he did was perfectly logical. He wanted to understand dying, to look before he leaped, so he went to war. He was a hero, because he wanted to take chances, get closer to dying. He loved a woman because C.K. had loved a woman, maybe two, and Moses Washington needed to understand that. He had a son because C.K. Washington had had a son. . . ."

"Moses Washington had *two* sons," she said, "and it's still crazy."

"Only if you're a Christian. Only if you believe in heaven and hell, and all those things. Moses Washington didn't; the old ladies always said he was a heathen, and he was—he spent all that time in the church and talking to preachers and reading the Bible because he wanted to be sure the Christians were wrong. You don't throw your whole life away if you're not sure that the dead really are there, waiting for you."

"That's not crazy," she said. "That's the Goddamned Twilight Zone."

I didn't say anything.

She raised up and looked at me; I could feel her eyes on me. "You don't think so, do you?" she said.

I didn't say anything.

"No," she said. "You don't. You not only think he did that, you think it was a perfectly sane and sensible thing to do, don't you?"

I didn't say anything.

"Don't you?"

I didn't say anything.

She lay back down. "Dear God," she said.

We lay there for a while, listening to the fire, to the first low hummings as the west wind began its song.

"Anyway," she said, "it's over now. You know what happened to Moses Washington, and all that—"

"I don't know anything," I said. "I don't know what happened to C.K., and that means I don't really know anything. I just know what Moses Washington knew when he got this far."

"Oh, great," she said. "So what does that mean? You're going to put on your little Dan'l Boone costume and take your little rifle down there and blow your brains out so you can go hunting with the old men, and sit around the campfire drinking whiskey and telling lies—"

"I'm going to sleep," I said.

We lay there for a while, not talking, not touching. The song grew louder. I tried not to listen.

"I'm sorry," she said.

"Yeah," I said.

"I'm *sorry*."

"It's all right," I said.

"Then hold me?" she said. "Please?"

I twisted around to face her, put my arms around her, felt her breath on my face, feeling the chill in it.

389

"Don't go away," she said. "Please."

"I won't," I said.

But I had gone away. When her breathing became slow and even, punctuated by the little catches and hesitations that, in her, meant deepest sleep, I slipped away from her, and went to sit at the table, staring into the darkness, listening to songs the wind sang as it fluted through the hills. I don't know how long I sat there; a long time. Long enough for the fire to burn low, its substance leeched away by the wailing wind. Long enough for the chill to come and set me shivering. I closed my eyes then, trying to escape the cold, knowing, as I did it, that it would not do any good. And then I heard her moving, getting up and going to the stove. I had opened my eyes and had seen her shadow moving, coming to me, bringing me coffee.

"I don't want it," I said.

"Drink it," she said.

"I don't want coffee. . . ." I caught the aroma then: strong, sweet, heady. A toddy. She had made me a toddy. I took the cup and sipped at it, once, twice. Then I drank it down, almost in a gulp, feeling the warmth spread through me. I closed my eyes. She came and took the cup from me and filled it again and brought it back, held it out to me. "Why?" I said.

"Faith," she said.

I didn't say anything.

"I know," she said. "You don't think I understand. You're right; I don't understand. But I can believe in you; I do believe in you. If you want to take that gun and blow your head off, I won't try to stop you; I don't know that I can help you, but I won't try to stop you. And I'll try to understand. And if you say you need something that I can't give you, something you need a toddy to get, then I'll make a toddy for you."

I wished the lamp were going so that I could see her face, but I could not, so I just reached out and took the cup from her hands and drank. She came and stood beside me, her hand on my shoulder, waiting while I finished. When I set the cup down she went to the stove and began to mix another. "You still hate him, don't you?"

I didn't say anything.

"That's what it is, you know," she said. "You hate him. You've hated him all along. You keep saying you made mistakes, or you didn't understand. That's true, I guess; I wouldn't really know. But I do know why you made all those mistakes. You were too busy hating him to really see him. It took you how long to figure out he killed himself? But you should have known. All the facts were there—"

"They covered them up," I said.

"'I study history because I want to know where the lies are.' That's what you told me. So now I'm supposed to believe you swallowed the biggest lie of all."

"How was I supposed to know?"

"'Why not study atrocities? History itself is atrocious.' You told me that too."

I didn't say anything.

"You know," she said, "you have to wonder. Here you are, hot-stuff historian, superscholar, able to leap to conclusions in a single bound, and half the people who know you think you're brilliant and the other half think you're crazy, but everybody agrees there's something special about you, even if they don't understand what the hell it is. You can make a bonfire by rubbing two dry facts together, so long as you're talking about the Punic Wars and Saint Francis of Assisi, or the Lost Chord and Jesus Christ. But let you come within twenty miles of where you live and it all goes out the window. Because you don't really want to know, John. You want to win. You want to beat Moses Washington and whatever—"

"No," I said. "Not now. Not anymore. Now I just want to know the truth."

"Then what's stopping you?"

"Facts," I said. "Don't you understand? There aren't any facts. All that about the runaway slaves and Moses Washington, that's extrapolation. It's not facts. I've used the facts."

"So get more facts."

"There *aren't* any more facts."

"Then forget the facts," she said.

"You were right to start with," I said. "You don't understand."

She brought the cup to me then, and I took it from her and drank it down, almost angrily. Drank it too fast. Because I realized suddenly that I had had too many toddies, that I was drunk. I set the cup down and closed my eyes, fighting off a wave of dizziness. I reached out and held tightly to the table feeling it solid beneath my fingers, knowing it was not moving, but feeling the room swirl around me just the same.

391

And suddenly I heard his voice, calling to me through the darkness, above the wind. No. Not calling, like a ghost. Just . . . talking. And I recognized the words, knew where they came from. For once upon a time we had stood on a hill, looking down at the river shining in the setting sun, running red like blood away to the south. We hadn't said anything; there was nothing to say. In the morning, just a little after dawn, I had laid for my buck and I had missed him. Or so I had thought, because he had gone bounding away through the forest, white flag hoisted in alarm. But I had followed up a ways, because that is what you do, and after fifty yards of trailing I had found the blood spoor. Not much. Just a spot. But enough. I had wounded; I would have to kill. I had trailed through the morning and into the afternoon, never seeming to gain on him, but always seeing the spoor, faint, almost nonexistent. In the afternoon Old Jack had found me—I will never know how—had seen me tracking grimly, and had fallen in behind me, saying nothing; asking no questions, because he had known what I was doing and why, giving no advice, because he had known I knew what I was doing and why, simply following, simply being there behind me, as we covered the miles, following a trail that would not grow and would not fade away. We had tracked until the sun was going, until the shadows were the same as blood, and then we had stopped on the hill, looking at the river. Then, for the first time, he had spoken. "You got him in a bad place," he had said. "Some place where it ain't bad enough to slow him, but where movin' keeps the wound open. You could say he wasn't wounded. . . ."

"Hell," I had said.

"All right," he had said. "But it's near dark. You can't trail him no more anyways."

I hadn't said anything.

" 'Sides, like I say, it probly ain't too bad. If you was to leave him be, a day or two, he'd probly be good as new. Scarred some on his belly or someplace, but none the worse for it. If you leave him be."

"I don't give a damn about him," I had said. "I want to know where the hell he's going."

He had nodded. "All right, then. We'll find him. But we'll have to wait for light. . . ."

"I'll do without light," I had said.

"How you gonna see the track?"

"I'll do without seeing it."

"How?"

"I'll figure it out." And so I had thought, estimating how much blood he had lost, gauging the wind, the lay of the land, taking into account all the things I had learned about him from laying for him and tracking him, and then I had moved off, extrapolating his line from all I knew, moving through the deepening dusk, going confidently at first, even though my mind was tired and my legs were tired. But assumption had piled atop assumption, and I had slowed, and slowed, coming, eventually, to a stop. It had been full dark then, and when he had spoken, his voice had come disembodied out of the darkness behind me.

"What's wrong?" he had said.

"I lost him," I had said. "I figured something wrong, or forgot something. We can go back now."

"Not yet," he had said.

"I lost him," I had said. "I don't know enough to—"

"You know you lost him," he had said. "You know that much."

I hadn't said anything.

"You figure too much, Johnny," he had said. "You ain't lost him. You jest lost your feel for him. He's still there. Quit tryin' to figure where he's at an' jest follow him."

"You want a story, do you?" I said.

"What?" she said. "I don't understand."

"Fetch the candle," I said. I kept my eyes closed, but I did not need to watch her; I could hear her hesitate, hear her move. I wanted to look then, to see if she would trip, or fumble. I didn't look, but I heard, and she did not. She came back with the candle, and the can of matches. I opened my eyes and reached out and took the can and opened it and took out a match and struck it, the flame springing suddenly out of the darkness, blinding me. But I touched it to the candle somehow, and the flame grew bright. I blew the match out. I held the candle sideways, letting the wax drip. When the pool had formed, when the candle was in it, sitting upright, burning, she took the can and put it back. And then she came and sat down.

Then it was as it had always been: the wind slipping through the chinks in the walls, stealing through the cabin, making the candle flicker, making the shadows dance; the air rattling and roaring in the flue. I didn't say anything. I listened: to the wood crackling in the stove, to the heat chimney, to the west wind singing to the hills.

"John . . ."

"Shh," I said. "Listen." She looked at me. I could see the light from the candle glinting on her eyes. "Listen," I said again. "Because the time is right: the leaves are off the trees and the ground is covered with snow and the west wind is blowing. Listen."

So we listened to the sounds the fire made, the sounds of our breathing, the low moaning as the wind went piping through the hollows. We listened for a long time. And then I heard a sound. "Hear them?" I said.

She didn't say anything.

"Do you?" I said. "Do you hear them?"

"No," she said.

"That's because you're trying," I said. "You can't hear them if you try. Don't try. Just listen."

"I can't," she said. "I don't know how to listen that way."

"Just listen," I said.

We were silent for a while. "I don't hear anything," she said finally.

"They're there," I said.

She moved then, sliding her hand across the table to cover mine—not holding it, just touching it lightly, so lightly I could hardly feel it. But I could feel it.

"I know they're there," she said. "I can't hear them. But I know you can."

"Yes," I said. "I can. I can hear them as they pass. I can't see them—it's misty. But I can hear them. They're running quietly, like Indians, never breaking the silence, never snapping a twig or turning a stone. You couldn't hear them at all if it wasn't for one thing: the breathing. They're running hard and they're breathing hard, and that's what you can hear, that's the sound that goes floating through the mist. That's what he hears. . . ."

I stopped and took a sip of the toddy.

"He's been listening for them," I said. "He's been listening for a long time. He started a day ago, when he came down out of the mountains to get supplies before the storm and Nelson Gates told him about the man who had come into town on the eastbound stage and taken rooms at the Rising Sun and started advertising to hire any man with a horse and a dog who knew the South County and didn't mind earning money tracking down a few slaves—a man named Pettis. He started listening then, wondering if somehow Pettis had found him, and he had gone around the Town, listening to people speculate as to why Pettis would hire all those South County dogs and men when just that morning a pack of mean-looking dogs and meaner-looking men had come up Cumberland Valley and into town, dogs that had the look of slave dogs, men that had the look of slave catchers, and, more important, dogs that were owned and men that were employed by the same man who was doing all the hiring.

"And then he had gone up to the Hill and listened to John Crawley say that he had gotten word that a group of slaves was coming north and had connived to get a local merchant to hire him and Graham to take a load of grain to Iiames' Mill, on Town Creek, in Southampton Township, and to wait while it was ground, and haul it back, giving them an excuse not only to go into the South County but to stay there and wait for the slaves, and a place to meet them. Then it all made sense. Pettis was there because of the slaves; slave catching was, after all, Pettis' business. The only thing that didn't make sense was the hiring of all those extra dogs and men. It was not a major question, but it was a question, and C.K. did not like questions—unless he knew the answers. And so he waited through the night, camping on the hillside at the south end of town, and then rising before sunup and making his way to the town square. There he lurked in the shadows until, in the predawn, he saw the first of the South County men arrive. He kept on waiting, but watching now, too, as more came, men on horseback, some with small packs of dogs. He watched as they milled about, their number swelling, finally completed by the arrival of those mean-looking dogs and meaner-looking men the townspeople had been talking about. It had been getting light then, and C.K. started to leave, but in the last few moments before dawn broke, he saw a man emerge from the Rising Sun, a man dressed in a severe black suit and a white shirt and tie, with a heavy gray riding cloak thrown around his shoulders. Pettis.

"And so C.K. stayed where he was, watching, as Pettis walked to the square and looked over the army he had hired. In a moment a black man came down the street from the direction of the livery stable, riding a mule and leading a well-kept bay stallion. He brought the horse to Pettis; Pettis mounted, sat in the saddle tall and straight, looking around at the other men. And then his eyes fell on C.K.

"He looked at C.K. long and hard, and C.K. looked back, staring into Pettis' eyes, cold, gray, dead-looking eyes, keeping his body motionless, inwardly cursing the curiosity that had kept him there even in daylight, but knowing it was too late to do anything except freeze and watch and wonder if, somehow, Pettis would recognize him. For a long moment it had been like that, their eyes meeting. And then Pettis nodded his head just slightly, and wheeled his horse and led his army east, out of town.

"C.K. waited again then, because he was shaken, and frightened as he had not been in many years. He wanted to turn and go, to fade back into the safety of the hills. But he could not. Because there were still things he did not know. He did not know why there were so many men and dogs. And he was not sure why Pettis had led his party not to the south, the logical direction, but east.

"And so he followed, not worrying too much at first about Pettis' route, because Pettis' men had come up the valley just the day before, and it was perhaps reasonable that Pettis might ignore it for now, and concentrate his forces on the other side of the mountains. But when Pettis reached the Narrows he did not turn south towards Rainsburg as C.K. expected, but crossed the river and headed east on the Chambersburg Pike, towards the town of Bloody Run. Then C.K. began to worry. Because it made no sense for a man to hunt northbound slaves by heading east. No sense at all.

"And so C.K. ran, not bothering to follow Pettis but staying on the south side of the river, making better time on foot than Pettis was making on horseback, reaching the western end of Bloody Run long enough ahead of Pettis to find good cover and take a stand overlooking the road. From there he had watched again as Pettis came, leading his party, stopping them and turning them and taking them down to ford the river.

"Then C.K. stopped wondering and worrying and started doing what he should have been doing all along: thinking. Really thinking. Not just gathering facts and ordering them; not just trying to follow them along; *really* thinking, looking at the overall pattern of things and figuring out what the facts *had* to be.

"The first thing he realized was that he had been underestimating Pettis, thinking that he was just another slave-catcher, and assuming that when Pettis went slave hunting he would go about it as other slave-catchers did. But C.K. knew enough about Pettis' history to know he wasn't ordinary. He was careful and he was organized. He was ruthless in his use of force, but he relied more heavily on intelligence—on knowledge. C.K. thought about that.

"And then, suddenly, it all made perfect sense—the extra dogs and men, the route, everything. Because if you assumed that a man was not just hunting slaves, but was hunting with knowledge of the Underground Railroad routes—gotten how, C.K. didn't know, but somehow gotten—that man would do just exactly what Pettis had done: sweep up the Cumberland Valley covering the most dangerous—and most unlikely—route, and then go east to Bloody Run and south through Black Valley, to the place where the other two routes merged. There a man, if he had enough men and enough dogs, could lay a trap that would be hard to avoid—probably impossible to avoid. If conditions were right, the air warm enough for the dogs to catch scent, the wind blowing out of the south—and it was—there would not even need to be a trap—a simple picket line would do. The slaves would be coming downwind and the dogs would catch the scent and take trail. The slaves would hear the dogs ahead of them and try to turn, but there would be more dogs and more men.

"It would be over then—the runaways would have no chance. Oh, they could run back the way they had come, but they would be running into the wind, leaving not only scent but trail, and they would be heading south, running away from the very thing that had kept them going. And so, one by one, they would fall. The weak-willed would fall first, even if they were young and strong—the will would be more important than youth or strength. Then the weak would fall, the very old and the very young. Then the chase would grow hotter, for what would be left after those had fallen were the ones that had to be caught: the strong-willed and the strong-bodied; the slaves who were not really slaves; the dangerous ones. It would go on for a while. But sooner or later, in an hour, perhaps, or two, or three, they would start to fall. Or perhaps they would turn at bay when they could run no more, turn and try to hide. There would be bloodhounds; they would not hide for long. Those that ran on would be slowing, nearing exhaustion, would see the hopelessness of it all, and just stop and stand and wait. That would be the end of it. Unless there was one. Sometimes there was one, one who ran on when everything—the pain and the sound of pursuit drawing near, everything—said to stop and give in. If it was a man, it was an older man, thin and wiry, a man judged not a good field hand at all. But more likely it was a woman, inured to pain by the agony of childbirth, rich in stamina, strong in will. Those things could make a difference. But not forever. Eventually she, too, would be taken, when even her stamina was gone, when even she felt the pain. She would still run, but she would run awkwardly, without grace or dignity, stumbling now as the panic took her, weaving from side to side as she turned to look over her shoulder at the galloping horses, the clods of earth flying up from the hooves, at the men crouched low in the saddle, ropes swinging in their hands. It would not be the men who took her, though. It would be the dogs that would come running, sleek and swift and low to the ground, making no sound, not even when they leaped and took her in the thigh or the arm and brought her slamming down. Then they would bay to call the hunters, their jaws wide, dripping saliva and, perhaps, a little blood.

"That was how it would end. And there was nothing C.K. could do about it. It was not even a question of the danger; there was simply nothing he could do. Nothing any man armed only with a pistol could do against thirty men and sixty dogs and F. H. Pettis, who knew the routes of the Railroad and God alone knew what else.

"And then C.K. realized that he, too, knew what else—Pettis knew about Crawley and Graham. Or soon would know. Because when the slaves were taken Pettis would surely question them, and learn about the mill. That much wouldn't matter, since the miller knew nothing, was probably as hungry for a reward as anybody. But Pettis would have to go to the mill to find that out, and when he arrived there he would find Crawley and Graham, two black men in the South County, at the very mill that was the destination of runaway slaves. It would be proof enough. But at least there was something C.K. could do about that; he could try to intercept Crawley and Graham and warn them away. And so he stayed where he was, thinking it through, figuring their route and their strategy.

"They would have left town already. They would have to leave early, because they would want to give the impression that they fully intended to make the trip to Southampton and back in a single day. But somewhere they would have to lose time, because they would want to arrive at the mill so late in the afternoon that they would have a perfect excuse to wait out the night. But they could not simply slow down or stop they would have to come up with something to explain their late arrival. . . .

"Then C.K. saw their plan, saw it as if it were one of his own: the early start, with them not only giving the appearance of speed but actually hurrying, going faster than any sane man would go, making an accident not only plausible but likely; a mad dash through Rainsburg, attracting attention by its recklessness, then, somewhere on the mountain, away from the eyes of the curious, sometime between eleven o'clock and noon, the faking of the inevitable accident, perhaps putting the wagon into a gully, and then making a good show of working feverishly to get it out, but nevertheless taking a long time about it. That was what would save them. Because having figured that much out, C.K. could run to meet them, cut them off, warn them, turn them back. And so he turned away from the river and headed south along the valley, trotting easily, taking his time, keeping alert so that he would not accidentally catch up to Pettis.

"By noon he had reached the forks and was halfway up the mountain, climbing slowly because there was no need to hurry—he could not miss Crawley and Graham. If he felt any urgency, it was because of the weather. As he had come down the valley he had seen the high cirrus twisted by a rising south wind, seen banks of low gray storm clouds come rolling up the valley.

"As he climbed the mountain, he speculated as to what effect the weather would have on Pettis' plans. The wind would be right for the picket line, but as soon as the sun went down the air would chill rapidly; it would be hard for the dogs to catch any scent. It was even possible that the runaways might slip by in the night. They would have their chance to escape then. But it was not likely that they would. Because sometime that day, possibly that afternoon, the snow would begin to fall, and the tracks in the snow would be plain to the eye. If it did not start until after dark, Pettis could simply abandon the picket line, send his men riding back and forth across the valley with torches, until one of them saw the trail. The runaways might still have a chance, maybe have enough of a lead to make a rescue possible. In any case, C.K. would have no part of it; it would be far too dangerous. For him to be taken would be bad, but for him to be taken by F. H. Pettis would destroy the work of a lifetime.

"He reached the top of the mountain and started down the other side, beginning to wonder, now, where Crawley and Graham were. It was possible that they had decided to fake their delay closer to Rainsburg, perhaps in the town itself, in order to provide themselves with witnesses. It would be an extreme measure, but the presence of a man like Pettis called for such measures. And so he went on, trotting quickly on the downgrade, filling the time with more speculation: what he would do if he wanted to rescue the runaways. The plans he came up with were ridiculous. One called for him to kidnap Pettis; that, he judged, was the least insane. Another called for him to start a forest fire and blanket the valley with smoke, destroying the dogs' abilities to scent and the men's to see. Another called for him to intercept the fugitives and lead them south and then east, over the mountains to McConnellsburg and perhaps Chambersburg, before turning north again; that one could even work—all he would have to do was to manage to find a group of slaves who would be busily engaged in avoiding any kind of detection.

"But in less than an hour the speculation had ceased to be idle. Because by that time C.K. was standing on the lower slopes of Tussey Mountain, looking down at the cluster of houses that was the town of Rainsburg, and the road in between, and not seeing any sign of Crawley, or Graham, or the wagon. No sign at all.

"He could not imagine what had happened. He went over the reasoning that had led to his being there, and could find no fault with it. He went over it again, changing his assumptions about the route they would follow, but it made no difference—even if they had gone south into Cumberland Valley to Patience and across from there, they would still have had to come up that mountain. But they weren't on that mountain. And that could only mean trouble, of one kind or another.

"And so he sat down and rested, letting his mind work on the possibilities. There were only three that he could see. First, that something had happened to keep Crawley and Graham from making the trip at all. In that case they would be safe. Second, that they had delayed their departure or encountered some kind of legitimate delay on the road north of Rainsburg. In that case, too, they would be in no danger, for either they would go back because of the lateness of the hour and the imminence of the storm, or they would arrive at the mill too late to be implicated. If the slaves had not been taken by then, there was a chance that the whole thing could still succeed as

400

planned. It was the third possibility that made a difference: it was possible that C.K. had figured wrong, that Crawley and Graham had made no attempt at all to wait on the mountain, but had gone straight to the mill. And if that had happened, all of them—the slaves, Graham, Crawley—would be caught in Pettis' trap.

"C.K. stood on the mountain above Rainsburg, looking down at the valley, thinking again through the alternatives, reminding himself of all the reasons why he could not take the risks, of all the reasons why he should not have to take the risks. And then he remembered the first time he had seen Crawley and Graham, and the look on the faces of the slaves who had gone to get on that wagon, to ride to freedom, or at least to ride closer to it, and he stopped. Stopped figuring the chances. Stopped guessing at odds. Stopped calculating, stopped thinking altogether, and he turned and ran back up the mountainside."

I stopped. My voice had started sounding hoarse to me—I realized that my throat was dry. I raised the cup, but it was empty; I set it down again. By the dim glow of the candle, I saw her rise and take the cup and go to the stove. I closed my eyes then, and listened to the wind singing. In a moment she was back, pressing the hot cup into my hands. I raised it and sipped, feeling the warmth on my throat.

"He stayed on the ridges, to keep clear of the dogs. He didn't know where they were; the mist was too thick for him to see much of anything in the valley, and it deadened sound too. But eventually he had to come down into the valley, even though he had no idea of where those dogs were, because the cove was starting to open out now, and the only place he had a chance to find the slaves was where it was narrow.

"So he came down from the mountain, coming down in a creek bed, using the water to hide his sound and his ground scent, just in case Pettis had bloodhounds sweeping the hillside. He probably came down Pond Branch, or one of the little streams that make up Black Valley Branch. Eventually he ended up on the valley bottom, in the middle of Town Creek. He stayed near it. Not too near—the sound of the water would have covered every other sound, and with that mist the only way he was going to find anything was by sound—but near enough. Because he had to assume that the runaways knew enough to follow the creek to hide trail and scent. And so his best chance of hearing them was there. But it was only a chance. And to make it bet-

401

ter he moved too, slipping back and forth through the woods, going silently, but moving.

"I know he moved, and I know why he moved, but I don't know exactly how he moved, because I don't know what would have made him move one way and not the other. It could have been the way the land rose and fell, or the way the underbrush had grown, or the movements of the air—it could have been anything. I don't know exactly how he moved or why he moved in that particular way. And so I don't know how it was that he came to be standing exactly where he was standing, listening as he was listening. But he was there. I know that. Because I believe that was how he found them, how he heard them, panting in the mist."

I stopped again, and sipped at the toddy, waiting for her to say something. But she didn't say anything. She was listening. I waited, listening to the singing of the wind outside, listening eagerly. Because now I knew what it was, knew and believed: it was singing. A song made by land and wind, perhaps, but singing all the same.

"I still don't hear anything," she said. Her voice was angry.

"You hear the wind," I said.

She looked at me. I saw her eyes shining. She nodded.

"He almost caught them," I said. "He waited a few moments, still listening, checking their backtrail to be sure that nothing was there. When he was sure, he went after them, moving as quickly as he could, keeping silent, trying to listen as he ran, wondering if the sound he had heard had been brought to him by a weird echo or a chance eddy of wind, wondering if they were there at all, and not a quarter of a mile away. And then he heard them ahead, the sound of their panting drifting back to him through the mist, and he ran faster, but even more silently, not wanting to alarm them, to make them run faster, more quickly to the dogs. He began to think how he could stop them without making noise, realized he would have to pass them entirely, circle around in front of them, head them off, and do it all in the gray mist, with only sound to guide him, and started to do it, slipping off to the side and running faster now, making a little noise now, having to, because he was winded too, was panting too, and hoping that if they heard it they would think that it was just another one of them running in the mist. He heard the sound of them slipping back, heard himself running with the sound of them all around him, and knew that in a minute, or two minutes, he could stop and whisper softly to them. And then knew that it was too late. Because from somewhere ahead he heard the hounds.

"He heard sounds around him, heard the gasps of panic, the shufflings and slidings as the runaways tried to stop, and knew that he should stop too. But he didn't. He ran on, straight towards the dogs, until he heard the sound of the runaways fade behind him. Then he stopped, waiting, listening again, but listening now to the dogs, yelping as they came upwind, looking for ground scent, looking for trail. When the sound of the dogs was close, he turned and doubled back, still going slowly, wanting to be sure. In a moment he was sure. The yelping stopped, turned into full-throated barking.

"He broke off then, and headed off to the west, still not moving too fast. In a few more minutes he heard the dogs turn. Then he knew that they were on his trail, and no one else's. Then he ran as fast as he could.

"He went hard for a while, putting space between him and the dogs, angling just a bit to the south in order to keep clear of any flankers. When he felt the land begin to rise, he turned and drove straight up the slope, using the momentum he had built racing across the valley bottom to carry him up. When that impetus was gone he slowed, catching his breath, listening to the sounds of pursuit. It sounded as if every hound in the South County was back there. But they didn't worry him; he had lost hounds before, better hounds than South County hounds, hounds as good as Pettis'. But losing them was not the question. What he needed to do was keep them, and take them with him as long as he could, perhaps decoy them up over the ridge and into the next valley, and lose them there. If he could do that, the runaways would have a chance. For they had surely heard the dogs turn aside, and would stop and turn back to the north, and be safe.

"So C.K. trotted up the slope, keeping distance between himself and the hounds, but not too much, slipping through the mist, across the carcasses of cornfields, over the fields that sloped too much for planting, that were good only for pasture, through groves of birch and pine. In half an hour he was high above any kind of cultivated land. He was tired, he longed to slow down. But he dared not. For even though the temperature was falling, and would fall more quickly when the sun set, eventually making it all but impossible for the hounds to trail him, there was plenty of light left, enough light to see a trail. And there was no way he could not leave a trail. Because now the snow was falling, falling just quickly enough to leave a cover over the ground, to clearly show his footprints, but not quickly enough to cover them from his pursuers. And so he could not slow down; he had to go faster, putting more distance between himself and the men, giving the storm time to cover his trail.

"That was what he had to do. But he could not do it. He simply did not have the speed. He had covered nearly forty miles since daybreak, and he was in no shape for sprinting. He listened carefully to the hounds, trying to gauge distance, not an easy thing to do in the mist. He was six minutes ahead of them, he judged. Maybe half a mile, at the speed that could be managed over the hilly ground. Not distance enough.

"And so he tried to run faster, and, at the same time, started thinking again, going through all the tricks of the trail that he knew. He found none that would help. And then he recalled a day, years before, when he had been hunting and reconnoitering, not on this side of the mountain, but on the other, and had come across a stream. He had noticed it because it ran south instead of east or west, its natural tendency to go straight downhill being arrested by the configurations of rock. It was not a large stream, but it was an old stream, and over the centuries it had cut down into the rock, creating a gorge, a jagged gash in the mountainside nearly three miles long. The gorge was deep, a hundred feet or more, but not wide—four or five feet at the bottom, opening out to nine or ten at the top—and C.K. had thought that if a man was desperate enough and strong enough, he could use that gorge, leading his pursuers to the center of its run and making the leap, leaving them with the choice of following and perhaps failing to make it, or of going around, a mile and a half to the end and another mile and a half back, to pick up the trail again. A man could make a lot out of a three-mile lead. Or so he had thought at the time.

"And so he thought now. Because he was desperate. His strength was going, more quickly than he would have thought possible, far more quickly than darkness and snow were falling to give him concealment. It would be that desperation maneuver or nothing. He only hoped he knew where he was, that he could find the gorge at all.

"He turned to the south, running along the mountainside. He was out of the forest now; the ground was almost pure rock, uneven enough to make him stumble, smooth enough to hold the snow, and dark enough to make his trail stand out like newsprint. But it was the kind of rock that lined the gorge. He stopped then, and listened, and heard the sound of water rushing over granite, a white rush of sound deepened by resonance. He moved towards it, not running, trotting, in order to keep his footing, mindful of the fact that to slip here could end everything, but mindful, too, of the fact that there were men behind him, men who were not as tired, not as afraid of falling, men who had a clear trail to follow, who were moving faster than he. The snow was heavier now, and the light was going; he hoped those things would cover his trail and slow the men up. But when he looked back he saw that the snow was not falling fast enough, the light not fading fast enough—his trail was clear.

"And so he rushed, a little, as much as he dared, turning his trot into a sort of desperate skating, a slipping and sliding over the snow-covered rock. The land turned upward, the grade grew steep. Low outcroppings of rock appeared on either side, weird dark fingers groping at him out of the mist. Suddenly a barrier appeared before him, a sheer wall of rock thirty feet high; he twisted desperately to keep himself from smashing into it, but his momentum was too great; he hit and bounced and fell, the back of his head slamming into the rock, stunning him.

"For a moment he lay there, trying to hold on to consciousness, barely succeeding, not even knowing that he had succeeded, because the gray mist above him could have been the mist itself or a film before his eyes. And so he closed his eyes and listened to the dull rumble of the stream, focusing on the sound, holding on to the sound. For long minutes it was vague, fleeting; the volume rising and falling, the direction shifting, spinning; then he knew how close he was to unconsciousness. But slowly the sound grew steady, the volume even, the direction constant. He focused then on another sound, the sound of his own breathing, controlling it, slowing it, listening as the sound of it responded to his will. When the response was perfect, he began to feel that he would not lose consciousness, that he could risk opening his eyes. But before he could do that he heard another sound, the scrabble of shod hooves on hard rock; first one set, then two, then four. Then there was no time for cautious eye-opening, or even for listening.

"He staggered to his feet, pumping his arms to gain balance, then groping around for the wall of rock that had stopped him, finding it, turning then and running along it, feeling, looking for some kind of opening. Behind him he heard the hooves and the jingling of harness and the heavy breathing of animals; the horses were winded from the climb. That gave him hope, and he ran more quickly than he thought he could, hands still groping. And then he heard another sound, a sudden scream from a human throat and a soft, almost gentle sound of the impact of flesh on rock. Then the mist was alive with cursing and the excited neighing of horses, one horse's neighing louder and full of pain; someone had galloped into that wall of rock. Someone had given him a chance.

"He made the most of it. He reached down into his guts and found a little more will, a little more determination, and turned that into a little more speed. He forced his mind to think, to make decisions; he had a lead, he dared not waste it—a hundred more steps and he would try and climb that wall of rock. He forced his mind to focus on the task of counting, forced his lungs to pump in cadence with the counting. Thirty steps. Forty. Fifty. And then his groping right hand felt empty air. Only for a second; then the rock was there again. But it was enough. He stopped, scrambled back, felt for the opening, found it. At his feet he saw a path, rough and rocky, choked, now, with a foot of snow, but a path. And a narrow one, far too narrow to allow a horse to pass. He started up it, feeling his strength return. The path had evened things: they could not run him down with horses now; it was man against man.

"He trotted up the path, the rock on either side falling away until it was no more than hip-high. The sound of the stream was so loud he could not gauge its nearness, could only peer through the gathering gloom, hoping to see the gorge before he stumbled into it. He slowed then, and crept ahead, wondering, hoping, then despairing, as the path twisted in a sharp dogleg and opened out onto a narrow ledge, and he looked down at the gorge, which was not ten feet wide here, but fourteen, perhaps fifteen, and out at the other side, which was two feet, perhaps three, higher than the side on which he stood.

"For a while he looked at it, remembering the day when he had looked at the gorge from the other side, probably underestimating the width of it, certainly thinking that if he ever tried to leap it he would be fresh, or at least not exhausted, and he would be jumping from the high ground to the low. Then, even if he had judged the distance right, the leap would have seemed possible. Now it did not; now it *was* not. And so he waited, listening, hoping that he would not have to try, hoping that his pursuers had lost the trail, had missed the opening in the rock. He stood there, panting, hoping. And then he heard the sound of men's voices, hard, excited voices, heard them even above the dull booming of the stream; they were close.

"Then he stopped hoping, stopped despairing. He stepped to the very edge of the gorge and stood for a moment, his toes hanging over nothing, and then leaped, his legs straightening and his arms slamming back to give him thrust, his body leaning out flat. For a moment he was rising, almost soaring, but then gravity took him. Halfway across, he knew that he would not make it; his feet were sinking down into the gorge, then his knees. But then his chest struck hard against the rocky edge. The breath was driven from him, but he threw his arms up, hooking them over the edge, let them take the shock as his feet slammed into the rock below. For a moment he hung there, gasping for air, but feeling the relief that came from being alive at all. And then he began to slide.

"It seemed slow to him, terribly slow. He had plenty of time to send his hands groping for something to hold on to, to find something, a knob of rock, to grasp it and hope, and then feel it crumble beneath his fingers, and then to feel the snow falling away as his arms slipped over the edge, to feel the skin of his wrists scraping away on the rock, to actually feel each hand, each finger, losing contact with the rock. It seemed that way, but it was probably not that way; probably all he felt was the loss of support and then the free fall, and then the awful pain in his chest as his body slammed into a rock outcropping seven feet below. He felt the pain, but he managed to curl around the outcropping and hold on.

"This time he did lose consciousness, long enough for the men who pursued him to come and stand above him, looking across the chasm. When he came to he heard them there, heard them speculating as to what kind of desperation would make a man try a leap like that, what kind of desperation would make it possible for him to succeed, and realized that they had not looked down, or if they had, they had failed to see him. He kept his eyes closed, listening, hoping. And then he heard a new voice, a voice that had command in it: Pettis.

"The voice came clearly, questioning, and the voice of someone else, the accent and inflection telling him it was a man from the South County, answering: Pettis wanting to know if they were certain

407

they had seen tracks on the far side, the man responding that it was too dark to say for sure, but it had looked like tracks; Pettis wanting to know if they were sure he hadn't fallen, the man saying they had been close enough to see him leap, and surely would have heard him scream if he had fallen; Pettis asking how long to go around, the man answering half an hour, maybe longer, in the dark.

"C.K. waited, but they said no more. He opened his eyes then, expecting to see nothing but mist above him. Instead he saw Pettis, still leaning out over the chasm. For a moment it seemed that Pettis had to see him, that he had seen him, was looking straight at him. But the shadows were too dense, or the light was wrong; Pettis turned away.

"C.K. gave them time to get clear, counting the seconds to make sure he would not wait too long, as a way of keeping his mind off the pain in his chest. When he had counted off three thousand seconds he eased his hold on the rock outcrop, felt around on the face of the rock. He found handholds with no trouble, even though his fingers were numbed by cold and shock, climbed up without difficulty. It was so easy he wanted to laugh. And when he had pulled himself over the edge and lay looking over at the other side, seeing how easy it would have been to leap the other way, he did laugh.

He lost track of time then; he could have lain there laughing for five minutes, or ten. But then his mind started working again, and he realized what he should have realized as soon as he had heard Pettis talking: Pettis had said 'he.' Not 'they'; 'he.' And he realized what that had to mean; that Pettis did not care about runaway slaves; just about one particular runaway slave. That what was going on was not a hunt for fugitives, but a hunt for C.K. Washington, with a bunch of fugitive slaves used as bait, their fates unimportant compared to the importance of capturing C.K. Washington. Pettis had set a trap within a trap. C.K. knew then that it was over for him. All of it. There would be no final season of selling moonshine, no leisurely retreat to Philadelphia. He would not dare stay in the County. He would not dare go to Philadelphia, either. For if Pettis had tracked him down this far, he had probably tracked him from Philadelphia. Perhaps Pettis had heard about a colored man who made whiskey and brought it across the mountains. Or perhaps he had heard one of the Philadelphia *bourgeois* complaining about a former member in good standing of the black middle class who had deserted the fold, and embraced not only moonshining but whoremongering. Or perhaps not. Perhaps Pettis had found him by accident. It didn't matter; because he could not afford to take the chance. He would have to head north to the cold of Canada; his choices were gone.

"He heard a single gunshot. They had killed the horse. Now they would be starting to make the circuit around the gorge, on their way to pick up his trail. He had half an hour's lead, perhaps a little more, certainly not much more. It was time to rise and run again.

"But his body was tired, and hurt; it was not going to be enough of a lead, no matter how soon he rose. The next valley was hardly a valley at all, just a hollow with no outlet to the north. If he made it beyond that he would be in Cumberland Valley; to turn north then would be to give up. But he knew he would have no choice but to turn north there. Because he could not climb another mountain.

"And so, because it made no real difference, he spent an extra minute resting his tired body, thinking. And then it came to him. He could double his lead, double it and perhaps lose Pettis altogether. All he had to do was stand up and turn around and leap that gorge again.

"He lay there thinking about it, thinking about how Pettis would come around in half an hour and find no tracks but think that it was only because the snowfall had covered them, and would send his men coursing down the mountainside, in a desperate attempt to catch a shadow; how he would curse; how he finally take a cadre back to round up the runaways, to try and salvage that much, and how they would find nothing. Because with an hour's lead and a storm to cover his trail, C.K. could get to Iiames' Mill and take the slaves and lead them up over Tussey Mountain and into town and hide them. Then they would be as safe as they could be. And C.K. Washington would be finished, but he would end with a success. It was nice to think about, and to try it made more sense than to run down into Cumberland Valley and find himself on the flat at daylight, hampered by the storm, or bogged down when the west wind piled the drifts.

"And so he stood up and leaped, giving it no more thought than that, and making the distance with ease, stumbling when he landed, falling hard against the wall of rock, throwing himself sideways to keep from slipping back, feeling the pain as his ribs struck the rock, knowing that the fall must have cracked one or more, but knowing, too, that he had made it. He let himself lie there for only a moment.

Then he rose and started back the way he had come, walking now, through the darkening mist, the scuffing of his footfalls echoing softly from the rock on either side.

"It was full dark when he reached the end of the path—so dark that he would not have known he had reached that point had it not been for the sudden dying of the echoes that had bounced back from the rock. He stopped then, standing in the darkness, feeling the mist wet and cold on his face, and listened. Because he had made the mistake of underestimating Pettis, not once, but twice, and he had been lucky enough to survive it, but he could not count on being lucky again. He would have to assume that Pettis was as good as he was, as sensible as he was. And the sensible thing to do would be to split the party into three groups, sending two to round the gorge at either end, leaving one, a small group of four or five men, to guard the backtrail; to leave them there, at the entrance to the path.

"And so he listened. Once he thought he heard the sound of harness jingling, and his hand went to his pistol, but when he focused on the sound he heard only the light tinkle of the snow falling through the trees a hundred yards down the slope. He waited, counting the seconds, knowing that time was slipping away, that soon he would have to take the chance. He waited. Five minutes. Ten. Then he moved, not because he was satisfied, but because there was always the chance that Pettis would be alerted by the lack of trail on the far side of the gorge, would turn and come back and find his trail and hunt him down by torchlight; he had to move now, to give the snow time to cover trail.

"He started down the mountain, still uncertain that he was alone, but hoping that if he was not, he would escape detection. There was a chance he would; it was so dark he could not see his own feet, could only feel the snow spilling down into his boots, the chill that came to his toes. He forced himself to move more quickly, in order to keep himself warm, even though the faster movement made his ribs ache. He ignored the pain, allowed himself to think ahead. A mile down in the valley he had a cache. Not a large one. Just emergency supplies: some dried meat, a jug of whiskey, a blanket, some clean cloth. He could pass by there, wrap his side with bandages, ease the pain in his belly with jerky, the pain in his side with whiskey. Then he would find the fugitives after that; they would all be safe."

My cup was empty again. I did not recall drinking the last of the toddy, but I must have, because when I raised the cup to my lips there was nothing there. Somehow she knew it, even though I made no sign; she took the cup and rose and went to the stove. So I watched as she made the toddy, not able to see her, seeing only her silhouette. She mixed as I would, using the thumb for the sugar, pouring the whiskey easily. She brought the cup to me and pressed it into my hands, letting her hands linger there for a moment, holding the warmth of the cup against mine. I knew then that I had underestimated her, and had done it in a way that cheated us both. She let go of my hands and took her seat again, and I could see her face in the candlelight.

"He could not take his eyes off her," I said. "He could not really see her—the interior of the mill was too dark, the crack through which he peered too narrow—but he watched her form, silhouetted against the glowing hearth, as she dipped a cup into a small kettle and then handed it to another woman, a small woman, who sat huddled a few feet away, a dark form clutched close to her breast. C.K. did not watch her; his eyes were on the first woman, and he watched her carefully, as she went again to the fire and knelt and stirred it. The coals glowed more brightly, and flame flared, and for a moment he could almost see her face—almost, but not quite. It didn't matter; he didn't need to see her face, didn't really want to see her face. For the moment he wanted only to stand with the cold wind knifing at his back, the snow in which he stood slowly numbing his feet and ankles and calves, and watch the outline of her; that was all that he could stand.

"He had found his cache with little difficulty, and the mill with even less. He approached it warily, looking for any sign that Pettis had somehow learned about it and set a trap there, determined not to underestimate the man again. But there was no sign of a trap. There was no sign of anything; the mill was simply a mill, not large, perhaps thirty-five feet by forty, two stories high, made of fieldstone and wood, dark and silent, the weir shut, the wheel still, the windows shuttered. The fire inside burned—there was the smell of burning coal hanging in the air—but only a wisp of smoke escaped the chimney; the fire had been banked for the night.

"Or, perhaps, for the duration of the storm. For the storm was growing. The snow fell less rapidly now, but the flakes were no longer soft and gentle; they were hard, icy spicules that came slicing out of

411

the darkness, cutting at his face. Soon the snow could stop, but the temperature would fall—faster, still, than it was already falling—and the wind would whip the snow on the ground into an angry froth, taking it back up into the sky and driving it across the land in great voracious clouds. That could last for hours or days—certainly it would last into the next day. And so the mill was shut down and the fire was banked; for no man, no miller, anyway, would venture out into that cold, that wind, that sea of snow. All any man with sense would want would be to be at home, with a fire on the hearth and wood stacked in the corner, with food in his belly and a toddy in his hand.

"That was what C.K. wanted, what he was thinking about when he finally approached the mill, forcing himself to wade in the icy water of the pond so as not to leave tracks, and coming to stand near one of the shuttered windows, in order to peer inside. But then he had seen the woman, bending at the hearth, and the thoughts had left him; he had forgotten the wind and the cold, had forgotten everything, except how to stand and watch her moving.

"She stepped away from the fire again, turned and looked into the corner of the room, then moved out of his range of vision. Then he became aware of the wind at his back and the numbness creeping up his legs. Then he found he could move, and he left the window and made his way slowly around to the door. The latch string was out; he wondered why she had left it that way, then realized that it made sense to leave it out, for if anyone came he would see it and enter unawares, and give her a chance to take him by surprise. . . . And then he realized what he was doing, figuring all that out: he was wasting time. Because he was afraid to go inside. Afraid of finding out that it wasn't her, or that it was; afraid of the truth. But the feeling was gone from his hands, and the rest of him was as cold as it had ever been, so finally he stopped trying to think about it; he just opened the door and went in.

"The room was dim, lit only by the glow from the hearth. But his eyes were accustomed to the darkness, and he could make out the shapes of all of them, three women and seven children, one a baby, and, in the far corner, the bent, frail form of an old man. He looked at them, not seeing them, really; looking for her. And then he heard a whisper of sound and threw himself forward, twisting his head just in time to see the knife that came stabbing down out of the darkness. But he need not have moved. Because the knife stopped inches shy of where his back had been, hesitated a moment, and then seemed to disappear into the shadows behind the door. And then she stepped out. She had a slightly sour expression on her face. She looked him up and down, taking in the snow-covered slouch hat, the snowy blanket, the gunnysack of supplies he held in his hand. And then she was in his arms."

I closed my eyes then and waited, waited for the question. But she did not ask a question. When I opened my eyes I saw her sitting, not moving, just sitting, and I realized that there would be no questions. And then I realized that something strange was happening. Because I was no longer cold. At first I thought it was because the wind had died, but when I listened I still heard it singing to the hills. And then I saw that the candle no longer flickered, that she had moved a little, just a little, but enough to block a draft, or perhaps create a new draft that balanced out the old one. I saw that she was leaning forward, her eyes shining in the light, fixed on the candle. And I looked at it too, at the steady flame, hardly a flame at all now, but a round, warm, even glow that seemed to grow as I looked at it, expanding until it filled my sight.

"He was warm now," I said. "He was warm, and the feeling was strange. Because he had not realized how cold he had been. He had known that his hands and feet and face were cold, even though they were so numb he had lost the feeling in them—he had known that because anyone who knew the weather and who knew how long he had been exposed would have known—and so he had not been surprised when the heat from the fire had caused the feeling to come pounding back into them. But he had not known about the other cold, the cold inside, the glacier in his guts that had been growing and moving, inch by inch, year by year, grinding at him, freezing him. He had not known that. But he knew it now. Because he could feel it melting. The heat that melted it did not come from the fire; it came from her, from the warmth of her body that pressed against his back, the warmth of her arms around him, the warmth of her hands that cupped the base of his belly. He lay there, feeling the warmth filling him, feeling the fatigue draining from him, feeling the aching in his ribs easing, becoming almost pleasant, and wishing that he would never have to move.

"For the moment, he did not. For the moment, none of them was going anywhere. That was what they had decided, he and Harriette, in a quick, whispered conference by the door. He had hoped to move immediately, to escape the danger of the narrow cove in the dark and while the wind blew the snow around to cover up their tracks. But she said that the others were too tired to move. They had been resting for only a few hours; before that, they had been running for more than twenty-four. That had exhausted them; the only reason they had been able to do it was because they believed that when they crossed the Line and left the South, they would be free. She had told them the truth, but they would not believe, and in the end she had let them run hard, because she had believed that when they reached the mill they would be met by men with a wagon, and they would not need to run anymore. But they had heard the dogs chasing C.K. and they had realized that what she had told them was true, that there was no safety south of Canada, and then when they had reached the mill they had found nothing: no wagon, no rescue, nothing. Then the hours of running, the miles of effort, the dashing of hope, the cold, the hunger, had come down on them. So they were exhausted; their bodies were, perhaps, a bit recovered, but their minds and hearts were far from that.

"C.K. looked at them, and realized that what she said was true. But he also knew that they would have to move, and move soon. And so he set about restoring them, using the tricks he had learned over the years. He went to them, speaking to each of them in tones so low that none of the others could hear, getting their names, gently touching them, asking about their pains, their fears, gently eliciting their stories, reminding them of why they had run in the first place.

"The first was a woman named Lydia, a short, small-boned woman, with ample hips, matronly breasts. Her age, she said, was twenty-five. She knew because the master had told her, once, berating her for being childless. She dropped her eyes when she told him that, dropped her eyes and lowered her head. It was not that she was not fertile; she had been pregnant eight times. But five of her children had died before their first birthday; she did not know why. One had been three when he died of cholera. The other two had been miscarriages. It hadn't mattered to the Old Master—she was an excellent midwife, good with children, good in the kitchen. But when the Old Master died his son had told her he was going to sell her, because she was twenty-five, and getting too old to breed. She had told that to Harriette Brewer, one day as they worked together in the kitchen. A

414

few weeks later, Harriette Brewer had said she was going to run away, and had asked Lydia to run with her. And Lydia had.

"The second was Juda, a young girl, perhaps fifteen, hardly more than a girl. She had had a lover, a field hand, but strong and determined to somehow become skilled. When he had learned she was pregnant he had run, hoping to reach the North, to somehow find the money to send for her and the child. She had waited for him to send word—had waited for months, worried that he had been killed, or that he had forgotten her. But then she had seen him brought back, his arms and legs chained, a man on a horse dragging him through the dust on his belly, like a snake. She had seen him flogged and branded. And when he had been sent back to the fields, he had told her that he had been wrong to run, that they would live together in slavery, that their child would grow to be a strong field hand. . . . But when her pregnancy had at last begun to show he had hanged himself with his chains. And so she had run with Harriette Brewer. The child had been born on the journey, delivered with the help of Lydia, in a Virginia barn. She held it to her breast, a tiny, wrinkled thing, sick from exposure, its tiny lungs choked with fluid. It would die soon; she knew that, and so she had not bothered to give it a name.

"Next was the old man. His master had called him Jacob, but that, he said, was not his name; his name was Azacca, he had been given it by his father, who had come from Haiti. He did not know how old he was, but he knew he was an old man because he had been a slave for a long time. When he was young he had learned to count to seven, and from then on he had counted up his Christmases. When he counted seven he would start over. He had started over seven times, and he was up to five and he was worried that he would not know when Christmas was, without a master to bring a trinket. If he did know, he would have another problem, because that would make seven sevens and six more and he would only have a year to learn another number, or to figure out how to keep track. . . . Of course, since he was an old man, he might go home first. His job had been to tend the gardens, the special ones that grew flowers and the vegetables for the master and his family. He had been very good at that, and he had liked it; he had known that he would go on doing that until he died. He hadn't minded that—he liked the garden. But he had wanted to be a free man, and the Old Master had promised that he would be, that he would put it in his Will. But when the Old Master died the

Young Master said there was nothing like that in the will. And so he had run with Harriette Brewer. But first he had plucked every flower and smashed every vegetable, and poured salt on the ground.

"The fourth was Linda. She was young and strong, in better health than the others, not only because of her youth but because she had not run as far as they had. She was from a different plantation; she did not know where it was, but it must have been farther north, because the others had passed it, and she joined them. She had not really wanted to run away, but she had always helped those who did. She had been bringing food to the others when she had been seen by another slave, a man, who said that unless she would sleep with him he would betray her. She had said she would, to play for time, while she slipped into the fields to get her three young sons, Daniel, Robert, and Francis, and they had run away.

"The children were already sleeping—Daniel, Robert, and Francis curled together on a sack of corn, the other three sleeping on the hard dirt floor. Two were girls. Harriette told him their names were Cara and Mara. The boy was William. He was the eldest, about ten, it seemed to C.K. And then he realized that the boy could not have been that old, because they were all Hariette's children. He looked at her, but she turned quickly away, going silently back to the hearth, where she was cooking a mixture of the corn meal they had found in the mill with water and the little salt she had carried. C.K. said nothing. He simply took the dried beef and dried apples from his gunnysack and gave them to her.

"They ate slowly, dipping with hand-carved spoons into the communal pot, not rushing because they were too hungry to really feel hunger. They looked as though the food was just another meal, not their first real one in almost a day. C.K. knew what the effect of the food would be; it would make them sleep, heavy and deep. But before that they would become cheerful. He waited for that, watching as they finished the last of the corn meal and beef, and chewed on half an apple each, watching as their eyes began to take on a little sparkle, their movements a bit more life; as the children, who had at first been more than a little cranky at being roused from sleep, began to act almost as children should act; the two little girls whispering to themselves and peeking at him from behind their spoons, the three boys, inspecting him with curiosity, edging ever closer to him, before slipping away to explore the corners of the mill. The fourth boy, William, was different; he sat calmly on the floor, his attention divided between C.K. and his mother. When C.K. rose and took the pot the boy followed him outside, stood silently at his elbow while he washed the pot and filled it with water, aped his movements when C.K. stood and peered up at the sky, looking at the clouds driving northwards. But when C.K. looked down he found the boy looking not at the sky, but at him. He smiled, but the boy did not; simply regarded him silently, and then trailed him back inside, watching as he placed the pot over the fire, only sitting down again when C.K. resumed his seat.

"When the water boiled C.K. took the jug of whiskey from his gunnysack and poured it into the kettle. He served the grog to them, one by one, using the only cup they carried. Then, when they had drunk, he stood up in the firelight and told them what they were going to do. How they would sleep for eight hours or so and then get up and make the run out of the cove while there was still darkness to hide them, and to hide their trails until the snow, driven by the south wind, drifted and covered it. How once they were clear of the cove they would simply climb the mountain, with the wind at their backs, and still in darkness. How after that they could slip into the cover of the deep woods and go north by trails he and no one else knew, how they would reach the Town the next night and be hidden and fed; how all it came down to was a simple run of a few miles to get them out of the cove, and then they would be safe. He watched their eyes as he spoke, saw the disbelief in them, the defeat, the distrust. He stopped talking then. Not abruptly, just letting it go, knowing that there was nothing that he could say to them that would really bring their spirits back to life. That would take a miracle. And so he fell silent, feeling, with sudden sharpness, the pain in his ribs, the fatigue in his muscles, the age in his bones. He sat down heavily. The others said nothing. After a while Harriette rose and went with Linda to settle the children for the night.

"The others began to talk again then, but C.K. did not pay any attention to them; he stared into the fire and listened instead to the rattle of the shutters as the wind gusted outside. But then he realized that one voice was a little louder than the others. Or perhaps not louder, just more distinct. He turned then, and saw her. She had left the children and was kneeling by the fire a few feet away from him, staring into the flames as he had been, but talking softly, as though she were talking to herself, and he and the others were only overhearing. But they all heard, C.K. and the rest of them, and they listened as she told her story.

"She told them how she had grown up favored, black, but in a place where black people had their own society, a society in which she, light-skinned and well provided for, occupied a high place. She told them how she had only known a good house and good clothes and good food and good schooling. And how one day the single, unquestionable sign of her womanhood had come, and her mother had told her what it meant. Then she had realized where the money came from, what her mother did to get it. Then she had begun to hate. To hate her mother for being a white man's mistress, for giving herself airs to conceal the truth from the world. To hate the white man, not because he was unkind, or ungenerous, but because he made it possible for her mother to debase herself, because he took it as his right that a black woman should do that, should be grateful for his generosity, should ask for nothing more. And to hate herself. Because even though now she knew where the money came from, and why, she still took the things it purchased: lived in the house, wore the clothes, ate the food, went to the school, and worse, did nothing for it, not even debase herself.

"She told them how she spent the first years after she learned the truth angry, troubled, hating more and more, hating not just the white man who came but all whites, and eventually, all men; not showing it, not even really feeling it, but rather feeling nothing, none of the stirrings that young girls are supposed to feel. Young men courted her—she was pretty and, more important, light-skinned—but found her cold. Not innocent and proper—they would have expected that—not even timid or prudish, but cold.

"She told them how, when she was eighteen years old, still a virgin and disinterested in becoming otherwise, she discovered a kind of passion; she met a man named William Still, the son of a woman who had twice escaped slavery, once by purchase, once by flight, the second time leaving two young sons behind. She saw how Still felt guilt at not having been one of them. She admired the way he used that guilt, dedicating himself to helping those who ran away. And she joined him, seeing in the work they did a chance to pay back for the struggle she had not had. The work helped her, brought her into contact with people who knew slavery, and from talking to them, she had come to understand how her mother might prefer genteel prostitution.

418

"And so, she told them, it became possible for her to know true passion, to love the man who came in the spring of 1850, offering to give Still what seemed amazing sums of money for the work of the Underground Railroad, providing Still would make efforts to foster and encourage the escape of slaves, especially women and children. Still was wary, but she saw the brilliance in the man's plan, and the daring in it. And she saw the dedication and determination in his eyes. And so she began to work with him, to plan with him, adding her ideas of detail to his broad outlines. She worried that he would reject her, because she was a woman, and because she had not known slavery. At first he did; but not, it seemed, for those reasons. It seemed he had reasons of his own. And so she went about the community, asking about him, finding that he was a man who had come, it seemed, from nowhere, probably from slavery, and who had become a spokesman of sorts, a respected man of property, and that his wife had been killed by a white man's hand and he had given his money away and disappeared, coming back years later with a hardened face and a wagon full of whiskey. By then he had come to accept her, to respect her, and the plans were no longer his plans amended by her, but plans created by both of them. And so it made sense that she would fall in love with him, that she would give to him the virginity that she had not so much been keeping but simply not been interested in losing.

"The plans, she told them, grew. Their love had grown. The man went back into the hills to make his whiskey. She worked on alone, except for the rare occasions, once, twice, when he would come to her for a night, or two nights. Then they planned how, when spring came, they would make their first trip south. But the time came when she knew that was never going to happen. Because she discovered she was with child.

"She had, she told them, cried when she knew. For by then she knew how much she needed to go, to make final payment for the debt she felt she owed. But she knew that by the time he was back it would be too late—her condition would show. But unless she went, unless she made that final payment, she would never be right for herself, or right for him. So she went alone, to steal away a few to freedom, and in doing it, buy her own.

"But, she told them, she had been a long time paying. For in southern Virginia, on the banks of the Nottoway River, she was taken. One of the women she had exhorted to flight betrayed her and the three others she had already enticed away, and all of them, betrayed and betrayer—the woman's master judged she had not spoken up as quickly as she should have—were sold.

She had been taken, she said, to Alexandria, and brokered by the firm of Franklin & Armfield, and later transported to New Orleans, where she was purchased, at a premium because of her light skin, by a young blade, the son of a rich planter, who wanted her for a concubine. But she escaped that fate by avoiding the consummation until her pregnancy was impossible to ignore, and then telling the young man and his father that the child was fathered by a man as black as the ace of spades. Neither of them believed her. But they dared not take the chance that a light-skinned woman, known to be the concubine of a planter's son, would produce a dark child. And so they put her to work in the fields.

"And then, she told them, she had paid the price in truth. She learned what it meant to be a slave: to rise in darkness and go to bed in darkness, to have the entire daylight of her life the property of someone else; to buy nothing, not only because she had no money, but because it was against the law for her to carry out even so simple a transaction; to hide her knowledge of reading and writing, to stand and listen to the master and his son, using words she was not supposed to know, discussing her fate and not be able to show anything; to do exactly what she was told in the way that she was told, to forget she knew better ways; to eat coarse food and drink brackish water; to beg permission to void her own waste; to see the man who had wanted to make her his plaything approach on horseback and, even though she had thwarted him, to lower her eyes and look only at the mud on his boots; to accept, when he chose, for no better reason than that he chose, the sting of his crop.

"That, she told them, had not been so bad. But in time she gave birth to her child, and then she really came to understand what slavery meant. Because there was nothing she could do for him. She could nurse him and protect him, but only so long as the Master willed it. She realized that she was her son's only protection, and that her only protection was to appear to accept slavery.

"And so she had adopted the poses of slavery. Covered the light in her eyes with drooping lids, the intelligence in her mind with halting speech, the aching in her soul with loud professions of belief in the tenets of the perverted Christianity that was fed to the slaves like corn meal and fat meat. She accepted her role: she was a woman and a slave, and such women take men and bear children, breed for Massa; she took a man and had two girls, covering the longing in her heart with the pumping of her thighs. And as a reward for her diligence, she was taken from the fields and placed in the house.

"That, she had said, had been her downfall. Because she looked back at the fields and was thankful to the Master for taking her from them; in feeling that, she accepted his right to put her where he chose. And as soon as she did that, she became truly a slave. She found her new role, her new status, obscenely comfortable. She gave her mind only to the care of the Master's house and the children that were, in reality, the Master's property, and she gave thanks each day that he did not sell them, or her, or her man. She stopped longing for a life of freedom and for the man she had left, not because she had forgotten either, but because she had forgotten herself; she had forgotten how to long for anything. She went through her days, doing her tasks without hatred, without bitterness. She no longer needed to hide anything, because there was nothing in her to hide.

"And then one day the Master had died. That was not a terrible thing, but it made a difference. Because now the son was the Master. She saw him eyeing her, knowing that he did not desire her as he once had, but that he still hated her. And she saw him eyeing her son, the child who, by his lightness of skin, signified her triumph of deception.

"And so, she told them, she had begun to reject slavery. It had not been easy. For she was surrounded by people, black and white, who thought of things a certain way. The wrong way, she knew, but she had forgotten what the right way was, was not sure that she had ever known. And so she began to practice. She practiced remembering all the things she had allowed herself to forget: her mother, the life she had led, the man she had loved. She was unfaithful to the man who, in normal society, would have been her husband, not with her body, but with her mind, thinking, when he came to her, of the other man, trying to remember how *he* had touched her, what *he* had said to her, what *he* had wanted of her, thinking of it as infidelity because fidelity was a concept denied the slave. She went through each day outwardly unchanging, doing exactly what she was told to do in exactly the way she had been told to do it, but thinking what she would have done, how she would have done it, had it been her choice. She practiced defiance, putting dirt and bits of soap and manure in the food she cooked for the whites, thinking of things to say to them that could have been taken two ways. At the same time, she worked

421

at appearing the model slave, better than before, anxious to please, bright and cheerful, but she worked at not believing her own deceptions, at keeping close to her mind and heart the things she really thought and felt.

"It had, she told them, taken months to throw off the servile habits of action and thought. And as she pushed those habits away from her she came to appreciate more the other slaves, those who had been born into slavery, who had never known anything else, to realize how difficult even the smallest act of defiance must have been for them; not so much to do it, but to simply *think* of it. She began to listen to the others talking in the evening, not passing the time as she had before when she was thinking as a slave, but listening to them, searching among them for the strongest, the most determined, those who might run with her. When she found them she encouraged them, allowed them to encourage her. She needed them. Because she was still not sure she could do what she had set out to do.

"But one night she had become sure. It was a midsummer night, she said, bright and clear, and she had been sitting in front of her cabin, her head tilted back against the logs, looking up in the sky, trying to recall the things she had learned about navigating by the stars. She had gone through the constellations, naming them, remembering their mythical significances: the Scorpion; the Twins; the Goat; the Archer; the Great Bear, the Small Bear . . . and then she saw, not a constellation, but a single star. The North Star. Saw it not twinkling fitfully but shining bright and clear and steady. And then she knew she *could* do it; all she needed was the will.

"And so, she said, she began to work at strengthening her will; she started taking risks. She stole from the kitchen, taking food and utensils, a kettle, a skillet, a cup, hiding them in the woods; taking a table knife and working, at odd moments, to grind it to a sharp edge and point, hiding it in her own cabin, knowing that if it was found there she would be flogged, sold, perhaps killed. She took to slipping about the house, listening at doorways, sneaking into the Master's study and reading his letters, learning his plans, stealing books from his library and reading them and then, rather than returning them, burning them, creating, in that shrinking inventory, the thing that would give her away eventually if her will should falter.

"But it did not. She made her final selections from among her fellow slaves, choosing not the young women who spoke angrily but lowered their eyes and bent their necks when the Master approached them, who made themselves seem smaller and softer when any man approached, and not the young men who bragged of acts of defiance, who claimed to have spoken sharply to the overseer, to have told him this and that, but who struck out with their fists, not at the overseer, but at each other and at their women and their children. She rejected them. She rejected the others too, the ones who feigned illness, who hid from work, who looked constantly for ways to rise in the plantation hierarchy. Instead she took the ones who were quiet, who calmly went about their business, doing their assigned tasks with more diligence than was required, who accepted praise with no joy, who bowed their heads when they had to but who never lowered their eyes. She did not choose the strongest of body, she chose the strongest of mind, the strongest of spirit. An old man, a young girl already with child, a childless woman.

"And then she had taken the final risk; she revealed herself to them. She placed her future in their hands, because she realized that, in some ways, she still thought like a slave, still believed the things the slavemasters had told her, that her brothers and sisters were incapable of their own salvation, happy to live the life of indecision, unwilling to give it up, ready to betray anyone who would force them to make any decision at all; and she knew that if she would win her freedom, she would have to reject the white man's truth. And so she took the final step in her own liberation. Then she waited, going through the days in constant anticipation of the moment when they would come to her and take her and she would know that she had been be-. trayed.

"But she had chosen well; she was not betrayed. And so, she said, when she saw a letter to the Master discussing the sale of a young boy of nine, quoting a price of ten dollars a pound, she told the others the time had come. And then she told her man, not saying she was going, saying only that she was afraid that her son would be sold, asking what he would do. The answer was clear: nothing. And then she said she might take the child and run away, telling him in the night, watching him the next day, knowing that he was troubled, waiting for him to decide, knowing already what he would say, knowing because she knew what kind of man he was, but having to wait for him to make his choice.

"Then her voice had grown quiet, her eyes had seemed to reach out and embrace the flames, as she told how she gave the signal, telling the others that this was the night by the song she sang as she came down from the house—'Steal away, steal away, steal away to Jesus'—and how she waited through the evening meal, waiting for her man to speak, and when he did not, lying beside him, thinking. And how he had spoken, finally, telling her that she did not need to worry, that he had spoken to the Master, that the Master had promised not to sell the boy. She said she did not believe that, that she had made up her mind, that she would run. He said that he would stop her. And she told him that he would not, that he was not enough of a man to stop her, waiting to see what he would do. He accepted it. He said that she would never make it alone. She said she was not alone, that there were others. And he said nothing for a long time. And then he asked their names.

"She had known, then, she told them, that it would be as she had planned. And so she refused to tell him, as she had planned, and accepted the pain he gave her when he forced her to tell, feigned remorse, repentance, touched him, gave herself to him. And then, when he slept, she rose and took the knife from the rafters. She roused him. And when he was awake, when his eyes were open, when he was looking at her, she cut his throat.

"And then, she told them, she had taken her children, her son and her daughters, and she had gone into the woods, and met the others, the ones with the strong minds and hearts and wills, and she had led them out of there.

"In the beginning, she told them, she had merely taken them north, navigating by the North Star, trying only to avoid pursuit. But in time she was able to make contact with the Underground Railroad, and then her route had taken on definition; she began to lead them not just to the North, but to a particular place in the North, where she believed the man she had loved would be.

"She had never forgotten him, of course; she had used the memory of him to free her, but that had been only a memory that had become less than that—a dream. But when she began to touch the Underground network the dream had come to life. For she heard his name, C.K. Washington, heard how he had been the bane of slavers from Virginia to Louisiana, how the prices on his head would buy a dozen slaves, but could not buy him. Then she had known not only that he was alive, but that the payment she had gone south to make had been made not once but many times. For she had recognized, in the pattern of his exploits, the workings of her own mind.

"And so she had bent her path towards the place where she hoped he would be. Where she knew he would be. Where she believed he would be. And, she told them, he was there.

"C.K. watched her face as she spoke, listened to her words and nothing else. But when she finished he became aware of the sounds of the others, the soft animated whisperings as they realized who he was. And he knew that she had done what he could not do, that she had provided the miracle. And as they had all composed themselves to sleep, he had known that when the sun rose they would be atop the mountain; that they would all be free.

"Now he lay with her against him, feeling the warmth from her, thinking beyond the dawn, beyond the last stages of their escape, to the life they would find somewhere, she and he and his firstborn son. His thoughts were not untroubled: he thought, too, of Lamen, his second son, and of Bijou. But the troubles were covered by the warmth he felt, the warmth that came from Harriette Brewer. He lay there, half-dreaming, listening to the breathing of the others growing easier as they drifted off to sleep, the snoring of the old man, the wheezing of the baby, and to the gusting of the wind outside, even that seeming to quiet, as though the storm itself were resting. And then he felt something change, some difference in the way she held him, not a motion, just a difference, a subtle softening of muscles, easing of posture, and he turned to her, slipping his hands, hands that seemed somehow too awkward, too rough, too dirty to hold her, around her shoulders. He tried to pull her to him, but he was too late; she was already there."

I stopped for a moment, sipped the toddy, waiting, while the rest of it took shape in my mind. I became aware of her hand, warm, resting on mine. Not resting. Squeezing. I imagined the rest of it then. I put the cup down.

"The silence woke him. He did not know it at first. At first he thought it was some sound that had come into his sleeping to alarm him. But when he listened he realized it was not sound that had alarmed him, it was silence; the wind had died.

"For a few moments he lay there, listening, hoping that it was only a momentary hiatus, that in a minute, or two minutes, or three, the wind would spring up again, strong and violent. But it did not.

The night was so quiet he could hear the chuckling of the creek, a steady dripping as the snow on the roof melted, the far-off barking of some farmer's dog. He rose slowly, heavily, throwing the sleep from him as if it were a blanket, and went to the door. He stepped outside, expecting to shiver in the chill, but the night was relatively warm, the snow beneath his feet damp. The clouds no longer boiled across the sky—they merely drifted, thinning, it seemed, before his eyes. He stood there, wishing he did not know the patterns of the weather, that he could have stood there in blissful ignorance, seeing the clearing sky as a normal man would see it, a welcome event, a time of thanksgiving. But he was not a normal man. He was C.K. Washington, and he had a dozen exhausted slaves looking to him for salvation, and now there was no friendly wind to hide their trail, no bitter cold to keep the hunters inattentive, to keep the miller home. The wind had died, and now they would have to run, and run hard, before the daylight came and took away their last concealment.

"He waked Harriette Brewer first. She came out of her slumber quickly, violently; he held her arms for a moment until she realized where she was, releasing her when he felt her struggles stop and he heard her speak the words that meant she understood: no wind. He didn't answer her, just moved to the others, waking them one by one, as gently as he could, hearing her moving too, waking the children, answering their sleepy protests with one-word orders that, despite their brusqueness, had good effect.

"They moved in ten minutes, turning eastward away from the mill and the main road, away from the mountain, for that route would not help them now. C.K. had to believe that Pettis would be searching for them, that by midmorning at the latest he would send part of his force sweeping up the valley, would find their trail. Then it would be a footrace, he and the fugitives racing to find concealment before the men and dogs found them. There was hope that the weather would change again, that the west wind would come to drift the snow and hide the path that they had taken, but that was a distant hope; their only real hope lay in covering ground as quickly as they could while darkness hid them, abandoning finesse, abandoning strategy, putting their hope in speed.

"And so he led them east. They went silently, falling in behind him, following silently in the trail he had broken, through the knee-deep snow, first Lydia, then Linda, the three of them taking the bur-

426

den of breaking trail, making easier passage for the ones who followed: the old man, Azacca, helping the girl Juda with her wheezing baby, then the children, William leading them, followed by Lydia's sons and Harriette Brewer's daughters, with Harriette Brewer in the rear, keeping the children moving.

"He took them east for half a mile and then he turned and led them up a low hill, forcing himself to climb quickly, to make it look easy, to lead by silent example. He had felt his ribs ache with pain when he had to breathe hard, and wondered if, when it came time to run, he could run; but he bit back the pain and ignored the thoughts and forged on up the hill.

"They reached the ridge, and there he found what he had hoped he would find: a long expanse of almost bare ground just below it, the ground scoured almost clear of snow by the wind. He did not pause but pushed quickly on, not seeing or hearing but sensing their spirits lifting as they found the going easy. He brought the speed up steadily and knew that they were with him, could hear the breathing as they ran behind him, the soft squeaks as their feet hit the snow, and he had felt his own spirits rise. They were running swiftly now, and he knew that they could keep it up.

"And then he stopped. Stopped dead. Because he realized that they would not make it out of the South County by daybreak. They would not make it out of the South County at all. Because ahead of them, arrayed along the valley floor, was a line of lights, torches; Pettis had blocked the escape.

"He said nothing. He simply stood and waited as the rest of them came up to him, while they stopped and looked and understood. And then he turned and started back. But before he could take more than a few steps he felt a hand on his arm, and looked up to see Harriette Brewer pointing behind them, to another line of torchlight, this one moving slowly, steadily up the cove. Again he did not hesitate; there was a choice to be made and he made it and turned to the east, but there was light there too, not a solid line of it, but the beginnings of one, a line that extended as he watched it, as men struck matches and lit their torches. He stopped then, not daring to turn to the west, knowing what he would see.

"And so he took refuge in his thoughts, in counting the torches and figuring how many men Pettis must have hired. Perhaps half the men in the South County. Or all. And then he felt her hand on his

427

arm and he looked down at her, not seeing her in the darkness, but looking at her anyway. She asked him how long they had.

"And then the horror of it struck him. Because her voice was different, was not the quiet, resigned voice of the woman who had told of planning and scheming to save her son from slavery. It was a small voice, a frightened voice, a cowered voice. A slave's voice. The rest of them were silent, even the children, waiting for his answer, waiting for him to tell them there was hope, that there was a scheme, a path, a way. But there was none. And so he looked at the line of torches moving in the south, the line growing thicker and brighter as the men on the flanks joined in when their positions were reached, and he made his estimates and told them: half an hour.

"For a while they stood motionless, looking to the south, to the line of torches moving towards them. C.K. could sense them, hear them, knew when they began to move; when the boys, Daniel, Robert, and Francis, went silently, almost calmly, to their mother, standing in front of her, almost as though they would defend her from the lights; when the childless woman, Lydia, pushed the daughters of Harriette Brewer to their mother's side; when the girl, Juda, began to nurse her baby; when the boy, William, came and stood in front of Harriette, close to him, but not touching him, not looking at him, just standing.

"And then he heard the old man, Azacca, humming softly, tunelessly, and then turning the hum into a wordless chant. He had listened then, and the others had listened. And the old man told them a story.

"It was an old story, he said, a story his father had told him. A tale of Death, some might say, but not those who knew the tale. Because as it went, the Great Sky God once, in the old days, had looked down and seen that men were not free, for they feared the Stillness That Comes To All. And so the Great Sky God had called for Papa Legba, the interpreter of the Great Sky God and the other gods, and had told him to take the message to men that the Stillness That Comes To All, that they called Death, was not an ending of things, but a passing on of spirit, a change of shape, and nothing more; that when the Stillness came upon those they loved, they should not fear or grieve, but rejoice, because the loved one had merely left the body that bound him to the ground and become a spirit who could fly wherever he willed. The Great Sky God had given the message to Legba, and told him to take it to men. But Legba was an old man, feeble, who walked with a cane. He was too fond of his pipe and his chair to make the trip. And so Legba had called to Rabbit, had told him to take the message. It was not a bad choice, for Rabbit was swift. But he was also stupid. And so, when he found the first man, a man with pale skin and straight hair and eyes as gray as winter, he had told him the Great Sky God's message, and thinking his task was finished, had gone away.

"But the man with pale skin was not stupid like Rabbit. He had listened to the Sky God's message and he had seen that if he lied to the other men, he could become the ruler of them. And so he went to the other men and told them that the Sky God had sent a message, sending it only to him. . . . But the other men would not listen, for they said, if the Sky God sent a message, why would he not send it to all? And so the pale man had gone away and thought. And when he had thought enough he came back and went to the other men who were pale as he was, and told them the truth. And then they all went together to the other men, the men with dark skins, and told them that the Sky God had sent a message to them. When the other men asked them why the Sky God would send a message to some and not to all, they said that it was because their skin was light, and that the Sky God said that meant they were better than other men, that they should interpret the meaning for other men. And then they told the other men that the Sky God said that when the Stillness came on men that they would cease to be; that their bodies would turn to dust and ashes, and that their spirits would be cast into a lake of fire to burn in torment forever—unless they did exactly what the pale men said. The men with pale skins all spoke the same, and the others became so frightened of the lake of fire that they began to do what the pale men said.

"But, the old man said, some of the men with dark skins guessed the truth. Those men did not fear the lake, for they believed that when the Stillness came upon them they would simply go away and live in a place where there were no men with pale skins who stole the spirit by telling lies. And so they did not do exactly as the men with pale skins said. And so they were beaten, and chained, and starved. But it did not matter. For they believed the truth. . . .

"And then C.K. heard the sound, a sharp sobbing sound. It came from Juda. And he then he realized that there was something he was not hearing; the wheezing of the child. And so he was not surprised when he saw her go to the old man and kneel before him and lay the baby's body at his feet.

"He knew, then, that they were watching him, all of them. Waiting for him to lead them. It came to him then that there was always escape, always, so long as one did not think too much, so long as one did not calculate too much; so long as one believed. And so he stepped away from Hariette Brewer and stood alone, and he took the pistol from his belt and held it high, so they could all see. For a moment he was not sure that he could lead them, was not sure that they would follow, but then he saw Harriette Brewer take her knife from beneath her shawl and hold it high, and then he heard her, heard her singing softly, then louder, heard the others join in, the words of the song growing, rising from the hilltop, floating down the incline, the words sharp and clear against the night: 'And before I'll be a slave I'll be buried in my grave, and go home to my God, and be free.' For a chorus or two, or three, the song was loud and strong. And then the song grew weaker, the voices that had raised it falling silent one by one, until at last there was only one voice, a strong soprano voice, carrying the song. And then that voice, too, fell silent. But the song went on. Because the wind had shifted again, and was blowing from the west; because now the wind sang."

The candle was gone now, the only sign of its having been there a small pool of wax and a tiny piece of wick on which the last of the flame writhed like a blue snake. I watched it twisting, wondering whether I should blow at it. But then it died of its own accord, leaving hardly an image on my eyes.

I got up then and took my cup to the stove, and pulled the kettle to the front. I stood there, not thinking, waiting for it to boil.

"Who buried them?" she said. "Who buried them there like that? Pettis?"

"I don't think so," I said. "I don't know why he would."

"Who, then? Crawley and Graham?"

"That's what Moses Washington thought," I said. The kettle hummed, on the verge of boiling, and I reached for the whiskey and the sugar.

"Make me one," she said.

I didn't say anything; I just turned to get her cup. The water was boiling then, and I measured and mixed and went back to the table. I gave the cup to her and stood there, sipping, listening to the wind.

"What do you think?" she said.

"They were buried next to a family graveyard. They died there, but they didn't have to be buried there. They were buried with the same spacing as the family stones. . . ."

"You're saying the miller—what's his name? Iiames?—you think he took the time to bury them like that, to figure out who loved who?"

"Yes," I said. "That's what I believe."

"But he was white," she said.

"I know," I said.

"Why would a white man . . . why would you think a white man . . . ?"

I heard the soft squeaking of the chair as her body stiffened, as she turned to try and see my face.

We left there in the morning. We rose early and washed and made breakfast; coffee and venison steaks. We packed our things. Or she did. I didn't bother with most things. Then I set the place to rights, bringing in wood and stacking it to replace what we had burned, washing the dishes we had used.

When I was finished I told her to go. She did not want to, but I said that I had things to do there, that I wanted to be alone to do them.

When she was gone I took the folio down and put the books and pamphlets and diaries and maps back where they belonged, ready for the next man who would need them. I sealed the folio with candle wax, as my father had done for me. Then I gathered up the tools of my trade, the pens and inks and pencils, the pads and the cards, and carried them out into the clearing. I kicked a clear space in the snow and set them down, and over them I built a small edifice of kindling, and then a frame of wood. I went back inside the cabin and got the kerosene and brought it back and poured it freely over the pyre, making sure to soak the cards thoroughly. I was a bit careless, and got some of it on my boots, but that would make no difference.

When the can was empty I set it down and went and got the folio and tucked it beneath my arm. I took the matches from their keeping place, took one out and closed the lid of the can and put it back in its place, so that it would be there when they wanted it. And then I left the cabin for the last time and went and stood before the pyre and stood looking at the cards and the papers, and thinking about all of it, one last time.

As I struck the match it came to me how strange it would all look to someone else, someone from far away. And as I dropped the match to the wood and watched the flames go twisting, I wondered if that someone would understand. Not just someone; Judith. I wondered if she would understand when she saw the smoke go rising from the far side of the Hill.